THE VENOM WE BLEED

SCORPION KINGS BOOK ONE

USA TODAY BESTSELLING AUTHOR
LUCY SMOKE

THE VENOM WE BLEED

SCORPION KINGS
BOOK ONE

LUCY SMOKE

Copyright © 2025 by Lucy Smoke LLC

All rights reserved.

No part of this book may be reproduced in any form or by any electronic or mechanical means, including information storage and retrieval systems, without written permission from the author, except for the use of brief quotations in a book review.

Editing by Heather Long, Kristen Breanne, and Alexa Proofreads

Cover Design by Quirah Casey

Formatting by Smoking Hot Covers

*To the therapy bill I'm most assuredly going to have after finishing this series.
Cheers.*

Everyone is going to die and no one is going to remember you, so … fuck it.

— BILLIE EILISH

CONTENTS

1.	Nolan	1
2.	Juliet	10
3.	Juliet	22
4.	Juliet	33
5.	Juliet	42
6.	Juliet	52
7.	Nolan	62
8.	Lex	69
9.	Juliet	76
10.	Juliet	85
11.	Juliet	93
12.	Lex	103
13.	Juliet	113
14.	Juliet	120
15.	Juliet	131
16.	Juliet	141
17.	Gio	148
18.	Juliet	163
19.	Lex	174
20.	Juliet	179
21.	Juliet	189
22.	Juliet	202
23.	Juliet	211
24.	Juliet	220
25.	Nolan	228
26.	Gio	237
27.	Juliet	243
28.	Juliet	254
29.	Lex	267
30.	Juliet	277
31.	Juliet	287
32.	Juliet	303
33.	Nolan	318
34.	Juliet	326

35. Lex	340
36. Juliet	346
37. Juliet	359
38. Juliet	367
39. Juliet	373
40. Gio	383
41. Juliet	391
42. Juliet	406
43. Gio	418
44. Juliet	426
45. Nolan	435
46. Juliet	440
About the Author	445
Also by Lucy Smoke	447

1
NOLAN

15 years old…

Most people fear death. When it inevitably comes for them, they cry, kick, scream, and sometimes pray to some otherworldly *being* to help them—to give them just a little more time. I don't understand why. Clearly no one's fucking listening. No one *ever* listens.

"Stop screaming!" Lex barks down at the man beneath us covered in his own blood, piss, and vomit. "It's giving me a fucking headache."

I have little sympathy for Xavier Pierce, but Lex has even less. When my father doesn't stop wailing about the gushing wound in his leg where the bone protrudes past the skin, covered in dirt and blood clinging to the pearl-white surface, Lex bends over into the hole and punches him in the head. I repress a snort.

Thud. Thud. Thud. It takes three blows for my father to shut the fuck up. He curls into a ball and tries to hide, covering his head and protecting himself from more of Lex's wrath. I'm surprised he hasn't passed out by now.

Thanks to him, I'm intimately aware that broken bones

hurt like a bitch. The pain of having one of your bones snapped in half and protrude through your fucking skin rips through your mind and makes it hard to focus on anything else except the fire burning over you. There's nothing you can do —not unless your father lets your mom help you, lets her drive you to the hospital to get fixed up—but he didn't because the fucker didn't want any cops or CPS knocking on his door. Three whole fucking days I'd waited until Mom grew brave enough to sneak me out in the middle of the night.

Now, it's my turn. I can't fucking wait to finish him off.

"Where the fuck is G?" I mutter, turning my back on the bloodied and sobbing man.

Almost as soon as I ask that question, a single dull headlight grows visible on the drive and the broken stuttering of a cheap dirt bike announces our friend's arrival. The headlight bumps up and down as he rides the hills, slowing as he gets to the ramshackle old cabin that Lex had inherited from his folks when they died. No one ever comes out here. No one ever even remembers this place. Not surprising considering his new 'guardian' is his aunt who forgets he exists most of the time.

Way to go, justice system; you really pulled through on repeat—first with my dad and then with Lex's family and G's. Well, we'll deal with his dad eventually. Even snot-nosed kids need to practice patience or so my mom says.

I'm grateful for this shithole tonight. It's far enough away from our town of Silverwood that people hardly recall that there's a mountain up here with a bunch of hunting cabins. It's not a good area for hunting anyway—not since a pack of wolves moved in some years back, and there's no money in hunting up in the boonies anyway. All the rich folks of Silverwood prefer their country clubs and business conferences.

Blackstone Mountain is the perfect place for our purposes, though, especially tonight.

Gio's dirt bike dies several yards away from where the dilapidated old cabin strikes a haunting figure on the hill, and it's only then that I realize my father is quiet. I crouch and stare into the hole that we forced him to dig before shoving him into it—the result now being his broken leg.

"He passed out," Lex says, and I see the truth of his announcement in my father's limp body. "What a pussy." My flashlight reveals the blood still oozing down his side. The moon above our heads is hardly enough light to see more than hints of the gruesome scene before us.

"Shit—fuck!" G curses loudly and comes stumbling towards us with two shovels in hand and a backpack. He doesn't seem to care about being heard. Why should he? There's no one out here. "Do you know how hard it was to bring this shit back on the bike?" he demands, pushing one handle at Lex before offering the other to me.

I shake my head at him and he groans before dropping the backpack and heading over to the mound of dirt my father had dug up an hour before. The shovel we'd forced him to use lies somewhere on the ground, splintered in several pieces.

The grunts of my best friends, as they begin to sling dirt into the hole, echo up the trees around us. The sound sinks into my ears. I close my eyes as it settles into my muscles and bones, letting it turn into the sensation of pure, unadulterated power. Something I've never fucking wielded before, much less over my father—it's heady, addicting.

Like so many of the deadbeats from Silverwood, Xavier Pierce will simply disappear. No one will look for him or wonder where he went. Everyone will assume he ran off to avoid his responsibilities to my mom who was too good for him and me, the kid who didn't deserve his wrath. Deep down, everyone will know that we're better off for his loss.

I hold up a hand to stop the other two. Lex and Gio's fast shoveling comes to a standstill while I reach into the back waistband of my jeans. The weight of the gun that Darrio Vargas, G's dad, had given me just yesterday when I'd agreed to work for him is lighter than I expect.

I lift the gun. My father's eyes flutter open. A part of me had hoped he would remain unconscious for this part. Awake or not, my decision is already made. His flat brown eyes, too much like my own, are fogged over with pain, yet they settle on me as I aim the Glock at him.

My hand doesn't even shake as I pull the trigger, but he does. The gun jerks in my hand as the gunshot echoes up the giant oaks that surround us and out towards the open field behind Lex's cabin, and I grimace as the kickback vibrates up my arm. Darrio had warned me that it'd do that, but it's still a bit of a jarring sensation. My father's body jolts as the bullet slams into his head, sending a spray of crimson liquid out the back of his skull to disappear into the earth. With a combination of the flashlight and the moonlight as my guide, I scan the bits and pieces of brain matter combined with skull fragments embedded into the ground like a halo around his head.

Stabbing the end of his shovel into the dirt, Lex props himself up with folded arms over the handle. I lower the gun. Several minutes pass in silence as the heat from firing it dissipates. Only once it doesn't feel like a brand in my grip do I tuck it into my waistband, pulling my t-shirt out a bit to cover it.

"That's it then?" Lex asks, canting his head in my direction.

When I don't answer, G speaks up. "You're really gonna work for that bastard?"

My gaze cuts towards him. "It's not forever," I assure him. There's no way in hell I'd ever let myself live under another man's thumb the way I've lived under my father's.

Gio stares into the darkened hole at the body. I expect to feel something when I follow his gaze. Regret maybe? Remorse or guilt. Yet, only a bone-deep relief fills me. I've never been one for sad sack poetry or some shit like what our English teachers force us to read for "education," but at this moment, I think I truly understand how some skinny starving artist types came up with all of their flowery words.

Writing was their release from a prison only they could see. Mine, it turns out, is killing.

"He's going to know you shot that gun," Gio murmurs. "He checks when they're returned to him."

"I don't care." I'm not afraid of Darrio Vargas. After tonight, I can't imagine being afraid of anyone ever again. I just put a bullet in the head of my demon. What else matters?

Gio doesn't respond right away, but his brows crease, forming twin lines between his eyes. I let my gaze drift back to the hole and the half-buried body there. If he could, G would do the same to his father. There are only two things that keep Darrio Vargas' heart beating:

One, Gio's mother still loves the bastard and forgives him for all of the insane shit he does to both of them. Two, Gio's respect for me.

Taking a step towards G, I hold my hand out. "His time will come," I assure him.

Gio stares at my outstretched arm before slowly raising his gaze to mine. "He keeps shit on everyone who works for him, Nolan," Gio says, his voice deeper than usual. "That's how he keeps them in line. He'll know what you used the gun he gave you for, and he'll use it against you."

I don't drop my arm, not even when my muscles begin to burn. Gio's words aren't a warning, they're a fact. It's too late now. Showing any sign of weakness or regret will only ruin all that we've done here tonight.

"Your father and I have an understanding," I say. Not dad, because that's not what the man is. "Despite what he'd have you believe, he's not infallible." Gio's honey-brown eyes glaze over, the minuscule light refracting off the sheen of tears there. "Trust me," I urge him, nudging him with my hand. His own lifts and we clasp forearms. I let the warmth of his skin on mine seep into my skin. "We'll use him until we graduate, earn as much money as his dirty profits can afford us, and then we're out of this shithole town."

"You want us to leave Silverwood?" Lex asks abruptly, turning to face us fully.

"Yes." I tighten my grip on G's arm when he moves to release me. His gaze meets mine and I speak—talking to both of them, but forcing G to hear my words and know their sincerity. "The three of us *are* getting the fuck out of Silverwood. We're going to make money and we'll go somewhere else. Somewhere far away." Where no one knows us as monsters or victims or eyes us with pity or fear. "But until then"—I bore into Gio's gaze, refusing to let go—"we're going to rule this fucking town and everyone in it."

Gio's brow relaxes and the hold he has on me becomes stronger, his grip tightening once again. One hard squeeze, then I release him and he steps back.

"Fuck them," he finally says, eyes sparking with something sinister—something that matches my own dark pride. "Fuck Xavier, fuck Darrio, and fuck everyone else that thinks we're garbage. We're gonna be the fucking Kings of Silverwood."

I nod. "Then we'll leave it all behind," I agree. "Until that day comes, though, no one will ever step on us again."

Lex remains silent for some time. His eyes are pitch black, sinking into the shadows around us as he glares at me.

I sigh. "You don't give a fuck about Silverwood," I remind him. "You have no ties to it other than G and me."

"What about *her*?" he spits out, anger coating his words.

My upper lip curls back. *Her?* He's fucking concerned about *her?* "She's nothing," I snap back. "She doesn't even know you fucking exist. Let her go."

A low, animalistic growl erupts from his throat and Lex's shovel drops to the ground as he stalks towards me. Gio curses and steps between us. I stand tall and straight, waiting. I'll be fucking damned if I shrink away from his violence now.

"Lex, man, stop!" G presses a hand into Lex's chest and the other man halts, though he continues to lean against the light hold.

"She's not nothing," Lex snaps. "She's *mine*."

"She's a distraction," I reply, crossing my arms. "Do you honestly think she'll give you the time of day?"

The specter of this damned girl haunts the air between us, a sore reminder of Lex's obsession with someone he can never have.

Juliet Donovan.

Her face comes to mind, pretty golden hair with dark roots and eyes the color of the clearest sky. She's far too perfect for someone like him—like any of us. Rich. Beautiful. Unattainable. I can't say I blame Lex for his one-sided infatuation with her, but it's been ten fucking years. Ten years since kindergarten and the one year that kids like us—poor, grubby, and damaged—were allowed to be in the same class as those on the other side of the tracks before Silverwood Prep had been finished.

"She was nice to you once, asshole," I gripe. "She pitied you." Somehow the bastard latched on to her and hasn't let go even though they haven't even spoken since then.

"You don't know her!" Lex leans harder against Gio, earning a grunt from our more reasonable friend.

I scoff. "And you do?"

"I know *everything* about her!" Lex snaps. "I know her favorite color, her favorite food. I know who she's friends with and I know about her nightmares."

"Because you fucking *stalk* her." I bite out the words, loosening the hold of my folded arms to let them fall back to my sides. "Tell me something, Lex, if she's so fucking important, why haven't you asked her out yet? Why let her date those stuck-up pricks at Silverwood Prep if she's so important?"

Lex goes still for a moment, and then, as if my words have the effect of a needle piercing a balloon, he deflates and steps back from Gio's hold. He doesn't answer me, not right away, but when he does speak, it's with a low voice that I have to strain to hear. "You don't know her like I do," he whispers. "She's different ... she's not like them."

I close my eyes and inhale a deep breath. The only difference about Juliet Donovan lies in the fact a veritable psychopath loves her. Or as much as any of us can love. I suppose I shouldn't be surprised. The three of us have always needed something to latch on to in order to get through our days. Lex doesn't have parents like G and I do. So, if his clinging to the dream of Juliet Donovan will keep him sane, then I have to let him.

Three years. That's all we have to get through anyway. Three more years until we're out of this life, out of Silverwood, and free from our pasts.

I sigh, then look back at the grave. "You can still watch her from afar," I say quietly. It's not like his obsession hasn't come with upgrades for G and me. Being so close and so far from the girl has allowed Lex the room to study methods through which he can follow her. Building his own computers out of scrap metal. Following her social media. Hacking into video feeds of her in her bedroom, her in class, her ... everywhere. Those are skills that when put to other uses, we can take advantage of.

"And if we leave and I want her to come with?" Lex asks.

I grit my teeth. "We are *not* kidnapping her," I tell him. Though I have no compunction about stealing someone else's freedom, Juliet Donovan is far too high profile and I will not let him put us all at risk just for some pussy.

"What if she wants to come?" Lex presses, sounding almost desperate.

Fuck me. That will never happen. The tightness in my jaw eases as I sink into those words. It'll never happen, so there's no need to worry.

I straighten and fix Lex with a look. "If Juliet Donovan

wants to follow you out of Silverwood when we leave," I tell them, "then we'll let her."

That's all it takes for Lex's mood to completely shift. All at once, he goes from a morose, angry bastard to peppy and cheerful. He gives me a brilliant smile and returns to his shovel. Gio glances between the two of us with a hesitant expression, but after a few more moments of watching Lex push more dirt into the hole, he seems to realize that the crisis has been averted and goes back to his own.

I pinch the bridge of my nose and stare up into the shadowy tree tops overhead. One thing those dead poets didn't have to deal with were brothers. Perhaps, though, that's why they're dead now. They didn't have assholes like these two to pull them out of the darkness. I do.

Because of them, I fear nothing anymore. Not even death.

2
JULIET

3 years later…

I know that ass. Well, sort of. Usually, I'm on the opposite end of that ass with his dick five inches deep in me. I used to think five inches was pretty good, but now, as I watch him use it on my best friend—scratch that, after this, she's definitely my *ex*-best friend—I think I'm realizing it's just … mediocre. I guess catching your boyfriend and ex-bestie fucking on your eighteenth birthday puts things into perspective like that.

Bran's ass bobs up and down a few more times and beyond him, I hear Avery moan. It pisses me off even more when it comes out sounding completely forced. I know her well enough to know what she sounds like when she's faking it. She's fucked nearly every football player on the team in one way or another and then dished the details to me for years, telling me all the ways they either rocked or sucked in bed and how to get through it, a girl has to sometimes just … fake an orgasm so they'll finish and be done.

The only player left is—or rather was—Brandon. *My* boyfriend. My *ex*-boyfriend.

Bran doesn't even seem to notice the high-pitched falsetto of her moan. He pumps his hips harder, cursing as he gets closer to climax. Neither one of them even realizes I'm here, standing in the doorway with my eighteenth birthday party still going hard behind me—a party *they* threw.

Lights flash. Music thumps. People pass by in the hall. It'd been a surprise party, and well, I suppose it's now a double whammy of fucking surprises. *Literally*.

Grayson Rowe stops behind me, the drink in his hand sloshing over the rim of a crystal glass—no red solo cups for the elite soon-to-be senior class of Silverwood Prep. He gapes into the room that I just walked into. Without thinking, I snatch the glass from his grip and tip it back, downing the mixture of rum and something carbonated fast, half-hoping that if I'm drunk enough this whole scene will change.

It doesn't.

"Holy shit!" Grayson yells. "Is that—"

"Move." I cut him off, shoving the now empty crystal glass against his chest as more people stop to see what all the drama is about.

"Oh, my God!" Avery's shriek fills my ears, but I'm already halfway down the hall.

Anger burns in my gut, churning around and around as bile builds up in my throat. I move quickly into the living room of Avery's parents' lake house where half of Silverwood Prep is currently grinding to the music blaring from the surround sound speakers.

"Hey, birthday girl!"

"Happy birthday, Jules!"

"Yo, Juliet!"

Feeling like I'm walking through another one of my nightmares, I ignore those calling out for me and make a beeline straight for the hallway between the kitchen and the four-car garage. Hardly anyone knows about the bathroom back there and it'll give me a chance to calm down and think rationally.

I slam into the semi-secret bathroom and quickly shut and lock the door behind me. My heart pounds against my chest, beating against my ribcage to the nearly same rhythmic thumping of the music on the other side of the door. My head pounds in time with the music and my pulse, a consistent maddening beat. My hands curl into fists at my sides, nails digging into my palm until pain spears through me and I have to force them to relax.

My hip hits the bathroom counter which runs the length of the wall, jerking me to a stop. I slap my palms against the rim of the porcelain surface and latch on with my fingers, clamping down on either side of the sink as I look up. Dark winged eyeliner. The perfect contour to both highlight my best features and hide my flaws. I turn my head from side to side and watch the reflection follow the movement, hoping to catch a hint that this is a dream. No such luck. Every movement is exact. Yet still, the woman in the mirror doesn't feel like me.

The phone I stuck between my bra and breast earlier in the evening lights up, illuminating a patch of my skin in the reflection. I take it out and seeing the face above the name that pops up in the center of the screen makes me want to throw the damn thing. I am living in a nightmare, only this one is real and no amount of drugs or therapy can make it end. I slam my phone down on the counter and stare at Avery's laughing squinty face and name until the phone stops ringing. It feels like an eternity.

A moment passes and then it starts up again. To my surprise, it's not Avery again. This time, it's my mom. No way in hell am I answering her call. The phone goes black and then trills a third time as another call comes through. My dad's name and face come across the screen. I'm not stupid. My dad never calls. It's Mom.

My racing heartbeat, the sound of the music pounding on the other side of the wall, my sweaty hands, the building rage squeezing the air from my lungs—it all combines into one massive lump that takes over my throat and chokes me.

I don't think twice; I pick up the phone and smash it into the counter—once, twice, three times. A long vertical crack forms across the 'crack-resistant' glass. Crack resistant, but not pissed off Juliet resistant. When the screen goes dark again, I turn and drop it into the toilet next to the bathroom counter. Then, as if I just have to make sure no one else can call me on it ever again, I reach up and press down on the handle of the toilet, flushing the phone.

It won't go down. It'll probably get stuck in the mouth and wedged deep where all of the crappy water can seep into the cracks I created, but that's not the goal. I don't care if it gets stuck. I just want to make sure I don't do anything even more stupid ... like try to answer it.

I stand there as the sound of the rushing water from the toilet slowly fades and then cuts off entirely and the silence of the small bathroom seems to wrap its arms around me. The walls grow closer, leaning into each other as if the tops are peering down at me, curious to see what I'll do next.

I feel watched.

Judged.

I can't fucking breathe.

When someone finally comes to knock on the door, the loud banging jolts me back into my body as the nasally sound of Lindsey Crawford's voice filters through the door. "Hey!" she yells, thumping against the wood again. "If you're done in there, some of us have to pee, too, you know."

I close my eyes and wrap my arms around myself as I sink back against the elegant floral wallpaper. The room closes in on me, the flat walls bending to cage me in. I have to go. I can't stay here. Where can I go, though? Home? Home, where my mom's probably drunk and annoyed because dad isn't there? Because he left his phone behind like he always does so she can't track him like she tries to with me.

Lindsey bangs on the outside of the door again. "Hurry up!" she shrieks.

With a groan, I move away from the counter. My ankle rolls as my heel catches on one of the black and white tiles, and I barely catch myself against the counter in time. Frustration pours through me.

"Oh, fuck this," I mutter, reaching down and removing the heels. Without a second thought, I turn and chuck them into the shower stall. The heels slam into the opposite glass wall, and a crack forms, but I couldn't give less of a shit if I tried. Not my house, not my best friend, not my boyfriend, not my fucking problem anymore.

When I turn to reach for the door handle, I feel my eyes begin to burn and I suck in a sharp breath. Crying won't do shit. It won't take back the last hour. It won't erase the image of my best friend faking an orgasm while my boyfriend fucked her. Ugh. What was the point if it wasn't even good for her? Why would she even bother?

The more I move, the less I seem to feel. The heels are gone but not the negative emotions. They swirl inside me like a massive tidal wave about to burst forth. I unlock the door and yank it open to Lindsey's waiting scowl.

"Finally," she snaps, stepping into the doorway as if she means to shove her way past me. "What were you doing in—" Then she gets a good look at my face. "Oh, it's you." I don't know why Avery even invited her; Lindsey has never liked me. Maybe none of my so-called friends have. "What's *wrong,* birthday girl?" She sounds almost amused.

I stare back at her, and I don't know why, but all of the pseudo-politeness I force myself to spew at Silverwood Prep just disappears. The need to always be perfect and maintain my composure disappears. I just don't. fucking. care. anymore.

"What's wrong with me?" I repeat, leaning into her as I

grasp the frame of the bathroom door. Lindsey seems to sense the rising tide of my rage, something no one has ever really seen, not even me. How long have I kept it all bottled up? Had I already known about Bran and Avery and just pretended? There's no way this should shock me. I should've seen the signs ... right? I shove away the swirl of questions that plague my mind and focus on the Barbie-wannabe in front of me. "What's wrong is that I've spent the last three fucking years letting you talk shit about me behind my back without a goddamn word, *Lindsey*." My voice is low, but my tone is biting. "What's wrong is that pathetic excuse for a nose job that your daddy bought you so that you'd break up with Joseph Meyer."

To her, Joseph had been little more than a rebellion against her parents. Maybe he had good dick. Maybe he was one of the few people in our world who was actually real with her for two seconds instead of blowing smoke up her and her trust fund parents' asses. Why that poor kid from Silverwood Public had been so in love with her, I'll never know, but he never deserved the write-off she'd given him when her daddy demanded she stop going out with a boy whose only chances of getting out of Silverwood were "the military or the grave," in Mr. Crawford's words.

Lindsey's artificially plumped lips part in shock. "What the fuck are you—"

"Get out of my fucking face," I snap, cutting her off as I shove her to the side and step into the back hall. "You smell like knock-off Chanel and desperation."

I don't have to look back at her to know that her face is red. "Y-you're a fucking bitch, Juliet!" she stutters out her insult.

"Yeah," I agree in monotone. "I am."

I walk away before I hear Lindsey's reply and find my keys on the counter next to the empty row of shots I'd been downing not thirty minutes before. I didn't finish them all, despite my gut churning like I had. Turning away from the messy kitchen decorated with various expensive liquor bottles and a shattered glass in the sink, I head for the foyer and run into the two people I'd hoped not to see before I left.

Avery and Bran are dressed this time, Avery in her skin-tight cocktail dress and Bran in a polo and pair of faded jeans with carefully placed patches to make the fabric seem old and worn when it's practically right from a catalog. My entire body goes hot where I was cold not ten seconds before.

"Jules!" Avery's voice is higher than average as she practically jumps away from Bran even as he reaches for her. "We've been looking for you."

I arch a brow at her and cross my arms over my chest. My bare toes curl against the tiled floor of the front hallway as I glare down at her. I'm by no means tall, but compared to Avery's four-foot-eleven height, everyone looks down at her—I wonder if that's why she feels the need to fuck every guy she meets. Does it make her feel powerful?

Avery's face pinches and she laughs as she reaches out, patting my arm. "Did you hear? Someone was fucking in one of the rooms and got caught, people apparently thought it was Bran and me." She rolls her eyes in a practiced move. "My parents are gonna be so pissed if they didn't clean up after—"

"Stop." I close my eyes as Bran comes up behind her and take a deep breath before reopening my eyes. "Just fucking stop." Avery might excel at playing the pretty dumb girl, but this is too pathetic even for me. Does she think I'm an idiot?

I mean she was fucking your boyfriend at your own birthday party, a snide inner voice reminds me. My hands curl inward and the metal teeth of my keys dig into my palm.

"What?" Avery blinks up at me, her fake lashes fluttering rapidly—a sure sign of her anxiety. "You don't think it was real, do you?" She forces a scoff. "Jules, I'd never—"

"Lie to me?" I cut her off before raising my eyes to Bran's

over her shoulder. He, at the very least, doesn't look as confident about getting out of this mess they've made. His brows are creased and the square cut of his jaw jumps nervously as he clenches and unclenches his teeth.

"Juliet..." He starts, but I don't let him finish as I step out of Avery's reach and circle them.

"Fuck off, Avery." I toss the words over my shoulder as I march to the front of the house. "You can have Bran for all I care—it's not like you actually came anyway. God knows I never did."

"Juliet!" Bran's shocked tone, full of outrage and a hint of irritation slides over my skin like sandpaper, but I don't turn around. Instead, the second I hit the door, I take off running.

Thanking God I ditched the heels, I sprint across the wide-open lawn down to the edge of the driveway where I parked my car earlier in the night. My feet slap the wet grass underfoot right before tiny rocks from the paved driveway dig into my soles. I can hardly feel them, though, as I unlock the BMW and quickly jump inside.

I don't bother with a seatbelt as my head screams at me to just get out! The engine purrs to life and my headlights flash over a Porsche in front of me as I turn and back out, nearly clipping the SUV behind me as I swivel the wheel at the last second. The car jerks and gears grind together, the wheels spinning as the back ones slip into the grass and dirt. I freeze as my gaze connects with a pair of semi-familiar cloudy gray eyes before swapping to those of the man sitting in the passenger seat.

Fuck me. As if my humiliation wouldn't be complete without *them* here. The fucking gangsters from Silverwood Public. The Scorpion Kings, or at least two of them. My upper lip curls back as I ease up on the gas and then press back down. Traction catches and I manage to get the car back onto the actual pavement.

Ignore them, I tell myself, ripping my attention away from their gazes. No doubt they're only here to do business—sell their drugs, fuck rich girls who think poor boys have bigger dicks, and generally make a nuisance of themselves with their judgmental looks. It's not my problem anymore. It's not my party anymore.

Hell, maybe after tonight, I won't ever see them again. It's not like I'll ever go to another Silverwood Prep party again. In fact, the second I get home, I plan to convince my parents to let me transfer schools. A nice boarding school in the Swiss Alps sounds fucking fantastic right about now.

Just as I hit the main road, I glance up and over the rusted roof of Alexio Medicci's old SUV. He and the other Scorpion King with him watch me through the windows, but I focus on the open door of Avery's parents' lake house. Avery and Bran stand on the porch, staring after me as several others from our school pour out of the house after them, likely having been called by the drama as they watch me speed off into the night.

Fresh tears well up and I swipe them away with the back of my hand. "Stop it," I order myself through a thick voice as the tears start to fall anyway.

My chest aches, winding tighter and tighter as everything inside threatens to shatter into pieces. Silverwood isn't far from the lake and black pavement disappears beneath my wheels as I drive back. The interior of the car is silent and I almost forget why—that is, until I remember what I'd done with my phone. That's fine with me. I don't need any more noise than what is already in my head.

Halfway home, I roll down the window. Hot summer air pours into the car, partially relieving the headache I have pounding against the inside of my skull. My stomach churns with bile and pain.

Forty-five minutes later, I turn into the gated community of my parents' home, and as I slow to a stop on my street, I look up and spot several police cruisers outside the three-story house I've lived in since before I can remember. The BMW idles at a stop sign as I gape at the scene before me.

The door to my house opens and my father is walked out with two officers at his back. His hands are cuffed and just as I'm sure I've fallen into some striking dream or alternate reality, a white van with a news logo painted on its side speeds past me and shrieks to a stop at the curb. That, more than anything else, has me taking my foot off the brake and easing forward until I'm close enough to park.

I turn the car off and get out as my mom runs out of the house after my dad and the police. "You're making a mistake!" she screams at one of the officers.

Several people pile out of the van. Some with cameras already in hand and another with a microphone and a haphazard suit thrown on—like they were rushed here last minute. I reach for my phone only to realize, again, that I'd tossed it in a toilet. Still, even without looking at it, I know that it's well past midnight.

"What the hell…" I move closer, stumbling up the pristine lawn of my house.

"Oh, thank God!" The second she spots me, my mother whirls around and hurries towards me. To say I'm shocked that she seems happy to see me is an understatement. A moment later though, she bypasses me and runs straight to someone else.

Turning, I spot my father's best friend and business partner, Morpheus Calloway standing on the sidewalk. He, too, looks like he was just pulled from bed in a soft pair of gray sweat pants and a white t-shirt. His face is lean, almost haggard, and a far cry from the normally immaculate man I'm used to seeing.

Pressured by the chaos around me, I turn and start walking towards them.

"Morpheus!" my mother calls out. "Do something!

They're taking him away. They say he did something terrible!"

My mother practically collapses in Morpheus' arms. Her loud, open sobbing ramps up. Something cold fills my chest. *He did something? What did he do?*

Almost as if he can hear me, Morpheus' face lifts and the look he gives me is one full of sadness and pity. I don't understand that. They couldn't have known why I was home already. Why would he be looking at me with pity?

"I'm sorry, Denise," Morpheus says, his voice low and gravelly. "It's true."

"*No!*" my mother wails. "No, it can't be!"

I stop in front of them and Morpheus' gaze lifts away from my mother, settling on me. His attention crawls over me, a visceral thing that feels alive the longer he stares. My insides churn and all of the alcohol I drank earlier in the night threatens to make me heave. Where he looked at her with tightness, he seems almost gentle with me. That gentleness is a lie. "*Juliet.*"

It's not the sound of police sirens or the news crew chattering animatedly that breaks that final shred of sanity inside me. It's not even my mother's sobbing or the click of the cruiser door as my father is ducked inside the backseat. It's my name, spoken in that quiet, broken whisper.

I thought nothing could make this night worse.

I was wrong.

As Morpheus opens his mouth again, all of the emotions I'd been feeling crash towards me at once. The hurt. The regret. The pain. The loss. The confusion. The anger. They hit me and that's it. I step away from him and my mother. My heartbeat slows down until it's a slug squeezing through my arteries. A distant ringing echoes against my eardrum, growing louder and softer … louder and softer. Tingles race up my arms and down my legs as goosebumps rise up on my skin. It's gone. All of it. The money. The protection. I cut my gaze to Morpheus and then my mother before they slide back to the blue and red flashing lights of the cop cars situated outside of my family's home.

It's the end of May. It should be warm. Yet, all I taste is the burn of ice on the back of my tongue.

Suddenly, I don't feel anything anymore. I don't want to. Not a *goddamn* thing.

3
JULIET

2 months later…

"Damn, girl, here again?" The sound of Cory's deep voice pulls me to a halt. Sweat drips down the side of my face, making the faded blue tendrils of hair that have slipped out of my ponytail cling to my cheeks and neck. "Why'd you come in so early? Ain't you in school yet?"

"School starts today," I answer the gruff older man, bending as I catch my breath without looking his way. One look at my expression and there's no doubt in my mind that Cory will guess the reason I decided to drag myself out of bed at five a.m. on a Monday morning for a workout before school. Hell, he probably doesn't even need to see my face to know why, but I keep my face averted regardless.

"Ahh, right." Cory's voice drifts off and the only sound that can be heard in the responding silence is the drip of my sweat on one of the plentiful faded blue mats or the churning cough of the fifteen-year-old air conditioner.

I slam my carefully taped knuckles into the punching bag

once more as Cory speaks again. "You're going to Public now, I heard."

I immediately reach out, catching the swinging bag as it jerks away before coming straight back. Holding it with both hands, I've never been more grateful for the lack of an early morning crowd in Cory's gym than I am now. His continued words, though, mean he's not intending to give me the stress relief I'm craving. He wants answers, and as one of the few people left in Silverwood who'll actually treat me like a human being, I owe him at least my respect and consideration.

I lift my head and give the gym owner a bland look. "Yeah," I tell him. "I transferred over the summer." He already knows that, but I don't point it out. As if he senses my inner thoughts, Cory shakes his head. The black dreads hanging down his back hardly move.

Turning away from Cory's dark and insightful gaze, I reach for one of the towels and spray bottles that are stationed around the gym for people to wipe off the equipment they use. Presenting the nozzle to the outside of the punching bag, I douse it.

"Can't says I blame you for coming here 'stead of getting ready for school," Cory mutters before lifting his voice a bit, "but you know you can't be coming around as often now, right? No slacking on your school work."

"I won't slack," I promise as I wipe down the equipment and replace the items in their rightful box. "I want out of this fucking town."

Any other adult might have chastised me for cursing. Then again, most of the adults of Silverwood would've turned me away at the door—membership or not—simply because of my last name. Three months ago, being a Donovan had meant something good and powerful here in Silverwood. Now, it's the name of a criminal. A pariah.

If anyone knows what's going to happen the second I step into Silverwood Public, it's Cory. He might have graduated over a decade ago, but he knows this town and its residents as well as anybody. He knows the tracks that divide the economic classes from obscenely wealthy to dirt poor, and even if he can't understand every nuance of my sudden downfall in such a short time, Cory knows that someone like me won't be accepted in Silverwood Public.

A fallen elite and the daughter of the man who wrecked half of this town by embezzling millions from the factories and businesses that keep most of them employed in some way or another. Those on the north side of Silverwood—other wealthy business investors and their prep school kids—managed to muddle through unscathed. Here, though, in the section of Silverwood where I now live because it's all I can afford, they didn't. Houses were lost. Life savings. Some of the more destitute even ended their lives when they realized how much they'd sunk into my father's businesses and how much they'd been scammed.

In the last three months, there have been more suicides in Silverwood than homicides. Considering the violence of the criminal organizations that run rampant on the southside, that, more than anything else, was the wake-up call to make me realize how bad it is going to be when I show up at Silverwood Public.

"I don't have a choice," I say, half to myself and half to Cory. "If I want to leave Silverwood behind, I need a scholarship." I put the spray bottle and paper towel roll back, glancing over at the gym's owner briefly. He arches a brow at me. "I think this year is going to be my best academic year by far."

Because I won't accept another outcome. Failure is not an option.

Cory sighs and his shoulders droop as he nods towards the front of the gym. "Go on home," he says. "Get properly cleaned up 'fore the bus come 'round."

Even though I'd been about to do just that, I check the old

digital clock hanging on the wall above the entrance. "Bus doesn't come for at least another hour," I tell him.

"Ain't you a girl?" Cory asks.

I cast him a confused look. "Has it taken you this long to notice?"

He snorts. "No, 'course not. It's just that girls need more time to get ready. Women always do."

I shake my head and don't offer a reply. Before? He would've been right. Before I wouldn't have even bothered to glance at this podunk little hole-in-the-wall gym as I drove by in the cherry red BMW my parents had bought me for my seventeenth birthday—after I'd crashed the white convertible that they'd gotten me for my sixteenth.

A lot can change in twelve weeks. *I've* changed and there is no going back.

"I'll be fine," I tell Cory as I head towards the cubby holes for members to leave any extra shit they brought with them. Yanking my hoodie from the uppermost corner hole, I slip it on and flip the fabric over my head.

My hair hangs around my face, a mass of different shades of azure waves. The color is an uneven cheap box dye because if there's anything a girl knows—regardless of which side of the tracks she's from—control starts with the hair. Coloring it, chopping it, or giving yourself bangs, it doesn't matter.

When the world is out of your control, you find something to latch on to and make yours.

For so long, I'd let my mom convince me that blonde was the perfect color. My one attempt at something different—a pretty sunrise red—she'd locked herself in her bedroom until I'd agreed to go back to her stylist and get it changed. Even then, her complaints hadn't ceased, but now she's not here. Neither of my parents are. My hair is my own.

Cory waves me off as I head towards the front of the gym with the only other item that'd been in my cubby—a ratty gym bag. Through the glass windows that frame the front of the gym, the sky is beginning to lighten. It's usually a thirty-minute walk from Cory's gym to the apartment complex I moved to after the authorities confiscated my parents' assets and I'd refused to live with Dad's best friend, Morpheus Calloway. I take a shortcut, though, jogging through an old junkyard sitting behind an abandoned grocery store. Still, I keep my hood up despite the warm August air in case someone spots me.

Hopefully most people haven't caught on yet about the changed hair, but eventually it'll get out. When I have to apply for jobs. When I go to school. There's no point hiding who I am long term, but for just a little while, I want to cling to my anonymity even if it's only a facade.

I hurry through a shower, the hot water running out quickly so I spend a good amount of time under icy spray just to get the sweat out of my hair.

When I hop out, I swipe a hand across the grimy, chipped mirror and take in my reflection. Dark circles underscore my eyes, and for a brief moment, the old me comes back and I wonder if I should try to cover it up with makeup. Almost as soon as that thought occurs though, I wave it away. There's no point in wasting what little money I have left on my looks.

Finished with my shower, I throw on a pair of jeans and an oversized t-shirt. At least the one good thing about switching from Silverwood Prep to Silverwood Public is the lack of uniform. I check the microwave clock and scramble to yank on a pair of sneakers, snatching up my backpack, before sprinting out the door.

I spy the big yellow bus rattling up the street from the outside upper deck of the two-story apartment building and bolt for the stairs. A collection of other students wait on the road to be picked up. I draw my hoodie back on and perform the same ritual that has become so normal over the last several weeks, flipping the hood up to mask my features.

The bus comes to a slow halt, brakes squealing in protest as red lights flash, and the stop sign swings out from the opposite side. I jog up the sidewalk and watch the others get on first before following their lead. I haven't ridden a bus since well before middle school, and even then, it was infrequent.

I hop up the steps into the bus, ducking my head lower when the driver looks at me curiously. Either my hood is doing its job or everyone is too tired from the first early morning they've had in months, but no one else spares me a glance as I move to the back of the bus and take a seat by a window.

Leaning back, I stare at the passing scenery as the bus speeds up and slows down to stop at frequent intervals. We pass by dilapidated brick buildings, millhouses with large patches on their roofs, and trailer parks as the vehicle begins to fill to overflowing. The bus even stops in front of a motel where one student hops on, their face turned down as they slide onto a seat towards the front since there's certainly no more room in the back. I sink lower in my seat and turn away from the two who have taken up residence on my row with me.

Perhaps it's the early morning, but few people bother to make conversation on the way to school. Instead, the sound of the bus's engine and someone's soft snores are all that linger in the air. By the time we roll up to Silverwood Public, I'm hopeful that I can get through the rest of this day as unseen as possible. Keeping my hood up, I exit the bus and follow the crowd toward the glass double doors leading into the school's cafeteria. I've never entered Silverwood Public as anything more than a rival cheerleader—and those days are long behind me now. The double doors open and I find myself hovering in place as students line up and begin moving in a restricted single-file line through the metal detectors directed by tired-looking teachers. That's something new to me. I don't comment and quietly follow the rest even as my heart rate increases. On the other side is the cafeteria where several students are already seated.

Keep your head down and keep your guard up. Cory's advice slides through my mind and I repeat it like a mantra. *Head down. Guard up.*

The ripe scent of stale weed and body odor slaps me in the face as I make it through and stride into the cafeteria. It's louder in here as students greet each other. Despite the early hour, a few boisterous guys are already passing a football back and forth across one of the tables. The teachers linger about, ignoring it all in favor of gossiping amongst each other. I scan the room before directing myself towards an empty table at the far corner, stopping only when a voice calls out.

"Hey, no hoods!" I stop and glance back, spotting a tall older man with graying sideburns glaring my way. "You know the rules," he barks.

I don't, but he doesn't know that. It's obvious he doesn't recognize me, but I know the second I take off the hood, he will, as will every fucking body else. I debate my choices. Take off the hood without a fight and hope I've changed enough for him not to realize who I am ... or ignore him.

I take route number two and start to walk away, moving faster than before.

Wrong decision, I realize a split second later as the sound of stomping footsteps follows me. "Hey, didn't you hear me? I said—" A hard hand grabs my arm and pulls me to a stop and my hood flies off my head. The teacher stops talking abruptly and releases my arm like I'm a snake ready to bite. Who knows? Maybe I am.

Several gazes fall on me and a hush falls across the cafeteria. *Mother fucker.* Just what I wanted to avoid. I want to pull my hood back up, but it's pointless now. "Got it," I say. "I'll keep my hood down."

The teacher glares at me with barely repressed disgust, as if trying to maintain a professional expression is too much for him. He nods towards the tables. "Take a seat."

He doesn't need to tell me twice. I spin away from him and finish my journey to the corner table, turning away from the crowd and facing the wall as I slide my backpack onto the seat next to me. It's quiet behind me for several seconds, and I can feel the burn of people's attention boring into the back of my skull. It only takes a few minutes for people to start talking again and once they do, their words penetrate me.

"—can't believe she actually showed up."

"The fucking nerve."

"I heard her dad got beat up in jail and is in isolation."

"Why is she here? I thought she'd have killed herself by now. I would've if I were her."

"Wasn't she supposed to be staying with Mr. Calloway?"

"He's too nice. I wouldn't trust her not to make off with whatever he has left after what her dad put him through."

Hold it in, I warn myself. *Do not react. It'll only give them more fuel.*

I rip open my backpack, yank out a worn library book, and flip it open. The words on the page blur in front of my eyes as the talking behind me grows louder. They're not even bothering to whisper anymore. Instead, they're just outright speculating.

Was she in on it?

Did she know he was stealing money from the town?

Did she laugh when people lost their homes?

A part of me wants to stand up and scream at them all. Of course, I wasn't in on it. If I was, did they honestly think I'd be here now? And no, people losing their homes isn't funny—not even to me.

I'm not sure how much time has passed when a hand slams down on the end of the table I'm sitting at. Slowly, I lift my head. The girl standing at the end of the table looks like everything my mother would hate. Her bleach blonde hair is dark at the roots from lack of upkeep and her dark eyes are lined all the way around with black liner. She glares at me as two of her friends hover behind her with their arms folded and their own expressions of loathing evident.

I sigh. "Listen," I start, "before you do anything, just know, I'm not here to fight."

"Why are you here then?" she demands. "You don't fucking belong here."

Because dropping out of school isn't an option and I can't afford Silverwood Prep anymore. I don't say as much though and simply hold up my hands in the universal 'I don't want any trouble' gesture.

"I'm just here to graduate like everyone else."

"You think you have a right to be here?" She scoffs and removes her hand from the table, rounding it to move towards me.

Irritation slithers through my veins. Looks like all of my hopes and dreams of managing to get through this day with my head down are dying right here ... and first period hasn't even started yet. *Go me.*

I rise up from my seat as she stops in front of me. There's no way in hell I'm going to let her hover over me and put me in a vulnerable position—not when I can see the barely repressed anger shaking through her whole body. She's skinnier than me, but she's got years at Silverwood Public—so I can't take anything for granted. I open my mouth to tell her she needs to walk away when she rears back and spits in my face. A wad of saliva lands on my cheek and then slides down my jaw.

I blink, frozen for a brief second. Reaching up, I touch my cheek, feeling the wetness there. I wipe it off with the back of my hand and stare down at the sheen on my skin. *So. Fucking. Gross.*

With a sigh, I shake my head. "I really wish you hadn't done that."

"Yeah?" Her friends hurry to join her at her back. "What are you going to do about it?"

In my periphery, I see the teachers from before, just as locked onto this dramatic scene as every fucking body else in the cafeteria. They haven't stopped what they know is coming, though.

Why?

Because they hate me too.

Everyone hates Juliet Donovan—the girl whose dad embezzled millions and ruined thousands of lives. So, what's a little catfight in the school cafeteria going to do? It'll give them some semblance of control, as if being cruel to a Donovan will somehow make them feel better about their own sad sack shitty lives.

I wanted to avoid this as much as I could, but now I know I was right to prepare. They think the pretty little prep princess can't fight and if they continue to think that, then people are going to be coming after me all year.

No one can be trusted. Not even him. Not anymore.

"Listen," I say, lowering my voice, "just walk the fuck away. Walk away and let it go."

Internally, I'm shaking. Enraged. Disgusted. I want to scrub my skin clean of her saliva. I want to shove this bitch to the floor and stomp her into submission. I hold it back. I hold it all back—the rage, the injustice, the cruelty that's bubbling up beneath my flesh.

"Make. Me," the girl says right before she pulls her fist back and slams it into my face.

First day of school and I'm already taking punches like a pro. My head snaps back, but I don't stumble. All of Cory's training and advice is about to come in handy, I realize. For some reason, a small fissure of glee shoots up my spine, filling my bloodstream with adrenaline.

I really hadn't been hoping for this. I know that for a fact. Yet, I also recognize that after three months of hiding and being treated like the town pariah, I've been wanting something to take out all of my rage on. Something that isn't a punching bag or a sparring partner that doesn't hate me. Too bad for this bitch, it's about to be her.

I reach up and run a finger under the side of my nose and it comes away wet with my blood.

"Would you take a good look at that. Looks like the silverbloods of Silverwood bleed red like the rest of us peasants," the girl taunts, and at her back, her minions cackle. "Why don't you do everyone a favor and just leave? No one wants you here. S'not like you deserve to even breathe the same air we do after what your family did to this town."

As expected, the teachers don't do or say shit. They just watch. Useless bunch of assholes. The girl pushes against my chest hard enough to send me back into the table. The backs of my calves slam into the attached stools, but I remain standing. I finish wiping away the blood with the back of my hand and take a deep breath, clenching my fists at my sides.

"Awww is the preppy bitch gonna cry?"

I look up. Cry? She thinks this will make me cry? "Sorry," I say, not feeling the least bit sorry at all as I clench my hand into a fist. "The preppy bitch you were expecting couldn't make it. I'm just a bitch."

4
JULIET

The second my fist flies for the bitch's face, the teachers make their move. Guess it's all right for *me* to get laid into, but the second I fight back, that's going too far. I expected as much. Which is why, even when I spot them hurrying toward us and hear their yells, I don't stop. I take the girl down to the ground and grip her by the throat.

"I tried to be nice," I hiss into her face. "I tried to tell you to back the fuck off, but you didn't listen."

Slamming my fist into her nose, the sound of crunching cartilage flies to my ears. I haven't gotten to bloody anybody up since I started taking lessons from Cory, so this is a whole new experience.

A heavy weight lands against my back and feminine fingers grip at my sides and arms, one even goes around my neck, as her friends try to pull me off. Nails dig into the back of my scalp as someone grabs ahold of my hair and yanks hard. I ignore it all, letting the pain fall over me and then slide right off. My hold on the bitch's throat tightens until she's clawing at my hands and kicking beneath me.

"But thank you," I say to her face, "for giving me a reason

to show everyone here that I'm not going to roll over and let you fuckers take your cheap shots."

"*Cunt.*" She squeezes the word out as black mascara-streaked tears leak down her face.

I roll my eyes and bat away the hand still holding on to my hair, yanking and trying to get me to let up. The girl pulls out several strands. I don't care. I'll go bald before I let this one get away without delivering a clear warning.

I punch again for good measure and she cries out as blood pours from her nostrils. "This will be my only warning to you," I snap. The sound of the teachers' footsteps is getting closer. "Come after me again, and I'll break your fucking legs. Stay away and I'll be good. I'll keep my fucking head down and I won't give anyone any trouble."

She spits at me and I dodge the flying saliva this time before shaking my head and compressing my grip around her throat. The sound of air wheezing from her mouth escapes. Her pulse hammers under my palm. Just a little more and I can completely cut off her airflow. Just a little longer, and she'll pass out. If she's unconscious, she won't be able to spit at me anymore. If she's dead, she won't be able to do anything to me anymore.

The silence in my head is overwhelmed by the cacophony of shrieks and curses. I lean closer, lowering my voice as my lips graze her earlobe. "Spread the word," I tell her. "You don't fuck with me, and I won't fuck with you."

Hard fingers wrap around my arm and pull, but I'm done saying my piece. I let go of the bitch without a fight and let the man holding on to me rip me up from the ground. Turning my head, I take in the bulky figure at my side. Angry brown eyes glare down at me, the same ones that I'd seen in the passenger seat of Alexio Medicci's SUV the night everything had gone to hell.

Nolan Pierce.

I take a step back, retracting my arm from his grip. He

releases me, but before either of us can speak a word, my name is shouted across the cafeteria.

"Miss Donovan!" The same teacher from before—with the graying sideburns—is standing there red-faced and angry. "The principal's office. *Now!*"

"Sure thing," I say, wiping some of the blood still leaking from my nose away as I turn and snatch up my discarded book. I shove it into my bag before flinging it over my shoulder. Nolan Pierce's gaze bores into my back as I go, but I don't give a fuck.

I know who he is and I know damn well why he thought he could step in and stop a fight. Unlike Silverwood Prep, where cheerleaders and jocks are the leaders, Silverwood Public has a different class system. Here, violent assholes and drug dealers are the Kings, and Nolan Pierce is their leader.

As I stride towards the front office, several students hurry out of my way—their eyes wide and shocked. *Good.* As far as first days go, this wasn't the worst way to start my senior year. Now, at least, they'll all think twice before stepping on my fucking toes. I move from the cafeteria to the front hallway, feeling the same teacher's angry breath on my back as I walk. He follows me to the front office and even takes direction when we reach the door, storming past me to slam it open and point inside as if I can't find my own way. I roll my eyes and walk inside.

At the front desk, an older woman with short curly white hair sits, wearing a dress that was likely ugly even back in the seventies. Her bespeckled face lifts when the door flies open.

"Coach Danley? What's this about—" She cuts off the second her gaze falls on me.

"Is Principal Long in?" he demands without answering.

The woman nods quickly, turning her rolling chair back as she looks over her shoulder. "Sh-she should still be in her office. She hasn't left for her walkthrough yet—"

"Good." Coach Danley's hand falls on my arm and it takes

every ounce of my self-control not to rip myself from his grasp as he drags me towards the back hallway to the door labeled 'Principal's Office.'

He doesn't bother to knock. Instead, he grips the knob and twists it open, thrusting me inside. Were this Silverwood Prep, he would be slapped with a lawsuit so fast that it would send his head spinning. But this isn't Silverwood Prep. It's Public and these people know I have no power.

The woman looks up from her desk with glasses perched at the end of her nose. Principal Long is one of those women who has a timeless face—she could be in her thirties or her fifties. The only tell are the slight lines around her mouth and the crow's feet at each corner of her eyes. As Coach Danley storms into her office, she looks up from the pile of paperwork set in front of her and arches a brow at the show of disrespect.

"Coach Danley." Her tone is even as she says the man's name. "Is there a reason you've barged into my office at"—she checks the clock sitting on her desk—"seven fifty-five in the morning without so much as a knock?"

"*This one* has already started a fight," Coach Danley gestures to me, practically spitting the words 'this one' out as if it's just as hideous as my name.

Principal Long turns her eyes on me, a mixture of colors swarming in their depths. Browns, greens, and a hint of gold. Her slate-brown hair is pulled back into a ponytail, making her face look more severe than the rounded curve of her jawline would suggest it normally is.

Unlike Coach Danley, she doesn't have any obvious signs of hostility—at least not directed at me. Her irritation is purely saved for Coach Danley.

The principal blows out a breath and sets down the file she'd been reading when I'd been unceremoniously launched into her office. She pinches the bridge of her nose for a moment before pointing to one of the twin chairs in front of her desk. "Take a seat."

Coach Danley moves forward and she holds up a hand, stopping him. "*Not. You.*" She glares at him. "I meant the *student.*"

Rounding the chairs, I drop into one of them. As uncomfortable as the seat is, unlike the stools I'd seen in the cafeteria, the faded cushion under my ass at least gives some barrier against the hardwood underneath.

"She caused a fight in the cafeteria," Coach Danley states. "There's surely security footage to prove it. I recommend expulsion."

Principal Long looks up at him, her mouth turning down in a scowl. "We do not expel students on the first day, Danley," she snaps, dropping the coach title. "And if a fight was all it took, you know very well that half our student population wouldn't be in school."

"But she—"

"Where's the other one?" Principal Long cuts him off with a harsh look.

Coach Danley frowns in confusion. "The other one?"

One eyebrow lifts. "You're not telling me that Miss Donovan got into a fight all on her own, are you? There should be two students in front of me, Coach Danley."

"I-I sent Megan White to the nurse's office," he stutters out. "*This one*"—he jams his finger at me, using the same tone as before—"attacked her and left her with a bloody nose."

Long looks at me and then frowns. "Seems like she's not the only one." She reaches forward and shoves a tissue container closer to me before pointing to a spot beneath her nose. "You've still got some blood here," she tells me.

I grab a tissue and dab it against my nostrils before glancing back at the coach whose face is quickly growing purple. "It's interesting that you send one girl to the nurse's office for a bloody nose but not the other," Principal Long comments.

"Megan White's injuries were more serious," he defends.

I don't even bother to hide the smile of pride that comes to my face.

The principal sighs and waves towards the door. "Go back to your morning duties. I will handle this," she snaps. "Next time, unless the other student is unconscious or in need of emergency medical care, you will send them *both* to my office."

The fact that at least someone is attempting to be impartial shouldn't give me hope. It doesn't. All it makes me feel is the sinister creep of distrust crawling up my throat. I clench my hands into fists and direct my attention forward, not even flinching when Coach Danley turns and storms out of the principal's office. I tighten my features when the door slams in his wake and the pictures and certificates on the wall rattle with his exit. I'm not sure who my dad fucked in Coach Danley's family, but I'd bet my last remaining dollar it was someone he cared about.

Principal Long waits a beat. I'm not sure why—maybe to make sure Coach Danley won't come stomping back in or to give the tension in the room a second to ease. After that beat, however, she directs her focus to me.

"So, first day at Silverwood Public and you've already gotten into a fight?" She shakes her head and reaches up, peeling her glasses off and setting them on the scarred surface of her desk. "If I were a gambling woman, I'd have bet it'd take at least a week."

I shrug. "Guess the animosity of the people can't be changed in a few short months."

She snorts. "I was really more relying on the intelligence I know you to have."

My upper lip curls back. "You don't know me," I snap.

Long arches one of those brows at me and the sight of it makes me realize exactly why Coach Danley had gone quiet when she'd done it to him. It's a strange sort of expression—

on someone else, nonthreatening, but on a woman like her? It's a little unsettling.

Long turns her head, a curl slipping loose from her ponytail.

"Regardless of what I know or don't know," she says, sliding into the main conversation with ease, "do you have anything to say?"

I cross my arms. "Does it matter if I do?"

"Of course it matters," she replies. "I'd like to hear your side of the story first before I track down Megan White."

"You heard the coach," I say, pressing my back against the hard spine of the chair. "There are security cameras in the cafeteria. I'm sure you can draw your own conclusions."

Principal Long eyes me for a moment more. "Interesting," she murmurs.

My jaw clenches tight. "What is?"

She doesn't answer for a long moment as we examine one another. Then she props her elbows onto the edge of her desk and steeples her fingers together, resting her chin there. "Why so hesitant to tell me your side of things, Juliet?" she asks.

"I'm not." Even as the words come out, I know they're a lie. I don't want to tell her the truth and listen to her pick apart every piece of my story. It's what people have done for the last three months—all of them wondering if I truly had no clue about my father's crimes and schemes.

Long hums in the back of her throat for a moment before rolling her chair back and standing up. My eyes go up and up some more. I hadn't realized how tall she was.

"If you don't want to tell me, fine," she says, shocking me, but then her next words set me on edge. "How about I take a stab at it and you stop me if I get something wrong?" She rounds the desk with her long legs and leans back against the wood, crossing her arms over an ample chest.

"I'm guessing you were approached by the student you attacked, and she said something about the fact that Mr.

Donovan is in jail and Mrs. Donovan has seemingly fled town."

The mention of my parents makes my whole body go rigid in the chair. She eyes me up and down, but despite her incorrect assumption, I don't say a word. I'm curious to see how far she'll take things.

"Before I saw you walk into my office here, I knew there would be some trouble considering the last few months. Now, that I've seen you—"

"I'm more trouble than I'm worth?" I guess, cutting her off.

She smirks and shakes her head. There's a note of sorrow and almost ... sympathy in her eyes when she looks at me again. I hate that. I don't want sympathy. I want to be left the fuck alone.

Instead of answering my question, however, she nods to the blue strands of hair that trail down either side of my face. "Dyed your hair to change your look, huh?"

I shrug. "Just felt like a change." It's not a total lie.

Long grins at me. "Sure you did, kiddo."

I scowl. "Don't call me that," I snap. "I'm eighteen. If I'm old enough to take care of myself, pay taxes, get a job, and skip the system then I'm not a kid."

"You're also old enough to get arrested for battery." Long's statement is delivered with little more than a quirk of her brow and I have no response for it. After a beat, she sighs and turns her head. One long, unpainted nail presses a button on the landline sitting on her desk. "Mrs. Rogers, can you please cancel my morning meeting?"

Above our heads, the speaker crackles as the bell signaling the start of first period sounds. Long returns to her earlier posture as the bell stops and Mrs. Rogers' reply comes through. "Yes, Ma'am. I'll make a note and send out an email."

"Come on." Principal Long straightens away from her

desk and uses two fingers to gesture for me to stand. I ball up the tissue still in my hand and get to my feet. She strides for the door, leaving me to follow behind her. On the way out, I toss the bloodied tissue into the waste paper basket and ignore Mrs. Rogers' curious gaze as I'm led out of the office and into the now deserted front hall.

"Where are we going?"

Without looking back, Long replies. "You'll see."

I don't like that answer, but short of beating a real response out of her, I don't think I'll get anything more. I've already punched one person today and made myself more than known to the school. Attacking the principal won't help. So, I keep following her instead of turning the fuck around and walking right past the added metal detectors at the front of the building and the doors waiting for me.

5
JULIET

I eye the girl standing before me in a pair of jean cut-offs so short I'm shocked they still manage to cover most of her ass. Principal Long doesn't even blink at the bare midriff the chick is sporting beneath the ripped black t-shirt that reads 'suck on this'—as if she's long since overcome the idea of enforcing a dress code amongst the crowd at Silverwood Public.

"Juliet Donovan, meet Roquel Lee."

The girl—Roquel—blows the gum she's chewing into a bubble that pops across her lips. Her tongue swipes out, gathering the sticky pink substance, and brings it back into her mouth before she finally takes a step forward and holds out her hand to me. "Nice to meet you."

I grimace but take her hand regardless and drop it quickly after the greeting is finished.

"Your punishment regarding this morning's fight will be an in-school suspension Tuesday through Friday," Long states. "I'd rather not start out today since, well, we don't have anyone to watch you and no one else will be there. I'll speak with Megan about what happened this morning. I'd put her in ISS too … if I thought the two of you could be trusted to be alone in a room together. As it stands, I don't. So, her punishment will either be the following week or something else."

I don't comment.

"Roquel here," Long continues, "is going to be your guard dog for the rest of today."

"Guard dog?" I blurt. Are principals allowed to say that?

Long reads me clear as fucking day because the second she looks at my face, she burst out laughing. "Yeah, kiddo," she replies, wiping one finger beneath her eyes even as she ignores my earlier demand. "Cory warned me you'd need one. Thanks for that—I lost our little bet."

"Cory?" She knew Cory? What the hell did my gym's owner have to do with Principal Long?

She smirks and leans down. I'm not super short, but I'm certainly no five-foot-ten model like she is. "Keep up the training," she says, lowering her voice. "If you're gonna make it through a senior year here, you'll need it." With that, she straightens, nods to Roquel, and turns around to walk away.

What. The. Actual. Fuck.

Seconds tick by and then Roquel pops around my side and leans closer. "You ready to go?" she asks.

I'm ready to move towns and change identities, but short of winning the lottery, I have no more money and no way to leave Silverwood. I'd sleep in my car if I could, but I sold that to be able to afford the rent and utilities on my new apartment and pad the money I'm relying on until I can get a part-time job.

"Yeah." I blow out a breath. "I'm ready."

"Great!" she chimes. "So, like Principal Long said, I'm Roquel and I guess I'm your school guide now. Do you have your schedule already?"

Without a word, I reach into my bag and pull out the crinkled schedule I printed off at the local library the week prior. She snatches it from my hand and holds it up to her face, squinting her already slenderly shaped eyes as she reads.

"'Kay, so it looks like you have homeroom with me," she says, pointing to the classroom she'd just been called out of. "So, remember this place, 'cause this is where you have to show up every morning."

"Got it." My foot starts tapping.

"Let's see what else you've got here…" Roquel drifts off and then releases a slow whistle. "Damn, your shit is packed. No study hall or anything?" She glances up at me.

"I want to graduate early," I say. The sooner I graduate, the sooner I can apply to a college and potentially get accepted for either an early semester or a summer program.

She clicks her tongue, popping a smaller bubble of gum with her teeth. "Yeah, well, if you can manage to keep up with these classes then you probably will." Her eyes scan the paper some more and in a quieter tone, she mutters, "Or at least you'll only be here for like an hour or two second semester." She shrugs. "Lots of the smart ones end up doing that and working overtime to earn money before they're completely on their own."

I don't feel the need to respond as she turns and starts walking, taking my schedule with her. "Come on, I'll give you a tour of Silverwood Public and then point out all your classes. First period will last for another thirty minutes, so you should be able to make second period without an issue."

To my surprise, there's no animosity in her tone. She makes it to the end of the hall before she realizes I'm not with her, and when she does, she stops and looks back, waiting for me. "You coming?"

I eye her yet again, but if she's not going to ask questions then I'm not going to encourage her to. I pull my bag onto my back and stride towards her. "Lead the way."

Roquel does just that. Though slightly shorter than me, Roquel's legs pick up speed as she walks. "That's the freshman hall—the sophomore hall—junior hall—library is up the stairs." Roquel gestures as she moves, looking up from my schedule as we move through the school. "Chem labs are down this way—you've got that fifth period," she states as we turn a corner and pass a row of empty pinboards anchored to the hallway walls.

Unlike Silverwood Prep, Silverwood Public isn't as well maintained. Though clean, there are portions of walls with peeling paint, scuffs on the cheap tiled floor, and mysterious stains on the ceilings that I'd rather not think about.

We're about fifteen minutes into the tour when I think it finally dawns on this girl that I haven't said a word in more than half that time. She slows to a stop at the mouth of one of the hallways and turns back to me. I pause, too, as her eyes travel up from my once-clean sneakers to my jeans and then up to my face.

She tilts her head to the side. "You don't like me, do you?"

"I don't know you enough to dislike you."

Roquel sighs. "I thought you'd be more stuck up—complaining about the lack of facilities and shit—but I guess after everything that's happened, I'm not too surprised by the attitude."

"What do you mean?"

She turns back towards the hallway and starts walking again. This time though, she lowers her hand and folds up my schedule before tucking it into her back pocket. I'll have to remember to get that back from her—I'd rather not have to catch another public bus to the library if I can help it, and with how things are going so far with teachers, I'm not entirely sure I'll be able to print it off again here at the school.

"You know," Roquel says, completely ignoring my question. "It would be better for you to at least try to be nice while you're here. They say you catch more flies with honey than vinegar."

"I'm not trying to catch anyone," I reply tartly. Who the fuck is this girl?

Roquel ignores my statement and continues. "Public can be pretty rough if you don't have any friends."

Is she offering to be my friend? I blanch. "What makes you think I want to make friends?" The only reason I'm even in school is because it's my last resort to get the fuck out of Silverwood. If I don't graduate then any hope of escaping to a decent college is gone.

Her short black hair shifts as she looks over her shoulder at me, and her lips twitch. "A princess from Silverwood Prep in a public school?" She snorts to herself. "Yeah, they'll eat you alive if you don't have anyone to back you up—whether you realize it or not, girl, you totally need some friends that'll back you up."

"I don't think I qualify as a princess anymore," I remind her.

I continue to follow Roquel until we come to a standstill, and when I take a look around, I realize we've traversed the whole school and we're back in the cafeteria attached to the main hall. The sounds of clanking and metal on metal grind my nerves as the lunch ladies hurry to clean up breakfast and move on to prepare the first round of school lunches. Roquel spins in a circle until she faces me. Clasping her hands behind her back, she rocks back and forth on her feet. She seems nice —polite even and not nearly as hostile as I was expecting— but that doesn't mean shit. Even nice people have dark sides to them.

"What happened this morning is only going to keep happening." She offers me the warning in a casual tone.

I tilt my head in her direction. "I figured as much," I admit, then with a slow smile, I lean back. "Bring it on."

She shakes her head. "I wouldn't be so cocky if I were you," she replies. "You caught Megan off guard, that's all. No one actually expected you to fight back."

"Or win." I deadpan as I push past her and head for the

front hall. Halfway there, I pause and turn back, holding out my hand. "I think I can take it from here," I say. "I'll need my schedule back."

One dark brow arches and Roquel smiles. "Sure, but first let me give you some advice."

I shake my head in disbelief. "Save your advice," I say.

She hums in the back of her throat, rocking back and forth on her heels once more. "Then no dice, chickadee. You want your schedule back? Then you gotta listen up."

I turn to face her fully. "Why bother?" I demand. "I'm not going to be around long. Once senior year is through, I'm fucking out of this godforsaken town and you'll all be a distant memory in my rearview."

She smirks. "A lot can change in a year."

A growl rumbles up my throat. "Fine," I snap. If that's the price of getting my goddamn schedule back, then so be it. "Spit it out."

Roquel's feet land flat on the ground and her smile drops away. "I know for a fact you were one of the rulers of your last school, Juliet Donovan," she states. "Public has a hierarchy, too, and unfortunately for you, you're now at the bottom of it."

I cross my arms. "And I should give a fuck, why?" Despite my sharp question and tone, I sense the direction of the conversation as I recall Nolan Pierce's hand gripping my upper arm in this very room. My fingers close over the same place now.

"You should give a hell of a lot of fucks," Roquel says. "Because unlike your old school—bullying around here is a bit different. We don't have any rich parties for you not to get invited to. Public plays rougher than that." She shrugs. "It's the only way we know how."

"Okay?" The word slips out through gritted teeth.

"People here go for the throat and they'll rip it out if you give them even an inch," Roquel says. "That girl this morning? That's Megan White. She's one of Giovanni Vargas' girlfriends."

The name slips off her lips with a sigh. Every muscle in my body tenses. If anyone is as bad as Nolan Pierce or Alexio Medicci, it's their best friend, Giovanni Vargas.

"I guarantee that if Megan can convince Gio that you're deserving of attention, your life will get a hell of a lot harder. The Scorpion Kings will eat you alive."

The Scorpion Kings. Even in Silverwood Prep they're infamous—the three bastards of Silverwood, not so much in terms of blood but in attitude. They're the worst of the worst. Drugs. Guns. Blackmail. Revenge. Despite the fact that they're all still in high school, the three men known as the Scorpion Kings are extortionists and runners for Darrio Vargas—the defacto crime lord of Silverwood's seedy underbelly.

To get involved with them would be the opposite of what I want—freedom.

Maybe a year ago, I would've cared about Roquel's obvious caution or the threat they present. Maybe before I'd been fucked over and left behind to take all the heat, I would've listened to the girl trying to give me somewhat decent advice and information about my new circumstances. Unfortunately for her, though, I'm not who I was and I just don't care anymore. Not about her and not about some group of assholes who consider themselves powerhouses to control the populace of Silverwood Public.

"Listen, Roquel," I say, stopping her when she parts her lips to start talking again. "Whatever the hierarchy is here—it's got nothing to do with me. If I'm on the totem pole, then you're right, I'm at the bottom. I'm fine with that. I'm not looking to climb shit. I meant what I said this morning—everyone leaves me the fuck alone and I'll mind my own business."

Roquel sighs and offers me a sad smile. "If you were anyone else, I wouldn't bother with this," she admits. "But you're not—you're Juliet Donovan. You're public enemy number one." Her sad smile falls away and a flat look enters her eyes. "I'm not saying any of this to scare you. I'm trying to save your damn life."

She steps closer until we're nearly chest to chest. "So, take the fucking advice and find a friend or two—whatever you have to do to make that happen," she says. "It doesn't matter how good you are, you can't handle the entire school alone. The Scorpion Kings aren't going to be fucked with if you step out of line."

I meet her eye to eye. "Then I won't step out of line." It's as simple as that. I'll keep my head down and I won't do a damn thing. I don't want to get caught up in their illegal bullshit anyway. One criminal in my family is all I can truly stand.

"You already have," Roquel replies. "Megan's dad lost a lot because of yours. Her parents are divorcing because her mom found out he invested practically all of their savings into your Donovan-Calloway enterprises. They lost damn near everything and she and her mom are currently living with her alcoholic grandpa. She *hates* your father—ergo, she hates you too, and she has every intention of making your life miserable."

Already there. "Okay," I say. "Let her try. Not like I can stop it. She'll learn that I'm not easy prey."

A soft growl erupts from Roquel. "You're not listening to me," she snaps. "She's fucking Gio and if she convinces him to get rid of you—he will. He might not even need to do it himself either. Nolan Pierce and Alexio Medicci would do anything for their boy. Everyone is pretty sure that Alexio Medicci kills people for the mob anyway."

The mob? I resist the urge to roll my eyes. He, like his friends, deals drugs—the fact is undeniable considering I've seen him so often at various Prep parties trading little bags of weed or white powder for cash—but there's no way the three of them are that dangerous.

"If Gio calls war on you because of Megan, you're as good as fucked." Roquel pauses a moment as if she wants that to sink in. "So, when I say find some friends, what I mean is when they come after you, and make no mistake, they *will* come after you—you're going to need a lot more than some good reflexes to protect yourself."

"I'm not here to fuck with anyone," I tell her. "I'm not going to go out of my way to pay them back either. I just want to get my diploma and get out."

She's already shaking her head before I've finished. Her grip on the paper tightens as I reach for it. "You don't get it," she snaps, nearly jerking it away until I close my own fingers around the edge of the page. "It doesn't matter what your intentions are. A lot of people lost their jobs—good people, people who were already living paycheck to paycheck, hand to mouth—and even if Mr. Calloway managed to save some, not everyone cares. Not everyone is as forgiving. They can't get to your dad, they can't get to your mom. All they have is you."

Nothing she's saying is new, but what is new is one person finally being brave enough to point out the obvious. With my dad in jail and Mom splitting town, there's no one else for Silverwood to blame. I'm accessible. I'm related. I'm guilty by association.

Adjusting the strap of my bag on my shoulder, I turn away from her, pulling my schedule from her in a clean movement. "Thanks for the advice," I say over my shoulder as I start walking. "But I'll handle myself."

"The Scorpion Kings are worse than Megan," Roquel insists, her voice bouncing off the walls.

One of the lunch ladies lifts her head and gives the two of us a glare. I ignore her and shake my head. "Then I guess I'll just have to be worse than them," I say over my shoulder.

"*No one* is worse than them," she bites out.

Before Roquel can offer a response, the bell for next period rings and I hold up the hand with my schedule secured. "There's a first for everything." If anyone can be worse than the Scorpion Kings—it's me.

6

JULIET

Despite my words, Roquel's warning sits in the back of my mind like a nervous tick throughout the day. I spot her in a couple of my classes, but avoid her for the most part even when she openly tries to talk to me. It's not that I dislike her, I appreciate the kindness she offered, but she's at least right about one thing: I have a target on my back. Friends might help … or it might place them in the line of fire.

When the bell rings at the end of the day, the noise drills into the back of my head even though I've somehow been placed at the front of my final class—well away from the actual speaker system the bell is run on. Before it's even finished ringing, I've started to gather my shit, stuffing books and papers into my bag before sliding out of my seat and heading for the hallway.

Footsteps sound behind me and a body shoves past one side just as I reach the door, a girl with long black hair glaring over her shoulder at me as my side hits the door frame. With a growl, I shove away only for the same thing to happen on my right side, nearly sending me to my knees this time.

"Motherf—" I cut myself off as I spin away from the doorway, not even bothering to see if the teacher is going to do anything about the obvious harassment. They're no more my allies than the students are. A body slams into mine from the back, shoving me face-first into the locker across the hall.

"Watch where you're standing, *bitch*," a woman's voice hisses in my ear before retreating.

I push away from the locker and send a seething glare at her back as a tall girl with hair in a low ponytail strides off, her shoulders wider than most men's. Several students glare at me as I shrug back my shoulders and stomp off, cutting a right out of the hallway and slamming into the parking lot.

The fastest route to the bus loop cuts through the school, but I can't be responsible for what I'll do if another asshole pushes me. Unfortunately, luck is not on my side. No sooner have I started to make my way around the main building, than I'm stopped by someone calling my name.

"Hey, Donovan!" Gritting my teeth, I turn back already lifting my hand to shoot whoever it is the bird. I don't get a chance.

Something wet, cold, and slimy slams into my front—dousing my clothes in the acrid smell of sour milk and vomit. Mouth gaping open, I stare down at the front of my shirt and the chunks of white and brown now covering me. I don't know what the substance is, but it smells like the inside of a garbage can that hasn't been cleaned in *years*.

A low masculine whistle sounds nearby and I lift my gaze to settle on a pair of dark red-brown eyes. The whistler is a big man—definitely one of the football players by the width of his shoulders. With his hair shaved along the sides of his head, the high cut of his cheekbones, and a thick, square jawline, he looks half-gangster and half-runway model as he grins at me.

"What's wrong, Prep Girl?" he asks, arching a brow with a deliberate shaved cut through it. "Not a fan of Silverwood Public greetings?"

"*Ha!*" I laugh, the sound loud and dry. First, Nolan Pierce. Now, Giovanni Vargas. All I need to complete this day is Alexio Medicci. *The Scorpion Kings.*

Rage pours through me. The anger so hot it burns the inside of my lungs, making me wonder if it's physically possible for a human being to actually breathe fire.

Cupping my hand and drawing it up through the mess clinging to my front, I start walking towards him. Gio Vargas sits at one of the picnic tables that surround the exterior amphitheater that I know hasn't been used since Silverwood Prep was built. Each step brings me closer and closer to him.

He doesn't move, doesn't shift out of his relaxed pose—back against the table, legs outspread—a trio of others gathered around him, two girls and a guy. All of them watch me with barely repressed looks of utter hate. All except him.

Gio's gaze remains on me as I move, but it doesn't hold any contempt. The arched brow slowly comes down and wary curiosity is all he exudes. I smile, calling back to my days as a cheerleading captain at Silverwood Prep. Bright. All teeth. Forced exuberance. Only then, does Gio's expression change, morphing from interest to suspicion.

"I'm a huge fan of Silverwood Public greetings," I say cheerily as I stop a few feet from him. I haven't moved my hand from where it rests against my stomach, holding a large portion of the foul shit that had been thrown at me. "Especially returning them."

I open my palm and swing my arm back before letting it sail forward.

"Oh fuck!" The guy at Gio's side dives away just as the other two girls scream bloody murder, their piercing shrieks like music to my ears. At least, it is until the clumpy gross mess slaps Gio right in the chest, staining the white band t-shirt he's wearing with the same mess that I am.

His eyes darken and he lifts himself from the table until

he's towering over me. I tip my head back, but I don't step away.

"Big mistake, Prep Girl," he growls.

Lifting both hands, I raise both of my middle fingers and shove them into his face. "Oh yeah?" I drop my arms and return his glare with one of my own. "You started it."

His gaze shifts to something over my shoulder. The anger seething in his gaze recedes some and he straightens, the fists at his sides loosening. A tingle of awareness creeps up my spine. *Fuck. Me.* Based on the smug expression Gio shoots at me, I know exactly who's arrived.

Gio's eyes meet mine once more. "You're in for it now, Prep Girl." He grins. "There's no hiding anymore."

I jerk my chin up. "I haven't been hiding at all," I snap. "If you have a problem with me then let's have it out here and now." I pause. "Or are you just gonna shove and run like everyone else?"

He snorts. "I'm not the shoving kind." Gio's tone is easy and relaxed now as two shadows appear on the sidewalk on either side of me. "Well, unless it's my dick," he continues, "then I'd like to shove my dick in your pretty—"

"*G.*" Cold. That one syllable, one letter, carries with it an extent of meaning. The tone, however, is like dumping ice over my entire body.

I turn slowly in the direction of the speaker and stiffen as if waiting for the next physical blow. Nolan Pierce stands next to Alexio Medicci with his arms crossed, glaring between the two of us. A shiver skates down my spine as Nolan's copper-colored eyes, like blood and chocolate pouring into a long river together, focus on me.

"She fucking started it," Gio snaps, sounding like a petulant child.

I scoff and shoot him a dark look. "I didn't start shit, *Playboy*," I growl before showing him my teeth again. "But I can certainly finish it."

Gio advances on me menacingly only to be called up short by Nolan's sharp bark, "Don't even fucking try it, G."

The three who'd been Gio's posse before the other Scorpion Kings showed up hover on the fringes of the group, watching with wide eyes. The guy—a tall, lanky dude with a flop of blond hair and ripped jeans—is the first to attempt to intervene.

"He's right, Nolan," the guy says. "She was—"

"I did not ask for your input, Decker," Nolan says, cutting him off.

The coward shuts his trap damn near immediately and shrinks back with the two girls. I roll my eyes, but then Nolan's focus is squarely on me and I know it's a dangerous place to be.

Unable to help myself, I let my gaze drift away from Nolan's and land on the man at his side. Alexio is a tall man, taller even than his friends and just as muscular. It's clear just by looking at the three of them why so many fear them. Where money makes the world go round on the north side of Silverwood, here in the south? Strength is king and so are these three.

Straightening my spine, I level the leader of the Scorpion Kings with a glare of my own and arch a brow. "If you've got something to say," I snap, "then say it."

"*Dumbass...*" one of the girls behind Gio mutters and I can't help but wonder if she's right when Nolan uncrosses his arms and moves forward. As if called by my challenge, he takes each step carefully—a predator stalking his prey.

Each second that passes makes something hot and wicked creep up my back. Alarm bells go off in my head. My breaths come faster, seizing in my chest. I don't move though. I remain firmly planted in place, waiting.

Nolan doesn't stop until he's standing squarely in front of me, his big body blocking out a lot of sunlight as I'm forced to tip my head back to meet his gaze. My fingers contract, twitching into an automatic fist, preparing for an attack. But that's not how Nolan acts. Despite all of his rough edges, the crimes he's infamous for, there's never been one rumor or hint that he'd hit a woman.

I'm well aware that there's still a crowd watching us, and I'm not just talking about Gio's posse. We're near the student parking lot and it's just after school. There are plenty of students still milling about, hanging out at their trunks, watching on with obvious curiosity. Goosebumps crawl up my arms. Hundreds of eyes are on us, *on me*. My stomach churns with acid and bile.

"No more fights," Nolan says, his voice no less commanding for its quietness.

I blink. Then I scowl. "I didn't start it," I reply, "but I have no intention of sitting back and letting your people take their cheap shots."

One corner of his mouth tilts up. "*My* people?" He chuckles, the sound low and vibrating. Fuck me—why does he have to sound like that? Nolan leans down, getting up in my space more. So much so that I almost take a step back, but that would be seen as a weakness. Instead, I grit my teeth and settle the weight of my body more firmly on my heels.

"These are the people your family created with their cruelty," he tells me. "They're your people now too, Princess."

A low snarl leaves my lips. "Don't fucking call me that," I say, but he's already pulling away—his attention going to his friend.

Nolan jerks his chin back at Alexio, a silent command for Gio to move places. I take the opportunity for what it is—a boon. Turning away from the two of them, I begin to walk around the side of the building towards my original destination.

I don't get more than a few feet before I hear Gio's voice. "Ah. Ah. Ah. No, you don't." I freeze as the sound of heavy footsteps echoes behind me and then a wide palm lands on my shoulder, stopping me.

I don't turn around or look back as I speak. "I highly recommend you take your hand off me before I break it."

Instead of listening, Playboy jerks me around and glances at Nolan. "You're really going to let her leave?" he demands, ignoring my words. "Just like that? She fucked up Meg's face. She got into a fight on our turf. We can't let her get away with that."

Nolan frowns at Gio. "I don't give two shits about your fuck buddy, G," he says. "Megan White can handle her own fights, and if she can't…" Those copper eyes are back on me and that frown of his shifts back up, as if he's amused by the sight of me. All the while, I'm slowly seething at Gio's hand still on my arm. "… then she deserves to get her ass beat."

I tug on my arm, but Gio's grip remains the same and he glowers down at me. My eye is starting to twitch.

"But you should take this as a warning, *Princess*," Nolan states, recapturing my attention as my upper lip curls back. The sound of him calling me 'princess' rings in my ears like the shrieking of an unwanted child's temper tantrum. "You're not in Silverwood Prep anymore."

My body begins to tremble, the rage I've kept so carefully contained starting to spill over. When I open my mouth, only one word comes out. "*Hand.*"

Nolan's brows furrow. "What?"

I look pointedly at Playboy's hand still on my arm. "Remove. Your. Fucking. Hand."

Playboy's eyes go from me and then back to Nolan. The hand on my arm falls away and finally, that small tingling sensation under my skin—the one that encourages me to go absolutely apeshit anytime someone tries to fucking touch me when I don't want them to—recedes.

I lift my shoulder, trying to shake off the last of the feeling before looking Gio right in the eyes. "Your girlfriend came after me," I state. "I told her to back off. She didn't. If you hit someone, you should anticipate getting hit back. That's all. No one touches me, I won't touch them."

"You won't touch anyone regardless," Nolan replies.

"This is our territory, Prep Girl," Playboy says. "You're the outsider."

"Okay." I wait a beat. "And?"

"*And?*" Playboy repeats the word with disgust, swiveling his head to look at Nolan.

Murmurs rumble through the crowd of onlookers and I switch my gaze from Nolan and Gio to the man behind them, silently watching. Alexio Medicci's eyes watch me with a dark emotion I can't quite name. The heat of his attention burns through me, like hellfire and dry ice.

Whipping my head back to the two nearest me, I take a breath and then carefully move myself away from them. Nolan catches the deft action and narrows his eyes on me as his hand finds Playboy's shoulder, gripping tightly as he takes a step forward. He moves, releasing his friend and I refuse to back up again as he comes up to me—chest to chest and eye to eye. Sort of. It's eye to eye so long as I crane my neck back and he dips his head. The guy has to be at least a good half a foot taller than me.

He leans down into my face. His lips part, but I beat him to the punch. "I know you hate me," I say. "This whole fucking town does. If you're planning on threatening me or telling me to drop out, then I'm sorry to say, that's not going to happen."

His skin twitches right below his right eye. "Is that a fact?" His tone doesn't sound angry. Instead, it sounds half-amused and half-curious. I don't like that at all. I am something new to their little pond. Something they don't know how to handle quite yet. I don't want to be a curiosity to these people. I want to be invisible and I'm doing a piss poor job of it.

"*It is.*"

Slowly, oh so fucking slowly, his lips stretch into a wide

smile. It's such a contrast to the seriousness in his eyes, to the rigidness in his jaw, that it sets me on edge. "If you want to stay," he says. "Then who am I to stop you?"

I narrow my eyes on him. "Does that mean this is done?" I ask. "You'll leave me alone?" *Please let it be that easy,* I silently pray, but just like all of the other wishes I've made in the past several months, it's futile.

Nolan chuckles, remaining right where he is. Face inches from mine. Shadow covering my frame, blocking out the rest of the parking lot. Red and brown swirl in his irises, daring me to come closer, to see just where the colors separate.

I don't want to. I want nothing to do with him or his friends or anyone else in this school or town. If I had any other option—any other family—to turn to, I might've run the second my mom had. But I didn't. All I have is myself to rely on and I'm not going to trust anyone else to fuck me over like the rest have.

Instead of answering me, Nolan simply continues to smile before finally leaning away. I inhale sharply, just realizing that I'd been holding my breath. He turns and starts walking back towards his friends, and Gio—sensing that this fight is over, turns and follows him—whipping his now soiled shirt over his head and tucking it into the back of his pants.

Holy... fucking hell. The rippling dips and valleys across Giovanni Vargas' back are a masterpiece of muscle. More than one girl he passes lets out a sigh and I think I even hear one of them moan.

Nolan lifts a hand into the air as he walks, calling back to me as the three of them leave. "Welcome to the real world, Princess. We'll be seeing you around."

I whip around and start jogging towards the building's side path. No one stops me this time, no one calls out, no one throws shit on me, but the lack of attention now doesn't dim my anger.

This isn't fucking fair. Life isn't fair. Fuck them and their hate. The hate that I have to give back. It's fucked up and wrong. I never did shit to these people, but still, they take it out on me.

I know this isn't the last I'll see of the Scorpion Kings. I've got a whole year trapped in this damn school with them. Graduation can't come soon enough.

7
NOLAN

Lex's little obsession is gone by the time I get to my bike, but the memory of her cold blue eyes glaring up at me is imprinted in my mind. She's different, that much is obvious.

Silverwood's once-rising socialite has completely changed, and I can't say I don't like the new Juliet Donovan. Outside of the expensive clothes, makeup, and elite attitude, I'd expected Juliet Donovan to shrivel and disappear into the background. I'd almost relished in the news that her father had become an even worse criminal than me.

The lives I destroy are already on the downhill slide—addicts and wannabe street thieves who see no other way out of their own lives. The people I kill are killers themselves. But Allen Donovan had one-upped the entirety of Darrio Vargas' enterprise by going a step further. Embezzling millions? A white-collar crime if I'd ever heard of one, but unlike other embezzlers, Donovan had targeted the people of his own town and he'd been stupid enough to get caught.

Gio steps up to my side, his gaze locked on the path she'd taken around the side of the building. I can feel the burn of Lex's gaze on my face as he stops next to the SUV parked by the Indian Scout Sixty I'd rebuilt practically from scratch.

"Are we just going to let her go?" Gio asks.

My eyes cut to him and then to the crowd still hovering. "Move on," I bark out, and that seems to do the trick. They skitter away, hurrying towards their own cars and cliques of friends without so much as a backward glance. *Fucking sheep.*

"Where do you think she's going to go?" I answer his question with one of my own and an arched brow. "She's got nowhere else to go. She'll be back tomorrow."

Lex's unspoken irritation is a searing burn against the side of my face. I slide a look his way, meeting his eyes. "Go on," I mutter. "Say it."

Lex shakes his head and glowers at me.

"You're too protective of her," Gio huffs. "Is she really worth it?" A snarl erupts as Lex swivels to face Gio, who quickly puts his hands up in the air in an obvious action of surrender. "Fine!" he says. "Fuck—you really need to see someone about that unhealthy obsession with her."

He's right about the unhealthy part, but I know that none of us have forgotten the promise we made. I'd never actually thought taking someone like Juliet Donovan with us when we leave this shithole town behind could be a true possibility—but the last three months have changed things.

She's no longer an icon that Lex can't touch, but she's also no longer the girl he'd fallen in love with. The sweet innocent perfect princess. I wondered how she would take to her new circumstances when news of her father's crimes came out. She hadn't hidden, hadn't cried, hadn't begged someone to save her. Instead, she had surprised me—and everyone else in Silverwood, poor and rich alike—by fighting back. Even when Denise Donovan skipped town, leaving her daughter behind, Juliet hadn't sought out her old friends. Then again, the reason was clear.

Lex and I had been there the night of her eighteenth

birthday—we'd heard the truth of what happened before Avery Carpenter and Brandon Pillard had gotten ahold of the rumor mill. Her best friend and boyfriend had fucked and fucked Juliet Donovan over. What a fucking cliché.

Still, I had to hand it to the girl—she was made of stronger stuff than I would've guessed. Lex's insane infatuation is starting to make sense. Had he seen beyond her exterior all these years to the core of utter steel that hides behind a pretty face and silk dresses?

"Lay off him, G," I order, shaking the thoughts free and refocusing on the present. Delving into my back pocket, I withdraw my phone and check the time. I open my mouth to tell them both I'll see them later—after my shift at the shop—when a flurry of movement out of the corner of my eye stops me.

Megan appears, storming through the last groups still hanging out in the parking lot, and makes a beeline straight for us. Her face is patched from this morning's fight with a big white gauze taped over her nose. I narrow my eyes on her. I don't know what Gio sees in her other than her tits and pussy, but for a girl that's grown up in the south side of Silverwood, she certainly hadn't been able to touch Princess Juliet.

Her face is a mask of anger, but beyond the emotion are signs of her failure this morning. Her broken or bruised nose has purpled out the sides of her face into her eye sockets, making it look like she's got a black eye split between both.

"Gio."

He's already marching out to meet her before I've finished saying his name, but it's too late. The two of them meet face to face only two cars down. Megan thrusts her shoulders back, the action jutting out her tits, practically shoving them into Gio's face as if she can entrance him to do whatever she says with them. I catch Lex's eye roll.

Yeah, I silently agree. Gio's a pussy chaser, but he's not stupid.

"Did you do it?" she demands, her hands going immediately to her hips. "Did you take care of her?"

Gio crosses his arms. "She's been warned away."

"A warning!" she shrieks, the sound of her voice grating on my nerves as she leans around Gio and glares my way.

I wait, arching a brow, but she knows better than to start on her bullshit with me. I couldn't give a fuck less what Juliet did to her face. As far as I'm concerned, Meg earned it. Ever since Gio's made her a regular fuck, she's been pushing her luck—gaining more and more traction as a *Scorpion Girl*. My lips twist down at that. Fucking stupid is what it is. There's no such thing as a Scorpion Girl.

"She needs to be kicked out of school," Megan spits, returning her gaze to Gio. "You said you'd take care of it. You promised. Everyone hates her anyway—it's her fault a lot of our parents lost their jobs!"

Gio lifts his shoulders in a nonchalant shrug, but it's Lex who answers. "It's not her fault." Lex's deep baritone causes Meg to stiffen. "The sins of the father don't become the sins of the daughter."

Meg eyes him with distaste but doesn't directly reply to him. Can't say I'm surprised. She shifts closer to Gio as if a baser instinct is telling her that he's the safest of us. He is.

I'm over Meg's whining and I let Gio know with a quick jerk of my thumb towards the glass double doors that lead back into the school building. "I'm heading out," I tell him. "I'll see you after work."

Gio nods and then with an exhalation, he uncrosses his arms and takes Megan by the shoulders, turning her back towards the student building and slapping her ass to get the girl moving. Megan's complaining tone rises over the noise of people talking and cars starting as he directs her back, leading her away and leaving Lex and me alone.

Megan better watch out. She might give good head, but her recent demands and possessive behavior have the makings of a bad breakup. She's gotten too full of herself, and even Gio is slowly losing interest. I give it less than two weeks before he dumps her ass. Gio sticks around chicks longer than Lex or I ever have—but it's always just been for the pussy. The second they become an inconvenience, he moves on. Meg's hit that stage. More than an inconvenience, she's become a fucking annoyance.

Lex turns and leans against his black SUV. The paint is peeling along the side and two of the rims are missing. I kick one of the tires and look at him when I notice how one of the wheels is slightly closer to the ground than the others.

"You should bring this by the shop and let me fix it up," I say.

He shakes his head. "No point. Don't want new shit on it for others to steal."

"Who would steal from you?" I ask, lifting a brow.

Everyone around knows he'd gut them without a second thought. Even now, I watch the way he slips his hand into his pocket, fingering the knife he keeps there, and somehow manages to get past the metal detectors every fucking day. It's impressive.

He shrugs. "Druggies, out-of-towners, idiots." Good point. In his part of town, there's almost always some nomad roaming around, and druggies don't give enough of a shit about themselves to care if they kill themselves via needle or a bullet to the head.

I sigh and lean back against it, watching him carefully. Lex lifts his gaze to mine but doesn't say a damn word. "You can fool everyone else, man," I say, "but you can't fool me. Say what's on your mind."

"Don't know what you mean."

Liar. As if the universe is hell-bent on calling the bastard out, a yellow bus rounds the lot from behind the school taking the side road meant solely for them. His eyes lock on one and I turn my head, immediately spotting exactly what he sees.

The face of Juliet Donovan in one of the dirty, finger-smudged windows. The longing in his expression is enough to make even the most romantic of men sick.

"We're still leaving," I remind him. "Right after graduation."

His eyes flash back to me. "You promised—"

I hold a hand up as his tone darkens and he leans away from the SUV, his hands clenching into fists. "I did," I say, "but you remember the stipulations. She has to agree to it. We're not kidnapping her."

"She will."

The confidence with which he says the words has me lowering my hand back to my side. I'm gonna be late to fucking work, but oh well—Pyke can cover for me like I've covered for him a hundred times before.

"You sound sure," I prompt him.

"I am."

"Why?"

Lex tilts his head to the side. Unlike other men, the action has an animalistic quality to it, the movement slow and precise. "Why are you so curious now, Nolan?" he asks me. "You didn't care about her before."

That wasn't quite true. I had cared about Juliet Donovan —but only in terms of how she could fuck up my plan for the three of us. His compulsion to watch her, to follow her, to learn all manner of fucked up shit that would be better spent getting himself out of this shithole town just so that he could see into her life was worrisome. Now, it might come in handy.

"She's on our turf now," I tell him. "She wasn't before."

"She might act different, but she's still the same in a lot of ways," he says.

"Yeah?" I don't know if he's just crazy about the girl or completely losing it. As far as I'm concerned, Juliet Donovan has done a total one-eighty on her personality. Gone is the preppy, pink-loving, blonde Princess. In her place is a blue-haired, violent-eyed rage queen. "How so?"

"She's vulnerable." That's the only answer I get from him, and when several minutes go by without an elaboration, I give up with a sigh, knowing it's all I'll get.

"Well, she better prepare because if she thought today was bad, then she's in for a rude awakening when her in-school suspension is over."

Principal Long is a smart woman and one of few that any of us actually respect. Megan White and Juliet Donovan will both spend the next two weeks in the detention classroom, trading weeks of in-school suspension for this morning's fiasco.

I had a feeling that Principal Long had done that on purpose to keep Juliet from the rest of the masses for as long as possible. There was only so much she could do though. Soon enough, the princess would have to step out again with the rest of us, and despite Lex's belief, she would have to face the consequences of her father's sins.

8
LEX

B<i>eautiful</i>. So. Fucking. Beautiful.
    I reach out, touching the tip of one finger to the length of pale skin that is her neck, and drag it slowly down to where the collar of her white button-up uniform shirt gapes open ever so slightly.

Blonde hair creates a golden halo of waves around a face made for worship. She'd been innocent the day we'd met. All chubby cheeks and big blue eyes. My attention leaves the first picture and goes to the second one. Although the faces are the same—the features of the second woman a direct replica of the first—there's so much that's changed.

If I thought Juliet Donovan was a dangerous obsession before, it's nothing compared to how I feel about her now. In the first picture, she's a year younger, smiling as she poses with a few of her previous classmates. My smile turns to a scowl as I stop on the brunette standing at her side and the guy standing a few feet away with his arms slung over another Prep student.

Avery Carpenter and Brandon Pillard. *Fucking cockroaches.*

I pull my hand away from the picture entirely and switch focus to the second one. She's not posing for this one but standing outside of Silverwood's public library at the bus stop. Though it was taken in the middle of summer, she's wearing a jacket with the hood drawn up.

Hiding, baby? I wonder as I stroke the curve of her cheek. There's no use. *No matter where you go, I'll always have eyes on you.*

And on those who fucking hurt you. Withdrawing my hand a second time, I turn away from the wall of images taped and held to the wall next to my desk. I take a seat and swivel my chair to the row of monitors.

Each screen is a different size. Some curved, some flat, and some held together by duct tape and a prayer. I'd spent hours digging through dumpsters behind old computer repair shops for decent scraps to put this setup together, and I'd studied far longer to learn how to make it all work again. Every single second had been worth it because it had been for her.

Now, I hit a button on the keyboard that's positioned at just the right height and the screens flare to life. Not all of them have clear pictures—some are static-filled, but most of them have something usable on them. I hit another button and the row in front of me shifts to the black and white grainy images of the CCTV cameras.

I haven't had an opportunity to get close to where she lives now, but using a face-processing software I traded for some hacking skills on the dark web, I can still pick up where she's been throughout the day. An image of the school cafeteria security cameras comes up and I smile as I watch Juliet throw a beautiful right hook into Gio's whore's face.

Megan White is annoying. I'd take a paid hooker over her any day, but then again, I've always had better taste than G. My cell buzzes, and I'm half-tempted to ignore it and continue watching Juliet take the bitch out on camera, but then I glance at the caller and know that won't be happening.

Scowling, I hit the green button and bring the phone to my ear. I don't speak. That's not how I operate. A beat of dead staticky silence passes, just long enough for the person on the other end of the line to realize I've answered and then they start talking. "Is this the Scorpion?"

I roll my eyes and remain silent, waiting for the bastard to get to the point. If he's smart enough to get this number then he's damn sure got to be smart enough to know that admitting anything over the phone is a one-way shot of getting caught. A low chuckle breathes over the silence.

"Right, dumb question. I'm just going to assume you are." The echo of nervousness is clear in the man's voice, making me wonder how the hell he even bothered to get my number if he's scared to talk to me.

I lean forward and switch screens, opening up the only browser I seem to use anymore, and type in my credentials. I tap my free hand against the desk as my screen name appears in black and white.

5C0RP10N.

"I have a job for you." I resist the urge to roll my eyes again. Too much of that and what my momma told me when I was little might come true—my eyes might roll right out of my head. Still, it's hard to take this guy seriously. Of course, he's got a job for me. Why else would he be calling?

Putting the phone on speaker, I let my fingers fly across the keyboard as I pull up the connection to my cell and start working to trace the number. By the time he hangs up— whether I take the job or not—I'll know every single one of his dirty secrets.

"I need someone on the outside who can help me," the man continues.

A map of the globe pops up on my screen and at the press

of a button, a square box appears over it—in North America. I knew that though. The man isn't using any kind of voice-modulating device and he sounds American—the flat cadence of his midwestern accent is an easy tell.

"I was told you could help me," he says.

I remain silent, waiting for the screen to catch up as another square box appears. The map zooms in over and over. Seconds tick by and the sound of crackling over the line has me tilting my head towards the phone, staring down at it. It wasn't necessarily crackling so much as the sound of a toilet flushing—but not the regular porcelain kind. That was the sound of water on metal. Prison toilets are made of stainless steel.

"I'm willing to pay—whatever your price. What they're saying I did. I-I didn't. I want you to prove that I was framed."

A beat stretches into the quiet, interrupted only by the harsh breathing of the man on the other end of the line. Then he curses. "You could say something, damn it," the man huffs into the phone. "I have a daughter to protect. She's—"

Idiot. I grip the phone and turn off the speaker as I slam the thing to my ear. Just before I speak, though, I reach up and press a button at the bottom that will automatically change the sound of my voice, making it come over the line deeper and grainier than it actually is.

"Stop talking."

There's a brief moment of silence and then an outraged scoff. "Listen, you, I—"

My grip on the phone tightens as I lean forward. The trace is almost there—zeroing in closer and closer. A dreadful feeling rises to the pit of my stomach. There's no fucking way. No way in hell … but the computer dings a split second later and an aerial picture of the Hansgard Correctional Facility comes into clear view.

"If you want to protect your daughter," I say, "you should know better than telling a criminal about your family." Allen

Donovan is a fucking imbecile. Had he called anyone else, he'd have put Juliet into an assload of trouble—more so than she's already in as Silverwood's pariah.

"I was just—"

"Making the biggest mistake of your life," I snap, cutting him off. "Shut up. You've done enough talking."

"But, I need—"

"I know what you need." His continued inability to listen to my commands is quickly growing on my nerves. One hand flies over the keyboard while the other keeps the phone pinned to my ear. In under ten seconds, I've got all the court documents of his upcoming trial pulled up as well as the mugshot that had been taken when he'd been hauled in three months prior. On her fucking birthday no less. If I didn't think it might make her hate me later on, I'd call in one of the favors I've got and have some POS in that facility gut him in his sleep.

I can always kill him later, I assure myself, but I can't bring her father back if I act too hastily. For Juliet, I can do anything—even help her dipshit father.

"Allen Donovan. Age forty-seven. Born in St. Trinity, Vermont. Graduated from Eastpoint University in the late nineties. Married to Denise Donovan in the early—"

"How do you know that?" Allen Donovan's shock is clear through the phone

I continue. "You're being charged with grand larceny of embezzlement and you're facing, at minimum, ten years in a federal prison."

Utter silence is all that meets my listing of his information. I didn't need to pull any of it up. Because of Juliet, I'd done a deep dive into everyone surrounding her the second I'd learned how to work the dark web without getting caught. Now, it seems, my skills are coming in more than handy.

"Let me guess," I say, pulling the phone away from my ear and turning the speaker function back on again before setting it down next to me. "You want my help to prove that you were framed." I fold my hands together and lean back. "What makes you think I'll believe you?"

"Because you have to!" Allen Donovan says, his volume rising as an edge of desperation takes over. "I really didn't do it—why the fuck would I embezzle from my own company? We weren't in any trouble. I was making millions—"

"Sometimes, millions isn't enough," I tell him. "Sometimes, a man wants more and more and more. Sometimes, he wants what he shouldn't." I know that more than most.

My eyes lift to meet hers—the picture I'd taken from one of her social media pages before she'd taken them all down over the summer. Her eyes meet mine from where she lies, spread out over someone's bed—a soft pink comforter at her back and her shoulders bare save for a few freckles. Her big blue eyes with a hint of gray glimmer with mirth, and my cock twitches in my pants.

"*I didn't do it.*" Allen Donovan practically sobs into the receiver of the phone. If he weren't my girl's father, I would've already hung up on the asshole by now. Instead, I contemplate his claim.

I'm not a lawyer he's trying to get to defend him. I'm not a court judge he's trying to convince of his innocence. In fact, if he's going to be honest to anyone—it would be me, right? The hacker he's contacting to find evidence, to help him prove his innocence.

"I'll know if you're lying to me, Mr. Donovan," I state.

"I'm not," he says. "I swear it. I was framed—I don't know by who and I don't know why, but I swear, I wouldn't be calling you if I was guilty of this. I've heard of your reputation here. I know you can find out anything. I'm willing to pay. Whatever it takes, but I did not do this."

My eyes go from the screen to the phone sitting on my desk as I contemplate my answer and my choices. I'm taking the job, there's no doubt about that—if there's potential for me to save my baby from anything, I'll do it.

I unlace my fingers. "I'll give you some advice, Donovan," I say as I hover over the red button on the phone screen. "Next time you call a criminal to help you, don't talk about your fucking daughter. I'll be in touch."

With that, I end the call. It's time to get to work.

9
JULIET

I peel off several bills from the wad of cash I hold in my hand, feeling my chest tighten with each one until the stack I've pulled free is considerably larger than the leftovers in my palm. I hand the cash over to Mrs. Ritchie, the apartment complex's 'receptionist' aka the landlord's wife who runs the front like a general at war.

She takes the money, glaring at me over the top of her cat-eye glasses. The old me might have haughtily informed her that they're about seventy years out of date. The new me could not give a shit less what she wears or looks like as long as she takes my money, and I have a place to sleep for the next several months.

"This ain't rent for one month," she states, eyeing me as if trying to determine where I got this kind of money when everyone in town knows all my parents' money is being held in governmental assets—the joys of living in Silverwood. Big enough to catch federal attention, but small enough that everybody knows every-fucking-body's business.

"Yeah," I say. "I want to pay the next six in advance." Who would say no to that?

"You want to pay out your lease?" Her tone is suspicious,

and though I hate the snide glances and the obvious disdain she has for me—this is the only apartment complex in town that hadn't slammed the door in my face. So, I offer a smile, albeit a tight one.

The rent is too high and their facilities are a joke and I'm not too stupid to realize that they charged me double the deposit because I 'don't have any rental history.' The real fact is, everyone knows I don't have a dollar to my name, but Mr. Ritchie is a sucker for drama and the closer I am, the more he and his wife can watch my life fall apart. They're givers like that.

"Yes, ma'am," I say as politely as I can manage.

"Hmmm." The old goat hums in the back of her throat as she licks her fingers and thumbs through the bills. After a moment, she hums again. "It's all here," she states.

No shit, Sherlock.

I try not to show my disgust as she licks her fingers once again and then fans the green stack out as if she's just double-checking despite her words. Doesn't she know how dirty money can be? Unfortunately, I do. I know exactly how dirty that money is. It's probably why I'm kinda grossed out by how intimate she's becoming with it. Maybe she wants the room.

"Great," I say quickly, spinning on my heel and shoving the puny amount I have left into my back pocket. I hope it lasts until I can get a job and make some money to cover food and other things. "Email me the receipt, please!" I call over my shoulder before pushing out of the office and ducking across the walkway toward my building.

I stomp past the green 'pool' Silver Creek Apartments boasts about in their lease pamphlet. Thirty years ago, it had probably been the same sparkling blue that the picture on the front portrayed, but now, it's nothing but a cesspool of disease and algae. They'd be better off just cleaning the shit out and filling it full of cement, but so long as it exists they can claim it's a part of their perks—even if the "closed for renovation" sign has been there for far longer than I've been alive.

The parking spot in front of my building that used to be relegated for my BMW just a few weeks ago is now empty, and the sight of it makes my throat squeeze with discomfort. It's the first time in my semi-adult life that I haven't had a car to get me places, but it's for a good reason.

Gripping the rickety metal railing, I climb the steps to my second-floor studio and then look over the exterior barrier across the street to the Dollar Mart. I glance at my apartment door with the number '2' hanging crooked. My stomach rumbles. There's nothing in my fridge aside from half a cup of saved ramen and a carton of milk.

With a sigh, I turn right around and head back down, the rusted metal steps creaking with each footstep. I hurry across the lot and then the road, the money in my pocket burning a hole. The door chimes as I step inside the cool air-conditioned corner store.

"Wel—" The attendant's pleasant voice is cut off and I duck my head, ignoring her hard stare as I grab a basket and head towards the too-narrow aisles.

A box of cereal. A couple of cans of red sauce. Boxes of cheap pasta. Mac and cheese. A loaf of bread and some cheese. I fill up the basket and head back towards the front.

The attendant scowls as I set the basket on the counter and then rock back on my heels. I wait, keeping my eyes averted as if doing so will keep both of us from acknowledging my presence so we can just get this over with. After another tense beat of silence, the middle-aged woman begins to unload and scan the barcodes in annoyed jerking movements.

I bite down on my lower lip and the tension in my shoulders finally eases. At least she's not going to kick me out. My eyes lift some more and I turn to watch the numbers on the till.

$11.98…

$13.49…

$17.97…

Come on, I beg silently. *Stay under twenty.* I'd calculated correctly. I know I did. Yet, still, the underlying anxiety that I missed something remains. What if I'd gotten the tax amount wrong? The last item passes over the scanner, and the woman looks at me, her thin lips twisted.

"That'll be nineteen fifty-six," she bites out.

With a relieved sigh, I withdraw one of the twenties from my pocket and hand it over. "Can I have change?" I ask, keeping my eyes off the small glass jar in front of her register. Who even tips a cashier?

Her scowl deepens and her movements turn even more aggressive as she presses a button to release the register and then rifles through it before slamming it again. The woman slaps the change into my hand. She does it so hard that a quarter slips between my fingers and hits the floor. She eyes me as if expecting me to dive on the floor for it. I'm not that fucking far gone, but I'm not leaving it either. Slowly, I bend down, pick it up, and then slip the change into my pocket before lifting my bags.

She turns away and begins fiddling with the displays of cigarettes behind the counter. I hesitate, sure I already know what her answer will be, but with how dangerously low my bank account is now that I've paid six months of rent upfront, I have to try.

"Um … do you have an application I could fill out?"

The woman turns around and eyes me as if I just asked her to clean out my cat's shit-filled litter box. "We're not hiring."

I grit my teeth and force a polite smile. "Still," I say, "just in case you are in the future?"

She narrows her gaze on me and then huffs before stomping towards the end of her counter. She ducks down and I can hear her cursing and grumbling under her breath as she riffles through some papers. A moment later, she stands up and practically throws a piece of paper at me.

I grab it before it can fall and then carefully fold it and tuck it into one of my bags. "Thanks," I say. "Can you tell me when the manager is in, so I can return it?"

"Tuesdays."

I nod, but she's already turned around again and ignoring my presence. I head back outside to see that the sky has begun to darken and the streetlights over the main road are already on. What sends me running isn't the sudden darkness, but the rumble of thunder in the near distance. Hoofing it across the street, I make my way back to my apartment in record time. I climb the stairs and slam into the nearly empty studio without a second to spare as the skies outside open up and rain begins to drizzle over the overhang of the balcony.

I go about unloading the groceries and putting them in the closet-sized kitchen before heading over to my futon with a bowl of cereal in hand. Exhaustion pours through me as I force myself to lift a spoonful of stale Wheat Rings in milk to my lips. Outside, the rain comes down harder. Once I'm done eating, I clean my bowl and spoon and pull out my homework.

Five minutes in, I hear the repeated banging against the wall opposite my bed where my only neighbor connects to me. At first, I try to tune it out, but then the moaning gets louder, filtering through the walls as it rises in intensity.

Are you fucking kidding me? I pass a glance outside where the storm rages hard against the glass. Leaves fly past and circle in the background. What spindly little trees there are around the grounds of the complex are practically bent in half with the force of the winds. Inside, though, someone else is having a storm of their own if the faster thumps against my fucking wall are anything to go by.

Irritation pours through me and I get up, stomping across the room to pound on the wall. The thumping stops for a moment, and then I hear the soft tinkling sounds of feminine laughter and the creaking and thumps start up again—harder and faster than before. *Assholes.*

Turning away from the wall, I go to the side of my futon and rummage through my backpack until I find headphones. Plugging them in, I quickly scroll through a hard rock playlist, select something from Linkin Park, and sit back down.

With the sounds of Chester Bennington's voice ricocheting through my head, I manage to finish the homework that the few teachers that didn't seem to care that it was the first fucking day back had assigned. Once I'm done, I tuck it away in my bag and reach for the folded-up paper I'd brought with me from the corner mart. I unfold it and lay it flat on my lap, looking at the black and white script. Few places actually still have paper applications anymore, but before I even put pen to paper, I feel like I already know how this will turn out.

Why am I even doing this? Why am I even trying?

I'm not going to be hired. No one with any sanity would dare hire the daughter of the man who ruined half of the town's lives. I'd done this song and dance before already. As my pen hovers over the 'name' section, I bite down on my lip and growl in frustration. Before I can think better of it, I jab the pen downward, stabbing a hole through the application. I do it again and again until the top part is littered with ink-stained holes. Then, I crumple up the page, balling it in my fist and squeezing it as tight as I can as if I can make it—and the emotions of unfairness and anger—just disappear.

It doesn't. Neither the paper nor my emotions.

I throw the ball away from me, tossing it across the room with no real direction. It's not like I have a parent coming through my apartment demanding I keep it tidy or a maid to clean up my messes anymore. Being angry is tiring, more exhausting than people know. It smothers me, squeezing around my lungs like it's trying to kill me. Sometimes, I wish it'd finish the job.

I've truly become pathetic.

A knock sounds on my door, dragging me out of my thoughts as it blares over the music in my ears. I open my eyes, not realizing I'd closed them, and then look out the balcony windows. The storm passed rather quickly—a fast summer rain, there one minute and gone the next. Now, everything outside appears dull and wet, but there are no more spirally leaves or bent trees.

With a grunt, I pull my headphones from my ears and get off the futon, stumbling through the short hallway to the front door. I swear to God if Mrs. Ritchie sent someone because she thought all that noise earlier was me, I'm going to—

My thoughts cut off as the door swings open to a somewhat familiar face. "Hey, just wanted to—oh, it's you." The man standing in front of me is none other than Gio Vargas, the fucking playboy. His hair is more rumpled than it'd been at school the other day, strands sticking in various directions as if someone had run their fingers through it repeatedly.

"What the fuck are you doing here?" I demand, shoving my side against the frame and dragging the door closed so he can't look into the rest of the apartment. I'm sure it's not hard to guess that I've got virtually nothing, but he doesn't need to see it.

Playboy doesn't seem put off by my unwelcoming response to finding him on my doorstep. In fact, as he stares down at me, the surprised expression on his face slowly morphs into a 'cat that ate the canary' grin. He rocks back on his heels as his eyes travel down my frame, pausing and lingering over my breasts. *Pig.*

He jerks a thumb over his shoulder in the direction of the apartment door next to mine. "I was pretty sure we pissed off the neighbors with our noise, so I *was* going to come over and apologize, but now that I realize it's you..." His tongue touches the bottom of his teeth, poking slightly out as he continues to stare openly at my chest.

A part of me wants to cross my arms over my tits to disrupt his view, but I don't want him to know that it bothers me, so I force down the urge and just glare at him. "Let me guess," I say. "Now that you know it's me, you're just going to go harder next time to piss me off even more?"

He laughs and the sound isn't completely hideous. It's deep and masculine. My scowl deepens. "Actually..." His hand lands on the frame above my head and he leans forward until I can smell the hint of a spicy cologne and something else. I'm forced to turn my face up just to keep my eyes on his. "I wasn't considering coming back for seconds, but if the little neighbor wants in on some of the action, I'd be all too happy to oblige."

"I'd rather suck on an exhaust pipe," I grit out, my nose wrinkling when I realize what that secondary scent is. *Sex.* He smells like pussy and I'm revolted.

"I've got an exhaust pipe you can—"

"Finish that sentence, and I'll knee your balls so far into your body it'll take a surgeon to find them," I warn him.

The sound of his laugh rings out into the air. I don't know what shifted between when I'd seen him outside of school to now, but he's in a far better mood, and seeing it is only managing to put me in a worse one. "If that's all," I start to ease the door shut, "maybe next time, you should keep in mind that other people live here too."

Then again, he had said he doesn't do seconds. I should be grateful for the manwhore's ways. I go to finish closing the door in his face only for the damn thing to bounce back as he shoves his foot in the way. "What the—"

Playboy tsks in the back of his throat, and gripping the frame tighter, leans in close until that scent overwhelms me. I crane my head backward. "Now, now, don't be nasty," he says gently.

"You're one to talk," I fire back. "You're the one coming over here stinking like used cunt."

His eyes widen and he blinks down at me as if shocked by the statement. "Stinking?" Playboy turns his head and sniffs at himself delicately. "Ah, you're jealous." He grins. "You want to mark me with your own scent?"

"No!" Finally breaking my internal desire not to touch him, I reach out and shove a hand against his chest. I push hard until he stumbles back and his foot and hand slip out of the way. "Now, get fucking lost, and next time—keep it down!"

I slam the door in his face and flip the lock, turning and pressing my back against the wood as I inhale sharp and rapid breaths. He's insane. I shake my head, but then I hear the sound of his laughter again on the other side of the door. It rumbles through the wood and pierces my stomach, flooding my insides. It's not attraction. Not even a little bit.

A thump raps against the outside—a hand hitting the door. "Deny it all you like, Prep Girl," he says, "but if you ever want to unleash any of that anger you're carting around, you know where to find me."

The echo of his footsteps lingers outside of my apartment door as he walks away. My chest pumps up and down and more rage infuses my soul. As if I'd ever let him fucking touch me, the disgusting prick. Sex is the last thing on my mind, anyway, and I'm not going to be as stupid as I was before. No one is getting past my walls this time. Even before my dad was arrested, I'd been betrayed. Now that he's in jail, the rest of my so-called friends have abandoned me as well. No one cares and even if they try, they'll never stay anyway.

10
JULIET

It takes me until the second week of school to realize that Principal Long did me a favor by putting me in ISS for four days. Because other than day one, the first week goes by without much fanfare. It's a pretty solid routine: go to school, do my assignments, get out, go job hunting, get turned down. Eat a shitty dinner. Try to sleep through the nightmares. Wake up tired as fuck. Rinse and repeat.

With it having been the first week of school, there was no one else in the ISS classroom with me. I was alone, save for the older substitute tasked with making sure I showed up and completed my assignments. It was actually kind of nice, and I have to wonder if I could make some sort of deal to just do this for the whole year, but I doubt it. At least, I managed to get ahead of most of my classes in terms of assignments and reading.

The second week, even though Megan is a nonissue because she's serving her time, is different. I finally get my locker number and code only to find that the info has been leaked and the inside has already been decorated with trash. I scowl as the metal door swings open and toilet paper falls out, landing on my sneakers. A used wad of gum pulls away from the inside, making long-ass strings of the pinkish-white substance stretch in front of my face.

"Trash deserves trash, after all." Someone laughs.

"Ew, what's that smell? Is that the locker or is it just her?"

So, it begins. I inhale and then slowly close the locker without doing anything else. Turning away, I look down and grimace, toeing away a wad of what looks like used toilet paper. If I have to carry my books around every day, so fucking be it.

I get maybe two yards down the hallway when a girl steps in front of me. I recognize her instantly as one of the girls who'd been with Megan the first day. She's tall and lanky with stick straight brassy hair and a nose ring. I contemplate just ripping out the piercing and seeing what happens. Hearing her scream in pain as I walk away would be like music to my ears, but I promised myself I would get through this school year flying under the radar.

I go to step around her only for her to move back into my path. I sigh. "Do you really want to do this?" I ask her, looking up as she crosses her arms and leans closer. "Really? After what happened last week with your friend?"

"If you make a mess, you should clean it up," the girl says in response.

"Excuse me?" I arch a brow at her and she nods behind me.

I glance back, where there's still a pile of trash and toilet paper sitting outside of my locker. "Maybe you're not used to it since you used to have our parents clean up after you, but things are different now, bitch. Go clean up your mess."

Slowly, I pivot to face her once more. "And what if I don't?" I prompt.

Both of her eyes widen as if she hadn't expected that response, but she quickly regains her confidence, scowling down at me. "Then maybe we'll make you."

"*We?*" The second the word slips out of my lips I feel both of my arms jerk behind my back. The books I'd been holding clatter to the floor and the lanky bitch kicks them away. Looking to either side, I spot the second girl from Megan's little trio and another I don't recognize. Just great.

My lips part, but before I can utter a single word, I'm dragged back down the hallway in the direction of my locker. Once there, the girls shove me, face first, into the row of brown metal doors and laugh.

"Now," Lanky bitch says, pointing to the ground, "clean up your mess."

I right myself and turn around. My backpack pokes into my spine, so I carefully slip my arms free and set it on the ground. I crack my neck to one side, lift my gaze, and glare at her. "*No.*"

One word. Full of hatred. Full of meaning. Full of my own internal desire for these people to fuck the hell off and leave me alone. Her face pinches and the amused confidence she'd had when she knew she was backed up by two others fades ever so slightly. What I don't understand is how she could anticipate another reaction when she'd been witness to what happened in the cafeteria days before.

She steps forward, between her friends, and opens her mouth just as someone else appears around the corner. "Teachers are coming." Lanky bitch scowls at her friend's words and moves back automatically.

"Scared of being caught?" I taunt her.

Lanky bitch points her finger at me. "Don't think this is over," she snaps. "Your year at Silverwood Public is going to get fucking worse, bitch. We suggest you drop out now."

I smile at her angry expression and wave as her friends look up and down the hallway. "See you in class," I say pleasantly.

She scoffs and turns away, whipping her hair over her bony shoulder and strutting off as if she's trying to pop a hip out of joint. My hand drops back to my side. I'm almost sad that our little fight was disrupted. As much as I'd like to not get into trouble with the administration again, I'm not going to sit back and let anyone think they can fuck me over. Not anymore.

I bend down, lift my bag, and swing it over my shoulder, almost clipping the girl who'd delivered the warning in the side. She jumps back and eyes me cautiously. Now that Lanky and Moody are both gone, the rest of the students have moved along and the hallway is quickly emptying. I give her a once over, noting the soft upturned tilt of her nose, her full cheeks with a smattering of freckles, and the golden blonde hair that cascades over her shoulders.

"The teachers aren't actually coming," she says quietly.

I pause and look back at her with a frown. Unsure of how else to answer, I arch a brow and offer, "Okay?"

She bites down on her lip and ducks her head. "Sorry, I just thought you should know that you don't need to run or anything. They're not coming—Lindsey and her friends won't come back though." She looks like a small animal with the way she avoids my gaze, but still, she doesn't turn tail and run, so maybe there's more of a core of steel in her than at first glance.

I tilt my head at her. "Am I supposed to thank you for saving me?"

Her head lifts again and light blue eyes widen up at me. "Oh no, that's not what I meant—I just..." She drifts off and her shoulders sag. "Sorry, I'll go now."

The short blonde turns and strides off, her head and shoulders low as she moves. I find myself watching her with a mixture of rising frustration and confusion. With a huff, I turn and head in the opposite direction even knowing that it means I'll be taking the long way to my next class. I don't want to see her. Knowing she tried makes me suspicious, but her response to my vitriol stirred guilt in me and Silverwood Public is no place for that shit.

Two periods later, a familiar figure drops down into the seat next to me in English Lit and leans over. "Heard you had a savior today." Roquel's curious tone only serves to aggravate the recently abated irritation.

I blow out a long breath. No matter what I do, I can't seem to get away from her. "I'm so not in the mood."

If my tone is a warning, she ignores it. "Kinda sweet if you ask me. Madison Torres doesn't talk to anyone anymore, not after last year. I think she felt bad for you because she knows how it feels to be the school outcast."

"Her pity is none of my business and I don't need it."

"Aren't you curious, though?" Roquel presses. "I mean why would anyone in this school feel bad for you after everything that's happened?"

She's right. It doesn't make sense, but I guess even rotten trees can produce a few good apples. I close my eyes and pinch the bridge of my nose. "Is there a point to you annoying the shit out of me or are you just here for shits and giggles?" I demand.

Roquel's laugh is like wind chimes, light and pleasant. "Just curious how your semester is going," she replies casually.

"Like shit," I admit. There's no point in lying.

"Oh? Just school or is there more?" She leans forward, her eyes alight with interest and I know I shouldn't confide in her. I shouldn't trust anyone in this school.

I bite my lip and open my eyes as more students filter into the classroom. "I can't find a job," I mutter.

The money I'd gotten from selling my BMW isn't going to last me forever. I've got a roof over my head for the next six months, but what about utilities? Groceries? The weight of reality is settling heavy on my shoulders. This is what it means to be on my own, to have no one to rely on but myself.

"Yeah, I heard you've been looking," Roquel comments.

"I'm not surprised you haven't found anything in Silverwood."

Even though her words annoy me, I can't deny that they're true. "What have you heard?" I ask, already hating that I can't help myself.

Roquel winces. "Dollar Mart turned you down?" The answer sounds more like a question coming from her.

"I didn't even turn in the application," I admit. "I knew what the answer would be."

She nods. "Have you thought about asking any of your old friends if their parents would let you take a part-time job? North side has better places than—"

"No." I shake my head, cutting her off. I'm desperate but not that desperate. Not yet. The longer I stay away from the north side of Silverwood, the more it feels like my old life was all just a dream. A beautiful lie.

South side is real. No one smiles at your face and pretends to like you when really they're just waiting to stab you in the back. No. At least here at Silverwood Public, they'll stab me in the face.

I can practically see my futile attempts to get a job to last me through senior year crash and burn. No one is coming to save me from being homeless in a few months if I can't make it work. For a brief moment, I think of my dad's best friend, Morpheus Calloway.

You can always come to me, Juliet. Whatever you need. You know that I think of you as my own.

Guilt eats away at my heart. He'd been so well-meaning, but I'd inevitably left him behind too. I'm not his daughter. I'm not his problem. How long would it have been before he, too, urged me to find my own place? To get out? If the last three months had taught me anything it's that it's better to leave someone before they can leave you.

I slump against my desk. Well, the businesses of Silverwood beat me to that punch. I'd bet all the money left in my savings account that the owners and managers where I've put in applications have collectively decided not to have anything to do with me.

Likely watching the play of emotions across my face, Roquel leans towards me once more. "If you still need a job, you're gonna have to look out of town," she advises.

"Yeah." I know that, but with no car, getting to and from work is going to be a pain in my ass. The idea of spending hours at a time riding to and from different towns that surround Silverwood in public transport makes me nauseous. How much time will I actually have to work if I spend half of the day just trying to get somewhere?

Roquel's attention doesn't leave my face, not even when the teacher closes the door and announces the start of class. I try to ignore her and dip my head as we pull out our textbooks and open it to the first choice of literature. *Hamlet*. The irony of the story of betrayal and revenge is not lost on me.

The hour passes in droning boredom as the teacher passes on the duty of reading aloud from student to student—thankfully bypassing me. When the bell rings to announce the end of the period and the start of lunch, I slam my book closed and stuff it back into my bag before grabbing it and heading for the exit. Roquel's shorter form trails behind me in silence.

I get halfway to the cafeteria when I decide against it and turn in the opposite direction. "Where are you going?" Roquel calls after me.

"Library," I say.

"I'll join you!" The sound of her footsteps squeak on the linoleum floor behind me.

I stop and turn back. "Why?"

She halts in front of me, the low-cut flowing black top she's wearing gaping open just enough that I can see the black lace bra she's got on underneath. "What do you mean, why?"

"Why are you coming with me?" I demand, my brows lowering. "We're not friends."

Roquel tilts her head to the side, the choppy strands of her hair fluttering above her shoulders as she does. "Maybe I want to offer my assistance."

"Your assistance…" I repeat her with no small amount of suspicion.

Her eyes roll. "Not everyone is out to get you, Jules." She waves her hand and breezes past me.

I turn to watch her go. "I'm not looking for backup or to make friends," I remind her. "Despite what you said the first day of school, I think it's best if I handle shit myself."

Several steps ahead of me, she pauses and turns back. "Yeah, maybe you can handle yourself in a fight," she concedes. Roquel touches her bottom lip with a single finger, pushing against the full pink skin as she eyes me. "But you need a job and maybe I can help."

She can help me get a job? My initial instinct is to turn her down and tell her to back off—distrust is easier to accept than hope. All around us, students pour towards the cafeteria, hunger and chatter heavy in the air. I debate for so long that it isn't until the hallway is nearly empty that I finally respond. "Fine," I say, crossing my arms over my chest. "You say you can help me get a job? What kind?"

Roquel grins and drops her hand. "No takebacks," she says with a chuckle before stepping ahead of me, and I'm left with little other recourse but to follow her and hope like fuck this job will be the answer to my problems.

11
JULIET

The public bus system runs from 7 a.m. to 11 p.m., and thankfully, one arrives in front of my apartment building not long after I get home from school on Friday. I manage to get into my apartment, change, and back outside just as the white and blue monstrosity pulls up to the curb.

I hurry on board and swipe my card in front of the bland-faced man sitting in his uniform before taking a seat towards the back. The smell of sweat and weed hit me square in the face and I wrinkle my nose as I pretend like none of this bothers me. As the bus makes its way towards the adjoining town, Tangier, where Roquel's great aunt owns a club, I can only hope the scents don't seep into my clothes and linger as I hop off an hour later.

Tangier has an almost urban feel amongst rural small towns. It's the only town nearby that's on the same level in terms of size and businesses. I stride down the main strip and take a right at the end, hiking up a hill and past a local cemetery until my surroundings change. I've arrived at my destination. I glance up and up some more at the red brick building with blacked-out windows and a sign hanging over the doorway that reads in non-illuminated neon script The Dionysus Lounge.

Nerves wear at the frayed edges of my mind. From the outside, it looks no different from a small town's version of a strip club. Roquel had assured me it wasn't. Still, I'm half-tempted to turn around and walk away before I even go inside, sure that I'd called it wrong and Roquel Lee is no different from any of the other bitches at Silverwood that had made it their mission to make my life even more miserable than it already was. It didn't seem possible for anyone to have this amount of bad luck but ... here I am.

My foot taps against the cracked pavement, and with a curse, I catch the door when it opens as a man exits and slip inside past him. Desperation fuels me as I stomp forward, but instead of poles and stages full of naked woman shaking their tits in old fucks' faces, I'm greeted by a rather impressive interior. In the place of stages, there are large, rounded booths spread throughout the place with women in done-up makeup and rather scanty cocktail dresses—though completely covered—pouring drinks for men in suits as they chat amicably. There's a sweet smell lingering in the air—something soothing like vanilla or lavender—and the music in the background is low and instrumental. It's not at all like the strip club I'd expected.

"Hello, how can I help you?" A tall blonde woman in stiletto heels with a thick Russian accent approaches me.

"Uh ... yeah, hi, I'm ... erm ... I'm here for an interview?" The statement I'm meant to make comes out more like a question and I feel my cheeks begin to heat. I smooth down the silk shirt I put on, hoping the ride on the bus didn't wrinkle it too badly.

I glance over the girl's attire—a black mini skirt and a twisted top that appears silver from the front but shifts into a multitude of rainbow colors when she turns away.

"Then you're here for Ms. Ma-Ri," she says. "Her office is this way. Please watch your step."

My heart blasts against my chest in rapid succession as I follow behind the much taller woman as she leads me around the side of the room. As she walks, I peek at the men and women on the floor. Most of them are sitting close, and I watch as several of the women casually brush against their partners as they listen to them talk, laughing at intervals and then frowning and nodding in commiseration at others. Are they workers? Or are they just here to drink with their partners? It seems odd that there are so many men in here with so many beautiful women just practically hanging on their every word.

The sight is cut off as I enter a back hallway and am led past a locker room and changing room. There are bathrooms, a door labeled for storage and inventory, and then finally, an office. The tall blonde knocks twice and waits until the sound of a woman's croaking voice comes from inside.

Instead of opening the door, however, she turns to me and gestures. "Go ahead in," she says. "Ms. Ma-Ri will see you now."

As I set my hand on the doorknob, the woman disappears back down the hallway towards the main floor and I let myself into the room. Smoke hovers in the air, so thick that I'm not two feet in before I start coughing.

"You'll have a hard time adjusting if you can't handle this, darling," a small, petite-faced woman says from behind a wide black oak desk. She reclines against a plush red chair with a long stick pinched between two fingers. Is that ... a cigarette holder? I didn't think anyone used those outside of the 1920s. Then again, this woman looks almost old enough to have lived through that time period.

Wrinkles line every open surface of her face, from the corners of her mouth to the edges of her eyes. Age spots are visible both on her hands and neck. Despite that, her makeup is perfectly done around her eyes and her lips are painted a bright red. Her pixie short black and white hair is styled with swooping bangs to one side.

Smoke drifts from the end as she puffs on her cigarette and then blows out a long train into the air. "So, I hear from my niece that you're looking for a job and you're over eighteen."

I take a seat in the only place available—the rickety foldout chair stationed in front of her desk. Despite the neatness of her office, it's clear she doesn't invite guests back here too often. The chair prepared for me looks like it doesn't belong and the hard metal hurts my ass, but I don't say anything.

"Yes, ma'am."

Her almond-shaped eyes narrow on where I sit. "You ain't lying 'bout being eighteen, are ya?" she demands.

"I brought my ID with me if you need to see it," I reply. "But I'm ... um, not sure exactly what kind of job you're looking to fill." It feels like a weakness to admit, but Roquel had been rather vague about her aunt's business. She only told me it was a club of sorts, that her aunt is looking for more hosts, and she's willing to pay under the table. Under the table means I wouldn't have taxes taken out, and I can use all of the extra funds I can get until college comes around.

Ma-Ri sniffs and crosses one leg over the other, making me realize she's dressed much the same as the other women outside—her black dress is low cut, showing off the little hint of cleavage that she has and it rides up her stocking-covered thighs. I look away and fixate my attention on her face, waiting for an explanation.

A laugh bubbles out of the woman, surprising me. "That girl didn't tell you anything, did she?" Ma-Ri guesses.

"Um ... she told me you were looking for more hosts and owned a club," I say. "I thought it was like a host at a restaurant or something."

The older woman shakes her head. "I am looking for more hosts, but this ain't no restaurant, sweetheart," she states. "It's a host club. You ever been to one before?" Before I can answer, she's already continuing. "My guess is no, considering it ain't all that popular in The States yet, but I've managed to build one up myself here that's done pretty well."

I bite my tongue, not wanting to ask and seem stupid, but I can't help it. I need to know. "What's a host club?"

"It's a place where gentlemen—or women, if that's your preference—come to relax and have a few good drinks with a beautiful woman on their arm," she answers.

My eyes bulge and something dark sprouts within me. What the fuck had Roquel sent me into?

"I'm sorry," I say, abruptly standing, "but I think there's been a mistake. I don't judge anyone by what they choose to do, but I'm not going to sleep with customers for—"

"Oh hush," Ma-Ri huffs and waves her cigarette holder at me. "This ain't no brothel. My girls don't sleep with my customers and if I find out they do then they get axed—that's precisely why I need help."

Confusion pours through me. "Then what—"

"The women here are simply *hosts*," she says, stressing the last word as if it means something to me. Even if it doesn't, it seems to for her. "The club is open from six p.m. to two a.m. every night. The only service my girls supply within the club is companionship."

"Companionship?" I repeat.

Ma-Ri nods. "Exactly. This ain't an establishment of *that* sort, so get that head right out of the gutter, young lady. The women here are expected to present themselves as works of art to their customers. They're simply something beautiful for our guests to look at as they drink their woes away. They pour drinks and listen to men complain about their lives."

"So ... there's no stripping or ... sleeping with them?" I clarify.

She scoffs. "Of course not. Don't insult me. I run a respectable business."

"So ... what, then? The girls just come in, dress nice, and drink with men?"

Ma-Ri lifts her chin at me. "Sit down," she commands. "Don't make me crane my neck at ya."

I sit automatically and blink back at the woman, waiting for further explanation.

"Lots of powerful men—and some women—too often don't have enough time to see a therapist to talk about their troubles. Their wives or husbands are too self-absorbed to listen or too busy handling the cleaning and child-rearing. This is a place for those powerful people to come to relax. It's *respectable*." She repeats the word. "Not as dirty as a strip club and certainly far more appropriate for businessmen to frequent. There ain't no funny business going on, I assure you of that, but you won't need to worry about such a thing."

"I ... won't?" Had she not meant to hire me as one of those women?

"You don't strike me as host material girl," she replies tersely, eyeing me up and down as I sit in the hard metal chair across from her. "Don't take no offense to this but you got some anger in ya. I dare say the first time a man puts his hand on your thigh when he's chatting you up, you'd be liable to punch him in the face or am I wrong?"

I flush but nod. She's not wrong after all. A sly smile stretches her lips. "I thought as much." Her words are proud as if figuring me out has given her some semblance of intelligence. I can't deny it, but then again, I don't think it's that hard to figure out. "You'll probably do better as a waitress and ya need to be eighteen to serve alcoholic drinks. You can manage that, can't you?"

I straighten my back. "Yes, I can. How much are you offering per hour? What kind of hours are you looking for?" The timeline of the club's opening works perfectly to not disrupt my school schedule and if I can manage to get a couple of full shifts during the week then I'll definitely be able to save up some extra cash.

Ma-Ri looks at me over the top of her cigarette holder as she puts the end to her lips and sucks in, igniting the red glow at the end. Another stream of smoke is blown out into the air around us and I wrinkle my nose once before forcing my face to even out.

"Waitresses make the minimum wage in my club," she says, "but there's tips in it for ya. Sometimes, even non-hosts go home with a couple hundred depending on who comes in and who they serve." Her eyes pan down to my outfit and her face blanches. "You'll have to wear something else though. Hosts dress up but since ya won't be sitting with the clients, all black will do. If you're showing a bit of cleavage, you'll gain more tips, but it's up to you."

Minimum wage isn't shit, but considering most waitresses are paid far below it because of the 'tips' it's a better offer than anything I've gotten so far which is a big fat nothing. I have a feeling if I don't take Ma-Ri up on her offer there'll be nothing else for me and at least The Dionysus Lounge is far enough away from school that I doubt I'll run into anyone from there. With tips, this could be a turning point for me.

"When do I start?" I ask, making the decision.

Ma-Ri's lips stretch into a smile. "You can come in tomorrow," she says. "Saturdays are busy, but the best way to learn is to throw ya in the deep end and see if ya can swim." Ma-Ri leans forward and presses a button on the landline phone sitting half-hidden behind a stack of papers and folders at the corner of her desk. She sits back again and returns to her examination of me. "We need a waitress that can handle her weight sooner rather than later, so I suggest ya get used to it quick. I understand ya go to school with my niece, but don't think that means you'll get preferential treatment."

"I don't expect anything else," I tell her. "Just a job."

She nods, clearly pleased. "Roquel tells me ya need the

cash under the table. I can do that. So long as you show up to your shifts and don't cause no issues."

"I will, thank you."

Ma-Ri waves her cigarette holder at me. "Six p.m. tomorrow night," she says. "Now go, I've got more business to do."

I stand as the door behind me opens and I turn, expecting the blonde woman from earlier. The giddiness of finally getting a job disintegrates almost immediately as I come face to face with none other than the asshole from school—the leader of the Scorpion Kings himself.

Nolan Pierce fills the doorway, backed only by the shadow of a second man behind him. When I damn near smack into his chest, he puts a hand out to steady me, but the second I realize who it is, I rip myself from his grasp and take a step back. Red-brown eyes carefully observe me. Full, masculine lips twitch in amusement. Why? What's so fucking funny?

Before I can ask, Nolan casts his attention over my shoulder to Ma-Ri. "Didn't know you had a guest, Auntie," he says.

"New waitress," Ma-Ri replies casually. I stiffen, wishing she'd kept that bit of information to herself. I should've known better. Even if Tangier is further outside of Silverwood, if Roquel's attached to this place, then that means others would be as well. Why did it have to be them? I contemplate retracting my acceptance of work right then and there, but I can't. I'm stuck and I fucking know it.

Nolan's gaze lands back on me and I feel my body tense. He grins as if he can see the guard that immediately slams up at his presence. Still, he doesn't move away from the doorway, blocking my only means of leaving. I bite down on my lower lip and debate my options. Shoving him out of the way is preferred but not in front of my new boss. Politely asking him to move would be the choice except ... from the glint of knowing in his eyes, I have a feeling he'd simply refuse. That leaves only one more option. Waiting him out.

I cross my arms and shuffle sideways, the silent gesture for him to enter the room. His lips curve up further, but he doesn't come inside. Instead, he chooses to speak over me to Ma-Ri.

"I'm here for the monthly expenses," he says.

Ma-Ri sighs and the creak of her chair sounds as she gets up. "You running errands for that boy again?" She doesn't wait for Nolan to answer as she strides out from behind her desk and now that she's standing at her full height, I realize she's even shorter than I expected. She barely reaches my shoulder.

Nolan shrugs at her words. "Gio's busy right now," he says. "Besides, who would pass up a chance to see your beautiful face, Ma-Ri?"

Ma-Ri scoffs and waves her hand, cigarette smoke burning my eyes. "Pah!" Her movements stop and despite the obvious scowl of her lips, there's a sparkle of amusement in her eyes, as if she's used to Nolan's words. "Don't try to butter me up when yer takin' my money."

Nolan grins. "I'm not buttering you up for nothing, Ma-Ri." He slides a glance my way and pushes his hands into the pockets of his jeans. I grit my teeth as he bumps his shoulder against the doorframe. "Seems like I might be coming back here a little more often if you're planning on hiring pretty girls to deliver drinks too."

Something vile blooms inside me. Vomit, maybe. I don't know, but it's sour and acidic and it makes me want to draw blood. I curl my hands into fists, stabbing my shortened nails into my palms until I can feel the sharp pain there more than my own irritation. I force my gaze past Nolan to the man still standing behind him in the hallway.

I recognize him too. Alexio Medicci. He doesn't say anything, and his presence does seem rather dull compared to Nolan's. Despite that, though, he's a monster in proportions.

Taller and wider than his friend, his head grazing the top of the doorway. When he moves, shifting forward, he doesn't make a sound. That's more disturbing than anything else, the way he moves with utter quiet grace.

"Well, I should let you get on with your business," I push the words from my lips, unwilling to wait this out any longer. "I should get going."

"Oh, am I in your way?" Nolan asks as if he didn't already know he is most definitely in my way. His grin spreads into a full-blown smile and instead of stepping completely out of the way, he turns to the side and gestures to the hall. Clenching my teeth, I take the opportunity to slide past him, hating that his chest brushes mine as I go. The heat that pours off him in waves sinks past his cheap cotton shirt and into me. Unlike Nolan, however, Alexio steps back against the far wall.

Now that I'm out of the room, I look up and get my first glimpse of his actual features. For all of two seconds, I'm stunned completely stupid. Not only is he tall and wide, his face looks as though it could've been carved to mimic an ancient Greek statue. A proud nose, distinct jawline, and coal-dark lashes so exaggerated that any girl would kill him to possess them. He's beyond handsome, and he's watching me.

Curiosity, maybe? is my first assumption, but no, the intensity of his stare has to mean something else. His eyes linger on me, not bothering to dip down to my body the way Playboy's or Nolan's had. Instead, they stay fixated on my face as if he's committing each feature to memory. There's something familiar about his face ... or maybe his eyes. I can't quite put my finger on it.

Then he steps in front of me and blocks my exit.

12
LEX

"Move." With pink lips, flushed cheeks, and a stubborn set to her jaw, Juliet Donovan glares at me. She looks right at me when she speaks, and even though it's clear she's annoyed, I can't help but relish in her undivided attention.

Vi et animo is Latin for "with heart and soul." My heart and soul stands before me now. Not in a picture. Not in a stolen moment of her life plastered to my wall, but as a real live woman. Flesh and blood.

My eyes fall to where her slender neck is throbbing to the beat of her own heart. I can touch her—just reach out and stroke my fingertip down the column of her throat and feel the *realness* of her existence. She's so close I can't help but hold my breath, I want to make this moment last.

It'd been over and gone too soon when I'd seen her back at school. She hadn't been focused on me then but on Nolan and Gio. That was all right. She can focus on them as long as she notices me too.

"Didn't you hear me?" she snaps. "I said *move*."

My cock is a damned iron brand inside my pants, throbbing behind my fly as if it can pry through the metal teeth of my zipper to capture her attention.

Instead of stepping aside as I know she expects me to, I widen my stance, blocking as much of her path as I can, inhaling the smell of what I assume is her lotion and shampoo. Cream and vanilla. I let the smell linger in my nose, wishing I could permanently carve the scent into my soul so I'll never forget. No matter how many pictures I take, how many files I hack, there's nothing quite like seeing the object of all my desires in the flesh.

"I heard you," I tell her, leaning forward. Punching one arm out, I slam it into the wall next to her head. She jumps, an action I know she hates because I see the way her lips curve around a silent curse right before her eyes are back on mine, narrowing. "I just don't feel all that interested in moving right now."

A volcano could erupt inside Ma-Ri's lounge and I would stand as still as the statue I would inevitably become if it meant I could be this close to her. Flecks of varying shades of blue swirl in the depths of her eyes. There's even some gray there.

The growl of irritation she unleashes is adorable. I picture her as a cute little puppy, barking and biting at me as I pick her up by the scruff. A puppy against a giant wolf. My eyes drop back to her bare throat. Smooth, unblemished flesh. How I want to sink my teeth into her and mark her for all to see.

"—fucking problem?" I'm so intent on devouring every minuscule detail of her features, her scent, her body, that I almost miss the entire question she asks me.

I blink, working my thoughts backward. What had she been saying? Ah, yes, she'd asked me what my problem was. That's easy enough to answer—my main problem now is that she has no idea who she belongs to. I recall the recent conversation I'd had with Allen Donovan, and a dark cloud descends over me. Before Nolan had called me out here to run some errands for Darrio so that Gio could help his mom out, I'd been ass deep in pulling up all kinds of records about the Donovan family.

It was difficult not to get distracted by all things Juliet. She's just so fucking pretty it's hard not to give her all of my attention, even when she doesn't want it. Not that she'll ever find out just how much of my attention she has or for how long. I'll remember. I'll know that for thirteen years. For nearly 4,745 days, I've thought about her, watched her, wanted her. But nope, those little secrets of ours will have to stay hidden with me. I can't have her running, after all.

I have to ease her into our relationship if Nolan is going to agree to take her with us. It'll take time and effort, for sure, but I can do it. I'm nothing if not persistent and dedicated. I'll close around her with such silent intention that she never even realizes she's been caged. I can do it now. There's no boyfriend, no parents, no more barriers in my way anymore. Yet, at the same time, I have a feeling I'm going to miss this part of our relationship. The distance and watching. The building tension between us that has my cock rock hard in my pants as I get close enough to smell her for the first time in forever.

"Hello?" Juliet snaps her fingers in front of my face when I've still yet to respond to her question. "Anyone home? Are you just going to block my path and be a dick or do you actually want something from me?"

I want you on your knees, my mind immediately responds. *Mouth open, tits bared for my eyes, legs spread, wet pussy on display.*

A groan works its way up my throat. I beat it back. "Maybe all I want is a kiss," I hear myself say before I can stop myself.

Her arms drop from her chest, the look of shock on her face so sudden that her features go slack for the briefest of moments. Then her brows lower and her lips curve into a scowl. Hands come up and slap at my chest. The heat of her palms where they press against me burns through my shirt and all I can think is *she's touching me. I want her to touch me some more.*

"Back off, asshole," she grits out, unaware of my thoughts. "Just because I'm not on the other side of Silverwood anymore doesn't mean I'm suddenly a prostitute."

"I've never thought of you as a prostitute," I promise her, letting my body curve around hers, blocking her against the wall. Her hands on my chest are perfect. Her little nails dig in past the thin cotton of my shirt. I want it harder. I want her to score me with her body, make me bleed for her.

The tiny point of her nose tips upward as she bares the flat whites of her teeth at me. A groan threatens to break free from me. "Then why the hell would you think I'd ever kiss you?"

I tilt my head to the side. Her scent is all around me, invading my nostrils, driving me mad, making me forget where we are. "Because you want to know what it feels like," I croak out.

She laughs, but the sound is unamused. "I've kissed before," she says. "I don't need to wonder what it feels like."

I reach up and touch her jaw, letting my fingers skim along the underside of her face. I'm oh so close to the pulsing beat of her racing heart. I wonder how she'd react to me putting my hand around her throat, squeezing, giving her a sense of my strength. Of what I could do to her or better yet, for her. "You don't know what it feels like to kiss *me*," I correct her.

One breath in. One breath out. She goes still and seconds tick by. Then her hand is punching into one of my shoulders, pushing me back. Disappointment is a sinking weight in my gut, but I let her go. The predator in me demands that I give chase as blue hair and eyes flash by me. My muscles tense and jump beneath my flesh and I clench my hands into fists, turning my head slightly as I watch Juliet Donovan sprint down the back hallway of The Dionysus Lounge.

She's taller than I remember, taller than she appears in videos and pictures. I knew that. All of her documentation says she's a solid five-foot-six-inches, but with her body so close to my own, she'd felt smaller. Breakable. I haven't been near her—at least, not *this* close—in years.

My eyes bore into her back and the rounded curve of her ass encased in black slacks that are a bit too long for her legs as she hurries down the back hall and then disappears around the corner.

Her fall from grace has changed her. Juliet Donovan had been a beautiful ice queen. Soft, innocent, naive, and worst of all, untouchable. I never expected those barriers to come down so suddenly. Gone is the softness of her childhood, and though she might still be innocent in some ways, there's no more naiveté left in the cold expressions I've seen her wear at school.

I didn't think she could become more stunning if she tried, yet she has defied my expectations yet again. The Ice Queen fell into the gutter and having her so close to me once again is a torturous exercise in restraint.

Now that her pathetic excuse of a boyfriend is out of the way, the beast that has watched her for the last thirteen years, categorized everything about her from what brand of makeup she uses to what her favorite foods are is ravenous to get to her. She's been abandoned by her family, by her boyfriend, and her friends. My upper lip curls back at the thought. They were all just vermin circling her anyway. She's better off without them in her life. My only point of contention is that I was not the one who got rid of them for her.

I unclench my fists and smooth them over my dark jeans, wiping away the sweat as my heart rate kicks up. The end of my nose twitches as I think of all the ways I could hurt them. Knowing how much of a whore Avery Carpenter is, I'm sure the girl has nudes out there somewhere. All it would take is a few minutes of my time to share them with the whole of

Silverwood Prep. Brandon Pillard, however ... I'll have to think of something special for him. Something painful. He'd had the perfect woman and he fucked her over. There's a special place in my personal hell for him and I intend to bring it right to his front door.

"Lex!" Nolan's sharp bark drags me out of my head, disrupting my fantasy of all of the devious things I'd like to do with Juliet's ex-boyfriend.

I jerk my head up and catch the last tendrils of Juliet's shampoo scent in my lungs. A groan works its way out of my chest. Nolan frowns at me. His head tilts down and he glances up the hall as if expecting Juliet to still be there. When he sees she's not, he flicks his gaze back to me and arches a brow.

"*What?*" I snap at him.

Nolan purses his lips. "Maybe you should ask one of Auntie's girls out, Lex. You're looking a little tight there, man." With a scowl, I lift one of my hands and give him my middle finger. He snorts and shakes his head before gesturing for me. "Come on," he says. "We've got work to do."

At his words, I sigh and turn, ducking into Ma-Ri's office before closing the door and flipping the lock on the off chance someone gets a bit too curious. Now that Juliet has fled, Ma-Ri moves to the painting hanging on her wall depicting an old Asian woman working a rather strange-looking contraption, spinning silk from the butt of a worm. It's always struck me as a bit odd, but I don't question Ma-Ri on her decor. Neither does Nolan.

She lifts the painting down, setting it to the side to reveal the safe beyond it, and with careful fingers, she twists the lock back and forth until the telltale sound of the door clicking open engages. Ma-Ri reaches inside and withdraws a stack of green hundreds, neatly wrapped with a paper flap around the middle. She shuts and relocks the safe, replacing the painting over it before heading to her desk and slipping a white envelope out. Nolan and I remain silent as she puts the stack into the envelope and seals it before handing it over.

"The fee, boys," she says, lifting her cigarette holder once more and putting it to her lips and sucking deeply.

"Ma-Ri." Nolan frowns at the envelope. "You know we have to count it."

Ma-Ri waves her hand absently at the now-sealed envelope. "Right, right, habit. Open it and count."

A muscle jumps in Nolan's jaw as he stares down at the unblemished and now closed envelope. It's nothing to rip it open, but doing so would also insult the older woman and while I don't particularly care if Auntie gets her panties up her asscrack about it, Nolan does. Still, after a brief moment of hesitation, he grits his teeth and slips his finger between the flap of the envelope, peeling it open so that the cash falls out into his palm.

Ma-Ri's lips firm a bit at that, but she doesn't speak as he quickly counts it. It's only when he's finished and tucking the flap back into the white paper that she opens her thin lips, blowing out a steady stream of smoke before she speaks.

"I take it your comment about coming back more often had everything to do with my new waitress," she comments lightly as Nolan lifts the back of his t-shirt.

A flash of black metal at the small of his back is there and then gone as he tucks the money into the waistband right next to the Ruger P89. I recline against the back wall of Ma-Ri's office as her gaze bounces my way and then back to Nolan.

As long as I've been coming here to run these little errands for G's dad, I know my presence makes her nervous. That's the point of my coming, though it'd been Gio's turn. I'm no longer as annoyed by it as I was earlier. Coming had given me a chance to see Juliet again.

"I'm surprised you'd offer Juliet Donovan a job," Nolan says to Ma-Ri.

Ma-Ri takes another drag from her cigarette via the long,

antiquated holder she carries around. "I need waitresses and I don't care what her daddy did. If she don't work out, I'll fire her. Simple as that."

"There might be a few from Silverwood who won't take kindly to her presence," Nolan warns her.

He's right. I've seen the treatment she's received since the start of last summer. Sad really, but at the same time, it's been almost … fun to see the change happening in real time. Almost as if I've been waiting for a new season of her life to start, for her to shake off the forced smiles she'd been using to hide the rising reality of who she is. This time, I'm not just watching from far away. I'm front and center.

"She ain't no host," Ma-Ri replies on a sigh. "She'll be delivering drinks and working the back end. 'Sides, Roquel asked me to give her a chance and my niece don't often ask for anything."

"Roquel asked?" Nolan looks back at me, his brows puckered.

I nod. "She's been hanging around Juliet more," I confirm. "They don't seem like close friends, but close enough considering she's the only one Juliet talks to." And if anyone knows what Juliet Donovan is up to, it's me.

Every move she makes, I'll be there—like that shitty-ass old song. Juliet Donovan is my muse, my obsession, and no one knows her better than me. Likely not even the girl herself.

Nolan blows out a breath and returns his attention to Ma-Ri. "It's your business, Auntie," he says, "but don't say I didn't warn you."

Ma-Ri smiles at him and pats him on the cheek. "You play rough, No-No," she says, using the old moniker she'd given him when he'd been a child. "You should give that poor girl a break."

Nolan flinches. "You're too kind, Auntie," he replies, shaking his head. "She's not as nice as you seem to think she is."

"*Oh, pah,*" Ma-Ri huffs out a breath. "She's just protectin' herself. 'Sides, it might do your little group good to try and go after some girls that don't fall at your feet with their legs already spread."

Nolan laughs. "We don't take advantage, Auntie. Gio's the only one who slips up on occasion."

Ma-Ri gives him a bland glare. "Don't try to fool me none, No-No," she says. "That boy does more than slip up *on occasion.* If he ain't careful, next time I see him, he'll be bringing me a babe to hold."

It would be difficult to deny Ma-Ri's claim. After all, between the three of us, Gio's drowned himself in the most pussy a man could likely take and still live. He's fucked more than half the female populace at Silverwood Public and though none would openly claim as much, several members of the Silverwood Prep Elite.

"You know I always look out for him, Auntie," Nolan says. "We've got plans of our own. None of us would do much good as fathers."

Ma-Ri shakes her head. "Just 'cause yer own daddies ain't worth a lick don't mean nothing, No-No," she says. "But you be sure 'bout Gio. All it takes is one wrong move."

"We got it." Nolan leans down and presses his lips to her upturned cheek, nearly bending in half to press the chaste kiss on the much shorter woman, the insult of counting the money long forgotten. "See ya next month."

Ma-Ri waves us off. As Nolan goes into the hallway, I trail him. The second the door shuts, his pleasant expression falls away. "This will be a problem for her business," he mutters.

"Like she said," I reply on a grunt, "it's hers to do with what she wants."

Nolan levels me with a glare. One that I neither reciprocate nor care for. "Darrio's not gonna give a shit if she's losing out on income," he snaps. "His payment remains the same regardless. Despite what she claims, if that girl's here, she'll bring Ma-Ri's profits down."

He doesn't know that. Not for sure. But I do and Nolan is forgetting that Juliet Donovan's new status as an outcast has brought forth a whole host of cockroaches. They've been subtle, but I see it—the look in the eyes of our fellow classmates, of the teachers, of even the pricks still in Silverwood Prep. Now that she's supposedly vulnerable, I have no doubt they'll try to take advantage.

"Let it go, Nolan," I urge, my voice deepening.

His eyes widen. "Are you defending her?" he demands. Before I can reply, he scowls and continues. "Don't let your little obsession get in the way, Lex. We have people to protect. Ma-Ri's one of them."

"Then perhaps we should think about doing something with Darrio," I bite out.

Nolan curses and turns away from me, stomping up the hall. I don't say a word, choosing to remain silent until we're out of the club and back in my SUV. I get into the driver's side and turn the engine on as he stews in the passenger seat. Several long minutes go by as I pull out of the lot and take the highway back to Silverwood.

Finally, he speaks. "It's Gio's call," he says. "If he wants to end this shit with Darrio, then he needs to be the one to make the decision. Not me. They're blood."

I nod my assent. Blood doesn't mean much in the long run. Just like Juliet's blood abandoned her the second they could or the way Nolan cares for Ma-Ri despite there being no familial relation, it ends up being water under the bridge in the long run. For us, blood just means responsibility. As such, it'll be Gio's decision to make regarding his own piece-of-shit father.

Once that decision is made though, Silverwood will see a new leader in its underworld. As far as I'm concerned, Darrio Vargas' days on Earth are already numbered.

13
JULIET

"Oh dear, you've had too much to drink, haven't you?" The somewhat familiar voice is a grating edge to my muddled senses. My head pounds to the beat of music I cannot hear. With a groan, I try to roll away from the man, but hands merely adjust me so that I'm on my back. Try as I might to open my eyes, they remain fixed closed, as if my own body is fighting against me—as if it's warning me that as soon as I open my eyes, the spell will be gone and I'll have to face reality.

A man's hand moves over my throat and down further. My skin itches, coming alive with the sensation of bugs crawling all over me. A low moan echoes up my throat and I resist the urge to gag. What did I drink? It wasn't enough to feel this drunk ... was it? Mom and Dad said it was okay—it was a party and I was fifteen, after all. All the European countries let their kids drink. It was fancy. It was cool.

"So pretty..." The voice speaks again. The compliment is accompanied by hands slipping between my breasts and lower still. Pressure against my front keeps me in place. I'm pinned beneath something—someone—much larger and heavier than a mere comforter.

Sickness churns in my gut as cool air wafts over my skin and further down. The hem of my satin dress rises up my thighs.

Don't open your eyes, a secret voice whispers. Don't ... open ... your ... eyes.

I blink blearily, my lashes lifting despite the dream's warning and I sigh when I spy the stain-riddled ceiling of my cheap ass studio. Relief courses through me, but on its heels is the exhaustion of a poor night's sleep. I hate those damn dreams; it seems like I can never fully escape them. At least they fade after I'm awake. Sometimes. I've had nightmares for as long as I can remember. When I was still with my parents—before shit went to hell—my mother had ordered the perfect cocktail of drugs to keep them at bay. It was one of the few motherly actions she'd ever actually performed without complaint.

Now, though, I've got no health insurance, no medical connections, and the last of my medication dried up two weeks after my dad was arrested and denied bail. Which means when morning arrives with a pounding headache that throbs against my skull, there's nothing but ibuprofen to manage it.

This time, I blame the untimely nightmare on the stress of looking for a job and running into the Scorpion Kings at The Dionysus Lounge—especially the one that had pinned me against the wall outside of Ma-Ri's office. *You don't know what it feels like to kiss me.* Those words circle in my mind, an annoying reminder accompanied by the fact that my eyes had gone to his lips, had focused on them even if only briefly, wondering...

I don't need to wonder about shit. I just need to take care of myself, finish out the school year, and get the fuck out of Silverwood.

A blurry gray morning, complete with drizzling rain, wakes me as it seeps into my studio apartment with a chill through the thin balcony glass doors. Blinking my eyes open and then promptly shutting them as my headache screams at me, a groan rumbles up my chest. Pinching the bridge of my nose, I manage to force myself to sit up and swing my legs over the side of my futon. Fumbling madly against the cheap table nearby, I feel my fingertips graze a small bottle. I peek my eyes open just to confirm it's the painkillers I need before popping the top, dumping out a full dose, and swallowing the pills dry.

There's a notification on my computer of new emails—contacts from my dad's lawyers. I ignore them. He made his bed and he can lie in it for all I care. I'm the one stuck here, dealing with the mess he made of Silverwood. The least he can do is leave me the fuck alone.

I wait another few minutes for the meds to kick in before I get up completely and start the day. I dress quickly and efficiently, thankful I laid out my clothes the night before. It's become my routine because I know that mornings are either early or late but never on time. I either wake up hours in advance on account of the nightmares or the lack of good sleep has me slapping the snooze button half a dozen times before I actually get out of bed.

Today is the latter which means I'm running late to the school bus and hiking it across the parking lot as the big yellow cab pulls up in front of the curb. With my backpack slapping against my spine, I hurry my footsteps and practically leap onto the bus before the driver can shut the doors in my face. He scrunches up his ruddy cheeks as if he'd been planning to do just that, but doesn't say a word as I pass him, panting and huffing, and slam into an empty aisle seat.

As we pass around Cory's gym, I realize I've not yet gone back. I haven't had time between school starting and job hunting and then spending the last weekend training at The Dionysus Lounge. Curiosity and confusion still prick at me.

Principal Long obviously has some connection with Cory, but what? And why would Cory and her talk about me?

There are no answers to be found on my own, yet still, the question permeates my mind as the bus finishes its route and makes its way back to the school. I spill into the cafeteria with the rest of the students, keeping my head low and making my way towards the front hall.

Unfortunately, my relatively peaceful entrance is ruined as a bold figure steps in front of me and I'm forced to either stop or run headlong into his chest. I choose to stop and look up with a scowl.

"There a problem?" I snap.

The guy is tall, probably another one of Public's football players, with bulky muscles straining his cheap cotton t-shirt. He grins down at me and crosses his arms over his chest. "No problem," he says, eyeing me, his gaze lingering on my breasts. Not much to see there—at least not with the hoodie I'm wearing—so I don't know what the point is.

"Great," I say. "Then move."

I step to the side when he doesn't and he follows. "Actually, I was wondering," he continues, "how much for a couple of hours? Me and my boys want to celebrate after next Friday's game. Oh, sorry, do you charge extra for multiples? We can do that."

His words leave me utterly confused. "What the hell are you talking about?"

The dude pulls out his phone and swipes across the screen before turning it around to face me. "Saw the ad you put out," he said. "Real ballsy, I've gotta say, but I get it if you're that hard up for cash—"

I snatch his phone from his hand without letting him finish and bring it closer to my face. A combination of horror and fury descends. Someone's taken an old photo of mine—one that looks like it used to be on Silverwood Prep's website for student leaders—and turned it into an ad promising private parties in exchange for money. I begin to shake.

"Yeah, so as I was saying, how much do you charge for three guys?" He leans forward, and the stench of cheap Dollar Store cologne hits my nose. "You've got three holes so I figure it'll save some time if we all just fuck you at once."

My insides tremble with barely repressed rage. Looking up into the fuckwad's face, I drop his phone to the floor and as his eyes widen, I lift my foot and crush it under my boot.

"Hey!" He reaches for my arm, but I react instinctively, punching him in the face as I bring my foot down a second time and hear the crack of his phone screen. The asshole stumbles back, holding his hand over his now bleeding nose.

I don't bother to offer any more of a response. I just lift my foot away from his phone and walk around him. I get about three feet when he shouts after me. "You can't do that!" he yells. "You broke my fucking phone!"

I pause and look back. "You were the one stupid enough to believe that ad," I tell him. "Play stupid games, win stupid prizes. You're lucky I didn't crush your balls as well."

I stomp away from him and the cafeteria, sensing the burn of all eyes on the back of my head and the sides of my face. I'll never get used to it—being a beacon of interest. Sometimes, I wish I'd been born into a moderate life. Boring. Plain. Invisible. Maybe then these types of things wouldn't get to me. Because worse than the actual post and ad, I saw one of the names that reshared the post. Even if she hadn't made it herself, it still stung that Avery would share it. I inhale hard and hold my breath as I keep walking.

It doesn't matter, I tell myself. *You cut her off months ago.*

Still, the open wound she caused on the same night I lost the rest of my previous life stings as if it's fresh.

No one else says a word to me the rest of the day about the obviously fake advertisement. It's clear that the creator meant for it to be used to humiliate me. I'm not humiliated. I'm not even embarrassed. What I am is fucking pissed. It's like anger is the only emotion I even know anymore. Despite that, when I spot Roquel in class, I don't avoid her this time. I take my seat alongside her and offer her a smile. It's been a shit day, but at least there's one bright spot—I have a job and that's all thanks to her.

"Hey, um, I went to that place you talked about last week," I tell her, working my anger into the back of my mind as I do what I know I should—acknowledging that she's the only one, other than Cory and Principal Long, who's actually tried to help me since my life fell to shit.

Roquel leans to the side and grins at me. "And?" she prods.

She already knows what happened. I can see it in her eyes. "I got the job," I tell her anyway. "Thanks for suggesting it."

Roquel sits back in her seat and her grin morphs into a smirk. "I'm glad it worked out," she confesses. "Aunt Ma-Ri needs more waitresses because everyone wants to be a host, but I figured you'd prefer that."

"Yeah, you could've warned me what kind of place it was though," I say. "I thought I was walking into a strip club."

The tinkling sound of Roquel's laugh makes a few people turn their heads at the front of the class, but we don't pay them any mind. "Totally not a strip club," she says. "Host clubs are a big thing in Asia. Auntie Ma-Ri used to be a big deal at one of the best ones in Seoul before she immigrated. Besides, I figured it'd be easier and better for her to explain the setup or for you to figure it out yourself."

"Yeah, well, regardless..." I lift my head as the teacher strides into the classroom, rolling a heavy-looking cart with a box TV towards the front of the class. "I'm still thankful. I appreciate it." More than she'll ever know.

For the first time, it feels like I'm actually going to make it through this school year. Fuck all of the bully tactics and high school bullshit. So long as I'm not in danger of starving or being homeless, things are good. Actually, better than that, they're looking up. I have a job. I have freedom.

The student chatter turns to excitement as the teacher explains that we're watching an old 90s version of Romeo and Juliet. She could've said we were going to watch reruns of old commercials and I think everyone would've still been ecstatic.

A movie day this early in the semester? I don't care if that means the teacher is a lazy fuck, I could kiss her for it. I've seen this version of Romeo and Juliet at least half a dozen times before, which means I might be able to catch a quick nap to make up for the shit sleep I got the night before.

Things are definitely looking up.

14
JULIET

My head continues to pound from several long nights and lack of sleep, but that doesn't stop me from hitting up Cory's gym after I finish my final shift of the week at The Dionysus Lounge. It feels like an eternity has passed since I've set foot in the dingy, cement room that makes up the majority of Cory's building. There's no need for me to change since I swapped clothes after I got off the bus and my warm-up had been the thirty-minute walk over.

Instead of heading straight for the locker rooms like normal, I go in search of the gym's owner, hoping to gain some insight into his relationship with Principal Long and possibly get a good spar in while I'm at it. As I move through the space, diving around big bulky men in workout gear, I frown. Normally, I avoid the gym during their busiest hours, but with school now in session and my new job, I don't have much of a choice but to come when I can.

I'd hoped that a Friday afternoon meant this place would be nearly empty, but as I catch sight of a familiar dark head and make a beeline toward Cory, the sounds of masculine grunts and dumbbells dropping onto padded floors make me rethink that assumption. Friday afternoons, it appears, makes Cory's gym a hopping place to be.

I keep walking, ignoring the stares I get until I reach the sparring ring towards the back of the big room. That's where Cory comes completely into view, leaning against the wall as he watches two fighters circle each other in the ring. I don't even spare the guys a glance, and instead, round the big roped-off section until I'm at his side.

"Hey, girl," he greets casually. "Ain't seen much of you 'round here since school started."

"Yeah." I recline against the wall at his side. "Been busy. Got a job."

"You did?" My lips twitch when his head swivels in my direction. I don't blame him for being surprised. The fact that anyone would be willing to hire Silverwood's number one pariah is shocking to me too. "Congrats."

"Thanks." A grunt sounds within the ring and I catch sight of one of the opponents as he stumbles into ropes across from us. His partner stands tall and firm with both feet spread apart and his back to me.

"So, funny thing," I start again, looking back at Cory. "I got into a bit of trouble my first day and ended up meeting the principal."

Cory chuckles. "Yeah, I ain't all that surprised by that. You was bound to attract some bad mojo."

"*Yeah*," I draw out the word as I side-eye him. "That's not what I'm getting at here." Cory doesn't look at me. He fixes his attention on the ring, but I keep going. "Principal Long seemed to already know a thing or two about me. Imagine my surprise when she admits that she got some of that information from *you*." I emphasize that last word. "Care to explain?"

Cory glances my way and then heaves a sigh. "Heather's a friend," he says. "We go way back. Thought it might do a girl like you some good to have someone *not* out to get you on your first day. You ain't gotta worry 'bout her. She's a fair broad."

Her fairness isn't my point of contention. "So, you thought that meant you could tell her my business?" I ask. "Exactly how much did you tell her?"

Cory arches one brow before scrubbing a hand over his trimmed but still curly beard. "It don't matter much," he says. "It ain't like everyone don't already know your business—in a town this small? Ain't nothing remain a secret for long."

"It matters to me, Cory," I tell him. "You know I can't really trust anybody in this godforsaken town anymore." He's one of the few and perhaps the last.

Cory sighs and then turns to face me fully. His hands come out and land on my shoulders. I don't push him away or brush him off. There are only a few people in my life now that I would let touch me so casually, but he's one of them. Even if he meant good, though, by informing Principal Long of my circumstances—even if I know she likely would have learned it elsewhere—coming from him, it feels like another betrayal.

"You remember what I told you when you first came here?" he asks.

I frown but nod. "Survival is about more than fighting, it's about learning *when* to fight and when to back down," I repeat his words and his face softens.

"That's right," he says. "You came in here looking like the world was tearing you down."

"It was." *It still is.*

He nods. "Yeah, but that don't erase the fact that I taught you the skills you needed to make sure it didn't rip you to shreds. Take this as another lesson. You can't do anything alone, girl. You might think you can, but at the end of the day, you'll need people on your side if you want long-term survival. If you want happiness."

Happiness. The mere notion of being happy again is such a faraway concept to me now. What would make me happy?

Getting back my life? Reversing time? No. If I'm honest with myself, I wasn't truly happy before my life fell to shit. I was just pretending to be. I was frustrated. Confined. Tired. The only difference now is that I no longer need to hide any of what I'm feeling to keep up the facade.

"I want to leave Silverwood," I tell him. "I think that'd make me happy." Starting over. A new life. A new city. That will be good for me. Maybe I'll even delete my email so that my dad's lawyer stops trying to get me to see him.

The edges of Cory's lips tilt up. "I think that's a good goal to have," he says. "But you've got months 'til you can make it a reality. In that time, you should think about making a few friends. Happiness ain't something you gotta wait on. You can make your own happy here too, for as long as you'll be here."

I shake my head and carefully step out from beneath his hands. "I trust you, Cory," I say, "and I respect you, but I don't think making friends in Silverwood is gonna do me much good. I'm just trying to live my day-to-day. I'll figure out 'happy' when this place is behind me."

Cory parts his lips, but whatever he's about to say is swallowed by the sharp sound of a body slamming into the hard floor. Not the padded bottom of the sparring ring, but the cold, hard linoleum tile above the concrete floor outside of it. In sync, Cory and I pivot towards the ring. I gape up at the man standing on the other side of the ropes with his arms propped and his face dripping with sweat.

"Well, well, well, if it isn't Prep Girl." Gio Vargas grins down at me from where he stands in the ring, completely oblivious to the groans coming from his opponent who stumbles back to his feet. I have to crane my neck to look up at him as he sets the bottom of one bare foot on the lowest rope separating the ring from the rest of the gym and his elbows on the highest one.

"What did I say 'bout throwing bodies out of the ring?"

Cory's voice booms out, the sound so loud it makes me jolt. Several heads turn.

Gio scrubs a hand back over his messy hair before supplying Cory with a sheepish grin. "That anyone who gets thrown out forfeits?"

Cory's expression darkens for a split second before he sighs. "That anyone dumb enough to get thrown out deserves it," he corrects.

"Yeah, well, I didn't expect the prick to be able to lift me!" The opponent, a rather bulky man himself, grumbles as he rubs his back and limps to the side of the ring.

"I bench two-eighty, big boy," Gio replies. "Think again."

"You're not getting back in the ring, Donner," Cory snaps. "So, don't even try it, old man. Get yerself back to the showers and grab a pack of ice."

"Awww." Gio grips the ropes between his fists and reclines back, pulling it as he tilts his head and whines. "Then who'll play with me?" His eyes light on me. "Maybe Prep Girl wants to go for a spin?"

"Not a chance in hell," I shoot back without hesitation. Getting in the ring with him? It's a bad idea all around.

He arches a brow and straightens as Cory moves forward, snags Donner by the arm, and directs him away when he seems intent on climbing back into the ring despite Cory's words. Anyone around here knows that, in the gym, Cory's words are law.

"Go on now," Cory says, shooing Donner away. "Get back there."

The man grumbles but finally gives in and walks away, still limping ever so slightly. I blow out a breath as I watch him go and decide that maybe it's not best to come to the gym on a Friday afternoon after all. This was a waste of a trip since it looks like the punching bag is already in use, and there is no room for me to even catch a treadmill to run on without someone up my ass.

"I think I'll come back later," I say as Cory turns back to me. "When it's not so crowded."

"Running away?"

I stiffen at Gio's provoking tone. With a careful expression, I look back at him. "There's nothing for me to run from," I say.

"So, you're not scared of getting your ass beat?" he asks with a laugh. "Good for you 'cause what I hear is that it's coming for you soon at school."

"Vargas—" Cory's tone is a warning.

Outside, I'm nothing but calm. Inside though? Inside, I'm fucking boiling. "You think I can't beat you?" I ask, stepping up to the edge of the ring and tilting my head back even further.

He chuckles. "What do you weigh? I'd bet anything it's little more than a buck fifty."

"You just said you bench two-eighty," I reply. "So I thought weight class didn't matter."

He whistles. "So I did."

I sense Cory's presence before I feel his hand land on my shoulder. "He's just bored, girl," he says. "Don't let him rile you up."

Too late for that. "I'm already riled."

Playboy looks far too happy at my words and he rips himself away from the ropes, bouncing back and forth on the balls of his feet as he holds one palm out towards me, face up, and curls his fingers. "Come on then," he says. "Let's do this."

"Got any extra pads?" I ask Cory without looking at him.

His low sigh is my only answer, but a few minutes later, I'm strapped up and ducking under the ropes to take my place on the fighting mat in the middle of the ring. I crack my neck one way and then another, hating how tight the headgear is on me, but then again, it's meant more for kids since none of the men's headgear would fit me.

"I want a clean sparring match," Cory says, directing his voice out over the gym as he stands back and crosses his arms.

"I won't go too hard on her, Cory," Gio replies.

I grin.

Cory sighs again. "I wasn't saying that just to you."

Gio frowns, but it's too late. The bell rings. The match begins. I dive forward and perform a quick series of jabs—relying on muscle memory to pound them out. For the last few months, while everyone else had been having a great old last summer before senior year, I'd been training for my fucking life. So, I know ... no one actually expects me to do well. Least of all a cocky asshole from Silverwood Public.

My first hit lands, but Gio's training kicks in for my second and he proves that he's no slouch either. He manages to dodge the following jabs and even make a few himself. I rear back and the two of us circle one another. Sweat coats my skin beneath my t-shirt, but I remain focused. My breaths come fast and hard, rocketing up my throat as we bob and weave across the mat.

Now that he's learned I'm not a slacker, Gio's face turns serious. Cory's eyes linger on me, his brow creased with concern, but I'm not going to let that bother me now. Playboy here was the one who wanted this fight and who am I to turn down a gift punching bag? It's better to get my anger out here and now than explode in school and risk another suspension.

"I gotta say, Pipsqueak," Gio calls. "Even if you need some more power behind your punches, you got speed on your side."

"I thought I was Prep Girl?" I snap. "Do you give everyone you meet a hundred different nicknames?"

He laughs. "Just trying to find the right one," he replies. "I'll let you know when it hits."

"Don't bother—fuck!" I shoot out of the way as he makes a dive for me and just when I think I'm clear, his hands wrap around my waist and lift me up.

I brace for impact, but all of the air in my lungs rushes out the moment my spine connects with the mat and his body moves over mine. "Maybe I should call you"—he pants—"Distracted Girl."

Bringing both my forearms up to cover my face, I wait for blows to land, but there's nothing. Uncertain, I peek out to see him grinning down at me. "What the fuck are you waiting for?" I snap, bucking against him.

His body lifts up slightly and then he readjusts and pins me back to the mat, coming back down harder than before. "Don't be so quick to anger," he says. "It'll do you no good in a fight."

"I can handle myself!" I bow against him, and unfortunately, despite my words, I'm proving myself wrong by being unable to break his hold.

"You telegraph your moves, you know," he comments lightly.

"Yeah, I been telling her to watch for that," Cory pipes in.

Gio turns his head towards him before flipping back to me. "Is it 'cause you don't have a sparring partner 'sides from Cory?"

"None of your freaking business!" I clench my hands into fists and punch at his side.

"Oof!" Gio grabs ahold of my arms and then suddenly, they, too, are pinned down—this time, beneath his legs. I freeze as his groin connects with mine. My eyes widen and I jerk my head down.

"You need to learn how to play nice with others," Gio says with a slow smile.

I realize one thing that makes my stomach twist and my rage grow. *His dick is hard.*

"Are you fucking with me right now?" I seethe, struggling against the hold he has on me. I wait for Cory to call the sparring match since it's obvious as shit that I lost, but surprisingly he doesn't and I'll be damned before I ask for an end to the fight.

Gio leans down further and puts his mouth as close to my ear as both of our headgear can manage. "You need a bit more practice before you take on the big boys, sweetheart."

"Why don't you let me up and I'll take you on again?" I suggest. The second his legs aren't pinning mine and my arms down, I'll fucking slam my fist into his cock hard enough to break it. The damn snake in his pants rubs against me again. *Just how fucking big is it?*

His low, reverberating chuckle moves from his chest against mine. "You know, I bet I know someone who'd very much like to take you up on your body's offer, Prep Girl."

"There's no fucking offer," I insist. "Other than the one that lets me kick your ass."

"Is that so?" Gio doesn't seem particularly bothered as I move again, shifting my body to the side as I try to break his hold and wiggle out. My face is hot and I feel flushed with both humiliation and exertion. What the fuck is Cory thinking letting this continue?

I try to seek him out but I don't get the chance. Gio grips my chin and tilts my face back to his. Dark brown eyes meet mine. "You think not?" His expression turns serious. "Tell me something, Juliet. If I slipped my hand into your panties right now, would you still say the same?"

"*Yes,*" I hiss back.

"Even if I found you wet and wanting?"

I stop moving and close my eyes. *One.* Breathe. *Two.* Nothing is going to happen here. *Three.* He won't do it. *Four.* Even if he did, Cory would kick his ass out. *Five.* But not before I had my revenge in the way of either my fist or my knee in his crotch.

"You're assuming," I begin, reopening my eyes and staring up into his face, "that I want you. I hate to break your heart, *Playboy,*" I snarl my own nickname back at him, "but I don't."

A clapping sound breaks the tension and Gio finally pulls back and releases my face. "Alright, that's enough. Time to give someone else a chance in the ring, you two," Cory calls.

I debate punching Gio in the dick again when I get to my feet and he casts me a smug grin before adjusting his basketball shorts. If he's concerned about sporting such a massive boner in a gym full of mostly older smelly men, he doesn't show it. Unfortunately, I know that if I hit him after Cory's called an end to the match, I'd have to find myself a new gym.

I'm grateful enough to Cory not to make him regret letting me use the place—especially when no other fucking gym in town would even consider my application. Small towns and even smaller businesses are shit when it comes to business, always letting community politics guide their decisions. Not Cory though. If it weren't for him, I'd have nothing but a few childhood karate classes to support my self-preservation for the next year.

"Good spar, Prep Girl," Gio says, holding his hand out.

I stare at it for a moment. Instead of taking it, I flip him off and grab the ropes, practically diving out of the ring as I rip the headgear off and begin to unwrap my knuckles.

"I take it you're gonna head home?" Cory asks as I shove the gear at him.

"Yup. Thanks for the referee." Fat lot of good it did me. I still lost.

Grabbing my tennis shoes and socks, I pull them back on and tighten the laces before heading for the door. I raise a hand in goodbye. "See ya later, Cory."

"Be safe, girl!" he calls back.

Thirty seconds after I exit the old gym building, the glass door swings open behind me and the sound of footsteps trails out, crunching over the gravel parking lot. The footsteps at my back linger past the lot, however, and I glance back with a scowl to find Giovanni fucking Vargas with a phone to his ear as he trails me.

"Yeah, thanks, man. See ya soon." He hangs up.

I stop and turn in a new direction. Guess it's the long way home today. Behind me, Gio's footsteps follow. I break into a jog, but five minutes later, I still fucking hear him.

Rounding an old bowling alley with a few cars stationed in the parking lot, I race for the chain link fence that lines the train tracks that run alongside the building. My legs burn as I pick up the pace, pushing more power into them.

"Shit." Gio's curse makes me grin.

I launch myself at the chain link fence and manage to get halfway up before a firm hand grabs ahold of the back of my shirt and yanks me down. My fingers peel away from the metal and I shriek as I fall backwards.

"Are you trying to kill yourself?" Gio demands as I land hard on my back on the concrete.

A low groan rumbles up from my chest. "Actually, the opposite," I cough back a reply. I get to my feet and wince when I feel a particularly sore spot right over one of my kidneys at my lower back. A quick look down to the ground reveals a rather large rock as the culprit. My luck just doesn't stop. With a sigh, I dust off my hands on my pants and face him. "Why are you following me?"

Gio, though, isn't listening. His phone is back out and against his ear for a second time. "We're behind the bowling alley," he says. "Can you—already? Great. We'll wait for you here."

Since there's no one else but me and him, I assume that his 'we' includes me, which can only mean one thing. I've got to make a run for it.

15
JULIET

I don't wait for him to realize my plan. I take off running. My sneakers squeak against the dirty, cracked pavement as I round Gio and sprint toward the opposite side of the parking lot. The dried sweat sticking to my skin that once cooled, heats up once more.

"Fuck!" Gio curses a split second before the sound of his heavy footsteps follows me.

I glance over my shoulder to see his hulking, big ass body barreling right towards me faster than I anticipated a man of his size to be able to run. "Shit. Shit. Shit." Pushing more power into my thighs, I pick up the pace.

Exhaustion clings to me and I regret how hard I went in the gym before this. All along, though, I hope he went harder and that it makes it more difficult to catch up with me. If I had to guess, he and the Scorpion Kings have a plan to fuck me up —no doubt Megan has been hounding them to do it and I just gave them the perfect opening.

My feet pound against the loose debris in the parking lot as I cut around the bowling alley and dive across the street. A speeding Camry honks, barely missing me, but thankfully cutting off Gio. His loud "Motherfucker!" is music to my ears.

Throwing my head back with a laugh, I call behind me. "Serves you right, asshole!"

"Goddamn it, Juliet!" Gio's voice follows me further as I continue my way up the street, running until I swear my lungs are going to burst.

My heartbeat races in my ears, throbbing in time with the rush of my blood through my body. Adrenaline courses through me. I laugh again as I catch sight of a chain link fence separating the end of one alleyway with an opening on the other end. Right next to it, however, is a double-wide dumpster. I hang a right into the alley, listening to the sound of Gio's filthy mouth at my back as I do.

"When I fucking catch you, Prep Girl, I'm gonna spank your ass so fucking red!"

"I'd like to see you try, Playboy!" I scream back.

A side door slams open and a man in a stained white kitchen uniform ambles out with two trash bags in each hand. As he heaves them up, finally spotting me, I dive around him and hook my hands onto the top of the dumpster. Using my momentum, I launch my foot onto the edge, praying I don't fall in as I reach for the top of the fence just beyond it. My fingers connect with thin metal wiring. With relief, I sail over the top of the fence, landing rather hard on the other side. I ignore the reverberation of pain up my calves. I'm not stupid enough to stop now. Gio's athletic enough that the fence won't be much of a hindrance. It's just something to slow him down.

Think, Jules. Think! Where the hell can I go to lose him? Do I go back to the gym? No, I don't want Cory to get involved. If I let Cory protect me once then I'll keep relying on him again and again. I need to figure this shit out myself.

Panting for breath, I slow my run as I make it out of the other end of the alley. Scanning my surroundings, I spot a park to the left and just as I pivot in its direction, a roaring SUV with a rusted-out underside skids up on the sidewalk nearly colliding with me. I jump out of the way as the vehicle jolts to a halt and the passenger's side door opens.

Horror descends as a familiar face appears around the hood as Nolan circles towards me. I back up, stopping as I slam into a second chest. Gio's hands land on my upper arms and grip tight. "I told you to stop running, Prep Girl," he heaves.

"Out of breath much?" I counter. In my head, though, I'm freaking the fuck out. How the hell had he managed to call and tell them where I was heading as he ran after me? Nolan opens the back door and gestures inside.

"Nope." I back up further into Gio's chest, shaking my head. "No way in hell am I getting into that car."

"We're not giving you a choice, Princess," Nolan replies. "I suggest you don't fight it."

"And I suggest you *fuck off!*"

"*G.*" That's all Nolan says, and yet the sheer tone of that single syllable and letter is enough to let me know that he's done with what he likely considers my bullshit.

Gio picks me up off the ground and in a matter of seconds, I find myself thrown over a big meaty shoulder and hauled towards the back of the SUV. "Oh fuck no!" I buck against Gio's hold and he curses again, slapping a hand over my ass more to keep me anchored onto his shoulder than to cop a feel, but indignation still rips through me.

"Hands off!" I shriek, bucking again, punching him in the back of the head.

This was exactly what I feared when I made the switch from Prep to Public—the nightmares come roaring back. Hands reaching out of the dark, grabbing on to my limbs, tearing my clothes. Teeth sinking into my flesh. Disgustingly lewd moans filtering into my ears.

None of it's real. It's not there. It's just the phantom of my nightmares, but the trigger is obvious. Gio's fucking hand on my ass. I struggle harder, fighting him and the feelings that are rising up within me faster and faster. My blood boils. The earlier adrenaline that had been waning comes back, crashing over me like a tidal wave.

I can't breathe, but I don't let that stop me. I punch the back of his head over and over again. I lift my legs trying to kick him or knee him in the face. I don't care if it means I'll land face-first on the pavement. I don't care if I get punched back or bruised. I just need his hand off me or I swear I'm going to throw up.

"Jesus, for fuck's sake!" Gio finally releases me, but only to toss me into the backseat of the SUV. I crawl away from him on my hands and ass until my spine slams into the opposite door.

Stay calm, I try to urge myself. Not that it does much good. Bile threatens to come up my throat. I'm honestly shocked it hasn't made its entrance yet.

Breathe. In and out. Count. *Five.* I reach for the door's handle. I need to get out. *Four.* Low masculine voices bite at each other behind me. *Three.* Locked. The door's locked. Fuck. *Two.* A body hops into the backseat with me. Not Gio. *One.* The front passenger door opens and closes and the SUV pulls away from the curb.

I close my eyes and breathe deeply through my nose. I picture all of my emotions and bundle them together. Rage. Hate. Fear. Anxiety. I squeeze them all into a ball and stuff them down, deep down. Further and further until I can't feel them anymore.

A firm hand touches my shoulder and when I expect to jerk back automatically, I surprise myself by not moving at all. Instead, my eyes open and I watch as Nolan leans around me, grabs the seatbelt, and pulls it over my chest before clipping it into place. His hand grazes my breast, but he doesn't stop or cop a feel. He just glares at me as if he hates my guts and can't believe he's doing this.

Why are *they doing this?*

When I speak, my voice is smooth and monotone. "Where are you taking me?" I demand.

Gio looks over the back of the passenger seat in front of me with a wild, annoyed look. He's holding on to the back of his head and scowling. "You just lost your shit on me and now you're calm?"

I frown at him. "That's what you get for kidnapping me, asshole," I reply.

My eyes flash to the man in the driver's seat. I recognize him now as the same one who stopped me in the back hallway of The Dionysus Lounge after my interview. He doesn't say a word to me, but he does release a low chuckle as if he finds my words amusing.

Gio ignores my words and rounds on his friend. "Don't fucking laugh at that, Lex," he snaps. "The bitch damn near gave me a concussion!"

Lex goes still and his smile drops away. Slowly, as Nolan sits back and sighs now that I'm buckled in, Lex turns his head to Gio and scowls. "Don't call her that," he growls, his voice deepening impossibly until I swear I can feel a reverberating bass deep in my ears.

Silence stretches between the two of them, sliding through the vehicle until it's filled with a strange sort of tension. I wait a beat and when none of the men say anything, I decide enough is enough. I jerk on the door handle, recapturing all of their attention.

"Let me out," I demand coldly.

In response, Lex turns his gaze back to the windshield and pulls on his seatbelt. Nolan shifts next to me and reclines against the seat.

"No," is all he says.

Scowling, I jerk harder on the handle, wishing I could break it off. My fingers squeeze the hard plastic to keep myself from planting a fist in the man's face. He's built like a

Greek god, all lean muscles and chiseled features, and I have no doubt I'd bruise my knuckles if I tried.

A thundering rumble from overhead keeps me from speaking again and I frown as I glance out of the window just as the sky opens up and it begins to rain. My hard grip on the door handle eases, but only a little. I cast a dark look at the man in front of me, but Gio is looking at himself in the pull-down visor mirror, turning his head one way and then the other.

When his eyes finally connect with mine in the reflection, his narrow. "Thank you would be the appropriate response," he gripes.

"*Thank you?*" I scoff.

Before I can tell him where he can shove that thought, his irritated expression morphs into amusement and he replies with a swift, "You're welcome."

I gape at him, my mouth opening and closing for several seconds as I try and fail to muster an appropriate response. What do I say to that? He certainly knows I wasn't actually thanking him. So, instead, I merely release the handle and sit back in my seat, folding my arms as I glare from Gio to Nolan and then to the third and final man in their trio. I start a bit when I notice that instead of keeping his gaze firmly trained ahead as he meanders down the back alley we're stopped in, Lex's eyes are focused on me in the rearview mirror.

What I once thought were dull brown eyes are actually not brown at all … they're a dark silver. Deep and covered in a layer of smoke that it took me until now to realize it. Brown is a normal color, it's the most common. Perhaps that's why I assumed his were brown. Now, I know better. Lex's eyes are the color of a switchblade, and they're just as threatening.

Unable to help myself, I look away and out the window to my right.

Moments pass and it isn't until the familiar sight of my apartment building and the shitty green and brown pool nearby comes into view that I realize they're taking me home. I sit up straighter as Lex pulls through the parking lot and slows over a few speed bumps before he finds a parking spot in front of my building.

The second the car stops, I unbuckle my seatbelt and reach for the door handle. Pausing just before my fingers touch it, I look back over my shoulder at Nolan. I expect him to be facing forward, ignoring my presence even though it's clear the three of them planned this. Nolan isn't ignoring me, though. Cinnamon eyes stare at me—through me—as my hand hovers over the door handle. I blow out a long breath.

"Say it," I tell him, lowering my hand with a scowl.

He arches one brow and I roll my eyes.

"I'm not stupid," I say in response to his unspoken question. "You obviously have something you want to get off your chest. You wouldn't have your boy kidnap me for a quick ride home to avoid the rain out of the goodness of your hearts." In fact, I doubt any of them have any good inside their cold, dead hearts, but I don't say as much.

Nolan straightens in his seat and nods to Lex. A moment later, the telltale sound of the door locks disengaging fills the quiet. I narrow my eyes on Nolan and wait.

"Consider this your last warning, Juliet," he says quietly. "If you want to survive the rest of this school year, stop making waves. Keep your head down and don't pick any fights."

That's why they chased my ass down and kidnapped me? To warn me off? I glare at the back of Lex's head, stewing in my rage. No. This wasn't just a verbal warning, it's a physical one. A silent 'look what we can do' as if they're telling me that they can kidnap me off the street and no one around will do a thing. Because no one in Silverwood cares about the daughter of the town's villain.

I close my eyes, not because I'm afraid, but because I can feel a fresh bloom of rage pulsing inside me. When I open them again, I fix him with a dark glare, ignoring the two sets of eyes on me from the front seat, and lean close to the King of the Scorpions. Closer and closer I draw until I swear I can smell the underlying spice of his aftershave in my nostrils.

"Newsflash, asshole," I murmur quietly, "I'm not the one making waves. If I need to defend myself, I will. Nothing will stop that—not the school, not this bumfuck town, and certainly not you or your boys."

Nolan's nostrils flare. "I know you didn't create the ad," he replies coolly. "But your response to it—you may not be aware, but we're on the team at Silverwood Public and we need our teammates to remain unharmed for their part in our games. Keep your hands to yourself in the future."

"*No.*"

He stiffens at my one-word answer and then he blinks. "No?" He says the word back to me slowly, as if the sound of it confuses him.

"No," I repeat. "You can't tell me what to do, Nolan. I'm not one of your minions." I cast a scathing look at Gio and Lex when both look over their shoulders at us. "If someone comes after me," I continue, returning my gaze to their leader, "I'm going to give as good as I get. You tell your boys to stay off my back and they won't get hurt."

Nolan unbuckles himself and moves closer to me, pressing me back into the car door. "You're ballsy for an ex-prep girl," he says quietly, threateningly. "You *do* realize I could *make* you listen to me, don't you?"

The idea of Nolan Pierce making me do anything only leads to one conclusion. He's threatening to fuck me to get me to do what he says? Bull-fucking-shit. I laugh, but the sound is hollow. The only thing I actually hear is the hard and fast beat of my heart rate speeding back up. "You think so?"

"I *know* so." Nolan deadpans. He lifts two fingers and captures a tendril of my hair that has fallen in front of my face. Carefully sifting the strand between the pads of his thumb and forefinger, he stares back at me. "No one gives a shit about the girl whose dad destroyed half of the town's finances," he says and I barely manage not to flinch at the words. "If I were to strip you bare right here and now, no one would come save you. I could do such awful things to you, Juliet Donovan. I could make you like it or I could make you hate it."

"I would hate it," I snap back, fear at his words slamming through me even as my hands curl into fists. "There's no fucking way on Earth you could ever make me like your hands on me."

"Never say never, Jules," Nolan says, shortening my name as if we're friends. He continues to stroke my hair, almost thoughtfully. "I can make many women love things they might not otherwise want."

"*Not. Me.*" I hiss the two words through clenched teeth.

He smirks as if he's not convinced. "*Nolan.*" That one word comes from the front, from Lex. It sounds like both a warning and a plea, and immediately, it makes the man in front of me release my hair and sit back.

"If you don't get out now," Nolan says, casually, "we'll take that to mean you agree to pay for this little ride."

I scoff and reach for the handle. "Oh yeah?" I snark. "With what money? You seem to forget, but I'm not a princess anymore."

The door handle clicks under the pressure of my hand and it swings out. Rain slaps the nape of my neck as I inch back out of the vehicle rather than turn and hop out like any normal person. I just can't do it. I can't turn my back when I know a predator—three of them, technically—is watching me.

Nolan grins as he leans out to grip the handle. "If you don't have cash, princess, then there's only one other way for you to pay," he replies. "With your pussy, of course—or if you want to give all of us a go, your pussy ... your ass ... and your pretty little mouth."

With that comment from him, I can't seem to get out of the

car fast enough. The second my sneakers hit the wet pavement, I turn and whirl away from them. The sound of two men's laughter echoes back to me as I rush for my building. Nolan and Gio's amusement follows me up the outside staircase. Lex's on the other hand ... isn't there. He doesn't laugh with his friends at the thought of force-fucking me.

As I reach the top of the staircase and the railing that looks out over the parking lot, I pause and look down. Through the windshield of the beat-up SUV, I see Lex's gray eyes staring back at me with that impenetrable gaze of his. A shiver skates down my spine and I hoof it to the end of the row, not stopping this time until I'm inside my apartment with the door shut and locked behind me.

16
JULIET

The Dionysus Lounge is a quiet place when there are no customers—or 'guests' as Ma-Ri insists they be called. Like we're all just hosting a bunch of wealthy men and pouring their drinks for them at our own houses. I roll my eyes at that thought as I finish wiping down a table and then tuck the cloth into my thin black apron.

A door opens in the distance, and Deb, one of the bartenders currently setting up, starts to say something behind me before she cuts herself off. Curious, I look over my shoulder when I reach the opposite side of the club and pause when I see a familiar head of spiky black hair. I turn back and wait as Roquel offers Deb a wave and then practically sprints towards me.

"Hey," I say, brows rising. "What are you doing here?"

Roquel slows as she gets closer, her cheeks flushed, and for a moment I think she's angry, but then she takes a breath and offers me a smile. "Just came to hang out before opening," she says.

I frown at that and start moving again. "You wanted to hang out here?" I scoff. "Why?"

The clink of glasses echoes towards us as Deb finishes

restocking the bar and getting it ready for opening. I head towards the back hallway to the service closet secreted away there.

Roquel follows and shrugs at my words. "Just wanted to," she says. "I haven't seen Auntie lately and I wanted to see how you were handling the job." She trails behind me, her soft footfalls nearly silent as I grab a bucket out of the closet and fill it up with fresh soapy water. Snagging the adjoining mop, I dunk it several times before rinsing.

"It's a job," I deadpan as I start mopping the floors in preparation for the hosts to come out and get settled. The schedule on the board in the back already let us know that there would be several parties of businessmen arriving a short while after the doors open and we need to be prepared for whoever they're bringing with them.

That's one thing I've learned from Ma-Ri since I started working at The Dionysus Lounge. This place is more than a bar and club with beautiful women acting as hostesses. This place is a meeting place for the rich and powerful—usually men, though I've seen the occasional woman or two as well.

"You liking it so far?" Roquel asks as she finds herself a perch on the back of one of the lounge couches.

I chuckle at her lame question. "I'm just delivering drinks and bottles to the girls," I remind her. "It's not difficult."

"Cool, cool." Roquel nods and looks away.

I give her a good side-eye as I mop around the area, expecting her to get to whatever it is she wants to ask me before I'm done. I'm not stupid. It's obvious by the nervous energy coming off her and the way her eyes keep flickering to me and away whenever I lift my head that she's not here just to check on me. She wants something. I finish one route around the room and drop the mop into the now-dirty water before I sigh and cross my arms over my chest.

"Alright, enough. Out with it."

Roquel lifts wide doe-brown eyes to my face. "Out with

what?" she asks. The pseudo-innocent expression she wears is not fooling anyone. Even Deb snorts as she strides by with two racks of glasses clutched in her hands.

"You're here for a reason," I prompt.

Slender shoulders under a thin spaghetti strap tanktop rise and fall. "I just wanted to see how you were doing because I suspect Megan and her little minions will try something before the end of next week."

A sigh rolls out of me and I let my arms drop as I turn and prop my ass against the back of the couch. "I expect you're probably right," I say, "but I'm not a psychic. I'll just have to deal with it whenever they do gain the courage to come after me again."

Roquel's eyes spear the side of my face, and I turn to meet them. "You don't sound that nervous about it," she points out.

I shrug. "I'm not." Whatever Megan and Lindsey try to throw at me, I've already made it more than clear that I'll pay it back tenfold. If they want to risk their own skins, then I don't give a fuck.

Roquel opens her mouth to say something else, but almost as soon as she does, the backdoor leading from the breakroom opens and a familiar face pops out. Madison Torres strides into the club as she gathers up her long blonde hair and ties it up into a ponytail.

I stiffen and go quiet as she lifts her head and pauses at the sight of Roquel. A soft smile appears across her lips and she lifts her hand in a hesitant wave. Roquel, as extroverted as she is, waves back eagerly.

"I take it you're the reason she suddenly got a job here too?" I inquire as Madison continues towards the bar to help Deb finish stocking.

Roquel lets her hand drop and shrugs. "She couldn't get a job in town without her parents knowing about it," she replies. "They've kind of locked down on her since the whole sex scandal from last year. I felt bad for her. She's trying to save up enough to move out."

I find myself following Madison's movements as she lifts stacks of glasses into place and then grabs a few towels to finish wiping down the bar, but I don't say anything. Madison Torres' business is none of mine.

"Okay," Roquel blows out a breath and captures the rest of my attention once more. "You're right. I didn't just come here to see how you were. I came to ask for a favor."

Tension crawls over the top of my shoulders, but I quietly force it down, reminding myself that I always knew there would be strings attached to this job. That's just how the world works.

"Hit me," I say, pushing off the lounge as I make my way back to my bucket and mop.

"There's a party this weekend and I was hoping ... maybe ... *thatyoumightgowithme*."

The words come rushing out, each one slamming into the other without stopping all in one long breath. "A party?" I repeat, before clarifying. "In Silverwood?"

She nods with a wince. I gape at her; she's lost her mind. The mere fact that she thought asking me to go to a party in the town where everyone hates my fucking guts is a good indication. Roquel is certifiable. She's crazy.

Before I've managed to piece together my 'hell fucking no,' Roquel rushes on to explain.

"I know you probably don't like them anymore, especially since everything happened with your folks"—that's an understatement—"but I have no choice. I really need to go to this party."

No one needs *to go to a party.* I open my mouth to say just that but Roquel continues on. "Besides, you know you need to start making more friends, especially since Megan is out of ISS and she and Lindsey are planning something against you."

"There's no proof that they are," I remind her. "Just your assumption."

Roquel gives me a bland look. "Don't be dumb," she replies. "I know Megan like I know the back of my hand; that girl won't just let it slide that you pretty much snubbed her attempt to conquer you. The fact that the Scorpion Kings haven't done anything to you..."

I wince at the reminder of those assholes and am surprised to learn that Roquel doesn't know about their little threat the other day. I would have assumed they'd have bragged about it to all their friends by now.

"—so please don't say no. I can't go alone, I just can't."

I blink and return my attention to Roquel's pleading gaze as she clasps her hands in front of her chest and stares at me.

"Don't you have other friends to go with?"

"Yeah, but they can't go—one of them has a family thing she can't miss and the other is going to be out of town—"

I hold up a hand, halting her excuses as a headache begins to throb in a band around my skull. "Just..." I hesitate, trying to think of any other good reason I can refuse. The nagging sensation in the back of my mind, however, doesn't let up. It reminds me that when everyone was shitting on me, Roquel was the only one who actually offered me a hand ... and she had gotten me this job. Without it, I'd be sucking down ramen for months and likely unable to pay my senior dues at the end of this year.

From the upper echelon to the gutter, I think to myself with no small amount of depression.

"*Pleeeassseee,*" Roquel begs. "It's just one party, and like I said, you need to show Megan that you're not afraid of her."

I scowl at that. "I'm *not*."

Roquel nods her agreement. "And going to this party will show her that," she insists. "It'll show her that you're not going to hide away and that you don't care what she thinks;

that you're not afraid of what she or the Scorpion Kings can do to you."

And just like that, I know I'm going to say yes. It's not showing Megan that I'm not afraid of her. The mere mention of the Scorpion Kings is what decides it for me. They, more than anyone else, need to know that they can't push me around. I might be a social pariah and I might be broke, but that doesn't mean I'm someone they can walk all over.

"What if I have to work?"

She must sense that I'm ready to give in because, at that question, Roquel claps her hands and grins at me. "Oh don't you worry about that," she says. "I already told Auntie about the party and that I was going to ask you. She was planning on giving you the weekend off anyway since you picked up extra shifts last week."

The sound of something clattering behind the bar has me jolting and both Roquel and I swing our gazes to where Madison pops up and comes around the side, grabbing up the stack of black check booklets that she'd accidentally knocked off the front.

I open my mouth to ask her if she needs any help only to be interrupted as Roquel calls across the club. "Hey, Mads!" The girl's blonde head pops up once more and she looks our way. "Are you off next Friday?"

Madison glances from Roquel to me and then back again before nodding.

Roquel squeals with delight and shoots me an accomplished smile.

Fuck. Me.

"Great! Then the three of us are going to the party," she announces. "I'll drive."

Gathering up the last of the booklets and setting them atop the bar once more, Mads tilts her head in our direction. "Party?" she repeats.

Roquel hops off the back of the couch and shoots towards

her. "Yeah, I just got Juliet to agree to go to Robby Cordin's party next Friday and we were hoping you'd come with us."

"*We* were?" I mutter to myself, rolling my eyes. Roquel ignores my comment and bounces up and down in front of Mads as she holds the other girl's hands.

"This is going to be so much fun. Robby's parties are fucking killer. His parents let him use the back of the junkyard property they live on and as long as no one gets too loud or gets the cops called then we can pretty much do whatever we want there."

This is a dumb idea, but as Mads turns her gaze from Roquel to me, something unfurls in my chest. It's cold at first before turning warm. Sympathy? Maybe. A groan rumbles up my chest, but I already know it's too late now. Roquel's made her mind up and if anything proves the girl is a force to be reckoned with, it's also the fact that she somehow managed to befriend me when I was sure I'd be able to make it through the entire school year without getting close to anyone.

I give Mads a nod of encouragement. "I guess you'll have to come now," I say before I jerk my chin towards Roquel. "She won't let up until you do."

Poor Mads doesn't even get a chance to respond. Roquel's over-excited scream is enough to seal both of our fates.

17
GIO

"Coach is trying to kill us," Nolan groans as we stride through the door into the house.

Heavy cigarette smoke lingers in the front room, but there's no hint as to how long ago my old man was home. He smokes so damn much that the scent has seeped into the walls. It always smells like cigarettes no matter how much my ma tries to clean up after his lazy ass.

Nolan drops his shit next to the couch and practically sags into the already weak cushions that damn near go concave under his weight. Coming in last, Lex circles me and collapses next to him.

"I'm fucking dead, man." I lean my head to one side, putting my hand on my neck, trying to crack it.

Each damn bone in my body feels as if it's been put through the wringer. Maybe it's because we're set to go up against Silverwood Prep in a few weeks, but our team had been hyped today. Even with the pads on, I'd felt each and every slam from our defense.

"My bruises have bruises," I mutter.

"Same," Nolan agrees before he sits up straighter and nods

toward the back hallway. "Mind if I use your shower before I head off to work?"

I know why he avoids using the showers at the school, but I don't comment. Slipping in and out of clothes is one thing, but walking around naked in front of a bunch of guys when he's sporting those scars of his is another matter entirely. Not everyone is as discreet as they should be and the fewer people remember he ever had a father who beat the shit out of him, the better.

I wave him towards the back of the house. "Fuck if I care. Go on."

Nolan is up and off the couch as if he hadn't just been acting like he could hardly move a minute ago. As he disappears down the hall, I grab the remote that controls the ceiling fan and take his place on the couch. I hit the button that'll start the rotation and hopefully get some air going as the sweat on my skin starts to dry. Several moments pass in near silence. Slowly, I let my gaze drift to the man next to me. Lex has his shaggy dark hair pulled back and away from his face, tied in a knot at the back of his skull. His phone is already out and sitting in his palm as he flips through various security feeds. When he pauses over a familiar face, I let loose a long-annoyed sigh. Lex looks up at me as I scowl at him.

"I've never understood why you're so hung up on that girl," I gripe, nodding down at the black and white still of Juliet Donovan standing in The Dionysus Lounge parking lot talking to Roquel Lee. "Just because she was nice when we were kids doesn't mean she's going to be okay when she finds out you've been secretly watching her for years. She'll be creeped out, man. You should really fix your sights on someone better. There are plenty of Public girls that'd suck your dick like a vacuum just to wear your jersey for a night."

Lex's eyes cut my way, but he doesn't turn his head. "I don't want those girls," he states. "Besides, are there any

Public girls who'd suck my dick that haven't sucked yours too?"

My lips twitch and a grin forms. "Probably not," I admit. "But that didn't seem to bug you before." My grin eases a bit and I gesture to his phone. "Not that you've touched anyone since Prep Girl fell from grace. You hoping she'll give you a chance now that she's in the gutter too?"

"Nolan said I could bring her with us."

The reminder of that long-ago promise makes me frown. "Are you seriously still planning on her coming?" I shake my head. "Come on, man. You know Nolan only said that shit so you'd chill. There's no way she's going to agree to follow us. Besides, why the hell would we want a spoiled needy little girl to weigh us down? We're trying to get out of this dump, not bring it with us."

Lex bares his teeth at me, his upper lip pulling back over the top row of shiny whites. "She's important to me," he snaps, "and she's not spoiled—not anymore."

I blow out a long breath. Talking to him about Juliet Donovan is as pointless as ever. "Yeah, yeah." I wave a hand. "Sorry, I didn't mean any insult or nothing—I just ... I've never understood what you see in her."

Those gray eyes of his, the color of smoke and burning ashes, go back to the screen. "She's different," he murmurs. "She cared about me when no one else did."

I punch him in the shoulder. "I care about you, you fucker," I snap. I wouldn't put up with his weird stalkerish tendencies if I didn't. "You aren't obsessed with me like that." Not that I'd want him to be, but if that's all it is drawing him to her then he's whacked out. I mean ... he's already whacked out, but he's Lex. That's his normal state of being.

Still, no man should ever be this caught up on some pussy.

"She was the one who reported my dad." The words are so quiet, I almost don't hear them. Almost.

My head whips back around and I gape at him. "What?"

Lex stares down at Juliet's picture, her face turned to give a smooth profile of her jawline and the delicate curve of her ear. He strokes it with a thumb. "She saw the bruises, and when the teacher ignored them, she threw a fit. She said that someone was being mean to me and that it wasn't okay. She told the teacher and when the teacher tried to calm her down, to tell her to be quiet, she refused." He doesn't lift his head from his phone as he stares at the nearly adult Juliet Donovan, though I'm sure he's thinking of her as the little blonde five-year-old she was back then.

"A lot of the teachers knew how shitty my parents were, but they didn't want to risk pissing off my dad," he continues. "He was a dick, but he donated to the school before Prep was built. They thought they needed the money. Juliet didn't care. She made such a big stink about my bruises that it would've looked bad if multiple teachers ignored her. It was because of her that they finally opened a case and then they found out all of the bullshit he was pulling behind closed doors—the gambling, the drugs."

I don't say a word as he tells the story I already know. When he lifts his gaze away from her image and looks me in the eye, I feel my chest cave in just the slightest bit. Parents always fuck up their kids, no matter if they're perfectly lovely and kind. Every kid grows up just a little messed up because that's just the way of society. Parents like Lex's though ... they are the reason psychopaths exist. If I believed in my mama's god, I'd thank the fucker every day that Nolan and I got to Lex before that happened.

"I might've died if she didn't tell," he admits. "Or I might've been in the house with him when he shot Mom and killed himself."

"Fuck." I sag onto the couch, forgetting about the television entirely. "Sorry, man. I didn't realize that's how it happened. I mean I knew about your ma and dad, but..." I let my words trail off, not entirely sure what to say.

Lex shrugs but then lowers his phone as the screen times out and goes black. "No need to say anything, but if you could do something for me?"

"What?" I glance his way.

"Don't hate her so much," he says. "I know Nolan didn't really mean it when he said if I could convince her to leave with us, he'd let her come—but I'm holding him to it. I want her."

My lips pinch together. Letting go of my hate towards her, I might be able to do. The idea of her coming with us when we leave Silverwood, though? It's still foreign to me. "What about us?" I ask him.

Lex tilts his head to the side. "What *about* us?"

I gesture outward. "Three guys and one girl?" I say. "You think that's a good plan? Or are you planning on getting your own place with her? Are you gonna leave Nolan and me and go start your life elsewhere with your fallen rich girl?"

For the longest second of my life, Lex doesn't say anything and then he shocks me. "Why can't we just be together?"

"Together?" My brow puckers. He can't mean... "Like ... *together* together?" I clarify.

He stares back at me. "Yes."

"You want *us* to have a relationship with her?" I shake my head. "Dude, you've been in love with her for years. Why the hell would you want to share her with Nolan and me?"

Not that I can't see the benefits. I've done a lot of shit in the bedroom and I've done it with a lot of people. Nameless, faceless people. I've played with threesomes before. I've fucked a girl's ass. I've done what seems like it all. Sharing with my best friends though? I don't hate the idea.

It would be one way to keep us all grounded, to keep us all together. Friends aren't meant to last forever. Friends grow up. They move on. I've heard that all too fucking much over the last year. The closer we get to graduation, the more I fear what leaving Silverwood would do to us.

We may not be blood-related, but the three of us are bound in something stronger. One girl … between the three of us? What better way to bind us all together and keep us from drifting apart when we escape this godforsaken town?

Lex puts his phone away and pulls a laptop out of one of his bags. "There's another thing I need to talk to you and Nolan about," he says, switching topics as he turns on the machine and his fingers speed over the keys.

"What's that?"

"Her father called me a while back to look into his case."

I blink. "Wait. Allen Donovan? Allen Donovan called you? To look into his case?"

"He called Scorpion."

Holy … fuck. "You took the job." It's not a question. The girl he's been in love with for over ten years' father asks for his assistance? Yeah, there ain't no way Lex has the kind of impulse control to say no.

"Yes, and I found something."

I lean closer, looking down at the laptop screen, but it's all a dark background with code appearing and jolting through various boxes that pop up and disappear too fast for me to even read them. Damn. I don't know how he figures anything out on the damn thing.

"Let me guess," I say. "Donovan claims he's innocent and he wanted your help to prove it." I roll my eyes. "Dumbass. All you'll do is pull up the truth and then he'll be shit out of—"

"I think he might be innocent." If it were possible for my jaw to unlatch completely from my skull and tumble to the floor it would do so.

"What?" There's no way.

Lex continues to type, pulling up box after box—only these show a series of documents, some scanned and some digitally created. "I went back into his banking history—through all of the income and profits of Donovan-Calloway enterprises."

"You're not going to tell me that the money isn't gone," I snap. "A lot of our friends lost their college savings because their parents couldn't afford to make ends meet. Silverwood is still recovering—"

"No, the money was definitely embezzled and stolen, but whether or not it was done by Allen Donovan is still a question."

"You're going to try and prove that it wasn't him, aren't you?"

Lex glances over at me. "I'm going to find the truth. If it was him, well he's fine out of Juliet's life then, but if it wasn't..."

"You know helping him and finding out that he was innocent might mean she'll have another option than going away with you when the time comes," I point out.

"She'll choose us." His gaze sharpens and I'm not sure if he's trying to convince himself or me.

I open my mouth to say as much when the front door opens. Lex has his computer shut and stowed back in his bag before I can blink and turn my head. When my brain catches up to the fact that he's back in his seat and the person walking in the door is Mama, I practically leap off the couch.

Carrying two plastic bags marked with the local grocery store's logo, she glances up as I hurry towards her, reaching for the bags before she can stop me. "Oh, amore mio," she murmurs, her Italian accent lilting, "you're home."

The sound of her accent soothes my anger. For a moment, I think it's too damn bad I never picked it up, but my papino had beaten it out of me every year as I aged. Though my mother is a proud Italian, the mixture of my father's Spaniard roots and the discrimination he's faced since immigrating to America made him ensure that his son would never pick up those small quirks from their homelands. Even if I do know some of the language, using it outside of the house is a disrespect he'd never stand for. Vile old bastard.

Mama doesn't fight me as I lift the heavy bags out of her hands and bend to place a kiss to the top of her head. As short as she is, I'm able to look over her and peer through the grimy storm door to the street beyond. With trash littering the sidewalks and overgrown weeds in the yards of the other millhouses in the neighborhood, the only thing out of place is the pristine black sedan sitting at the curb.

The car's not brand new, but it's well-kept. I'd seen a few of the dealers driving around in something similar—though I know they prefer the SUVs. The blacked-out windows aren't different either. I can't tell if there's anyone inside, but there's some warning bell inside me blaring that there is. That we're being watched.

"I am, Mama," I reply distractedly as I stare at the car. "Practice ended half an hour ago."

"Hi, Lex," Mama murmurs.

"Hi, Mrs. Vargas," Lex replies with a nod.

"Do you want me to fix you boys something to eat?" She circles me and moves further into the house. "Is Nolan here? He's probably got to work tonight. I can whip up some panzanella for him before he goes."

"No, Mama," I say, still eyeing the sedan with increasing irritation and concern. "We're okay." My eyes flash to Lex. He's glaring at me still, but there must be something on my face because in the next moment, he's up and off the couch, our spat forgotten.

"Gio, why are you still standing at the door?" Mama asks, tsking. "Go on and close it and bring those bags into the kitchen. Your papino will be home soon."

The mention of my father has me gritting my teeth, but instead of responding, I just give Lex a look of meaning and nod out of the storm door towards the black sedan. He doesn't need words. He merely nods and nudges me out of the way before opening the door and heading outside. I wait a moment to make sure he makes it to the car and is safe before I half-heartedly kick the door so that it swings shut, but not all the way. Then I follow my mama into the kitchen and set her bags on the scratched counter before unloading.

"Let me grab you something to drink. You sweat too much at those practices of yours," Mama says as she moves towards the equally beat-up refrigerator.

With a sigh, I set one can of tomatoes on the counter and turn, catching her around the waist with one arm. "Mama, we're fine," I say, cupping her cheek. The dark circles under her eyes have grown. "You look tired. Why don't you go rest and I'll finish unpacking this."

"I'm not an invalid, Giovanni Luis." Her face tightens as she uses my first and middle name as if that'll get me to do what she wants. It used to … when I was eight. Now, however, I stand a good six inches taller than her and more than double her body weight.

Still, I stroke a strand of her black and gray hair back and give her my most beseeching smile. "You are tired, Mama," I repeat. "I am a grown man; I can make my own food. You've been at work all day. You should lay down before Pa—Father—gets home."

The asshole will likely only interrupt what little rest she manages to get by demanding his dinner and criticizing the unkempt house that he seems to wreck whenever he comes through. It's better she get as much now as she can.

Mama grumbles and glares at me. "You never listen to me anymore, amore mio," she gripes. "Ever since you shot up"— she pauses to smack me—"it is as if you lost all respect for your mama. I raised you to be a better man than this."

I bite down on my tongue to keep from laughing at her poor attempt to guilt me into letting her work. I shake my head. "Not going to work on me, Mama," I tell her. "You raised me to take care of those I love and that's what I'm doing."

With firm hands on her shoulders, I turn her around and push her towards the hallway just as Nolan exits the bathroom down the dark interior. His half-naked form appears and he offers Mama a wave as he ducks his head and disappears into my room to, I assume, get changed.

Mama gripes and complains and guilt trips me every step of the way, but finally, I manage to nudge her halfway down the hall. Far enough for her to get the hint that I'm not going to let her do anything until after she lies down. Her smaller frame dips into the room she and my father share as the front door opens and Lex appears.

My gaze shoots to his and I frown. "Who was it?" I demand.

Lex tips his head around me, trying to look past the living room into the kitchen and I sigh. "I just got her to go lay down," I say, lowering my voice as I answer his unspoken question about whether or not Mama is still there.

Lex nods and moves back towards the couch. "That was Mattias," Lex murmurs, lowering his voice as a door opens down the hall. I look up, spotting Nolan as he moves towards us, wearing a pair of my jeans and a dark t-shirt.

I frown at him. "Wash those before you bring them back," I say. "I don't want them back covered in grease."

Nolan flips me off without looking my way as he finishes towel drying his hair and then lets the worn gray fabric just hang around his neck. Shaking my head, I return my attention to Lex, less concerned now that I know it was just one of my father's men checking up on me. I fucking hate it when he sends them without warning, but telling him to stop would only result in another fight and Mama crying. I'm tired of seeing her fucking cry.

"What did he want?" I ask Lex.

"The collection money from Ma-Ri," Lex replies.

Nolan moves into the kitchen and starts up the task of unloading Mama's groceries that I'd stopped earlier. "Good thing you had it," he says. "The handover went fine?"

Lex nods and moves up next to the counter, grabbing a carton of juice and turning to stow it in the fridge. Together, the three of us make quick work of unloading the two bags and at the bottom of the second, I pull out the receipt and scowl.

"Fuck—when the hell did shit get so expensive?" I mutter, crumpling the little piece of paper before I remember that Mama likes to use the coupons on the back. With a huff, I set it back on the counter, straighten it out with the flat of my palm as much as I can, and then toss it onto the stack in the junk drawer.

"Everything's expensive nowadays," Nolan comments as he pops a can of soda and then starts to chug it.

I grip the edge of the countertop and bend over it, inhaling slowly through my teeth.

Even if it comes out that Allen Donovan is innocent, the damage has already been done. There will always be a dark cloud hanging over his daughter's head and people will still believe that her father was the one that ruined half of the town's lives.

"You should tell him," I say, catching Lex's gaze and nodding towards Nolan.

Nolan lowers the soda can. "Tell me what?"

Crossing my arms, I wait, but Lex remains curiously quiet. I sigh. Nolan watches the two of us but doesn't say a word. A beat of silence slides through the room, then I throw my hands up in disgust.

"He's working for Allen Donovan," I offer up and sit back for the shitshow.

Nolan stares at Lex. "Tell me he's joking." His words are a low growl, a demand.

Lex shakes his head.

"Goddamn it, Lex." Nolan crumples the aluminum can in his fist, the sound of sharp cracks resounding around the room. "I told you when you started that hacking shit that you shouldn't accept work close to home."

"Allen Donovan is being held in Hansgard Correctional Facility, three hours north." Lex's statement earns a hard glare from Nolan.

"He's from Silverwood," Nolan snaps. "You know what my stipulations meant; don't get technical on me."

"That's kind of his job," I say, reclining against the counter and crossing my arms again.

"Shut up, G." Nolan doesn't even look at me as he bites out the words. His sole attention is focused on Lex. *It always fucking is.*

I wince at that thought, but keep my mouth shut as Nolan lays into Lex about his dark web practices and taking jobs that won't get him arrested or found out by local authorities. In the beginning, it used to be just Nolan and me. Lex was too quiet and reserved to really be of interest to a couple of five and six-year-olds. Since Lex's dad was outed as an abuser, though, we've been ten times closer. The three of us realized that few people would actually care if our fathers killed us—at least they wouldn't care until it was too late.

Unlike me, though, Lex hadn't been able to manage normalcy for a long time. Nolan worried about him and constantly talked about keeping him under control. In some ways, it feels like Nolan and I are Lex's keepers, and up until three years ago, it bugged the shit out of me.

Now, though ... Lex is as much a part of me as Nolan is. There shouldn't be any room for jealousy. Yet ... their abusers are gone. Both are dead either by our hands or by their own. Mine remains in the same house as my mama and me. I can't help but resent the fact that my monster still lives when theirs are long gone.

"—what I want when it comes to her, this involves her." I

withdraw from my thoughts and take in the last bit of Lex's words.

I don't have to hear what he said before to know what he's talking about. Everything concerning Juliet Donovan is under Alexio Medicci's purview. He knows all when it comes to her. He knows her favorite soda, her preferred music, and probably even down to the color of her thong on any given day. At least, she strikes me as a thong wearer. Maybe, along with all of the other things that have changed about her in the last several months, that has too.

"Helping her criminal father is not something I would be okay with. You knew that," Turning, Nolan tosses the now-crumpled soda can into the trash bin before fixing Lex with his impenetrable gaze. It's the same look he gives to some of my father's men when they think they can fuck with the three of us just because we're younger than them. "I want you out. I don't care what you have to tell the bastard, you end the job."

Lex is already shaking his head. "No."

Nolan's expression darkens further and before his top can blow, I step between the two of them. When I originally outed Lex's little secret, it hadn't been to cause a fight between them, but because for our group to work, we can't keep secrets like that from each other.

"Alright, that's enough," I say, pressing a hand against Lex's chest when he leans forward. "You two need to take a fucking pill. She's just a girl."

"Not to him." Nolan jerks his chin in Lex's direction. He's right. To Lex, Juliet Donovan is an idol, his savior, his perfect woman.

I blow out a breath. "Regardless, the fact of the matter is that if you want shit to continue smoothly with Darrio and after we graduate, then we need money." And no doubt if Lex manages to find out that Allen Donovan is innocent of the charges against him, the payday from that will set the three of us up for a good long while after we get the fuck out of Silverwood.

"We don't need the money that badly," Nolan argues. "I've been pulling more shifts at the shop and with the income Darrio generates—"

"That income won't last forever." I cut him off, letting my hand drop from Lex's chest as I turn to face one of the two men I'd both kill and die for. "You didn't just make a deal with Lex when you decided that we're out after graduation," I remind him. "You made one with me too."

At the end of this year, it'll all be over. No more Darrio. No more constantly looking over our shoulders to see what bullshit my psycho of a father has dragged down on all of our heads. He'll be gone. Mama will be safe and we'll be on the road straight out of town.

Nolan doesn't say anything for a long moment, his gaze switching from mine to Lex's as the big man stands behind my shoulder. It's rare for us to form a front against Nolan. More than that, though, this is the first time it's ever been about a damn girl.

She's beautiful, I'll give Lex that much. Hot as hell and stronger than I would've given a prep girl credit for. She's a fighter. When I first learned that she hadn't skipped town like her mother, I assumed she'd be out before the end of the year. I was wrong.

Juliet Donovan is not the same girl from years past. I don't know if that girl had been a facade or if this one is, but I'm rapidly growing curious about her. *Fuck*. To think I'd given Lex shit about her over the last thirteen years and then end up just as interested in her as the lovesick idiot. Is crazy a disease you can catch?

Nolan finally straightens away from the counter at his back. He tilts his head, first at me and then Lex. Something passes between the two of them, a silent conversation. I try not to let the fact that I'm being left out of whatever is being said get to me again. I really fucking do, but the longer the silence reigns, the tighter my muscles wind.

With a sigh, Nolan shakes his head. "You're right," he finally says, his gaze returning to me. "I made a promise to both of you and I'll keep it, but Juliet Donovan is a distraction none of us need." Despite his words, when he says her name, there's a glimmer of something in his eyes. I know what it is.

It's a dangerous curiosity.

Nolan glances back at Lex. "I know I can't convince you to just let it go, but at the very least, I hope you'll keep us in mind—whatever actions you take don't just affect you, they affect all three of us."

Whether we want to admit it or not, Juliet Donovan is affecting us all.

18
JULIET

Friday arrives, and I'm ready to chew my own arm off to get the hell out of my apartment—even if it means attending a shittastic party. When I still had my BMW, I used to just drive into the city for the weekend and get trashed at a club with Bran or Avery to unwind. Now, I have little else in the way of entertainment options other than Roquel's party invite.

A week of dealing with insults from Megan and her crew and the childish pranks of trash in my locker, gum on my seats, and worms in my lunch have me strung so tight that I'm ready to beat someone to a bloody pulp. Yet, still, I haven't made it back to Cory's since seeing Giovanni Vargas there. My safe haven has become a place to avoid and I hate him all the more for that.

Nothing is sacred anymore thanks to the Scorpion Kings.

Lights flash from the parking lot of my apartment building, spearing into the thin window above my kitchen sink. Before Roquel can flash them a second time, I'm out the door and heading down the stairs leading to the parking lot. Unlike what I used to wear to Prep parties—heels, club dresses, and thousand-dollar diamonds—tonight I've opted for the fashion of a wallflower. A pair of ripped jeans, a black tanktop, and a black and gray flannel. My blue hair is pulled up in a high ponytail at the back of my head, swinging against my neck as I jog down the metal stairs and hit the pavement at a light run.

Roquel's car—an older gray Toyota Camry—sits towards the back of the lot, pointed directly towards my building. I hit the sidewalk and make my way over, pivoting towards the passenger's side door. I pop the handle and slide inside to find her touching up her lipstick in the cracked visor mirror before slapping it back up and tossing the Dollar Store brand tube into the console.

Her eyes widen when she takes a look at me. "Wow, Jules," she murmurs, her eyes roving down my clothes with no small amount of dismay, "I was never invited to the Silverwood Prep parties, but ... is this what the rich kids are wearing these days?"

I roll my eyes and gesture to the frayed jean skirt she's wearing over fishnets and the ripped black band shirt tucked into the waistband. "It's going to be cold outside," I tell her, not bothering to answer the question. "You're going to freeze wearing that getup."

I slide my seatbelt on as Roquel backs out of the parking spot at the speed of light. My heart jumps against my ribcage as the seatbelt immediately constricts across my chest. *Fuck.*

"Get enough alcohol in me and I won't even notice the cold," she says.

"Aren't you driving?" I remind her pointedly as I try not to focus on how close she gets to the curb as she speeds out onto the main road.

She shrugs, unconcerned. "You can drive back."

I sit back, annoyance flaring to life. I hadn't planned on drinking—there isn't anyone I trust in this town to see me even remotely intoxicated—but I'd at least wanted the option. Roquel chatters on about the guy she's hoping to see at the party. She says the guy's name so many times I'm sure it's ingrained in the back of my skull by the time she slows down and turns onto a dark street. I sit up a bit straighter and glance around as she shuts off her headlights and slows the car down to a stop halfway up the block. She puts the car into park but doesn't turn it off as she lifts her phone from the console and swipes it open.

Confused, I glance from where she sits typing out a text to the dark street ahead. "What are you doing?" I finally ask.

Roquel finishes typing out her message and hits send before replying. "We're picking up Madison," she answers. "Her parents are…" Roquel grimaces and sighs before unclicking her seatbelt and turning fully to face me. "Madison's parents are a bit strict," she says. "Remember how I told you about last year's fiasco with her old boyfriend? What he did?"

I nod and Roquel's lips pinch together briefly before she continues. "She isn't allowed out," Roquel says. "Not to go to work, not to go to parties—"

"Wait, but you got her a job at The Dionysus Lounge," I remind her.

Roquel tips her head to the side. "Yeah, and her parents have no clue. She has to sneak out to go to work too. I doubt she'd ever say anything, but I'm pretty sure she gets into trouble every time they catch her gone."

"Where do they think she's going?"

Roquel shrugs. "Dunno. That's her business."

I sit back against the cheap faux leather seat. "I don't blame them for being protective," I murmur as a pit opens up in my stomach. "If some asshole released a sex tape of my kid, I'd fucking kill them." Not that I'll ever have kids. With parents like mine—a criminal and a coward—I doubt I'd be much of a mom.

The sound of Roquel's scoff brings my attention back to her. "They're not *protective*," Roquel mimics the last word as if it's a filthy curse. "They're controlling."

"At least they care." Unlike mine.

The reminder hits me in the chest. The numerous emails from my father's lawyer asking me to see him aren't the only things I've been avoiding. My dad's best friend, Morpheus Calloway, is another piece of my past I don't want to think about. He's been emailing me a lot too, asking to meet up and practically begging me to reconsider his offer. Unlike my parents, Morpheus is a good person. He feels guilty for his best friend's daughter—even if that best friend almost made him lose his entire business.

He's the one person in this entire fucking town that doesn't hate me and isn't trying to use me. He just wants to make sure I'm taken care of, and it almost hurts that I won't let myself rely on him. I can't. No one gets my full trust anymore. Not even him, even if he probably deserves it. Anger curdles in my stomach, flaring to life.

"Just because some parents are around doesn't mean they should be," Roquel murmurs quietly—almost too quiet for me to hear, but I hear it. Slowly, I turn my head again to face her. She's no longer looking at me though. Instead, her eyes are locked on a distant point through the front windshield. "Sometimes, leaving is the better choice. If all they're going to do is ruin our lives and fuck up our futures, then they can get lost and leave us to our own devices."

There's obviously something there with her words, some dark past or maybe even present. Though a part of me wants to offer my condolences or even reassurances, I keep my mouth shut. If anything, my current predicament pretty much solidifies that I have no business trying to help anyone. I can't even help myself. A quiet tension settles in the vehicle as we wait several more minutes and then a dark figure appears at the top of a fence two houses down from where we're parked. My eyes widen as I lean forward and realize it's Madison.

The girl is agile as she climbs and swings both of her legs over the fence before dropping down into a crouch. She stays hunched over and runs down the length of the first house and then the second before she straightens and slows her pace.

"Her house is another street over," Roquel quietly explains. "She asked me to park here so her parents wouldn't get suspicious and she just climbed her back neighbors' gates."

"Damn," I breathe. "She should be an athlete with those skills."

That comment more than anything else, I think, breaks the awkwardness and Roquel flashes me an amused smile. "She is," she admits. "She runs track and field." Almost as soon as the words are out of her mouth, though, her lips twist into a scowl. "For people like us, you have to either be an athlete or a genius to get ahead. She'll get a scholarship eventually and get out from under her parents' thumbs."

I nod my agreement as Mads gets closer to the vehicle, peers in, and then smiles and waves as she moves toward the back passenger door next to the sidewalk. The door opens with a metal creak and then thuds shut as she scoots inside and pulls on her seatbelt.

"All set?" Roquel asks as she flips her lights back on and buckles herself.

"Yup," Mads responds, offering me a small smile.

Roquel does a three-point turn, forgoing pulling into one of the driveways, and soon we're off, heading towards the edge of Silverwood.

I'm not one for small talk, but with Mads, she makes it easy. As Roquel drives us farther and farther from the town limits of Silverwood, I focus on Mads to keep myself from throwing up or grabbing the wheel from her fucking hands. If I'd known how bad of a driver Roquel would be, I don't know that I would've agreed to come to this thing.

Mads and I chat about anything and everything. To my surprise, she's not just good at hopping fences, but she's a straight-A student. Makes me wonder how she came to have such a douche for a boyfriend or how he managed to take advantage of her last year. Then I think of Brandon and Avery and remember that I'd had the same kind of douches for both a boyfriend and best friend. Unwilling to let them take up any more space in my head, I push them out of my mind and focus on the passing scenery as Roquel's Camry starts to slow, rattling as she turns onto a dirt driveway, splitting a line of dark trees.

There are no streetlights out in the country, so the dual headlights at the front of the car are the only illumination—sending dusky yellow beams out over the dirt road. We travel several more minutes until the line of trees is disrupted.

I didn't even realize that I'd been tensing up until the sight of an old, dilapidated farmhouse comes into view along with several bonfires situated around the property. There are dozens of cars all parked haphazardly around each other at various angles as if the drivers were either already drunk when they arrived or that was their attempt at making sure no one could box them in.

"We're here!" Roquel crows excitedly, her little car slowing even more even though her body seems to be vibrating in the driver's seat.

The Camry jerks to a stop and my chest slams into the seatbelt, knocking the air from my lungs. Before I manage to unbuckle myself, Roquel has already hopped out. Mads and I exchange a look before following her out of the vehicle at a much slower pace. The second we get out, the scent of cheap alcohol and gasoline hits me. My upper lip curls back in disgust and Roquel flashes me a warning look as she adjusts her top a bit lower.

"Don't start," she says. "We're here for a reason—to have fun."

"And to show Megan that Juliet isn't scared of her?" Mads adds in a questioning but amused tone.

Roquel and I both turn to look at her.

She shrugs. "I'm not stupid. I knew that was the only way you'd convince her to come," she says to Roquel.

"I don't give a fuck about Megan." I roll my eyes and cross my arms as a breeze drifts by. I'm glad I opted for the longer-sleeved flannel rather than something like Roquel's outfit as she shudders and then turns to march toward the fires.

"Come on!" she calls over her shoulder. "Let's grab a drink."

Mads hesitates, glancing at me. "Isn't she driving?" she asks.

I shake my head. "I'm not planning on drinking," I tell her. "I can drive us back."

Mads considers that for a moment and then sighs. "Do you have her keys?"

My eyes widen when I realize I don't, and Roquel is already halfway to the party, leaving the two of us behind. "Fuck," I mutter and start to pick up the pace.

Soft, feminine laughter at my back has me pausing and glancing over my shoulder as Mads chuckles. "And that," she admits, "is the real reason I came. Roquel's pretty known for not being able to come to parties on her own, but then ditching whoever she's with the second she gets here if they can't keep up. She means well, but…" Mads shrugs as if to say there's nothing anyone can do about it.

A groan rumbles up my chest. "Ugh, I really don't want to do this," I tell her, reaching up to pinch the bridge of my nose. "If I knew she'd ditch, I would've—"

Sharp, squealing laughter echoes down from the top of the hill we parked on towards the farmhouse and bonfires. I cut myself off and glance up just in time to see Roquel rushing towards a beefy guy I think I've seen sitting around the footballers' table in the cafeteria at school. Hudson Grey—the guy's name is stamped to my mind because of how much she talked about him from my place to Madison's.

Hudson's face scrunches up for a split second when he

spots Roquel, but he doesn't push her away when she dives for his arms and hugs him. I shake my head with sympathy. She's obviously way more into him than he is into her, but like any teenage boy, he leers down at her low-cut top to the rounded curves of her tits. Then he cops a feel of her ass and she laughs, swatting at him playfully. I grind my teeth together until my molars ache in protest.

I'm not sure if we're friends or not, but there aren't many classmates who have been as neutral as Roquel. At the very least, I appreciate the fact that she helped me get a job. I really hope that asshole doesn't break her heart. The Silverwood Police Department would likely love nothing more than to arrest me for shattering his kneecaps with a baseball bat.

Mads sighs. "There she goes," she murmurs. "We probably won't see her again for the rest of the night."

"Why did you bother to come if you knew she would act like this?" I ask, curiously.

She shrugs again. "I hate being left alone," she answers quietly. "When you're alone, especially when you're surrounded by people, you just start to think about all of the ways you're inadequate. I didn't want you to feel like that."

I stiffen at the insinuation. "I'm fine being left alone," I say sharply. "In fact, I prefer it." Jabbing the toe of my Converse into the dirt under my feet, I frown. "I didn't want to come to this stupid fucking party and if I'd known Roquel would just abandon me the second I got here, I'd have resisted a bit more."

Mads eyes me. "You came because you felt like you owed her." She shrugs. "I'm the same. She's a bit flighty, but she's a good person."

I don't know what makes a good person anymore, but I certainly know that I'm not. I turn away.

"Are you going to leave?" Mads calls after me.

Pausing, I pivot back to face her and catch sight of the

worry on her smooth face. She bites down on her lower lip as her eyes dart from me to the top of the hill and back again.

"I can't even if I wanted to," I remind her as I gesture around us and then up the hill. "Roquel's my ride too, and she still has her keys. I doubt we can get a rideshare this far out here." Not that I could afford to waste the money on one right now, but I don't say as much.

My words seem to comfort her as the tightness in her face eases a bit. Mads' shoulders slowly lower back down.

"Why don't I go grab her keys?" she offers, taking a step back. "It's probably better for one of us to hold on to them anyway. I can grab us some drinks too—soda, of course."

"You don't have to stay sober," I remind her. "I said I'd drive us back."

Even as I'm speaking, Mads shakes her head. "Nah, it's no fun being the only sober one in a group of drunk people." She hops back and grins at me. "Soda is good with me—better even. My parents won't be able to say I was out drinking if they test me."

"Test you?" My brow creases as Mads freezes where she stands, half-turned to race up the hill toward the crowd gathered around the bonfire. It's clear from the look of shock on her face that she hadn't meant to admit that much.

Sympathy unfurls in my chest, an old emotion I hadn't expected to feel again after everything that's happened. Somehow, though, Mads brings it all back. Drawing in a breath, I let the question go and don't press her to answer it. Instead, I glance up towards the farmhouse and the laughing Silverwood Public kids drinking and dancing to someone's old radio with shitty and static-filled music.

"Actually, do you mind if I stay down here?" I ask. "I'd rather avoid those crowds and just..." I don't know how to end my request, the sentence trailing off awkwardly. Like me, she's wearing longer pants and sleeves. Even if we're far from the bonfires, we won't freeze, so I hope she says yes.

Mads' expression shifts into one of relief and then amusement. "Sure," she agrees easily enough. "I'll go grab Roquel's keys and some sodas. We can hang out by the cars and chat until she's ready to go."

I nod, thankful, and then stand there, watching, as she makes her way up the hill. A feminine shriek that sounds too much like one of the girls from the parties I used to frequent—a sound that's faked outrage—echoes down towards me. A girl is lifted into a big guy's arms and he jostles her up and down as if he's lifting weights, her tiny skirt flying in all directions and revealing that if she's wearing anything underneath it's not covering much.

My gaze switches back to Mads as she slips between the other students as easily as breathing. She disappears into the masses and no one even seems to notice. *Interesting.* Where I'm a pariah and Roquel is a partier, Madison Torres is like a ghost. An obviously lonely one if she thinks being my friend will do her any good.

I pivot back towards the Camry, intent on hunting through Roquel's backseat for a blanket, when the sight of two broad-shouldered guys with a girl between them catches my attention. The three of them form a pattern of swaying shadows as the guys urge the long-haired girl between them towards the treeline, each of them reaching for her arms.

The girl stumbles and giggles lamely, her hair flipping over her shoulder as she glances back and up at them. A familiar look of unease crosses her face but then she gags and cups a hand over her mouth as her features morph into one of panic and disgust.

"I'm gonna puke!" she warns them just before she stumbles and races between the trees.

Let it go, I order myself. *It's none of your business, Jules.* I grit my teeth and drag my eyes back to the Camry just a few short feet away. When I turn back, though, the guys are following her into the darkness.

Ice floods my veins as one of them, the shorter of the two with an uneven jaw and a tattoo peeking out of the collar of his shirt, looks over his shoulder and up towards the hill. It's not the look of someone wanting help, but the careful observation of a predator making sure no one is watching.

Fuck. I close my eyes and once again, try to remind myself that whatever happens between the three of them is none of my business.

Somehow, though, my feet don't get the memo because when I next open my eyes, I'm already moving away from the Camry, back up the hill, and towards the treeline to the place where they all disappeared.

19
LEX

What the hell does she think she's doing? A deep, visceral need to storm across the open space of country lawn and drag the blue-haired vixen I just witnessed stride right into the woods back by her fucking throat assails me. *I'm going to spank her ass.* The thought pops up in my mind along with an image of Juliet Donovan bent over, that perfectly heart-shaped ass of hers settled over my lap as I paint her backside a pretty shade of crimson with the flat of my hand. In my imagination, she'd like it.

Oh, she'd cry and scream and beg me to stop—maybe she'd even threaten me with bodily harm—but she wouldn't mean any of it. Or if she did mean it, well, I'd let her stab me if she let me fuck her.

Gio nudges me, bringing me back to myself and reminding me why I'd had the thought in the first place. "There goes your girl," he murmurs, eyes locked on the space in the treeline where Juliet had gone not but thirty seconds before.

Nolan tips back his beer and glares at the dark forest that surrounds the dilapidated old farmhouse where the students of Silverwood Public have gathered to escape the reality of our lives. "We're going to have to take care of those two," he murmurs, no small amount of rage burning in his eyes.

Gio and I exchange a look. He's not talking about Juliet, but the guys we'd watched disappear into the trees a few minutes before she'd made her way after them. Thrusting his bottle up, he drains it in a split second before tossing the now empty container to the lawn and leveraging away from the hood of G's Firebird.

"I'll take care of them." Nolan freezes as the words leave my lips and both Gio and Nolan slowly turn to face me. Nolan narrows his gaze.

"You never care about shit like this," he snaps, and I have to remind myself that it's not me he's mad at—it's the two shit stains that are currently leading one of Silverwood Public's cheerleaders into the forest to do to her what we've heard they've done to so many others.

The girl is a nameless, faceless nobody to me. To Nolan, though, she's someone's daughter, someone's sister, someone's best friend, and if we don't do something she'll likely end up raped and intimidated into silence before the end of the night.

Perhaps it makes me a bad person—though, I've always known that I'm not exactly morally in sync with everyone else—but he's right. I *don't* give a shit about *her*. Why should I? She's never done anything for me. Not like Juliet has. Juliet saved my life. If not for her, I would have been under my father's roof the night he decided to kill my mother and himself. He would have killed me too. I owe her *everything*.

But Nolan is my brother—not by the blood in my veins, but by the blood on our hands—and if he wants to save some future teen mom some trauma then I'll do it. I'll do it for him, and for the fact that if I don't, Juliet might end up wandering into the path of those two asswipes and paint an even bigger target on her back.

"Because you want it to stop," I say, answering Nolan's

comment, though it hadn't been a question. "Because this is the first time we've ever been close enough to get proof of their actions. You want them done for? I'll make it happen."

Nolan eyes me as if he's not sure whether or not I can be trusted. The longer we stand here, however, the longer Juliet is in the woods with those two, and I highly doubt the cheerleader is going to help her out if they get into a scrape.

After a beat, Nolan curses. "I want Josh and Rich out of here," he states. "When you're done with them, send them towards the road—not the party."

Josh and Rich have been smart until now. Their actions have only ever been spoken of in whispers. No one has ever been able to catch them and none of the girls are willing to speak up—not to friends and certainly not to anyone fucking else. Nolan's expression makes his intention clear. He's out for blood.

I glance at Gio who tosses his glass bottle onto the lawn and heads around the side of the Firebird. "You'll be there?" I guess.

"*I'll* be there," Nolan corrects before jerking his chin at Gio. "You—go with him."

"You don't think I can handle it myself?" A scowl overtakes my face. He should know better.

Nolan's dark eyes find mine. "Around her?" he prompts with a shake of his head. "No. Take G as backup—dickheads like Rich and Josh would rather run than get caught. I won't let them run off only to deny their actions later. Bring them out towards the road and we'll finish their asses tonight."

Gio tosses Nolan his keys. "Mile marker twenty-two," is all he says before Nolan turns away and slides around the Firebird to the driver's side door.

Slapping a hand to my chest and pushing me back, Gio diverts my attention as he nudges me out of the way of the car. Nolan quickly backs it up and swivels towards the dirt path that leads back to the road. Annoyance lingers in my blood, heating my veins.

"I can handle this," I insist, turning the emotion on G.

Gio simply shrugs and starts moving. "Of course you can, man," he says. "Don't mean you need to."

"But you don't even care about her," I snap, throwing Nolan's earlier words out into the open.

G pauses with his back to me. A second passes and then he turns, giving me his profile. "You think I give a fuck who's out there with Rich and Josh?" his sneer curls his full mouth. Shadows cling to the hidden side of his face, creating an almost inhuman skeletal mask over one half of his features. "Juliet Donovan might be a pariah, but we both know what that dumbass was doing when she followed them into the woods."

Almost as soon as the words are out of his lips, a familiar figure appears at the treeline. I jerk and gape as Cara Macey comes stumbling from the woods, huffing out breath after breath as she pivots towards the hill and begins to make her way up to the farmhouse. Gio must notice my expression because he swivels back to the woods. Then he, too, watches as the girl makes her way back to the party.

A beat passes and then another and another. Juliet doesn't return. Neither do Rich or Josh.

A low growl erupts from my throat and I practically sprint forward. Josh Michaelson and Richard Glean are going to regret ever putting their hands on the girls of Silverwood Public, but if they put their hands on what's mine, they'll regret their very fucking lives.

"Fuck." Gio's curse echoes at my back, but he doesn't tell me to slow down or to wait up. Instead, he simply hurries to catch up and our legs eat up the distance to the trees and shadows.

I crash through the trees, ducking beneath a branch as the

light from the bonfire and party instantly dims. Darkness surrounds me.

Violence is what built us. Violence is what made us choose this path. And though we'll eventually leave Silverwood, violence is in our blood and we crave it.

Tonight, Josh and Rich will see some of that violence and if they know what's good for them, they'll disappear afterward. If they know what's good for them, they won't force us to *make* them disappear.

20
JULIET

It's darker in the woods. Not surprising. What is surprising, however, is that the two men several yards ahead of me don't act like they're having a hard time at all making their way deeper between the trees. The girl stumbles along, throwing a glance back over her shoulder every once in a while even as she pauses every so often to gag and try to hold back the vomit likely arching up her throat. None of them notice me following, but I notice her expression when she's not fighting the urge to puke. Anxious, even as she tries not to show it.

Her sharp, pitchy laugh sounds in the near silence of the shadows and she speaks. "A-are you guys trying to make sure I d-don't crack my head open?" she asks, continuing with her nervous little giggles.

Poor girl. I can tell that, even in her inebriated state, she understands what they're doing and she's probably not sober enough to figure out how to stop it. I bite down on my lower lip and move faster. The three of them are a good distance ahead of me and even though I've had nothing to drink, the roots of the trees seem to jump out at my feet, tripping me up with each step forward. It's probably why I didn't manage to lose them completely despite them being so far ahead of me to start with. Panting and huffing with both annoyance and concern for the girl, I step over another ragged stump of a root and nearly go sprawling when, in the darkness, I don't see the next one.

"*Fuck*," I hiss a curse, catching myself upright on a near tree branch. My ankle throbs.

I jerk my head up a moment later, belatedly, to see if the guys caught wind that someone is following them. Fortunately, that isn't the case since the two of them have now surrounded the girl like she's the prey to their predator.

Moving a bit faster now, I hop over the next root and around another tree as the two guys back the girl further into the dark and up against a tree. How they haven't heard me coming when I feel like I'm stomping madly through the underbrush is a mystery to me—though if they've had a lot to drink then that would certainly impair their awareness.

I send up a silent prayer that they are a bit worse for the wear drink-wise. It would be just my fucking luck that I decide to help some girl and get raped myself.

"R-rich, I don't know, I-I've had a l-lot to drink." The girl's voice echoes back to me, her laughter completely gone, and in its place, fear. She appears to have forgotten the urge to puke as she focuses on the men surrounding her.

Unwilling to let them get on with their plans, I stomp down harder on the next branch underfoot in response, eliciting a sharp, loud *crack* that rings through the air. A gasp from the girl is followed by the sound of footsteps and rustling as the two guys ahead peer around a thick tree with matching scowls.

"What the fuck?" the shorter of the two says. "It's just the Donovan bitch."

I raise my eyes to meet his as I move towards him. "You haven't seen me be a bitch, yet," I tell him matter-of-factly. Carefully stepping over another branch, I advance on them.

The girl comes back into view as I finally catch up to the three of them and though her eyes are still a little glazed from all the alcohol she's had, there's a familiar expression of relief on her face.

Damn. She must be in a bad position if she's relieved to see me. Almost as soon as it happens, though, she covers it up and straightens away from the tree they'd crowded her against.

With a scoff that sounds more forced than not, she flips a strand of hair over her shoulder and scowls at me. "What do *you* want?" she sneers.

I roll my eyes. She doesn't have to like me, but she sure is fine at pretending like I didn't just save her ass. My annoyance at her attitude evaporates a second later as she makes the first smart decision since I watched her walk into these woods. The girl stumbles forward, using my presence as an excuse to leave the ring the two guys have formed around her without letting on what she's really doing—escaping.

We might not be friends—she and I—but here, in this place, we're both familiar with what it means to be female in a world that always wants to take something you might not be willing to give.

"Your friend saw you coming out here," I lie easily, eyeing her with meaning. "She told me she's been looking for you." My gaze remains on her, even as I sense the men behind her shifting uncomfortably.

If I'd had to hazard a guess, I'd say they didn't expect that anyone would know where the girl they brought out here went. To be fair, I don't know if she's even got friends at the party—but the less the guys know about our virtual aloneness, the better. Even if she is drunk, this girl can't be stupid enough to call me on my lies though. Not with the way her eyes flick to the side without turning her head. She's watching them just as I am, in her periphery.

The taller of the two with a shorn haircut and a shadow of

stubble over his jaw sneers. "You're not seriously telling me you know this chick, do you, Cara?" he demands.

Cara shrugs and glares over her shoulder at the guy. "Shut up, Rich. She goes to our school. Just because we have class together doesn't mean I know her."

We have class together? I'm not sure if she's just lying through her teeth to get out of this uncomfortable situation or if we really do have class together. Whatever the case, though, the guys groan but take her at her word.

Cara doesn't seem nearly as drunk as she had when first entering the woods, but even as she takes another step away from them—towards me—she stumbles and nearly collides with me. I reach for her only to have her hiss at me and draw back.

"Don't fucking touch me," she gripes, the words slurring slightly.

"Whatever." I hold my hands up. "I just didn't want your friend to lay into me. That's all."

"If it's Janice, then she'll come barreling out here at any moment to get you and I don't want to deal with that cunt." The second guy, not Rich, is slightly skinnier than his friend with longer hair that's pulled into a ponytail at the base of his skull.

"She's not a—oh fucking forget it." Cara cuts herself off and shakes her head before she moves past me in a fury of awkward jerking movements. She doesn't offer me a look of gratitude or whisper any words of thanks as she passes. She just stumbles farther and farther away, back in the direction of the farmhouse and the party.

I wait a beat, side-eyeing the guys to make sure they don't try to stop her. When she's far enough away that I can't really hear her stumbling steps, I shift on my feet, turning back the same way.

"Hold up there!" I freeze as a hand locks on my shoulder.

I don't even think about it. I just react—reaching up and

latching on to his fingers and then keeping a hold of them as I duck out from under his arm, taking it with me. It's the one with longer hair I see a split second before I yank down on his hand and twist it behind his back, jerking his hand and arm up his back until I know it hurts.

"What the fuck!" he bellows and I'm pretty proud of my reaction time. Or at least, I would be, if I didn't try to shove him forward and trip over yet another twisted root on the ground. Instead of pushing him, I end up letting him go completely to catch myself before I land on my knees.

The other man laughs, a low grating sound. "I don't think she likes you much, Josh," he says, sounding amused.

Great, at least now I have their names. Rich and Josh. I straighten away from the two of them as Rich steps off the tree he'd had the girl—Cara—previously pinned against as Josh rounds on me with a scowl.

"Fucking bitch," Josh spits, rotating his arm as if trying to relieve the ache there. "That hurt."

"I promise you," I snap back. "It won't hurt nearly as much as what I'll do to you if you touch me without my permission again."

My heartbeat thunders in my ears. I take a step back and the two of them follow the movement with not just their eyes. The sound of leaves shifting under their feet seems to echo into the night. The gates holding back my adrenaline are shuddering, waiting to be opened.

"Whatever you're thinking," I say in warning, "I suggest you don't."

"Don't what?" Rich asks with a sneer, his eyes moving down over my loose flannel and black tank. I'm not dressed to impress, but somehow, he must still find me worth looking at because his sneer turns into a smile. "We don't want to hurt you."

"Yeah, we don't want to hurt you at all," Josh agrees, his earlier anger at me dissipating quickly. "In fact"—he grins, sidling closer—"we're more about pleasure than anything else."

Blood rushes in my ears, the sound so incredibly loud. I flick a glance back. I'm too far from the party now for anyone to hear me if I scream … or to hear if *they* scream.

"Play bitch ass games. Win bitch ass prizes," I grit out, the warning like acid on my tongue as I take another careful step back.

I reach out, feeling along a tree to keep steady. Something rough and hard bumps against the back of my ankle. It's a bad idea to let my desires get the best of me here. These guys might be dumb assholes, but there are two of them and only one of me.

"Ah, come on. Don't be like that," Rich says, advancing forward. He offers me a placating smile but I know it for what it truly is—a fucking mask.

Everyone wears a mask in this world; I know that for a fact. I was raised in a masquerade of smiling faces and razor-sharp teeth. It's where friends stab you in the back, fathers fuck you over, and mothers abandon their only daughters to the not-so-tender mercies of the world.

"Don't even think—" I start to say but nearly bite down on my tongue a second later as Josh dives forward, fingers locking around my wrist.

Twisting out towards his thumb, I silently curse when instead of breaking his hold, Josh's other hand comes up and wraps around my neck, thrusting me backward. A gasp startles out of my lips as my spine slams into the bark of a tree. The air rushes from my lungs on a wheeze.

"You should be grateful anyone wants you now, *Donovan*," Josh says my last name like a filthy curse. "Your rich prick of a boyfriend dumped you as soon as he heard about your dad."

I curse and raise my other hand up against his chest. "I dumped him, *dickhead*." I match his tone as I shove hard against his sternum. He doesn't move, though that's not much of a surprise.

My breath saws in and out as I try to think back to Cory's training. It all flies out of my head—just like that. I thought I would know what I was doing when something like this happened. Now, I know the truth. I'm fucked. All those long weeks of working out in the gym and going up against trainers and sparring partners ain't shit in the face of real danger.

All I have left is the festering anger inside—wickedly sharp and volatile. I could unleash it. It would be so easy to let it all go. To start swinging and see what happens. A small, invisible rope snags around it, though, holding me back.

I close my eyes and draw in a long breath even as the hand around my throat tightens marginally. What will happen if I finally just ... let it go?

In a blink, I see what could happen. Blood spurts from Josh's nose as I shove the base of my palm into his face. My knee slams into his groin and I relish in the soft whoosh of air escaping his lungs right before I grip the back of his skull in two hands and bring my knee up again. If his nose isn't already broken from my first attack, it would be by my second.

Red on my fingers, wetness oozing down the side of my throat—a lingering spurt from his nose? I like that idea. Bathing in someone's blood. Fucking them up and releasing all of the rage I've held in for so fucking long.

Good girls do as their mother tells them, Juliet.

Good girls listen to their daddies.

Good girls don't ask questions.

Good girls don't care if their boyfriend cheats on them.

Good girls forgive their best friend for fucking their boyfriend.

Good girls smile even when they want to scream.

Good girls don't cause problems.

Good girls ... get shit on by the world.

I don't want to be good. Not anymore.

I blink again, and reality invades once more.

The image of me attacking Josh evaporates, and in its place, I'm right back where I was—with my back pressed against the unyielding bark of a tree and his hand on my throat.

Why don't I want to let the rage go again?

"I always wondered what Prep pussy felt like," Rich comments as he hovers over Josh's shoulder. Josh squeezes my throat roughly. I don't fight back. Not yet.

Instead, I eye them both. The two of them have got to be athletes at school, they're built big and thick, each of them a solid five inches or more taller than me. That doesn't mean I'll take this lying down though. No. I won't let this happen to me. I can't.

I force myself to take a calm breath, squeezing in as much air as I can around Josh's hand as I stop fighting. I let my arms fall back to my sides. Spots of black and white dance in front of my vision. Out here, it's so dark that the only way I can even see the two of them is because the moon is shining down through the treetops.

Cascading light spears through the leaves and over their heads and I spy a third man hovering in the shadows just behind Rich. My heart thuds rapidly against the inside of my ribcage. Fear spirals through me as well as the urge to maim. I'm not going down like this. I won't let this happen.

The third figure is bigger than both Rich and Josh, though not by much. He's taller than both, but his features remain in the shadows. His silhouette is all I can make out. I inhale sharply as he moves closer, silent somehow in the underbrush full of twigs and crunchy, dry leaves. A tingle of awareness creeps into my limbs. The third figure moves through the shadows like a wraith, silent and deadly. My heartbeat picks up speed, but before I can do anything—attack or scream—

Rich is gone from behind Josh. He disappears as if he evaporated into nothing but thin air.

Shock slams into me a moment later. Not that his friend, Josh, even seems to notice. The idiot somehow takes my sudden stillness as his opportunity to bend down and brush his mouth along my throat. I barely feel it. My focus is on what's happening behind him.

The third man—the shadowy stranger—reappears and lifts Rich up by his throat, the smaller man's voice disappearing as he clamps down and silences him. He dangles there, back and forth, feet swaying just a few inches above the ground. A hysteric snort bubbles up out of my nose and I reach up, slapping a palm over my mouth and nearly smacking Josh in the face.

Oh, right. *Him.* I forgot he's still there. Josh's head lifts a bit and he scowls down at me, not the least bit aware of the peril his friend is in. Instead, he's solely focused on me as he moves his mouth to my face. I turn my hand and push it against his mouth and chin, and using my back to brace against the tree, I shove him back.

"Don't even fucking try it."

Since Josh had dipped down to kiss my throat, his grip loosened and it makes it far easier to twist out of his hold. Reaching up and pinching the back of his hand, I spin out of reach, the sharp crack of a branch snapping under my sneakered foot.

Josh's furious gaze meets mine. "Listen, you little cunt, I—"

He doesn't get to finish whatever he's about to say because a second shadow appears next to the first and a fist collides with Josh's face. The abrupt attack sends Josh sprawling to the ground into a tangle of roots and curses.

I back up, hissing when something sharp slices across the back of one calf, digging into my jean-clad leg.

"What the fuck!" Josh barks as his friend coughs and hacks.

My gaze goes to the new men. The hoods both are wearing fall back, revealing a pair of familiar faces. The last I would ever have expected to be grateful for—or welcome seeing. Two of the Scorpion Kings appear as if formed out of the shadows themselves. What little light there is gleams on the murderous intent in their eyes.

Rich and Josh are so fucked.

21
JULIET

Curiosity holds me tight in its wicked grip.

Lex and Gio look like dark avenging angels as they stand in the little clearing Rich and Josh chose to lead their prey to. Dressed in black jeans and an equally dark hoodie, Lex cants his head to the side, eyes sliding from the man in his hold to me as Gio reaches down, hauling Josh up from the ground and holding him aloft.

A flash of silver catches my attention and my eyes drop to a chain that dangles out of one of Lex's jeans' front pockets. It spans around the side, disappearing into the back. Unlike Josh and Rich, whose attire—worn jeans, sneakers, and faded jerseys—speak of their athleticism, Lex looks more goth than jock right now. Gio's not far behind.

"G-Gio, man," Josh stutters as his eyes span quickly to Rich's and back. "W-what are you doing out here?"

Like a snake watching its quarry, Gio Vargas tilts his head and scans down Josh's frame before returning to his face. If Josh expects an answer, Gio doesn't give him one. I slide back against the tree I'm braced against, my hand reaching out and skidding over harsh bark until a splinter digs into my palm.

A hiss escapes my teeth as I yank my hand away. In the

dim lighting, Lex's head jerks towards me and a low growl emits into the air, freezing the blood in my veins. I go still, my breath shuddering to a stop in my throat. That growl ... that sound ... there's nothing human about it. It's the sound of an enraged animal, violent and ready to tear through bone and flesh.

"Don't kill them." Gio finally says, but it's not what any of us expect.

The responding growl thrums through the air, growing in volume before tapering off. Sweat coats the back of my neck and the adrenaline that had hit me when I realized just how much danger I'd placed myself in by coming out here to save that Cara girl screams back to the surface.

Lex scrubs his free hand down his face and then back over the longer strands of ink-black hair at the top of his head. The glint of metal under the moonlight reflects against the rings he wears. I find myself focusing on them, needing something to ground me in the scene before me. One ring is a simple, plain band. Another is shaped in small links—a chain. And the middle one is a skull.

A shiver skates down my spine.

"W-we were just fucking around, G," Josh continues in a rush of air. He's not fighting Gio's hold, but neither is he comfortable.

My eyes flash over Gio's face. Unlike his friend, he's standing directly under a beam of moonlight that floods the clearing, the light illuminating the raw anger in his expression. The muscles in his forearm bunch and bulge, forcing his veins to stand out next to the seam of his shoved-up hoodie sleeve. Black inked lines circle his arms and disappear beneath the fabric.

"We both know what you were doing out here, Josh." Gio's voice is a cool mask of indifference even though his face is anything but.

"You don't know fuck all!" Rich snaps, kicking out against

Lex in a futile attempt to break free. "Why do you even care? No one wants that bitch around anyway. Donovan is the reason all our parents lost their fucking jobs!"

I stiffen, the pain in my hand and calf temporarily forgotten in a brief moment of all-encompassing fury. Before I can step forward and correct him though, Lex's fist jolts out and slams into Rich's face. Once, twice, and by the third strike Rich sags, his head lolling to the side as he goes unconscious. Not that his awareness, or lack thereof, seems to stop Lex.

No. Instead, Lex continues to beat Rich's face in. The sharp crunch of cartilage breaking under his knuckles echoes into the night and the sound seems to break something in Josh.

"Dude, he's killing him!" Josh scrambles, bucking against Gio's grip. With a sigh, Gio releases his captive and steps to the side. Josh stumbles at the sudden freedom he finds and catapults himself into a nearby tree.

At first, I think Gio's letting him go, but that's not the case. He turns and plants his hands on his hips, watching on as Lex releases his unconscious victim and attacks Josh. With a barely stifled shout of dismay, Lex takes the other man down, gripping him by the head and slamming it against the ground.

"Stop!" The begging yell is swallowed by the sound of Josh's skull meeting the hard-packed earth. The air in my lungs becomes stifling, swallowing in on itself until all I can taste is foul carbon on the back of my tongue.

Josh goes silent a few minutes later and his body collapses into the leaves and underbrush. I wait a beat, wanting to see if Lex will stop now that his second victim is also unconscious. He doesn't. He just keeps pounding away in near silence. I don't even think he's breathing particularly hard or with any effort.

A minute passes. Then another. And another.

Someone should stop this. They should tell Lex he's done enough, but I don't want to be the one to end Josh's torment, even if he isn't aware of it. That cruel, wicked sensation from earlier rises back up inside me.

I wait to feel guilt start to creep in, but it never does.

In its place, I feel nothing but satisfaction.

I glance at Gio to see if he's going to end Lex's actions any time soon, but he's no longer watching his friend. His eyes are fixed squarely on me.

I jerk back, nearly falling on my ass as something smacks the back of my legs. He advances on me and I don't have time to step over the root that stopped my retreat before he's on me, grabbing me by my upper arms and pressing me against the very same tree Josh had.

"Hey!" I shove a hand against his chest, forgetting about the splinter and biting back a curse when the action forces it deeper into my flesh.

Gio's dark eyes narrow on me and he hovers closer. "Don't fucking think you're blameless either, Prep Girl," he snarls. "What were you thinking following these guys out here?"

"None of your damn business." Balling my hands into fists and ignoring the ache in my palm, I press him back a step. "But if you're done going caveman on me, I'm leaving."

"No, we're not done," he says. "Not by a long shot." Then he turns his head and barks over his shoulder. "Lex! Get your ass up and stop beating them. They're too unconscious to enjoy it."

The consistent thudding of a fist meeting an unresisting body ceases and the shadow that is Lex appears over Gio's shoulder. The irony of trading Josh and Rich for two of the Scorpion Kings is not lost on me. When Lex moves closer, his big body remains shockingly silent as if he's not real but a wraith, a creature belonging to these woods. My ribcage constricts tightly around my heart and lungs.

Rich and Josh might have been two men high on the power of being strong, but Lex and Gio are different. In the world of Silverwood, they are filthy kings. Monsters in their own right.

I tip my head back and wait for them to pass their royal judgment, but no words escape their lips. They remain silent as the noises of the forest return gradually to replace the silence I hadn't even realized held us in a bubble. A small animal chitters nearby as it squirrels away in the underbrush. The scream of insects seeking a mate echo into the night. A strange sort of pressure keeps me locked in place.

Neither of them had hesitated to attack Rich or Josh. Gio had known what Lex would do if he released his prey. Turning my cheek, I gaze past them to the two men collapsed on the ground, their faces each beaten to a bloody pulp.

Josh's nose is at an awkward angle that tells me it's certainly broken and blood runs down under his nostrils over his upper and lower lip, dripping down his chin. Gravity grabs ahold of that dark crimson liquid and drags it further down, coating his Adam's apple with it. I'm so consumed by watching the blood drip down Josh's face that I almost forget I'm standing here, held up against a tree by a man I certainly don't trust. Gio's hands ease on my upper arms and move up until they're cupped on either side of my throat—the feeling catapults me back to reality with all the subtlety of a raging bull.

Yanking my gaze back to his face, I scowl up at the handsome playboy of Silverwood Public. "You gonna let me go?" I demand.

Gio leans closer, and Lex does the same. I'm surrounded by the scent of fire and musk, the two masculine bodies against me now so very different from the ones before. My belly drops and my thighs tremble as an emotion I thought I'd left behind months ago burns to life.

Arousal.

Oh. Fuck. No. I shake my head and try to dispel the sensation, but it doesn't leave.

"Did they hurt you?" Gio asks, the question quiet in the otherwise too-loud night sounds.

My heartbeat races in my ears, rushing along with the sound of my blood through my veins. I shake my head again, though I'm not sure if it's to answer him or to try and get rid of the unwelcome attraction swarming my body.

As disturbed as I am by my body's reaction, all it does is make me viscerally aware of the two men crowding me in the dark. Their large frames make everything else disappear—blocking out the rest of the clearing so I can no longer see the bodies collapsed on the ground. All I can see is *them*.

My breathing picks up, growing faster and faster as Gio's thumbs rub soothingly along the sides of my throat. Damn him. I don't want to be soothed or comforted and definitely not by him.

I switch my attention from him to Lex. "Let me go," I demand.

Lex doesn't say anything. Instead, he just stares at me with those dark, soulless eyes of his. Air dries up in my lungs and I choke when I want to say something, though I'm not sure what. Silence lingers between the three of us, cold and filled with tension. Their shoulders rise and fall with the effort of their own breaths, and after a moment of carefully examining Lex's face, I realize that it's speckled ... with freckles? No, not freckles. He's speckled with blood. My insides clench but not in fear. I stifle a groan of disbelief. I can't find a man covered in blood sexy because that would make me fucked in the head. Damn it, I *am* fucked in the head.

"Who the fuck brought you here tonight?" Lex demands, his voice a deep gravelly rasp.

I blink. "Why does that matter to you?"

He stares back at me, but his expression is so imperceptible I can't tell if he's surprised or angry. "Answer the question and I'll step back," Gio murmurs.

I latch on to the bargain without a second thought. I need to get the two of them away from me. I need them both to stop fucking touching me. "Not that it's any of your business, but my friend Roquel brought me tonight."

The heat burning my insides diminishes but only marginally as Gio makes good on his promise and takes a step back, forcing Lex to do the same. I sigh and fold my arms over my chest, shooting them both a dark glare.

"You want to explain what you thought you were doing, following these two out here?" Gio reintroduces his earlier question with a much calmer tone than the one Lex had used.

I glance over their shoulders to Josh and Rich before returning to meet their gazes. "Not particularly." They don't need to know.

Gio bends slightly as he looks at me, gaze scanning my face and lower. The color of his eyes, already nearly ebony turns into darkness itself. My lashes brush my lids as I stare up into his face. It's like looking into a never-ending void. You know what they say ... once you look into the void for long enough, it begins to look back into you.

Right now, I very much think it is. I think *he* is the void.

This is insane. *They* are insane, and I need to get the fuck away from them before it's too late.

"Listen." I blow out a breath as I reach up and put a hand over Gio's chest, pushing lightly to give myself some more breathing room. Not that it helps. The motherfucker doesn't budge a single inch. Instead, his breath hitches and he makes an odd sound in the back of his throat. I whip my hand back in an instant but don't comment.

"I appreciate you coming to help me." The words are pulled like nails from my throat. I really don't want to say them, but I'm not so much of a bitch that I won't admit when I've been given a break, even if that break is from one of the bastards trying to wreck my life. "I didn't ask for your help, but it's done now and it's not like we're friends—quite the opposite actually—so—"

I shuffle to the side, sidling out from the wall of muscle

that surrounds me. A thick arm, corded with muscle snaps out and halts my escape. Tilting my head back, I gape as Lex captures my hand—the same one that had touched Gio. He pulls it towards himself, pressing the flat of my palm against his chest.

"Why are we the opposite?" Lex's question is full of an enigmatic emotion, but the deep baritone of his voice vibrates across every molecule of my flesh.

The heat of his hand on mine, keeping me in place, is like a brand to my nervous system. It takes my brain a second longer than usual to catch up with his words. "*What?*" Is he serious? "Because you hate me. Everyone in Silverwood hates me."

"Hate?" Lex's head tilts to the side, and though I can't pick up the fine details of his expression, I can tell that the movement is one of either confusion or curiosity. I tug against his hold. He doesn't release me. Doesn't even react to the action. "I don't care what anyone else thinks, but I don't hate you, Jules."

Jules? My upper lip curls back, baring my teeth. *He doesn't get to call me Jules. We're not fucking friends.*

"*Let go.*" I hiss the words between my teeth, pulling harder on my trapped hand. The muscles of his chest are impossibly hard. I try not to think about how close our bodies are.

"No," he snaps in answer to my demand.

My eyes skip back to Gio, expecting him to step forward and do something to stop his friend. To my utter shock, the corner of his mouth is tilted upward and he stands back, folding his arms as he watches on with *amusement* twisting his expression. *Asshole.*

"This is stupid." I tug on my hand again to no avail. My scowl deepens and I yank harder on the hand holding mine in place, right against his pectoral. "Don't pretend—you and the entire fucking school have been out to get me from day one," I snap.

Lex glances at Gio. "Are you still out to get her?" he asks. At least, he's admitting that my words aren't all false.

Gio snorts. "Not that it would do me much good if I was, but no. I'm not out to get you either, Prep Girl."

I swivel to gape at him. "You could've fooled me." Sarcasm and rage drip from my words. "Your girlfriend is still after me."

Gio's amusement fades in an instant. "I don't have girlfriends," is all he says.

I'd feel bad for Megan except ... I don't. She's a fucking bitch. I stop fighting against Lex's hold—it's getting me nowhere.

"Fine," I grit out. "Then your fuck buddy—I don't care what you call her. The fact remains, you haven't exactly made my life easier since I transferred to Silverwood Public. You'll forgive me if I don't necessarily trust you enough to tell you about my life."

"I'm not asking about your life," Lex says, drawing my attention back to him. The lock he has on my wrist remains ironclad.

"No?" I laugh, but the sound is a dry, ugly thing. "Then what are you doing?" I flex my fingers against his chest, feeling the throb in my palm from the splinter there.

He lifts my palm, dragging it up with his hold. The press of muscles covered by fabric under my hand distracts me just long enough for him to pull my hand all the way to his mouth. I hiss out a breath as his tongue touches the exact placement of the sliver of wood embedded there. I jerk back, a pained noise escaping my throat.

"What's wrong?" Gio is there, his big body pressing against my side as he forces me closer into Lex.

"Nothing, it's just a—" A gasp interrupts my words as Lex's teeth bite down. The shard of bark shifts and I realize a split second later that Lex isn't biting me but the splinter. With careful ministrations, he pulls my hand straight down as he extracts the painful little piece of wood from my palm in a practiced fashion. More heat pours into me, lava flooding my stomach and sinking lower to the place between my legs. *Damn them.*

"That hurts." My complaint falls flat both because it's no longer true and because of the breathless sound of my own voice.

"It shouldn't anymore." Gio's voice is a quiet weapon. Sinking into me just as much as the warmth from both of their bodies.

"Why are you doing this?" It doesn't make sense.

In places like Silverwood—where the rich and poor can be separated by little more than a series of train tracks separating the rich from the poor and the luck of birth—the reality is simple. Power goes to either those who are born with it or those who will do anything to achieve it.

For men like the Scorpion Kings, power isn't a byproduct of birth. Power is in their blood, sweat, and sacrifices. They may not have money, but they have everything else—strength, brotherhood, and respect. People fear them as much as they envy them. Women want to fuck them. Men want to *be* them.

Not me.

"Why can't you let someone help you without complaining?" Gio asks, ignoring my question.

A low snarl erupts from me and I try to pull myself back from them. In response, Lex and Gio step closer, forcing me between them—crushing me with their fire and strength.

"We're not friends," I snap back.

Lex moves closer and for some reason—some insane illogical sense that he won't cause me harm at this moment—I don't flinch away from him. "Do you want to be my friend, Juliet?" he asks.

The sensation of familiarity at those words niggles at the back of my head, an old memory cropping up. *Do you want to be my friend, Juliet?*

"Juliet?" Lex's questioning tone brings me back to the present and I shake my head, warding off the strangest sense that I've heard him ask that before.

"No," I say, not sure if I'm telling the truth. "No, I don't want a friend." What I want is freedom. I want to get away from this place, from this godforsaken town, from the destruction my family caused. I want to go somewhere else where I can start anew and be someone else, find out who I am without the past haunting me and turning me into someone else.

I close my eyes and inhale deeply, trying to stave off the worst of my rage lest it completely overwhelm me. When I reopen them, it's to find that both Lex and Gio have released me. A cold autumn wind cuts through the trees and fills me up, a balm to my overheated flesh.

"Give me your phone," Lex demands.

I blink up at him. "I don't have one."

Now it's his turn to blink. "*What?*" His voice takes on a new pitch, rising in shock. "What the hell do you mean you don't have a cell phone? You have to have one."

I shrug even as my voice comes out defensive. "Not sure if you're aware of this, but cell phones cost money and I don't have any." Humiliation burns a hot wave of acid through my stomach at my admission. I'd *had* a phone months ago and it went the same way as my life—to shit.

"You have a job," Gio points out. "How does your work get a hold of you?"

I look away from eyes that, even in this darkness, see too much. "I still have a laptop," I answer. "There are programs and shit you can get to make it look like you have a phone number. It'll record a voicemail and send those and texts to your email. I usually check it a couple of times a day when I'm at home." In my lone studio apartment with the barest necessities.

My, my, how the mighty have fallen.

A tense, silent moment passes. Lex's grasp on me loosens

enough for me to pull free and shake my hand out. I put my palm to my chest, rubbing it absently, feeling the heat of his skin elevate. The splinter is gone, but the ache remains. "Are we done here?"

Silence and then a hand rises up. I stiffen, but all he does is hover it near my face for a brief moment. The heat of him is right there, so fucking close, and yet he doesn't touch me. It's almost as if he's waiting for me to come to him, for me to ask for it. Fat chance of that happening.

Instead, I take a healthy step back, away from Lex's big shadowed body, and glance at Gio. Between the two of them, G seems to be the safer bet.

"Thanks for your help," I say again, sounding far less grateful than my words would lead someone to believe. I can't help it. The two of them make me feel vulnerable in a way I won't allow myself to be ever again. Not to anyone. "I gotta head back to the party."

"I will take you back." Lex drops his hand as he makes the offer.

I wave a hand through the air. "No, thanks. I got it."

"I wasn't asking," he says, reaching down and finding my arm with his fingers. Lex steps up to me and I nearly jerk back another foot, only stopping the automatic action by sheer force of will.

"*Lex*." Gio's voice is hard, but there's a wealth of meaning behind the single syllable.

A bolt of electricity races through my nerve endings at the feather-light touch of his hand on my arm, and I'm grateful when Lex releases me quickly.

"I don't need your help."

Lex's eyes aren't on me now though. They're on Gio's face. "She needs—"

"We have our orders," Gio says, cutting off Lex's argument.

I pass a look between them even as I shuffle back towards

the path that I came through before. "I can find my way back." Though I mean for the words to sound reassuring, they come out a bit thready.

Two pairs of equally dark eyes meet mine, and though I know they're two different colors, in the shadow of the woods, they look the same. Like two wild creatures watching me as I back away from them.

"Be careful on your way back, Prep Girl," Gio murmurs. "Don't stop to rescue any other idiots."

I nod, and the second I feel I've been dismissed, I turn and make my way out of the clearing. When the trees part to reveal the shitty cars lined up along the forest's edge, I glance back one last time. Nothing. Not even the hint of their shadows. More shivers move up and down my spine. Closing my arms around myself, I turn and trudge toward the party-goers. If I have any luck at all, I'll find Madison and Roquel fairly quickly. I don't care if it makes me a shitty friend, either, but the second I do, I'm getting the hell out of this party and away from the likes of the Scorpion Kings.

22
JULIET

When we get back to my studio, Roquel pulls up with a scowl and narrowed eyes glaring at the brick building lit by the dull illumination of her headlights. I don't bother to apologize for ruining her night. It took far longer than I would have cared for to find her. When I had, she'd been bent over one of the threadbare beds in the farmhouse with that jock, Hudson, railing her from behind. Mads and I had waited until the shrill cry of her orgasm faded and all we could hear were their panting breaths before we'd banged on the doorframe and hurried her along. She'd been annoyed and had refused to leave at first.

I'd been so keyed up that I hadn't cared and was ready to drive off with her ride with or without her. Mads must be Mother Teresa reborn, though, because she'd taken Roquel off to the side, said something in low whispered words, and came back with an agreement that would get me back to my apartment sooner rather than later.

Roquel's quiet fury is still festering when she parks the car. I can't find the energy to care as I hop out of the front seat and mouth a quiet 'thank you' to Mads as she gets out of the backseat and switches to the front. Roquel doesn't even glance my way as Mads closes the passenger side door, and soon the Camry is backing out and gunning for the exit.

What-the-fuck-ever.

I jog up the steps to my second-floor studio, my ankle twinging slightly, forcing me to slow my pace. The second the door is locked behind me, I strip off my clothes, toss on my pajamas, and pull out the futon. I draw the shades along the side of the sliding glass doors before slipping beneath the sheets and blankets and closing my eyes to shut out everything around me. I start counting seconds into minutes.

Do you want to be my friend, Juliet?

I flop onto my side and punch my pillow. Questions and curiosities circle my head like vultures ready to devour a carcass, forcing me to squeeze my eyes shut and pray for sleep. I don't even mind if it comes with my latest round of nightmares as long as I can escape reality. My whole life, I'd taken advantage of my parents' wealth. Money is a protection—or at least, it was for a time. If you have money, then you have power and most people will think twice about hurting you. Most people…

Now, there is no more money. No medications. No therapists. No more protection. Now, here I am, raw dogging my fucked-up-ness like everyone else and it sucks just as much ass as I expected.

The memory of Lex beating Josh and Rich to unconsciousness plays on repeat in the back of my head. There's no guilt, no fear, no sense of wrongness. They deserved what Lex gave them. They earned that pain and whatever else the Scorpion Kings plan to give them.

My eyes open and I flop onto my back once more, staring up at the stains on my ceiling without truly seeing them. *Have I always thought like that or is there something seriously fucked up with me now?* Maybe it's both. Maybe I've always had a darker side but pushed it down because there was never any need for it.

Phantom warmth trails down my arm and invades my palm. Unclenching it from where it rests over my stomach, I lift my hand into the air and flip it over. There's a thin red line where a piece of bark had pierced my flesh. Though it's gone now, the mark lingers. My stomach clenches at the faint recollection of blunt teeth scraping my vulnerable skin and then the pain receding as Gio held me in place for Lex to remove the splinter. Gritting my teeth, I let my hand drop back down. There *is* a need for my darker side now, I remind myself. I'm in survival mode and if I want to get the hell out of Silverwood at the end of this year, then I need to tread very carefully. The Scorpion Kings could ruin everything for me.

My dreams, when they do come, are not the usual collection of nightmares. There's no black abyss, no angry mobs, no zombies chasing me down. Instead, my twisted mind supplies me with a different kind of hunt. Dropping me back into those same woods I escaped mere hours ago, releasing me into the wild where I'm all alone.

Until I'm not.

"Pretty, pretty girl…" A whimper escapes my mouth as those words trail into my ears. "Pretty girls like it when the boys look, don't you, Juliet?" I try to roll away, but my limbs are far too heavy. My thighs are pressed open. My dress is lifted. Cool air slides across my breasts, my pussy. I can't open my eyes. I don't want to. I'm scared to know who's on the other side of this too-familiar nightmare.

Hands move down, down, down. The darkest oblivion reaches for me and I latch on to it. If I fall, then I won't have to endure this.

"Juliet." My head turns towards the familiar voice—different from the one before. The one that always compliments me but makes me feel like something sticky is clinging to

every pore. This voice is deeper, gruff with a hint of feral danger. Somehow, I know it's safer.

My heart pounds against the inside of my breast, an internal warning. The darkness surrounding me devours all of my senses, dropping into an abyss where I've never been before.

"Juliet." My name echoes back to me in the shadows. Another voice, just as dangerous, but almost lighter—amused —as he calls to me.

Ragged breaths crawl up my throat. In and out, I breathe and I wait.

"Juliet." Closing my eyes against the darkness doesn't bring me any relief as their voices resound around me. There's no pinpointing their location, and if that's true, then there's no escaping them either.

Still, I try. Stumbling forward, I place one foot in front of the other. Again and again, picking up the pace when nothing reaches out to stop me. Wind rushes up into my face, and every so often, something soft brushes against my sides, letting me know I'm not alone—that there are other things surrounding me. To my surprise, though, I never hit anything. I don't run into any trees. I don't trip over any roots. My legs find it quite easy to simply keep going. Through the woods and into the darkness, I run. And though I can't see them, I know I'm being tracked.

"Run, Princess," I hear someone say. "If we catch you … we eat you."

'We.' If I wasn't already sure I was being hunted by more than one of them, that statement confirms my suspicions. My bare feet fly across the soft earth, crunching dead leaves underfoot. A shiver of warning slithers down my spine and I stop in my tracks just as a pair of eyes appear before me. Crimson and glowing in the shadows, they hover a foot or so higher than my own—growing bigger and bigger the closer they come. I know I should turn and run in the opposite direc-

tion, but my feet don't move. My legs hold me in place until I'm little more than a captive before the monster that steps from the gloom.

Big and broad, Nolan Pierce glares down at me. Moonlight suddenly fills the area, turning the void back into something I can see. We're surrounded by thick trees and when I glance back, I see no path—no hint of where I came from and no sign of where I can go to get away.

"Juliet." I close my eyes as Nolan's voice skirts over my ears, deep and vibrating.

My hands shake at my sides, trembling against naked skin. Naked ... skin? My eyes pop back open and I glance down to find that I'm not wearing clothes. I'm completely nude and so is he.

Hands slip from the darkness—more than one man's hands. Gio and Lex appear on either side of me, caging me in as they had in the forest next to the farmhouse party. My throat closes completely, allowing not even a single gasp of air to pass into my lungs.

A light-headed feeling enters my veins, making the whole dream seem hazy.

"Pretty..." Rough, masculine fingertips brush my arms and then move down. Lex grabs my hand and lifts it once more. Except this time, there is no wound for him to make better. He sets his teeth to my skin and bites down.

"Are you ready to be eaten, Jules?" he asks. Something tells me that he's not talking about cannibalism.

With eyes the color of dead embers, he crowds me closer to the others—both Nolan and Gio pressing against me to keep me locked between them. This is what was missing in the real world. There had only been two kings against me in the woods. Now, I have all three.

I swallow roughly, my head swimming. My body thrums with barely repressed desire, a need so volatile and extreme it threatens to set me aflame and burn my bones to ash. The darkness recedes a bit more, the silvery light of the moon sprawling across the four of us, revealing the dips and hollows of perfectly sculpted bodies.

All around me, holding me, caging me, protecting me.

When has anyone ever protected me?

A pair of lips descends and meets the skin of my throat. I tip my head back, my lips parting on a cry as fresh oxygen rushes in. I feel branded, claimed.

Tingles race up and down my spine, spilling into my bloodstream and stealing away all logic. If this is what insanity feels like … I never want to be sane again.

"Give in to us," Nolan whispers.

Sweet, cruel words, but it's alright. In this world—in my dreams—I don't have to deny them. Here, I can take the pain and I can take the pleasure.

So, I do.

I wake to dull sunlight coming in through the thin blinds over the sliding glass doors next to my futon and my laptop's notification alert dinging. Though all I want to do is close my eyes again and try to go back to sleep, there's only one reason my notifications can be going off.

With a groan, I fling the covers off my bed and reach for the damn thing, dragging the computer from its spot on my scarred coffee table into my lap. There are a series of fresh emails from my dad's lawyer. As I scan through them, I see that he's been sending them at least once every few days. Without reading them, I drag the lot into the trash and delete them before moving on to the newest one.

Through bleary, sleep-heavy eyes, I rub my finger over the trackpad to the voicemail-to-text email application I set up to receive calls from The Dionysus Lounge. Past the date and time stamp that tells me the information came through less than thirty minutes ago, there is a request from one of the waitresses at The Dionysus Lounge asking if I can pick up an extra shift. I quickly check the timestamp of the notice and then the time it is now. If I hurry, I can make the next bus into Tangier, so I type back a quick reply to let her know I'll be there.

After hitting send, I crawl out of bed and head into the shower. Standing beneath the spray, I think about last night. The woods. The dream. The Scorpion King that had chased me through both.

Do you want to be my friend, Juliet?

Lex's voice penetrates the silence in my mind and I lean forward, twisting the knobs with jerky movements until ice-cold water slaps me in the face. With a gasp, I scrub both hands down my cheeks to ward off the freezing sensation but decide not to change the temperature back until I'm done. The feeling of someone else's presence not just in my head, but in the safe haven my studio is supposed to be lingers as I get out of the shower and hurriedly dress in my usual black uniform.

There's a red stain on the corner of my shirt, but I tuck it into the waist of my pants, thankful that the inside of the lounge is always dark unless we're in the process of cleaning. Unlocking the front door, I pocket my keys and turn to go—nearly tripping over the plain brown box sitting in front of my apartment when I exit.

"Shit!" Catching myself on the opposite railing, I scowl down at the offending package before glancing down towards the end of the row of apartments.

I might think it'd been dropped off at the wrong place were it not for the name scrawled in big, blocky letters on the top. I stare at the box and then where the stairs wait, empty of people. Whoever dropped it off is long gone. For several beats, I contemplate leaving it right where it is, but at the end of the day curiosity killed the cat for a reason and I can't deny myself. It has my name on it after all.

Picking up the package, I rip open the brown paper

covering it, pausing only when I get to the electronic logo stamped into the side of the box. The lightness of the box alleviates some of my earlier anxiety and concern that it might be dangerous. Then I remember the legend of how the Silverwood Scorpions got their name and my grip on the box tightens and freezes.

Though Darrio Vargas might be today's version of a crime lord, the power dynamics of Silverwood are ages old. Decades before, when an old Italian mobster had made Silverwood their home, he'd announced his enemies by sending them packages of scorpions. My fingers curve around the edge of the box and I wait, listening for any movement inside. There's nothing though. No hint of little creatures hiding in the box's contents. Slowly, though, I turn the box around in my grip.

"Just fucking open it," I order myself as I let my nails dig under the edge of the cheap duct tape used to hold the flaps closed.

I slip the sides open and instant relief fills me. No scorpions. Inside the box is a second, smaller box, and immediately, I know who it's from. As if the image on the outside doesn't give it away, I lift the offending item out and scowl at it. I open the top part and stare at the black, brand-name knock-off. It's a goddamn phone. A fucking *cellphone*.

The image of stabbing Lex in the face comes to mind and I find that I don't hate it. I'm not even slightly disturbed. If anything, I'm excited by the prospect.

He gave me a fucking cellphone. I'm so stunned by the fact that I can't even contemplate his reasoning. I don't know how long I stand there holding the box in a death grip, staring at the phone's blank screen. A bubble of hysterical laughter escapes me and I release one side of the box to slap a hand over my mouth. With a shake of my head, I dive back into my apartment and fling the box onto the counter of my small galley kitchen.

Why? The question echoes into my head. *Why would he*

send me a phone? Then I shake my head because it doesn't matter. I'm not using it.

Shoving the top of the box back on, I debate chucking the gift into the algae hotbed apartment complex 'pool' on my way to work. A moment later, the sound of an engine approaching the building forces me to forgo that plan and abandon the box in my kitchen to be figured out later.

I leave my apartment, hurrying to lock the door before I catch sight of the public bus ambling up the street. Stomping down the creaking metal stairs, I race towards the bus stop on the opposite side of the parking lot.

Fucking Lex. Fucking arrogant son of a bitch. Fucking Scorpion Kings and their stupid faces and their reign over the gutters of Silverwood. No matter what I do, it feels like everywhere I go I'm reminded of them.

There's just no getting away from the Scorpion Kings.

Not at school. Not at work. Not at the gym. Not even in my goddamn dreams.

23
JULIET

I work double shifts over the rest of the weekend just so I don't have to think of the Scorpion Kings, but each night as I lie down on my futon—praying I've exhausted myself to the point of no dreams—I'm disappointed to return right back to that damn forest. By the time Monday morning rolls around, I regret ever wishing that my usual nightmares would disappear. I'd take being chased by zombies or falling from a twenty-story building over the three assholes now haunting me every night anytime.

When the bus arrives Monday morning to shuttle me and the others waiting in the pre-dawn light, I keep my hood up and over my head and don't look at anyone. Despite my obvious desire to remain invisible, there's really no avoiding notice at school now. Maybe I should've thought better about the bright, electric blue hair—but then, it'd been something I'd always wanted to do before and I have no parents now to tell me no.

"*Bitch*." Someone hisses at me as they pass by.

The first bell of the day rings, announcing that school is about to begin. I ignore the stink-eye from a few of Silverwood Public's finest and make my way to my locker to grab my books. Despite hoping I could avoid using it due to all the vandalism, the more assignments that pile up, the more space in my backpack is needed. That means resigning myself to dealing with daily trash and cruel notes.

A shoulder slams into mine as I turn, slapping the locker door shut.

"*Whore.*"

I grit my teeth and don't respond. I'm doing so much better at this turning the other cheek thing—it's hard, but hopefully the more I ignore the comments and general shitty behavior, the fewer people will go out of their way to antagonize me. After all, there's only so much patience a person can have, and even if I try my best, I know I'm bound to snap one of these days. I'm honestly more shocked it hasn't happened yet.

The first half of the day flies by. I spy Roquel in the halls, but keep walking when she ignores me in favor of the football jock she'd banged at the party. Mads waves to me with a remorseful smile as she hurries by, her arms laden down with a bunch of papers. I stop to consider whether or not I should offer to help her, but before I can make a decision she's out of earshot as she dives around a corner and disappears from view.

With a sigh, I turn to head to my next period when something soggy hits the back of my head. Jerking to a stop, I reach back and my fingers come away covered in some sort of red-brown sludge. Laughter echoes back to me. I turn my head slowly, lifting my gaze to the end of the hall where a trio of girls stand against the lockers, smirking at me. It doesn't take a genius to figure out who launched the attack.

Megan White's angular face twisted into a self-satisfied smile. Next to her is Lindsey and on her other side is some girl whose name I'm sure I know since she's in at least two of my classes, but I can't quite recall at this moment. The nameless girl is the one my focus lingers on. Her back is against the lockers, her hips jutting out as she rolls a piece of shit BIC lighter between her fingers. They're banned from campus along with cigarettes, but that doesn't stop students from bringing them in. I'm about to teach the bitch exactly why she should've left it at home.

My hands fall to my sides and I take the first step towards the trio. Megan leans away from the lockers and moves to the front of her posse. My eyes remain on the third, nameless, girl. As if they all share one brain cell, the three of them straighten and meet me halfway down the hall.

I don't stop until I'm right in front of them.

"Do you remember what happened the last time you did this?" I ask, tilting my head to the side.

The third girl flicks her BIC between her fingers, glancing from me to her friends. On Megan's other side, Lindsey sneers, "You got off easy because the teachers got involved."

I switch my gaze to her, my eyes dropping to the off-brand Mexican soda clutched in one hand. It's half-empty, but that's not what catches my attention—it's the fact that the bottle is pure glass. I file that information away in the back of my mind before turning my gaze to Megan.

"Don't start this shit again," I snap. "You won't like how it ends."

Megan scoffs. "I wouldn't have to do this at all if you would take the hint." She leans close enough for me to smell the scent of spearmint on her breath. "Get out of Silverwood, Donovan. No one wants you here."

"I'm well aware of that fact." It's not like they've kept it a secret thus far. "But I've got a lease to live out," I continue, "and I need my diploma if I'm going to go to college. So, like it or not, I'm here, Megan. Deal with it. This is your final warning; leave me alone or else."

Her hand slaps my shoulder, sending me back a step. "Or else *what?*"

I tamp down the rage that threatens to boil over by

reminding myself that they feel wronged. Their anger is valid. If someone ruined my family's finances, I'd be pissed too. Hell, my own father ruined our family. I *am* pissed. We're the same, the students of Silverwood Public and I. They just can't see it, and they can't get to the one responsible, so here I am, taking them on simply because, in their eyes, I'm guilty by association.

"Just..." I take a long breath as two shadows appear around the corner, catching my attention. My entire body goes stiff when I spy Gio and Lex and Nolan round into the hallway and stop. Fuck, I do not want to be around them right now. I might not be able to escape them in my dreams, but reality is different. Even if it means giving up on beating Megan's face in, I'll give in just to get the hell away from the trio of assholes that won't let me fucking rest.

I focus on Megan again and straighten my shoulders. "Just let it go," I snap. "You don't fuck with me and I won't do anything that we'll both regret."

The last part is a lie. If she stops her bullshit, I won't have to do anything, but if she doesn't, well, the only one of us that will regret my actions will be her.

Another breath and another step back. I turn away, wiping off the crust of whatever nasty trash they'd thrown at me against my jeans. Five feet. I get maybe five feet before I feel nails digging into my scalp and a hand locks onto my hair, tightening and yanking back.

Game. Fucking. On.

The feeling in my limbs goes dead as I spin, giving her no warning. A rushing sound slams into my ears as my fist flies toward her stunned face. Why she's so surprised when she attacked me first, I won't ever understand. Cartilage collapses under my knuckles and blood runs red from both her nostrils. Megan's eyes widen and she stumbles back, running into the two girls behind her. Lindsey's soda bottle crashes to the floor, orange liquid smearing across the flat surface as she breaks

Megan's fall. The third girl jumps forward, a snarl on her face as she reaches for me, dropping her lighter that clatters to the ground.

Oh, hell no. I dive away from her grasping hands, turning and slipping around her back when she tries to grab ahold of my hair like Megan had. The strands flutter against the base of my throat as I take the nameless girl down to the cold, tiled hallway floor.

"Lindsey!" She immediately starts screaming as several students nearby take out their phones. I already know this is going to end up on the internet before Lindsey's hand wraps into the back of my shirt and yanks me up.

The nameless girl swivels, getting to her feet, and I grin as I slam my sneakered foot into her gut before I twist out of Lindsey's hold. The BIC lighter catches my attention where it slid up against the wall of lockers. Before I can think better, I dive for it.

"What the fuck!" Hands grasp at me, yanking me back as my fingers close around the cylindrical object. I shake it, checking to make sure there's actual liquid inside.

Fingers dig past my neck, wrapping around my throat and my lips curve upward. Flicking my thumb over the wheel and depressing the button as I shove the flame that sputters to life right against the hand on my neck. Heat warms my own skin, but the responding scream and the sudden release is music to my ears. My chest heaves up and down as I slowly get back to my feet and turn to face the trio of bitches that started this whole thing.

Megan's still clutching a hand over her nose as she glares at me. The twin lines of red dropping past her fingers over her chin are far too familiar to her face.

"I warned you," I say, sucking in a breath. "I told you not to fuck with me."

The first day had been a warning—this isn't that. They've had enough warnings. I switch my attention to Lindsey, who's staring down at her shaking hand as if she can't figure out how I burned her. I shake the lighter again and smile wide when she finally lifts her gaze to mine. Her features contort into a mask of rage, her too-big nose scrunching up as her thin lips scowl back at me.

"You fucking bitch!" she screams.

When she launches herself at me, it's easy enough to take a single step to the side and let her run face-first into the lockers. Not that I'll let her punishment stop there. Oh no. I grip her by the back of the neck and hold her against the rusted metal doors before glancing over my shoulders. "I tried to tell you," I say, the words dark and wicked. "I tried to warn you—told you to let it go and leave me alone, but did you listen?" I switch back to where Lindsey bucks under my hold.

Depressing the button on the lighter again, I hold the flame right up against her cheek. She immediately goes still—the threat of being burned enough to stop any further resistance. A pitiful whimper escapes her.

"I don't want shit from any of you except to be *left. The fuck. Alone.*" I grit the words out through clenched teeth.

Lindsey shakes under my hold, her slender body trembling against the lockers as she tries to edge away from the fire in my hand. I glance at it, watching the flame flicker and sway, dancing in my grip…

It wouldn't be hard to put it closer to her face, to hold it down against her flesh until her skin bubbles and splits. A scar would show her—would show them all—what happens when they fuck with me. Hurting her won't take back all the shit they've done. It won't erase my father's actions, or my mother's abandonment. Hell, hurting her probably won't bring me more than a single moment of satisfaction—of the knowledge that I'm stronger than the ones who are trying to take me down.

I know I shouldn't, but I still want to. I want to hurt her.

As if my body moves on its own, I bring the flame up and

hold it in front of her eyes. "You see this?" I ask, moving it closer as her hands slap against the metal doors and she screams in shock and fear.

"Stop!" Lindsey forgets herself for a moment and jerks back.

"If I recall correctly," I say, my voice far calmer than it should be as I lower the flame until the ends of her hair curl away from the heat. "That's exactly what I told you to do. Are you going to leave me alone now? Have you learned your lesson?"

"Yes! Yes! I'll stop. Oh, my god!" she screams as more of her hair curls away from the flames. "Someone get this psycho off me!"

"*Princess.*" I release the lighter's button as that low voice whispers against the side of my cheek. I'd been so focused on Lindsey's struggling body that I hadn't noticed when Nolan had gotten close. Now that he is, though, and I recognize it, I'm viscerally aware of the heat of him pressed to my side.

He reaches for my hand, fingers circling my wrist, and forces me to take a step away from Lindsey ... then another and another until we're across the hall from her.

"Gio! Do you see what she did? She's fucking crazy." Megan's shrieking enters my ears, but it's like listening to sounds in water—muffled and laborious.

"I saw that you started shit, Meg." Gio's voice pops the bubble, coming through clearly as he steps into my line of sight. "She told you to stop—you didn't."

"She could've scarred Lindsey for life!" Megan shoots back.

Lindsey sobs and collapses to the floor as her friend—the nameless third girl—approaches and puts her arms around her, glaring in my direction as she does. I take comfort in the note of fear that shudders her expression when she can't seem to hold my gaze for longer than a few seconds.

"I doubt you would've been kind about beating the shit out of her," Gio says.

Nolan reaches down and gently retrieves the lighter before passing it off to someone on his left. I jerk my head up and to the side, watching as Lex takes the lighter and slides it into his pocket. Gray eyes meet mine and he holds a finger up over his lips as if telling me to stay quiet about where it's going.

I don't care. I turn away from both of them, only drawing up short when my feet refuse to keep moving. I glance down. It's not my feet but my arm. Nolan is still holding on to me, his fingers a manacled grip on my wrist.

"Let go." The words are quiet but no less steely.

"Not yet," is all he says back.

My jaw clamps down, clenching tight enough that the bones beneath my ears begin to ache. I am so done with people touching me, grabbing me, trying to control me.

"Nolan," I choke out his name, "if you don't want me to lose it on you right here, then let. Me. Go."

Nolan turns, his body blocking out the rest of the hallway. "Look at me."

I tip my head back, meeting a pair of crimson-brown eyes —like blood-soaked chocolate. "Take a breath," he orders, and somehow I find myself doing just that.

Sucking in one mouthful of oxygen and then the next and the next until I no longer feel like I'm about to scream or shatter into a million pieces. His fingers release my wrist and he takes a step back just in time for me to see a familiar figure come barreling around the corner. A low groan emits from my throat.

Nolan grins. "That's what you get for losing control, Princess," he says, the taunt in his tone obvious. "Next time, when you plan to fuck someone up—do it somewhere private."

"Giving me advice now, asshole?" I shoot back. "Careful, someone might think you have experience." It's on the tip of my tongue to ask what happened to Rich and Josh, but I swallow the curiosity back.

Nolan's eyes narrow on me and he leans in again until my entire field of vision is filled by him. "Experience is something no one can take away from you, Princess," he whispers and the words sound more like a promise of sin. It immediately makes my skin go tight.

With a vicious growl, I flip him off before turning to face the music and worse ... Principal Long.

24
JULIET

"You want to tell me why you attacked that student, Miss Donovan?" Principal Long has mastered the art of the disapproving scowl. Despite her relative youth for a principal, her face is a mask of deep lines and narrowed slits for eyes.

I shrug. "I was defending myself."

"Hmmm." The sound that escapes her makes it clear she's not buying my story—even if it is the truth. A moment passes and then another. Silence fills the office and I have to smile because I know what she's doing. It's something my father always preached about. People feel uncomfortable in silence, and if you let them sit long enough they'll weave enough rope to hang themselves just by talking. I'm not uncomfortable in silence—not anymore. I find peace in the silence of the world because it's certainly not silent in my head.

Principal Long disrupts the quiet in the room first. Leaning forward as her chair creaks, she clasps her hands together on the edge of the desk that separates us. "Grief is hard for everyone," she states.

I close my eyes and inhale deeply, trying not to allow

myself to act on the annoyance those words bring out in me. "I'm not grieving," I reply, opening my eyes and fixing her with a bored look. "No one's dead."

Yet.

I'd wanted to though. I'd wanted to burn her skin off. Scar her for life, maybe even slit her throat. The power I'd wielded over her had been a drug, and now that I'm coming back down from the high, I realize how dangerously close I'd gotten to the point of no return.

It would be my luck that a Scorpion King had pulled me back from the edge.

Had I always been this way or is this what happens when everyone abandons you and you find yourself in the gutter, struggling for survival?

"There are other types of loss, Juliet," Long says.

On a good day, I don't like it when people look at me with sympathy. Even if it's kindness that spawns the emotion, it feels far too close to pity for me to feel even remotely comfortable with it. Considering Principal Long had been on a wrathful war path up until we crossed the threshold of her office not but two minutes ago, this is too much of a one-eighty for me.

Sitting back in the thinly cushioned and frayed chair that's positioned before her desk, I crack my neck to one side, stretching the muscles there. "What's the verdict?" I ask. "What's my punishment?"

Expulsion? Suspension? Being strung up by the angry townspeople and beaten with the business end of a bat?

Ironically, that last option doesn't scare me as much as it once might have. Pain is an emotion. It's a sensation. Right now, I feel like anything would be preferable to this icy numbness that's crept up my insides and flooded my veins.

Long sighs and props her elbows up on the edge of her desk, steepling her fingers together before she leans down and rests her chin on them. Her eyes are too knowing, too compassionate. They make me feel like bugs are crawling up my spine and all over me, but always in places I know I won't be able to reach. No scratching can make the sensation go away. She sighs, the sound an echo of her disappointed expression. "I don't know yet," she admits.

Fuck. That can't be good.

"Of course, you'll return to ISS for the rest of the week," she continues, reaching forward and ripping a tissue from the box stationed on the corner of her desk.

She offers it to me and I glare at her, but take it anyway. I'm not going to fucking cry, but I use the offering anyway, balling the material in my fist and crushing it, wishing that it were a good stress ball.

"I understand that things aren't easy for you here at school and I know you've got other things going on, but what you did today can't happen again." I nod my agreement. What I almost did today can't be repeated—certainly not in public. Nolan was right. If I'm going to lose control like that, then it needs to be somewhere out of the public eye. I need to have plausible deniability.

"Being out of control isn't good for your mental health," Principal Long says.

I almost smile at that comment as I loosen my hold on the tissue and then flatten it out on my thigh. Staring at the white, gauzy material, I slowly and methodically begin to rip it into lines, up and down, up and down. Despite what Principal Long may think, I wasn't out of control today. It was the opposite. I haven't felt that in control of myself in a long time.

Riiip. Riiip. Riiip.

"I want you to have regular sessions with our counselor here at school too. She's trained in more than preparing students for what happens after school. She's a licensed therapist."

I snort. "You think therapy is going to help me figure out my fucked-up life?"

"I think you're on a very dangerous path, Juliet," Long replies, eyeing me. "Your whole world has shifted in a very short span of time. You've gone from relying on friends and family to…" She drifts off.

"To not having any friends or family?" I guess aloud, arching a brow in her direction.

Her lips press together briefly before she starts talking again. "Something needs to change or you'll find yourself in trouble when the real world hits."

My hands still over the ripped tissues in my lap. "The real world has already hit me." It hit me months ago on my eighteenth birthday when I lost everything. Literally. No home. No parents. No boyfriend. No friends. No money.

The old Juliet Donovan died that night and sometimes I think I'd have been better off if I'd died with her.

"I'm already in trouble," I murmur.

Not with myself but with this fucking town. Silverwood is a wound. A festering, ugly, puss-seeping wound full of bacteria and infection. I don't want to cure it. I just want to get out.

"This isn't a suggestion or a recommendation." Long's eyes harden as she makes her decision. She lifts her head away from her steepled fingers and lets her hands fall. "This will be part of your punishment—counseling with Mrs. Beck. Now, where'd you get the lighter? Are you smoking?"

I shake my head. "I don't smoke." It's not a lie, but there's no point telling the principal it was someone else's addiction that gave me the weapon. Long hums in the back of her throat, narrowing her eyes on me as I go back to ripping the tissue paper. The strips turn into tiny squares.

"I'll talk to our counselor and arrange for your meetings with her. She should be ready for you to start by the time you leave ISS. You can decide when you see her. That's your decision to make, but you *will* see her." She glares across the desk at me as if her expression can force me into compliance.

"One missed session"—she stops and holds up a single finger—"just one and we'll have a problem. You could go to jail for what you pulled today—not juvie but *jail*." She repeats the word and the intended effect strikes home. My heartbeat stutters and my hands fall still. "It was dangerous," she continues. "You threatened another student."

"She shouldn't have started what she couldn't finish." The words, despite sounding tough, fall flat. She's right. Fighting in school is one thing, but I am eighteen now and if they wanted to, those bitches could press charges. Maybe they don't know that yet, but how long will it take for them to figure it out?

Long's fuzzy ponytail waves against the back of her head as she shakes it back and forth. Leaning over to the big, boxy computer set to the side of her desk, she types something on the wired keyboard. "The counselor will reach out and discuss what time you two can meet regularly when she's ready," Principal Long says, ignoring my statement.

My eyes linger on the computer. In quiet places like the principal's office, the differences between Silverwood Public and Silverwood Prep become so obvious that it's difficult to ignore. The Prep Academy had been built within the last fifteen years. Everything from the desks to the computers used by both teachers and students was updated yearly. Principal Long's computer looks like it's been here since the nineties. There's even a curve to the front monitor and when she types. I close my eyes and my hands still over the shredded mess in my lap. There's no point in noticing these differences. My custom laptop had been left behind along with my several thousand dollar wardrobe when my father had been carted off to jail. The rest ... doesn't matter.

The sharp click-clack of Principal Long's keyboard stabs into my ears like ice picks, pulling me back when she speaks again. "Alright, the email is sent," she announces. "I'm going to walk you to your locker where you can gather the rest of your things and then you'll go to ISS for the rest of the day."

I frown and glance down and around, realizing I'd dropped my backpack in the hallway when everything was happening, but—oh—there it is. Someone must have gathered it for me and set it just inside Principal Long's office door. I don't even remember hearing it open, but I'm relieved to see it there. I get up along with her and reach for the strap before realizing that standing had sent a rain of ripped little tissues to the floor. With a groan, I bend down and gather them all up, tossing them in a nearby waste paper basket before meeting her at the door.

"Just one more question, Juliet," Long says, her tone lowering as her hand hovers over the doorknob.

"What?"

She looks back, eyes settling on my face. "Have you heard from your mother or talked to your father since everything happened?"

My spine goes rigid as I quickly adjust my backpack strap over one shoulder and look away from the penetrating look she's giving me.

"No," I grit out. "My mom dipped the second she could. She knows as well as I do that no one in town would've been kind to her had she stayed." It was just too bad she hadn't thought to take her daughter with her. Selfish bitch. "And I have no plans to talk to my dad after everything he did."

"He's still your father," Long says. "Life is already hard enough when you feel so alone. I know he's being held in a prison that's only a few hours away. You might consider visiting him."

I cut a hand through the air. "I don't want to talk about my parents," I snap. "So drop it."

Principal Long's hand falls away from the doorknob and she turns completely, pivoting to face me as she folds her arms. The stretch of the gray pantsuit she's wearing makes her look severe even when her fuzzy curls stick out all over at the back of her head, held in place by the thinnest of hairbands.

"You could've stayed with Morpheus Calloway," she states. It's not a question, so I don't respond. I do, however, take a healthy step away from her and give her the evil eye, waiting to see what else she'll say. For a while, the two of us just stare at each other.

Silence permeates the room, broken occasionally by a ringing phone outside in the front office. The sound of the office secretary's voice, her words muffled by the thin walls that desperately need an upgrade, fills the room along with the buzzing of ancient electronics.

Finally, Principal Long asks her real question. "Why didn't you?" Her head tilts to the side. "Your life could have remained virtually the same had you stayed with Morpheus Calloway. He's a kind man. I know he offered to pay for your prep school tuition and even help you get into the college of your choice." She unfolds her arms to wave around her office. "Why would you give all of that up and come here?"

Because I couldn't trust that it wouldn't all go away again. Because Morpheus isn't my father and he's not my uncle—not really. They were business partners, friends. Not blood. Morpheus Calloway isn't my blood, but even if he was—I still wouldn't trust him. If my own mother couldn't hack it in this town for her own daughter, then why the fuck would someone who has no responsibility for me do so.

I eye her for a moment, the words on the tip of my tongue. Hefting my backpack higher on my shoulder, I step past her and reach for the door. Just before I turn the knob, though, I pause and the words escape. "When everything you've ever known is ripped away from you and all of the people you've trusted turn their backs on you, there's no such thing as trust anymore. The only person I can rely on now is myself. If I'd stayed with Mr. Calloway, I would have just been pretending like everything didn't happen, but it did. I'm not my mother." A mother who is, no doubt, off somewhere at the bottom of a bottle, acting like her husband isn't in jail and her daughter isn't half-starving in a town full of piranhas. "I'm not going to close my eyes to the truth," I tell her.

Not again.

25
NOLAN

Sweat drips into my eyes as I push up from the ground. Grass digs into the palms of my hand as Coach's sneakered feet stride by. He barks out.

"Down!"

We go down.

"Up!"

We lift back up.

The muscles in my upper arms are burning today, but all I can really think about is the look on her face. The emptiness. The hollow panic that invaded the second she'd realized what she'd almost done.

Juliet Donovan is a danger to us all.

"Megan's become a problem." It takes a moment for me to recognize Lex's voice.

I turn my head in his direction, giving him a solid nod, and then I flip to the right to eye Gio. "You need to take care of it," I inform him.

The coach yells out again and we do another push-up, holding for as long as he forces us to. Gio hisses out a breath between clenched teeth before responding. "I'm not fucking dating her," he snaps. "I've told her to back off now."

Knowing Megan, she won't. She'll blame Gio's loss of interest on Juliet and if she tries to attack her in a less public setting ... well, I'm not worried about Megan so much as I'm worried about what will happen if Juliet takes a page from our book and kills someone.

Wait, I'm worried about her killing someone? The realization slams into me and I nearly slip on the already slick ground, but I catch my sliding hand and stabilize my position. *No,* I tell myself. *It's not Juliet I'm concerned with. It's Lex. That's who I care about.* If Juliet ends up in jail, there's no telling what Lex will do to get her out. He'd probably even risk burning his hacker identity—the 5C0RP10N.

Which reminds me ... my eyes slide back to Lex, but I clamp my lips shut as Coach passes in front of us once again. When I'm sure he's clear, I direct my question to the man on my left.

"Have you had any more contact with Allen Donovan?" I ask, keeping my voice low so only the three of us can hear.

Lex pushes up, the muscles in his arms bulging even beneath the black t-shirt he wears. "*Yes.*" He hisses out the word as the three of us drop to our bellies once again.

"And?" I press. My fingers flex and the black lines that stretch over my forearms shift as we lift back onto our palms.

"I'm working on it," Lex grits out.

If Lex hasn't figured shit out by now then the chances that Allen Donovan is as guilty as everyone thinks he is just shot up.

"Why are you even bothering?" Gio bites out, the strain in his voice adding to the shaking of his forearms when I look back at him. "Whether or not Allen Donovan is guilty or innocent won't change anyone else's mind."

No, but it would mean something different for the girl that Lex is in love with. "Quiet," I snap as Coach's footsteps approach.

Coach Kale stops before the three of us. "Keep it up," he

calls out over our heads. "If you want to beat those preppy motherfuckers then I wanna see your asses sweating."

The corner of my mouth tips upward. No other coach would ever get away with talking to students like that, but here at Silverwood Public, the coaches are as real as the rest of us. They know what's on the line and they know what will get us motivated. It's not promises of pizza parties and polite preaching.

Practice passes in a haze of pain and sweat. By the time Coach calls an end to the run, reminding everyone of the upcoming game a few short weeks away, I have no interest in heading over to Laurenti's Auto Shop. The other players all groan through their after-practice showers, moaning about soreness and exhaustion that I understand all too well.

Planting myself against the row of lockers older than even our parents, I let my head slide back against the metal and wait for the room to empty out. The guys are smart and quickly get their asses moving, offering up hands and goodbyes as they head out. Once there's no one left but Gio, Lex, and me, I get off my ass and strip down to my skin.

"Tell me what you've found," I order as I head into the nearest shower, twisting the knobs and gritting my teeth at the icy spray that shoots out over my chest.

"If Donovan is being framed, then the cover-up is well done. It's professional." Lex's voice echoes in the near-empty space of the shower room just beyond the thin plastic curtain separating us.

The water slowly begins to heat up and my muscles unclench enough for me to reach for the bar of soap waiting on the rack beneath the shower head. "Are you still convinced he's innocent?"

"I'm not convinced of shit," Lex admits, "but if he is, I want to know."

"I'll be honest," Gio pipes up, "when everything first hit, I thought it was weird. I mean, why would a guy who has everything risk it all by embezzling from his own company?"

Working up a lather, I scrub down the front of my chest. As I move, the skin of my back—stretched beneath the scars—tightens, an old ache building up as the nerves beneath resist the movements. Gritting my teeth, I force myself to move beyond the pain.

"People are greedy," I say. "He didn't think he had enough."

"Yeah, I'd get that if he were like an employee," Gio agrees, "but why wouldn't he embezzle from his partner's funds or even one of their associate partner companies? He had to know he would get caught."

"I agree," Lex says, "and I've been following that trail. All of the money was well hidden, but they found it fairly easily and every link directly comes from one of Allen Donovan's accounts."

A silent curse threatens to break free when the soap slips from my fingers and my back seizes. I slap a palm to the wall and breathe out.

"You good, Nolan?" Gio's concerned voice rises up over the shower wall and curtain and a man's shadow hovers on the other side.

"Fine," I bite out. I reach back and work my fingers against my spine, every vile, disgusting curse I can potentially think of screaming through my mind as the pain nearly overwhelms me.

"Coach went pretty hard on us today," Gio continues. "You might need to take it easy tonight—ice your back."

He's right, but damn it, I don't have the time to do that. Darrio wants me at the shop tonight when they bring in the next job. I'm supposed to take apart an Escalade they lifted from some business magnate in Tangier and Darrio doesn't want any of the other mechanics' hands on the fucker.

"I'm fine." This time when I say the words, they sound at

least marginally more believable. I straighten and sigh when my back doesn't offer any more protest. Finishing scrubbing myself clean, I shut the shower off and rip the curtain back before stepping out.

Gio steps back and Lex tosses me a towel from where he reclines against the row of sinks on the opposite side of the room. I deliberately ignore the foggy mirror behind him and head back towards the lockers. They follow. Quiet falls over the room as I open my locker and pull out a pair of jeans so worn through that they're more white than denim colored and a black sleeveless shirt. The three of us finish cleaning up the locker room before heading to the student parking lot. It isn't until we reach the back of the lot where G's Firebird, Lex's SUV, and my Indian are parked that any of us speak again.

"Things with Megan are over," G says. "I told her to back off Prep Girl, but if she doesn't—then you'll have to come up with a different plan. Short of making her one of ours, there's no way we can keep the students off her ass."

Making her one of ours might be our only choice. I sidle a look Lex's way. Without commenting, though, it's hard to figure out what he's thinking as he slides on a pair of black sunglasses and crosses his arms.

"We need to address the other thing," I say, keeping my gaze locked on Lex's face even though half of it is now hidden from view. He doesn't speak, doesn't even move a muscle. I sigh. "What did you do to Rich and Josh, Lex?"

Gio frowns. "Why does it matter?" he asks. "They were pieces of shit. Let them disappear."

"I wasn't talking to you, G, though it's good to know you approve."

"They were going to rape her." When Lex speaks, it's in a voice so deep and low, I have to strain to hear it.

I lift my head and scan the parking lot. Once I'm sure we're alone, I return my gaze to him. "They were missing from school today," I say.

Lex doesn't respond.

"Did you kill them after we finished roughing them up the other night?"

Nothing but silence meets my question. I curse. "Damn it, Lex."

"No one will find them," Lex says. "It won't blow back on us."

"We don't kill where we sleep," I snap. Gio snorts and I swivel to glare at him. "Got a fucking problem, G?"

He rolls his eyes. "Just with hypocrisy, man," he shoots back. "If we don't kill where we sleep, then what the hell was your dad?"

I shove my finger at him. "That was necessary," I bite out.

"So was this," Lex argues. "They annoyed me."

The pulsing behind my eyes drives into my skull. "You can't just kill someone because they annoy you."

The asshole merely shrugs. "Too late. Already did." Before I can say anything more, he fixes me with a look. "They already hurt several of the girls in school. They were going to rape her too. I took care of a problem. You would've done the same thing."

But I hadn't. I'd left them alive for a damn reason. Josh Michaelson and Richard Glean were pieces of shit, but they were too close to us that if anyone ever actually did find their bodies we could come under scrutiny.

"You wanted to," Gio agrees, reaching up to clap a hand on my shoulder as I lower my arm. "I could see it in your eyes when you beat them to a bloody pulp that night." Not that I'd been able to tell the difference after both G and Lex had dragged their already bruised bodies through the woods and thrown them into the trunk of Gio's Firebird.

He's right though. When they'd woken up and claimed to not understand why we'd come after them, I'd wanted to pound their faces—and I had. It wasn't until later when they'd finally realized they'd been found out that I'd truly lost my shit. That was when the excuses had come—those girls had wanted it, they were teases, they asked for it. Why would they dress like whores if they didn't want to be treated like one?

Each sentence makes me want to cut out their tongues. I'd barely held myself back from slitting their throats myself. Even now, it's a struggle not to applaud Lex for his actions. The only thing that holds me back is the worry that if people start asking questions about where a couple of Silverwood Public's basketball players are, it'll come back to us ... and to her.

"She saw you two drag them away," I snap. "If someone finds out that they're dead, she'll be the last one to have seen you two with them."

Lex shrugs, his big body barely moving as his shoulders lift and lower. "She won't say anything."

"You can't be sure of that," I say.

"It's done," Lex says. "There's no taking it back."

"And what are you going to do if she does decide to talk?" I ask, narrowing my eyes as I jerk my arm out from under Gio's grip. "Are you going to be able to silence her?"

Lex stiffens and then uncrosses his arms, taking a step towards me. Gio hurriedly jumps between us, putting both hands up. "Whoa, whoa—calm the fuck down!"

"You need to fix this," I snap. "I don't care how you do it —but make sure she keeps her mouth shut."

"Don't threaten her," Lex growls.

I blink and lean away from Gio's hand. "I'm not threatening *her*, asshole." My upper lip curls away from my teeth. "I'm threatening *you*!"

Almost as if those were the magic words, Lex's earlier tautness evaporates and he relaxes. "Oh, that's fine then," he says.

I shake my head. "You fucking psychopath."

Gio sighs and drops his arms before speaking. "No one is

going to ask questions about Josh and Rich," he says. "I've already started working shit on my end."

Both Lex's and my head turn towards him. "How?" I demand.

With a smug grin, he shoves his hands into the back pocket of his jeans and waltzes backward toward his own car. "Rumor is that Rich and Josh were planning to head up to Eastpoint." His tone practically drips with satisfaction. "Someone might have mentioned that Rich has a cousin that lives up there—and that maybe that cousin works for the mob. People who work for the mob disappear all the time."

Lex reaches up and removes his glasses, a smile curling his lips. "You fucking smart bastard." He laughs. Yeah, because that's Gio. Lex loses his shit and we fix it—or rather, usually I'm the one that fixes it, but it's good to know that Gio can do it all on his own.

My pocket buzzes and the creeping grin I feel stretching my face falls flat the second I slide my phone out and see who it is. "Shit." Gio stops walking, and as one, both he and Lex look at me.

"I gotta go," I say, shoving my phone back into my pocket and circling the Indian.

"Dad?" Gio guesses.

I press my lips together but offer him a short nod as I lift the helmet from my handlebars. Just before I slip it on, though, I lift a finger and point at him. "I want you to keep an eye on the princess," I say.

He blinks. "But I just told you that we're in the clear," he says.

Pressing a hand flat to the seat of the bike, I swing my leg up and over the back. "Rumors are just rumors," I say. "We're not sure we're in the clear yet. Until we know, you need to watch her."

Gio groans, turning and shoving his hands into his hair. "How the fuck am I supposed to do that?" He swivels back to face me as I straddle the bike and lower the helmet onto my head.

I flip up the visor and then buckle the strap beneath. "Don't care," I tell him. "You were fucking around with that chick that lives next to her, right? The one that works at *The Veil*."

Gio grimaces as if remembering something foul. I wouldn't be surprised if she hadn't been a good fuck. In all likelihood, she'd probably been just shy of a fleshlight. Everyone knows that the girls who work at the strip club on the outskirts of Silverwood are the desperate kind.

The Veil is the place where people go to get cracked out. There are more drug deals in the back rooms than there are lap dances. Were it up to me, I would've steered clear of the place forever, but they're under Darrio Vargas' protection, which means the regular visits Gio makes are business-related. Still, he should've known better than to get involved with one of the strippers.

"I don't do seconds," Gio states.

"And I don't make unreasonable demands." Lifting a hand, I point his way for the third and final time as I turn the engine of my bike over. "You're closest to the girl. Use her however you want, but you're in charge of keeping an eye on Juliet Donovan while Lex figures this shit out with her father. I'm not going to ask again. *Watch. Her.*"

26
GIO

Cancer fills my lungs as the cherry red end of my cigarette burns hot in the night air. "Gio?" The husky female voice at my back makes my muscles bunch ... and not in anticipation. "Are you coming back to bed?"

My skin crawls. I don't know what the fuck I was thinking the first time I followed this chick back from *The Veil*. I can't even remember her name—Jen? Jess? Something with a J.

Removing my lips from the cig, I turn my head to the side and let a stream of smoke blow out before responding. "Yeah, be in once I'm done with this." I hold the cig up as an excuse for my escape. I've already fucked her once tonight and it was hard enough to get it up when I wasn't inebriated or high. If I manage to get it up again, it'll be a miracle.

Jen-Jess presses her side against the sliding glass doors of her apartment and pushes her tits out in my direction. "Don't keep me waiting too long," she murmurs, the intent and desire in her raspy tone evident.

I close my eyes and turn back to the gray horizon. "I said I'll be back in when I'm fucking done," I snap, not caring about her feelings. I don't even want to be here. The only reason I am is the damn girl next door.

The stripper huffs out a breath and then disappears back into the apartment, slamming her sliding door with enough force to make the whole rickety thing shudder. I put the cigarette back between my lips and then clamp both hands over the railing. Wood splinters crack under the pressure. This whole building is falling apart. No doubt, Mr. Ritchie has been bribing the inspectors who infrequently come by to make sure everything is up to code because there's no way this two-story apartment building is anything more than matchsticks waiting to go up in flames. My mind begins to circle back to my reason for even being here. Cool autumn air filters over the back of my neck and further down my bare back.

Watch her.

That's all any of us have been doing since Juliet Donovan fell right into our laps. Straight down from her castle in the sky to the gutter where we've lived all our lives. My fingers grip the railing tighter, the wood creaking in protest. Jerking my hands away, I lift shaking fingers to the cigarette hanging from my lips and release another stream of smoke. I'd give anything for this to be more than nicotine right now. A good joint would do me a world of good, but if I'm watching Prep Girl then I need to have my head clear.

Turning away from the darkened sky, I quickly stamp out my half-finished cig on the shitty patio that looks like it hasn't been cleaned since well before the current occupant moved in and head inside. The tiny apartment is more like a shoebox than a place to sleep and Jen-Jess is already naked and sprawled out on her bed. Her tits are small but perky, and the rosy-brown nipples peak as she writhes against the mattress.

My eyes scan to the coffee table that's set between her bed and the rest of the studio apartment. The sight of white powder residue lingering in the center and a cracked credit card discarded nearby makes my chest ache. *Fuck.*

My eyes shoot back to the girl as her lids lift and she offers me a smile. "Gio…" She moans and reaches out. "I'm so hot for you, baby."

I stand stalk still. The sensation of insects crawling all over my body roots me to the floor. Disgust rolls through me in waves. The walls close in. My head fills with water and smoke.

God … no.

"Gio." Sickness creeps up my throat as Jen-Jess groans again and rolls back and forth on the thin mattress set atop the box spring on the floor. "I'm hungry for you."

She rolls to the side and begins reaching, hands stretching past the edge of the mattress until she latches on to my belt loops. I stumble forward and she practically attacks my zipper. It was hard enough to do this before when she wasn't drugged out of her fucking mind. Now, my cock remains flaccid as she reaches past my jeans and into my boxers to take it out. Her bony fingers tighten and stroke me in practiced moves. I grit my teeth and force myself to remain still though I'd love nothing better than to shove her off my body. Nothing about her attracts me now that I'm sober. Nolan was right—I should've stayed the hell away from the chicks that work at *The Veil*.

Swallowing back bile, I reach out and capture her hand, removing her from my dick as she turns wide, blown-out eyes up to my face. "What's wrong?" Her lips are dry and cracked, and she licks them, leaving behind a shiny trail of saliva.

My gag reflex works hard against my resistance. "Nothing," I tell her. "I want to focus on you first."

I want her to hurry up and pass out so I don't have to pretend that the reason I'm here is because I want her. My eyes cut back to the coffee table, wondering just how much cocaine she's had. Is she a regular addict or just a social one?

A soft sigh escapes her lips, drawing me back to the present as I press Jen-Jess onto her bed and leverage up over her. Transferring her hands to one of mine, I yank up my jeans and boxers, tucking my cock out of sight before holding her down.

"Close your eyes," I order.

"Gio…" Her eyes slide shut as my name leaves her lips. I'm not an incredibly kinky bastard—not like Nolan or Lex—but right now, I'd give anything for a ball gag. I don't want to hear my name from anyone, much less her, but I have a job to do.

Watch her.

Even as I press the girl whose name I still can't remember into her sheets, my thoughts are on the woman next door. Juliet Donovan is uncontrollable. She has us all on edge. I used to give Lex so much shit when it came to his obsession with her. Now, her poison has spread to all of us. She's in our heads. In our dreams. Fucking everything up.

"Yes, yes, yes…" The whispered words from the girl beneath me drag me back to reality as I lower my head and graze my lips over the curve of one breast. In my mind, it's not her I'm touching.

In my mind, Juliet Donovan is the one stretched out under my muscles, her naked body on display for me. If I close my eyes, I can picture her perfectly. Pale skin, gleaming in the shadowed room. My cock twitches in my pants, finally showing some interest. I let my mouth trail over her breasts and lower to the nearly concave hollow of her belly. Prep Girl isn't this skinny. She's not half-starved. No, her curves are lush and round. Her tits bigger than the nameless, faceless girl's in my arms. A hunger I've never known assails me, driving me against the girl as my cock lengthens and hardens, pressing into the fabric of my boxers and jeans.

It would take no work at all to have Juliet beneath me, to spread her out like a feast, and find my way to the place between her thighs. Wetness against pouty lips, juice oozing down her sensitive flesh. I let one hand move between the legs under me and press into the bundle of nerves there, rotating as the girl's back bows and a cry of pleasure escapes her.

What would it feel like to have Juliet Donovan screaming for me? To spread her open and force Lex to see how filthy his innocent little angel can truly be?

The fantasy fills me up and I grit my teeth against the urge to cum. Around and around, my thumb strokes a quivering clit just begging for some attention. I keep my eyes squeezed tightly shut, unwilling to let reality invade my illusion that I crave more than my next breath—Prep Girl under me, writhing for me, crying out my name as I drive her higher and higher towards the precipice of pleasure.

I want her to forget everything—all of the hate and fear and vitriol that consumes Silverwood. If anyone might accept my brothers and me, surely it's the girl who hates Silverwood as much as we do.

A feminine cry fills the air as I sink two fingers deep inside a soaking cunt. Rotating my hand, I curl my fingers inward and stroke the spot just behind her pubic bone. Anatomy is good for one thing. I might be average in school, but here—when I can put my hands on a subject—I'm an A-plus student.

"Oh God!" The hips beneath me bump and twist as I finger-fuck the girl to completion. Harder. Faster. She screams and a sudden rush of wetness preludes the hard clamping of inner muscles squeezing my fingers. All at once, Jen-Jess sags into the mattress, panting heavily and my eyes open. The fantasy disappears and disappointment invades. Thankfully, though, so does obvious exhaustion. Jen-Jess opens her mouth on a hard yawn, nearly cracking the bones of her jaw in the process.

"Ugh, that was so good," she mumbles. "Gimme a sec and I'll take care of you…"

I withdraw my fingers and stare down at the clear fluid encasing the digits. In my mind, it's Juliet's orgasm coating my hand and I want to know what she tastes like. I want to put it between my lips and suck her clean. But it's not. This isn't her cum on my hand. It wasn't her cunt squeezing me. That fact disgusts me, and what's worse is the knowledge that I want her enough to fantasize about her.

So, I get up and head into the bathroom. I turn the knobs on the sink until steam billows up from the scalding water flowing into the cracked Formica. Shoving my hands into the boiling water, I scrub with the cheap soap on the countertop until my fingers are lobster red. When I feel marginally clean —or rather, I don't think I can stand the small enclosed cubicle of a bathroom any longer—I head back into the room to find that Jen-Jess has passed out on her mattress.

Relief courses through me and I head for the balcony, pulling the cigarette pack from my back pocket as I go. Withdrawing another, I press it between my lips and exchange the pack for a lighter. The red and gold flame dances in front of my face, warming my skin as I light the cig and drag more of that evil cancer into my lungs, sucking it down and praying it kills me someday before it's too late.

27
JULIET

*S*cratch. *Scratch. Scratch.* My eyes shoot open and dart around the room.

The sheets surrounding me have long since stolen the heat from my body and a shiver moves through me. The nightmare lingering at the back of my mind hovers close, blurring the line between the waking world and the dreaming one. *Is he here? Has he come back for me? There's nothing stopping him now. He can do whatever he wants. Again and again.*

I blink, taking in the familiar surroundings of my own apartment. No, it was a dream. It's not real. *Scratch. Scratch. Scratch.* My body stiffens beneath the covers. All remaining drowsiness evaporates, and I'm suddenly wide awake. My heart hammers against my ribcage as adrenaline surges into my veins. Something had woken me. A sound that should not be there.

Forcing my body to go lax beneath the blankets over me, I remain still, not wanting to give away my consciousness just yet. My breath saws in and out as I strain my ears for any other sound in the darkness. Then it's there again. The soft snick of a lock clicking out of place.

No, maybe I just *think* that's what it is. It could be a

scratching of one of the trees on my window ... never mind that the branches don't reach that far into the balcony. It's possible with wind, right?

Creak. Swoosh. Creak.

I close my eyes with a silent curse. There's no denying that sound nor the sudden rushing chill of air flooding my apartment. I don't need to roll over to know that the glass door leading to the tiny balcony off the main room of my studio is open. All of my hopeful thoughts die bloody deaths.

Idiot. I'm such a fucking idiot. I hadn't blocked the track because I'd thought being on the second floor would be enough of a deterrent.

To my surprise, it isn't fear that streams through me at the realization that someone has broken into my apartment—it's pure, raw fury. It burns hot behind my eyes. It's not fucking fair. As if my life isn't hard enough with the shit I have to put up with at school, but now some asshole thinks they can break into my home—even if it is a shitty excuse for one—and terrorize me.

I lie still, letting them draw closer as I consider my options. Even if I manage to call the cops, what will they actually do? Silver Creek Apartments is under the Silverwood Police Department jurisdiction, and no one there will care if anything happens to Allen Donovan's daughter. My fingers curl inward as more rage pours through me. It's not fucking fair. I didn't ask for any of this.

The quiet in the room is full of phantom tension. It ramps up and up some more as the heartbeat in my ears makes it impossible to listen for the intruder. There's only one reason a stranger would break into my apartment and it's not to steal.

They're here for me.

Bile coats the back of my tongue with an acidic flavor that makes me want to vomit. I stem the urge, swallowing against the need to both puke and scream. Pinpricks touch the bare flesh of my arms and travel both up and down, covering the rest of my skin as alarm bells sound in my head. *It's as if they're yelling, "Danger! Danger! Danger!"*

Yeah, I already know that. Now, I have to do something about it.

Not allowing myself to think better of my actions, I fake a yawn and stretch beneath the sheets. The footsteps on the floor of my apartment freeze. I keep my eyes slitted as I roll over on my futon and face the open sliding glass doors. The dark figure standing just inside, barely three feet from my makeshift bed, is every one of my nightmares come to life and it pisses me the hell off.

Whoever the man is, he's tall and lanky—though there's no denying his gender. The rotten stench of cigarette smoke and male body odor permeate the air, invading my senses like a disease looking for its next host. He takes a step towards me, and a stream of moonlight glances over his face—his uncovered face.

He's older than me by at least a decade or two. His face is a mask of lines and a scruff of beard growth covers the lower half of his face. Dark eyes glitter through the darkness and I can't make out their color. There's something wrong with this image. He's not even bothering to cover his identity. Does that mean he plans to kill me? Or ... that he knows no one will care what he does to me. Whatever the reason, the image of his face—a human version of a monster—sends me into action like nothing else. I bolt forward. Sitting up and flinging the covers free of my legs, I launch myself from the futon and tackle him to the floor.

I don't even stop to consider whether or not the intruder has a weapon or what he could be here to do—murder me or just to scare the shit out of me. I'm too angry for any of that. Adrenaline surges through my body, making the world slow down as I throw the first punch, slamming my fist into the side of his face. The responding grunt is all masculine annoyance.

I find myself atop a solidly built chest and despite the wiry form, I can tell that he's got at least fifty pounds on me.

"*Shit.*" The curse hisses out of my chest. Bulky arms close around me and the man rises to standing—an impressive feat considering I'm bucking and kicking the shit out of his thighs and calves and pretty much anything my legs can reach. Not that he seems to notice. No, the man just walks back over to my bed and slams me down.

Stomach acid threatens to come up my throat and I bow upward, trying to throw him off to no avail. My heart beats double-time as my breaths come in shorter bursts. I punch at his chest. He comes down on top of me. Hard hips press into mine, pinning me to the sagging futon mattress, and hot breath, stained with the acrid smell of tobacco, invades my lungs. This time, I can't stop the gag as I force myself to turn away, pressing my cheek into the sheets even as my hands are gripped and brought up over my head. *No. No. No.* After everything else I've been through, I can't bear this too. Not again. The universe is asking too much.

Or maybe the universe isn't asking at all. Hell, there's no explanation for my twisted luck over the past few months. Dad in jail. Mom MIA. No friends. No boyfriend. No one to care if this man takes one more thing from the town pariah.

The only one who can save me is me—the only one who cares is me. Still, I can't help the words that come out of my mouth in rapid pants. "Why are you doing this?"

The man doesn't respond. The only sound echoing between us is the heavy breathing. The only smell is nicotine mixed with old and new sweat.

I grit my teeth. "Fucking tell me," I demand, bucking again, throwing my hips against him in a fruitless attempt to throw him off. It doesn't work. Surprise, surprise. He doesn't answer and I close my eyes as I contemplate my options. I try to think back to Cory's training, but the harder I try to remember the more my mind races away from it. Frustration wells up inside me, and my eyes begin to burn. Then the nearly soundless click of a switchblade opening has me jerking against his hold and my eyes shoot open once more. A flash of metal passes in front of my face and the intruder finally speaks.

"Don't move," he warns me, voice deep and gravelly—like a man who's smoked at least two packs of cigarettes a day for a decade or more. "Or you'll regret it."

Ice floods my arteries. *Or I'll regret it?* Why do *I* have to be the one with regret? Why can't it be everyone else?

I barely feel the blade as he skims my cheek with the flat side. The metal is no colder than the ice inside me. Down, down, down—the blade disappears from my sight but not from my body. The metal presses against my lower stomach where my sleep shirt has ridden up to reveal the stretch of skin above my pajama bottoms. The man turns it deftly, as if the weapon is a part of his body and easy to maneuver. With a sharp jerk, he yanks his hand up. My shirt pulls tight before it loosens far more than it should. When the thin cotton fabric of my pajama bottoms does the same a moment later and air slides over flesh exposed to the air, the room begins to spin.

Like that scene from the Wizard of Oz, everything rises up and floats for a moment before it begins to swirl at lightning speed, taking me with it. Around and around, I go until all I can feel is the wind against my sides and face. Witches on bicycles. Spinning Houses. A tornado from another world forces me to leave this plain even as my body remains firmly planted on the futon and the stranger cuts away the rest of my clothes and then my underwear.

This place feels frighteningly familiar. Like I've been here before and just like back then, I don't fit.

Cool air washes over my sex, the sensation so unnatural in this circumstance that it brings me back to reality. I crash into my body with all of the grace of an inexperienced skydiver. When I slam back into my flesh and bones, I realize that the man has released my wrists to reach for the front of his pants. My head turns slowly, latching on to the silvery metal of his switchblade tossed haphazardly on one of the pillows nearby. Moonlight pours in through the still-open sliding glass door, half the glass muted by the layers of grime I can never quite get off no matter how much I try to clean it. I reach out, seeking the knife with my fingers. Not that the intruder notices. No, he's far too fixated on the fact that he's managed to free himself from his pants and has a cunt in front of him. Gripping me by the hips, he drags me closer, hooking my legs over either side of his thighs as he shoves the scraps of my sleep shirt out of the way and grips a fistful of my breast, squeezing tight.

Frost on the back of my tongue slides into my throat, choking me as my fingers close around the switchblade's handle. I tighten my hold as sickness wells up within my chest, setting fire to the ice that's consuming me. I'm so fucking over people trying to hurt me because I'm my father's daughter. I'm not the one who stole from them. I'm not the one who ruined their lives. Do they care who they hurt, though? No. They are just as bad as him.

Principal Long's words come back to me. She wants me to talk to someone, to go see my father? I don't need that. What I need ... is a way to excise the rage spreading its poisonous veins through my body.

The intruder fumbles between my legs, not seeming to bother holding me down now that I've stopped moving—getting closer and closer. A strange sort of ... anticipation rests inside me, coiled like a snake waiting to strike. He fists himself, stroking up and down, pumping his cock as if it's not already hard.

The floaty Oz sensation changes. I can almost see myself lying here, eyes on the ceiling despite the fact that I'm more than aware of everything the man over me is doing. He mumbles something in that raspy voice of his, but I only catch a piece of it. "—cunt's gonna be good on my cock."

I tap the edge of one fingertip against the switchblade. Once, twice, three times. I stare up into the yawning darkness as I feel the hard plastic and rubber of the knife's grip. This is going to be messy. My mother would be so disappointed. Good girls aren't supposed to make messes. My lips curve upward. I'm not her good girl anymore—certainly not after tonight.

"They told me you'd fight harder, but I guess you want this, huh?" the guy says, his hand moving up and down his cock as he shifts forward on his knees.

My mind latches on to those words. *They? Who the fuck is they?*

My breath rushes in and out of my chest, filling me up, and yet I still feel lightheaded. It's as if a bubble has formed around me and keeps my mind and attention separated from my body. I continue to tap against the knife's handle as I consider where to stab him first. The side? No, not damaging enough. Maybe his kidneys. Yeah, one little slice to those fuckers and he'd bleed out fast. He'll die.

I like the thought of killing someone. Of finally being the one who gets to decide what the hell happens to me ... and what happens to the man trying to rape me.

The stranger pauses and I know without looking down that he's about to begin. He rises up between my legs, hand on his cock, directing it forward. Just as he means to drive himself into me—no preamble, no attempt to make sure he'll even get inside considering I'm as dry as a fucking bone—I twist my hips and the head of his cock slams into the crevice between my thigh and pelvis.

"Fuck!" He shouts. "Fucking bitch!"

A hand swipes out, his fist barreling towards my face. My head snaps to the side, pain radiating through my jaw, and I'm done—so. fucking. done.

Arching up and shoving my free hand against his chest, I reach around and slam the blade home. It cuts through the fabric of his shirt and then the flesh of his lower back easily. Muscle is a bit harder, though, and I have to grit my teeth—digging in even as he screams in pain. Laughter threatens to bubble out of my chest. I shove down on the blade, twisting the handle until I'm sure it's buried deep.

Then I rip it out and punch it in again. The first scream melds into another, rising in pitch as he shoves away from me. Finally, the laughter festering inside me breaks free. I look down at my hands as the man stumbles from the bed. They're covered in crimson.

"F ... uck. Ugh." I look up to see the intruder turning around, wavering on his feet as a dark stain blooms across the back of his gray shirt. I tilt my head to the side and watch him for a moment more as he tries to reach for the blade and pull it out. It's not going to happen.

Slowly I rise from the futon and look down at myself. I'm naked from the waist down, the only thing clinging to me are the remains of my big t-shirt, though the bottom part is cut up towards the underside of my breasts. The man's body slams into the opposite wall across from my futon, tripping over my backpack. It tips over and the items inside scatter across the floor.

I'm not sure if I actually hit his kidneys or not—the dim memory of Cory showing me which parts of the body were the most dangerous to get hit play like a grainy old black and white film in the back of my head. I take a step forward and another and another. The man moves away from me, back toward the balcony. I pause as my toes squish into something wet. Blood.

There's no remorse, no sorrow, no emotion. I feel decidedly numb as I lift my head and continue towards my would-be rapist.

"Get ... it ... out!" His voice is slurred, garbled as he tries to shout the words. His side slams into the wall that separates me from the apartment next to mine. I follow him at a much slower pace. He's grunting and cursing and acting for all of the world like a rabid animal. It's kind of funny. I bite my lower lip to keep from laughing again.

Behind me, the distant sound of a deep voice echoes through the barrier of my front door. I ignore it and focus on the man in my apartment as he curses and spins again, hands reaching out to remove the knife in his back. He doesn't even seem to be aware of me anymore. Then his head lifts and his eyes lock on mine. They're black, I realize. Well, maybe not black, but they're dark, and his pupils are so dilated that there's no hint of any actual color.

Rage infuses his expression, the pain receding as he growls and reaches for me, hands outstretched as if he wants to choke the life from me for hurting him—as if he wouldn't have hurt me even more. I stand still. When he gets close enough, I dodge in a circle and he follows. He spins towards me, following me right out onto the balcony.

"B-itch..." The slur in his voice rises above the yelling at my front door.

I might be a bitch, but at least I'm not a dead bitch. Not like him.

Without really thinking about it, I shove him, using both hands to push him right into the wooden railing. The flimsy decades-old barrier breaks, a loud *crack* sounding upon impact. His eyes widen in shock and then he screams. The sound echoes into the moonlit night as he careens over the edge. Right. To. The. Ground.

I pause at the edge, air sliding over my nearly naked form as I stare down at the man's twisted form. One leg is bent at an unnatural angle. His neck is twisted to the side and something white and red sticks out from his left arm. He doesn't move again. As the dust settles around the outline of his body, reality slams back into me.

The vomit I'd kept down earlier comes spewing forth. I turn and heave. The cheap mac and cheese meal I'd made for dinner splatters right onto the balcony's edge. Retching over and over, I barely notice the sound of splintering wood that filters in from the front of my apartment. I'm still on my knees, breathing through the heaving of my stomach as it cramps and tries to expel everything it no longer holds.

"Jesus Christ, Jules." Gio. I close my eyes. "What the fuck happened?"

I press my lips together, resisting the stabbing pains in my stomach to stop myself from vomiting again—or laughing. The wind whips through the balcony, the lack of a railing making it obvious that something terrible has happened here. I close my arms around myself and look down. I'm damn near naked. The stench of my own vomit permeates my nose.

Pretty girl ... pretty, pretty girl ... Those words circle around and around my head just like an evil witch's cackle. Except ... I think even the wicked witch wouldn't be so fucking cruel. I'm no one's 'pretty girl,' but I am ... a killer now and I'm not sorry.

"Fucking hell." Gio's bark makes me jump, but almost just as quickly as it sounds, soft fabric slides over my shoulders. My head snaps back. Gio stands over me, his face half-hidden in shadow, though not enough to hide the expression of confusion and surprise that deepens the crease between his brows.

"Baby?" The feminine voice comes from the front door and Gio turns, blocking me with his body.

"Go back to your apartment," he barks. "Don't fucking come here."

"But—"

"What the fuck did I say?" His tone is deep, angry. "Get lost!"

She gasps at the insult. Whatever she says next is lost on me, but she's gone a moment later and that's all that matters. Then Gio is bending down next to me, crouching on his toes as those soil-rich brown eyes of his bore into me. "You're okay," he says, his voice far lighter and kinder than it had been to the other woman. "You're going to be okay, Jules."

I blink back at him. Am I? I want to ask if he means that, because I don't feel okay. I feel like I did the night my dad was arrested—out of control and dead inside. It's as if I packed up all of my emotions into a box and shipped them somewhere far away.

Gio reaches into his pants—jeans, *was he sleeping in his jeans?* I wonder dimly—and pulls out a cell phone. I watch him punch at the keys before lifting the cell to his ear. I don't have to ask to know who he's calling. Who else would it be but the very men I promised myself I'd never trust?

Gripping the edges of the blanket that Gio had given me, I pull it closer, wrapping my body with it, hiding the truth of what happened. Of what I did.

I killed a man, and I liked it.

A bubble of hysterical laughter rockets up my throat. I shove my knuckles between my teeth and bite down to repress the sound, but a muffled noise makes it out. Looking back at Gio, I realize that his gaze is still locked on me, though seeing him is difficult through the curtain of water in my vision. *What the fuck—*

"It's okay," Gio murmurs, voice soft as he pulls me against his chest, against his warmth. "You can cry, Jules."

Cry? I shake my head. No. I don't need to cry. What I need is a mental hospital.

My thoughts splinter as I inhale, gasping and choking. Somehow, though, with Gio so close, the smell of his soothing cologne, spicy and rich, overwhelms me and erases the filthy odor of sweat and blood and a tainted memory that needs to remain buried.

28
JULIET

I'm cold, which is ironic since I'm pretty sure the body heat the three hulking men in my already tiny studio are throwing off should be enough to make this place feel like a sauna. Instead, I'm bundled up, kind of wishing I still had the expensive parka my mom had gotten me for Christmas three years ago. I'd only ever used it once, but it'd been big and fluffy, heavy enough to survive the frost of Aspen when we'd gone skiing for Christmas. I'm sure it'd warm me now.

The Scorpion Kings have stationed themselves throughout my apartment. Gio is out on the balcony, taking a look at the damage a man's body flying into the already piece of shit railing has caused. Lex is against the wall, arms crossed, expression indecipherable, but eyes eerily focused on me where I'm sitting on my futon that's now been shifted into its upright position.

"Okay, let's run through it again." Nolan's commanding presence seems to evoke a desire in me to throw something at his head. I glare at him but keep still on the futon as I hold the edges of the blanket together to hide my near-nakedness. Maybe if I throw something at him and see his reaction, it'll thaw some of the numbness I'm currently feeling.

"What's there to run through?" I ask. To my utter shock, my voice is raspy and raw. I cough and blink, frowning when the tightness in my throat doesn't ease. I shake my head and refocus on the man hovering above me. "I told you everything that happened exactly as it happened."

"That man came in, attacked you, and you stabbed him," Nolan says, repeating my earlier words. "He tries to escape and he falls over the balcony. I get that right?"

Well, I pushed him and therefore, killed him, but other than that, he's got everything right. I bob my head. Then a thought occurs to me. "Should I call the police?" Would they even give a fuck that the town outcast was nearly raped and murdered in her own apartment?

"No." I'm so caught up in my own thoughts that at first I think the answer is referring to my internal question before I recall that it's actually in response to the idea of calling the police.

Gio steps back into the apartment and closes the sliding glass doors before engaging the lock. For all of the good it did the first time. "No police—and most definitely not the police in Silverwood."

Nolan agrees with a nod. "He's right. All of Silverwood was affected by the embezzlement. The police department wouldn't bother to do much more than file a report—and that was before you killed a man. If they find out, they won't waste the chance to get rid of you just as anyone else would."

At least, they're honest. Their healthy dose of reality reminds me of the reason behind my current circumstances. "Do you think he was out for revenge?" I ask, glancing to the balcony.

"Probably," Gio says.

"Am I going to jail?" I ask the question in a quiet monotone, no inflection to reveal how I'm feeling about the possibility.

All three men exchange looks as the room goes silent.

When it stretches out, I glance up at them curiously. Each of their expressions are hard masks, and I sit there watching them talk in silent ticks and chin jerks, a language that's all their own. It's one I can't understand.

Turning away, I glance at the faded glowing digits on the microwave in my kitchen. 2:59 a.m. The witching hour. The hour when bad things happen. When nightmares come to life.

I'm the daughter of a criminal. Abandoned by my mother. Betrayed by my friends and ex. Now, I'm a murderer.

After a tense moment, Nolan speaks. "No," he says, drawing my attention back to him. "We're not going to let that happen."

Nolan's irises look like cinnamon in the light of the bare bulb that throws dull illumination across the floor of the apartment from my cracked bathroom door. A part of me wonders if they assumed my attacker wasn't acting alone, but if he hadn't been, then wouldn't someone have already come for his body?

I know if I go out there on the balcony right now, I'll look over the edge and find him still there—splayed out on the ground like a broken doll no one wants to play with anymore.

We're not going to let that happen. Nolan's words circle in my head, dizzying me with their insinuation.

"Why?" I ask, lifting my head and staring him down with a frown. "Why would you help me?"

Once again, there's that annoying exchange of looks between them and that secret, silent language of theirs. My upper lip curls away from my teeth. I hate being left out of the loop. It makes me want to stab something. Again.

Nolan sighs and looks back at me. "Don't worry about the whys of things," he says. "You need the help. We'll provide. Just accept it."

Just accept it? No. I move to stand, but the blanket around my knees gapes open, reminding me that I'm still mostly naked. For a moment, I contemplate sitting back down, but then decide to hell with it.

"You hate me," I remind them as if they've forgotten. "This whole town does. There's no way in hell you're helping me now out of the goodness of your heart. How do I know you weren't a part of this?"

I keep my gaze trained on Nolan, but it's Gio who moves towards me, jolting me out of the stare-down between his leader and I. Gio doesn't stop until he's shoved his way between Nolan and me.

Dimly, I think of how shitty a night it's been for my downstairs neighbors. No doubt they're getting about as much sleep as I am with all of the noise. It's almost lucky that I live in a shithole apartment complex. People in this neighborhood know to mind their own business. Even if they're annoyed or cranky, they keep to themselves and they don't ask any questions.

With his hands clenched into fists at his sides, Gio looms over me and growls, "We are not responsible for a man breaking into your apartment with the intention of raping you."

Rape. I'm proud of the way I don't flinch at the word. I never truly knew how powerful words could be until this moment. The word grows in size in my head, filling it until there's no spare inch not covered in a layer of what it means.

Someone broke into my apartment, pinned me down, threatened me, and...

I cut myself off at the reminder of how he'd held himself in front of me, stroking his cock as he'd prepared to put it inside me. I should've cut it off with the knife instead of stabbing him in the back with it.

My eyes rise back to Gio's. "How do I know that?" I prompt him. "It's not like we're friends. If anything, the three of you are part of the reason shit at school has been so difficult."

His brows shoot up to his hairline and his already hard jaw firms even further. "If you think we're like that asshole, then you don't know us very well."

"My point exactly." I nod at him. "I don't know you. So, why the hell should I trust you?"

Honey brown eyes narrow on my face. "Because we—"

"Gio." Nolan barks his friend's name, cutting him off and making me even more curious to know what he'd been about to reveal. Gio whips away from me and stalks back across the room until he's in front of the mangled door that he apparently kicked in when I didn't answer during my attack. I stare at his back for a moment before scanning the entryway.

The lock is a broken mess and the framework is completely splintered. The door itself is propped against the gaping hole to give the illusion of some privacy. He kicked it in and now it's useless, but I can't find it in myself to be frustrated. Even though it means I'll probably have to find a new place to stay until it gets repaired, I have to admit that at least he came when he heard trouble.

No one else would have.

No one else did.

The back of my head throbs and I sink back onto the futon, cupping my skull with a groan. "Fuck." Now I have to think about staying somewhere else.

Motels might seem cheap as shit, but no matter how inexpensive a place is, the cost inevitably builds up over time and there's no telling how long it'll take for my apartment to be livable. The Ritchies don't strike me as particularly caring towards their residents. I'd found dead bugs painted over the walls when I moved in. What's worse is that I can't afford any other place now that most of the money I had is sunk into the advance rent I paid weeks before. If I can't stay here, I doubt the Ritchies will refund me. Scratch that. There is absolutely no doubt that they'll happily kick me out for damaging their property and keep my rent payments as compensation. I'd considered myself lucky I even managed to get this place after the bullshit of my father's embezzlement and the fact that I had no previous rental or job history.

I'm so caught up in the loss and figuring out my immediate future, that I've almost forgotten about the three men taking up residence inside the destroyed apartment. That is, until the sound of male voices brings me back to the present. I raise my head and frown at Nolan and Lex as the two have moved closer together, their heads bowed as they speak in low tones. The crease of Lex's brow and the hard set of Nolan's mouth tells me they're arguing.

"She's welcome wherever I am," Lex snaps.

I straighten up. "What?"

Both Nolan and Lex glance over at me. "You can come stay with me," Lex says before gesturing to the door Gio's blocking. "At least until your door is fixed."

Gio places a hand against the wood, the inked tattoos on the back of his palm flexing with the movement. "The maintenance team of this complex is pretty lax," he states. "It'll take at least a week for them to fully fix the damn thing."

Gio looks back but not at me. He focuses on Nolan. "I think we should board this up before morning. Otherwise, she's liable to have raccoons getting inside ... or worse." I don't have to ask what the 'or worse' could be. If tonight has taught me anything, there's always a worse.

My gaze remains firmly latched on Lex. "You want me to come stay with you?" I ask, my brow furrowing. From what I remember of his background, he lives on the outskirts of Silverwood with his aunt after his parents' deaths.

Lex nods even as Nolan lets loose a curse. "Not fucking happening," Nolan growls.

Lex's stone-gray eyes collide with Nolan's. "She *can't* stay here," he argues.

"And she won't," Nolan replies. "She'll stay with me."

For a moment, I think I've somehow fallen asleep and

entered another of my nightmares, or maybe this is the Twilight Zone.

"Um." I raise a hand, drawing all of their attention. "Do I get a say in this?" If it comes down to a choice between Lex and Nolan, I'm not even sure which would be the safer option, but all in all ... a motel is probably in my immediate future. A week might set me back savings-wise, but if I tell Ma-Ri I'm willing to work some host shifts at the lounge, then I'm sure I can make up for it. It won't be forever.

All three men shoot me looks and answer as one. "*No.*"

Well, that solves that question. I lower my hand and sigh. "Well, regardless of where I'm going after this, I need to get dressed."

Gio frowns as I get to my feet, keeping the blanket locked around my legs. "What about a hospital?" he asks. "Do we need to take you to see a doctor?"

My feet come to a stop in front of my closet door. I glance down at the floor, at my bare feet peeking out beneath the quilted puke green and brown blanket I'd picked up in a Goodwill clearance bin because it looked like it would be warm. *What if he had an STD?* He hadn't managed to put his cock in, but he had touched me. He'd bled all over me too.

Blood is filthy. It's full of bacteria and disease. I stare at the red splatter on the edge of my hand, at the creases in my skin that are full of crimson. I need a shower. A scalding, disgustingly hot shower. Even then ... I don't know if I'll get rid of the feeling of his hands on me, of his cock getting so close.

It didn't happen, I remind myself. Even so, my head floods with images of what could have happened and what might still happen in the future. *I didn't let it happen.*

I begin to shake uncontrollably. My whole body trembles beneath the blanket as something akin to rage and horror dawns over me.

"Jules?" Gio's voice sounds far away and my ears are full of wind.

Bodies move around me, coming closer, but all I can do is lock onto my body hidden beneath this hideous blanket and wish for x-ray vision. I want to be able to see past flesh and bone and muscle, to know if I've been violated in another way, a new, sicker way. I swallow reflexively to keep vomit down.

"I need a shower," I mumble to myself. "I need..." *Clean.* I need to get clean. I want to scrub my skin until it's raw and bloody and there's no cell left on or within me that has ever been touched by another person.

A hand that feels too hot lands lightly on my shoulder. I'm gently turned around and then Nolan's face is in front of mine. "We'll get you to a doctor, Juliet," he says quietly. "Don't worry. Whatever happens, we'll make sure you're checked out."

I part dry, cracked lips. "He—" I stop and swallow again before trying anew. "He didn't..." The words are a struggle to get out.

Nolan seems to understand what I'm trying to say though. He nods sharply. "Okay, but if you still want to go, we'll take you. No questions asked." His eyes bore into mine. The tight muscle in his jaw throbs as he clenches his teeth and then releases a slow breath to speak—as if he's trying to calm himself.

"I don't want…" I shake my head. Fuck. Why can't I just talk? Nothing even happened to me. *Almost* isn't the same thing as actually being raped. Still, my skin crawls with invisible insects and my stomach cramps with the urge to vomit all over again.

Once more, Nolan seems to understand my non-words. "No one will know," he assures me.

"No doctor?" I don't even feel his hands on my shoulders anymore as I stare up into eyes like blood-soaked earth. Cinnamon and chocolate in his gaze.

His jaw flexes, an obvious sign that he doesn't like my decision. "We can't force you, but if you start feeling weird, you *are* getting checked out. I'll drag you to a clinic by your hair if I have to, do you understand?"

No. I don't understand a damn thing, but I nod anyway as all the breath in my lungs escapes.

Nolan releases my shoulders and nudges me toward the bathroom. "Go ahead and get showered," he says. "I'll grab you some clothes." His eyes move down my body, taking in the threadbare blanket, the blood on my hands, and my bare feet against the floor. "Don't take too long. We can't stay. Get clean and make it fast or I'm coming in after you."

With a scowl, I step back and slip into the bathroom, shutting and locking the door behind me. The blanket loosens and then slips to the floor. I turn and regard myself in the cracked mirror over the sink. Slowly, I scan the length of my reflection. One side of my face is flushed red. Bruises are already forming on my hips and thighs. None of that bothers me. I lift my hands and hold them in front of me. My left hand has a droplet or two of blood but is otherwise pristine. My right hand though ... is covered in dried, flakey blood.

I can't bring myself to look in the mirror again. Instead, I lower my hands and turn to the cubicle of a shower—cranking the hot water knob until steam billows out from behind the plastic curtain. I find a towel under the sink and set it on the lid of the toilet. My hands are steady as I reach up and remove what remains of the t-shirt I'd worn to bed. Letting it join the blanket on the floor, I step into the piping hot water and let the warmth drive back the ice inside me.

The first pass of soap over my skin gets rid of the flakes of blood, but it doesn't change the way I feel. The second pass is a bit better, but it's as if that asshole's blood has turned invisible. I stare at my hands as I scrub until I see no more evidence of him on me. Even when I can't see him, though, I can still feel him. I grit my teeth and scratch at my wrist and arm. I scrub and rub soap over me until the water runs cold. Nothing helps. The feeling of him is so far beneath my skin that it's burrowed into my very pores. A knock on the door stills my hands.

"Hurry up in there," I hear Nolan call out. "Your time is almost up."

My hands and arms are an angry red, but I have no doubt that Nolan Pierce means it when he says he'll come in here and drag me out if I put off facing them. I can't afford another broken door. So, I switch to my hair, shampooing, conditioning, scrubbing, and scratching at my scalp as though that'll alleviate the feeling of bugs crawling all over my skin. It doesn't.

The second knock on the door a few minutes later halts any plans to start washing all over again. "I'm coming!" I call out, shutting off the water.

"I've got a pair of sweats and a tank here for you. I'm going to set it on the floor here." Nolan's deep baritone enters the room as I hear the door creak open. I go still. I locked the door. I know I fucking did.

Gripping the edge of the plastic curtain, I yank it to the side, making sure to cover my nakedness as I glare across the small room at him. "How the fuck did you open the door?" I demand. "I locked it."

Nolan lifts his head, cinnamon eyes sliding down to my bare shoulder immediately before slowly lifting to my face. One dark brow arches. "It's a cheap lock, Princess," he says. "It's not difficult to pick." He nods down to the clothes he laid on the floor. "Gio and Lex are going to run out and grab a few things. Get dressed. They'll be back soon."

My mouth hangs open as he shuts the door behind him.
What. An. Asshole.

I shut off the water and step out, grabbing the towel off the toilet and drying off as I pick up the clothes he left for me. No bra or underwear. Nolan probably thought I was wearing them.

I shake my head. Guys don't understand that girls don't wear bras any more than they have to. As for my underwear ... I clench the elastic tie of my sweatpants' waistband as tight as it'll go. There's no use pointing out the reason I'm not wearing any. My pajamas weren't the only thing my attacker had cut away.

Nolan stands in the combo living room and bedroom with his phone in his hands as he types furiously away. When the bathroom door swings shut behind me, making a creaking noise, he looks up. His eyes move from my face down to my breasts and I know just when he realizes what he forgot. He blinks as his lips part. My nipples pebble against the thin fabric of the tank, but I don't rush to hide them. There's no point. I just turn away, rubbing my hair with the towel to hasten the drying process.

After a beat, Nolan clears his throat. "You good?" I snort and rub faster. "Okay," he amends, "do you feel any better now that you've had a shower?"

I glance at him. "Marginally," is all I say.

With a frown, he turns away and stalks across the studio. Leaning into the tiny closet that acts as storage and clothing space, he flips through my meager belongings. A moment later, he pulls back and turns, holding out a giant oversized sweater. His upper lip curls away from his teeth as he skims an eye down the jagged pastel stripe print that belongs on a '70s paper cup.

"Couldn't find anything uglier?" he asks.

Rolling my eyes, I rip the towel away from my hair and drop it to the floor before stalking towards him. I rip the sweater from his grasp and yank it on before crossing my arms over my chest.

"I'll let you know when I'm taking fashion advice from a guy who thinks motorcycle boots go with his football jersey."

He glances down and then back up with that same arched brow as if to tell me 'I'm not wearing my jersey.' I narrow my eyes. The fact that he's not wearing it *right now* doesn't matter —I'd seen him wear them in tandem at school many times before. When neither of us voices the internal battle we're having after a few more moments of pure, spiteful silence, I turn away.

"So," I begin, glancing from side to side, looking for the others before I remember what he'd said about them running out for something. I return my eyes to him. "What now?"

Nolan moves into the kitchen and leans down to pick up a duffle I hadn't noticed before. It looks like one of the sports bags given out to all of the guys on the football team, but the top is unzipped, revealing clothes from my own closet. And that's not all. The box with Lex's cell phone gift in it is packed right on top and beneath it, my laptop.

"Now, I'm going to take you home and you're going to get some sleep." With his free hand, he shuffles the broken door out of the way and holds it for me to pass under his arm.

"You really expect me to come home with you?" I blink at him. "Just like that?"

He tilts his head to the side, a dark lock of hair falling over one side of his forehead. "Do you have any better choices right now?"

I press my lips together, hating that the fact is I don't. Even if I can find a motel to stay at, there aren't any close to the school. With a sigh, I glance around and find my sneakers half-buried beneath the futon. I don't bother looking for socks and just stick my feet inside before reaching down and fixing the back lip so it doesn't get stuck and folded beneath my foot.

Ducking beneath Nolan's arm, I spy Lex's SUV turning into the parking lot. The headlights are off, which means he doesn't want anyone to notice him. I watch him as he drives past Nolan's bike and the dark red car parked at the front of my apartment building, heading around to the back. Half-turned, I peer back at Nolan as he follows me from the apartment, turning to grip the broken door and angle it back over the opening.

"What about the—" I cut myself off with a grimace before I say too much. Even if the people of Silver Creek Apartments mind their business, it'll do me no good to borrow trouble and say anything out loud.

They're going to get rid of the body.

Nolan's eyes glitter in the darkness of the night as he looks back at me, hefting the duffle bag up higher on his shoulder. "Gio and Lex will come back and board this up for you," he says, not answering my unfinished question.

There's no question about whether or not the Scorpion Kings are dangerous men. A murder happened here tonight, and not a single one of them flinched. They're taking the body of the man I killed, and they're making it all disappear. What should fill me with relief, only fills me with wariness.

"This is a debt." One I'm not sure I'll like paying back, much less be able to.

Those red-brown eyes of his are twin pools of something hypnotic. When a thumb touches the side of my cheek and I flinch at the sudden pain it brings, I realize he's not looking into my eyes so much as he's examining me. I'd seen the redness on my cheek in the bathroom mirror, but I hadn't realized how much it hurt until he touched it.

"Don't think about what you might owe us, Princess," he tells me. "For tonight, just think about getting some rest."

I shouldn't trust him. I shouldn't trust any of them. I know that. Yet ... I'm fucking tired. More tired than I've ever been in my life and I just want to close my eyes and pretend like tonight never happened. If that means I'll owe the Scorpion Kings a debt in the future then so be it. Some things are worth selling your soul—killing the man that tried to rape me is one.

29
LEX

"Do you know him?" Gio's question isn't a surprise. If anyone is familiar with the criminals that infest Silverwood, it would be me. Though, considering that all three of us are more than familiar with backdoor deals and murder, he could be asking himself and Nolan that same question.

Unfortunately, he won't have to because my answer is yes.

I lean over the man splayed out on the ground in the narrow walkway between Juliet's building and the next. My nose twitches at the acrid scent of urine and shit. Reaching into my back pocket, I feel around for a cigarette pack. When I come up empty, I curse, but Gio is already there, holding one out for me as well as a lighter.

With a grateful grunt, I take it and put the cigarette between my lips before responding. "He's a criminal for hire," I tell him out of the corner of my mouth. "Name's Otis. I've seen him around."

Flame bursts to life in front of my face as the two of us stand over the body of the man who attacked Juliet Donovan. I burn the end of my cigarette and then return the lighter to Gio. The bastard is lucky he died before I got here.

Gio's stare burns into the side of my face. "Is Otis a first or last name?"

I shrug.

Gio shifts at my side, crouching down and using a nearby stick to poke at the man's head, moving back the hair so we can get a better look at his face. The burn scar that covers his jaw and moves down his throat is enough of an identifying marker, but no doubt Gio isn't familiar with him. Otis kept away from the actual gangs of the town.

"You think someone hired him or he came on his own?"

The nicotine rush is much needed after a night like tonight, especially since my girl is going home with Nolan and not me.

"He didn't strike me as all that smart," I say. "Not a real self-thinker." Someone put him up to this. Someone wants to hurt Juliet. When I find out who, I'm going to enjoy flaying them alive.

Gio drops the stick and gets back to his feet, hands on his hips. The longer I look at the piece of shit on the ground, the more my gut twists. What if Gio hadn't been here? What if he hadn't heard her fighting with the bastard? An insidious urge swells within me and I have no reason to keep it contained. After blowing out a long tendril of smoke, I put the cig back between my lips and hold it in place as I reach for the front of my pants and unzip.

Gio's head whirls towards what I'm doing before he really thinks about it. A curse slips free of his lips as revulsion rolls across his features. "Seriously, man? Here?"

"You can leave if you want, but I gotta take a leak." The words form around the cig in my mouth. Holding my cock, a jet stream of piss rockets out of the head and right onto the corpse of the man that attacked my girl. Gio throws up his hands and turns around completely.

He's seen his fair share of death and violence, but he's still a halfway decent person. I'm not, and I don't give two shits about desecrating the body of a bottom feeder. I shake the last few droplets over the fucker's face before tucking myself back into my pants and zipping up.

"We should hurry up and get this place cleaned up," he suggests. "It'll be dawn in a few hours."

He's right. The people on this side of Silverwood know better than to poke their noses into shit that ain't none of their business. They know better than to peek their heads out at the sounds of a domestic disturbance and ask questions. A nosy bitch is a dead bitch. Still, it won't do to leave Otis' corpse rotting out here any longer than necessary.

"Get the tarp," I order, jerking my chin toward my SUV a few yards away where the pavement ends and the grass begins.

"Roger that." Gio jogs away and I pinch the cigarette between two fingers, ashing it over the body at my feet. *Shit-stain motherfucker.*

My upper lip curls back as rage, white-hot and violent, spears through me. I know the reason Nolan took Juliet away, the reason he'd refused to let me take her home with me. Of the three of us, his place is the most normal. She'll need normalcy. Not the isolation I could offer out on my aunt's farm. It's unspoken that she wouldn't be safe at Gio's either. If anyone would off the daughter of Allen Donovan just to prove a point—that he's the most badass motherfucker in Silverwood—it'd be Darrio.

Gio returns in record time, unfolding the dark swath of plastic material on the ground. I hold the cig in place as I go for the legs, and together, we lift Otis' body onto the tarp before wrapping it up like some morbid Christmas present. A snort escapes and I nearly drop my cig from my lips as I fold one corner of the tarp over the body.

"What?" Gio glances up and frowns at me.

I shake my head, but then, because the thought intruded and I can't seem to help myself, I ask, "You think if we dropped this on Pillard's front lawn he'd shit himself?"

"Brandon Pillard? Prep's defensive lineman?"

The shriek of duct tape pulling away from its roll is loud in the night as I rip off several strips and toss the roll to Gio. "Yeah, her ex," I say by way of explanation.

He catches the flying roll of duct tape. "You're a fucking psychopath," he mutters with a shake of his head, then smirks. "But yeah, that little fucker would probs shit his pants and pass out."

The two of us chuckle at the image as we get to work. Within five minutes, we've got the body taped shut. We lift the big ass form and cart it over to the still-open back of my SUV and with a swinging toss, Otis' body crashes against the floorboards. The bloody stains inside the plastic make me grin. Then, I notice an odd sort of bulge around the lower side of his back.

The knife, I realize, as her recollection of the attack resurfaces in my head. She'd stabbed him in the back. I make a mental note to pull the knife free before we start the process of stripping the body later. If I clean it well enough, she might like it as a gift.

I blow out another stream of smoke and shut the hatch. "What about the cameras?" Gio asks, nodding up to the burned-out light pole and a black half-globe that's stationed towards the top. I roll my eyes and drop the cigarette to the pavement, crunching the end under one boot before reaching down and lifting the remains to deposit into my pocket.

Killing is one thing. Body disposal, another. But littering? Completely unnecessary.

"It's fake," I tell him. "They haven't replaced those lights in months. This complex is cheap as fuck." Something that has been a constant annoyance since the day Juliet moved in. I'd had to rely on traffic cameras and security feeds from the stores across the street to spy on her. The lack of light had probably emboldened the motherfucker that had attacked her. Bet that made him feel real safe climbing into her apartment and—I cut that thought off with a curse and turn away, stomping towards the front of the SUV. Gio follows and gets into the passenger seat.

Cranking the engine, I keep the headlights off as I ease around the side of the apartment building. "What are you doing?" Gio swivels to look at me, his brows creased with confusion.

I gesture to the front of Juliet's apartment. "Got some planks in the back seat," I tell him. "We need to make sure no one is breaking in while she's away."

"Oh, right." Gio climbs out of the seat and reaches into the back to withdraw the wood planks and some nails. I stay in the car, keeping my eyes on the rearview mirror and the area as he does his job. Twenty minutes later, he clomps back to the SUV, hammer in one hand and a familiar backpack in the other. When he hops back into the SUV, he stows it at his feet. "Nolan forgot it when they left," he explains.

My chest swells with excitement. Returning her backpack will give me another reason to see her.

"We'll have to come back for Nolan's bike," Gio says as he looks over at the Indian parked by the curb.

I grunt my response. "Later." We ease out of the parking lot, just under the speed limit. "No one will mess with it," I say. "Everyone in town knows it's his."

"He better not fuck up *my* ride," Gio huffs. "I don't like anyone—even him—driving my baby."

Once we're on one of the main roads, I flip my lights back on and slow at a red light. "If she ends up back in that apartment, I want cameras inside."

The sharp sensation of someone watching me pricks at my senses. I don't have to look over to know Gio's staring at me. "Because you want to protect her or because you want to stalk her?" he asks after a beat.

A snarl of warning works its way up my throat. "Stalkers escalate," I snap. "I haven't fucking touched her." No matter how much I want to. No matter how much I crave knowing what it feels like to have her naked body under me, on top of me. To taste her sex. To pin her down and fuck her until she screams. To lead her into my den of deviancy and show her everything—all of the pictures and videos of her that I've kept over the years. To have her accept me ... and ultimately, to let me keep her.

"It's only a matter of time, bro," Gio says.

I grit my teeth and punch the gas as the light changes to green. Seething in the silence that follows, I try to tamp down the desire to take out all of this anger on the man sitting next to me. Gio and Nolan aren't my enemies. They're my brothers. Bound in blood. Forged in fire. Raised in darkness. Without them, I'd be too far gone to even be remotely human.

Without them. Without *her*. I am nothing if not a bag of skin, bones, and blood walking.

"I still want cameras in her place if she goes back," I repeat.

With a groan, Gio laces his fingers together and stretches them forward in front of himself and then up. "If I can get in, I'll make it happen," he says. "It'll be safer all around to have you look after her anyway—Nolan should be fine with it too, just in case she catches wind about Rich and Josh disappearing."

My head swivels to the side as I slow around a bend in the road. "She killed a man tonight," I snap. "Why the fuck would we care if she finds out now?"

"Jesus, watch the fucking road!" Gio shouts, his hands slapping the dash.

I snap forward and curse, swerving around a deer skipping across one side of the road. "Shit, sorry."

Gio leans in and breathes. "God, I thought you'd almost wrecked this shit. Nolan would've been pissed."

I roll my eyes. "No, he wouldn't. He wanted to do upgrades on the SUV anyway. No doubt, he'd love the opportunity, but back to the cameras. You're good with putting them in if needed?"

"Unless you'd rather do it yourself?" Gio releases the dashboard to sit up in his seat.

Get back into her space? Touch her things? Languish in her scent? My cock throbs. No. It's not a good idea at all. I shake my head. "No, it's probably better if you go."

We drive out of Silverwood, hopping on a back highway that lost most of its traffic the day a nearby interstate exit had been built. Now, it's mainly used by farmers and locals looking to avoid slow-downs and wrecks.

Several minutes pass in near silence and then, Gio speaks up again. "I don't want you getting close to her while she's with us."

My hands tighten on the steering wheel. "I don't know what you mean."

His attention sears against my jaw. "Yeah, you do." Spoken in a low tone but no less firm, the words strike at me. "You're in love with her. She's not sticking around."

"Then why are we helping her?" I demand. "Why is Nolan taking her back to his home? Why are we getting rid of the body of a man she killed?"

For a long moment, Gio doesn't reply, but when he does, I almost swerve right off the road. "For you. We're doing it for you."

If I weren't driving, I'd close my goddamn eyes at that statement. "Nolan and I know you're no virgin, but you might as fucking well be," he continues. "Those chicks you take back to the carriage house? They're not girlfriends."

No. They're not. The women I fuck in the rebuilt carriage house I live in on my aunt's property are paid for their time. And despite their choice of employment, I make damn sure they enjoy everything I do—as if they're the woman I want more than my next breath, more than my own life. As if they're Juliet Donovan herself. I don't mind Gio knowing my business. I'd have gone crazy by now if I didn't have someone to confide in. But what I do mind is the fact that his words—his claim—are a lie.

The front of the SUV shudders as I push the speedometer past seventy, flying down the darkened highway and beyond Silverwood's town boundary.

"You want her too." The words hang between us, the silence in the air before and after them making them louder than they actually were. Gio doesn't say anything. He doesn't refute it but neither does he confirm it.

"You tested her when she first came to Silverwood Public," I continue. "You were curious. You wanted to know why I've watched her for so long." If Gio knows me down to my core, then I know him just as well. "She surprised you, and now you get it. You see what I see."

Juliet Donovan is more than a woman. She's an addiction. An obsession. Every look, every touch, every breath she takes is a slow-acting poison. By the time you realize you're dying, you're too fucking hooked to ever let her go.

An hour later, after we've hit the edge of Silverwood's town limits, I slow and pull down a dirt path. The SUV's 4-wheel drive gets a workout, bouncing along the unpaved path. The headlights wash over the darkness of the forest, illuminating the base of the trees that line the road. Finally, after another fifteen minutes, I slow when I spy the gates that are held closed by a twist of rusted metal links. Gio pops the passenger door before the vehicle even fully stops. I watch through the windshield as he stomps towards the chains and unlocks them before pushing the gates open wide enough for the vehicle to pass through. I get to the other side and let the SUV idle as he closes the gate once more and jumps back inside.

It takes another five minutes from the gate to get to the old hunting cabin my parents used to own. I ignore the cabin's driveway set before the slanted metal roof, smudged windows, and sagging front porch. The SUV bumps and sways as I drive right up over the boundary line of the grass and around to the even older outbuilding in the back.

When I stop, I cut the lights and the engine. Both Gio and I get out of the SUV, circling around to the back. "Chainsaw still in there?" he asks, nodding to the dilapidated shack that doubles as a garage when we need it.

"Where else would it be?" I pop the back and stand back to let the door rise all the way up.

The scent of death is thankfully muffled by the tarp. There's no point in using any of the cash I've squirreled away on getting a new car when I can keep this one from smelling of urine and decay.

"After we're done here, we might want to double-check Juliet's place for any more evidence. She said she stabbed the guy, so we'll have to scrub the floors and balcony."

I never thought I'd be so grateful for the summers we spent helping Gio's mom make extra cash by cleaning houses. We know all we need to get blood out of anything. God, I want another cigarette. I eye Gio, debating on if I should ask him for another, but we're about to open up a shit ton of chemicals. I better not.

"I'll send an email to Mr. Ritchie and tell him we took a prank too far or something to explain the door and other shit." Gio scrubs a hand down the back of his head. "He'll be pissed, but I'll send him a couple hundred to cover damages."

I snort. "That's more than either of those doors or the railing was worth."

"It'll keep him happy, though I doubt he'll be fixing it any time soon," Gio replies. "You know how he is—always has to find the cheapest deal for any repairs."

Having Juliet reliant on the three of us for longer? That's just fine with me.

"Alright." I return my attention to the body in the back of my SUV. "Let's get this fucker inside and start the process."

G stares at the tarp-wrapped corpse for a second before releasing a snort. When I arch a brow his way, he shakes his head. "I'm rocking a B in chemistry," he tells me as if that explains the sudden outburst of amusement.

"So?" I reach for one end of the body and use the loose plastic around it to drag it closer to the edge of the compartment.

Gio reaches for the other side. "You'd think I'd do better in a subject I'm so damn good at outside of the classroom."

I pause, the body still lying sideways in my trunk. "Huh." I crack my neck to one side. "I never considered that."

It does take a considerable amount of knowledge and know-how to disintegrate a human body, bones and all. We'd learned that a few months after killing Xavier Pierce. We'd returned to the hunting shack only to find a bunch of wild animals digging the old man up. There'd still been pieces of him left. One thing to be said for the human race other than the fact that we breed like rabbits is that we're durable even after death.

With a groan, Gio takes his half and I take mine. "On three, we lift," he commands. I wait and as his lips form around the numbers, I heft the body up onto one shoulder as he does the same. "Fuck, this asshole's heavy," he complains as we head for the shed.

"Not for long," I remind him. With enough lye solution and time, any amount of human weight can be overcome. Human remains are much easier to handle when they're watered down, and more than that, I hate burying bodies. It's honestly one of the least effective ways to make one disappear.

30
JULIET

Nolan's place is not what I would have predicted. When he pulls into a gravel driveway in front of the one-story, cottage-style house, I expect him to back right out because he missed the correct address somewhere amongst the various streets and turns we took to get here. He doesn't.

Instead, Nolan shuts off the Pontiac Firebird that might have once been a bright cherry red, but over time has become a faded orange-red. From what I'd heard of Gio's love for his Firebird, I'm surprised Nolan appeared so comfortable in the driver's seat. A car is a luxury for the kids of southern Silverwood, and yet it's clear that the Scorpion Kings share their things—even if they're important to them. It almost makes me respect them, or at the very least, their comfort and trust in one another.

What would it be like to have that?

The lights of the Firebird dim and Nolan gets out of the car, pocketing the keys before popping the front seat forward to retrieve the duffle bag of my stuff. I open the passenger door, and the loud groan it makes causes me to jump in the near silence of the rest of the neighborhood.

Looking around, I take in the darkened street corners and empty sidewalks. It's not a bad neighborhood, more well-maintained than my complex for sure. Although some of the lawns are overgrown and there are plenty of fences in need of repair, there aren't any boarded-up windows or cars on cinder blocks.

Nolan appears at my side, shutting the car door with a quick movement. I go still at his nearness and then slowly lift my gaze to his. At first, I think he's going to mock me for living in a place that's below his own. Perhaps he'll scoff and snarl that I shouldn't get used to this because I'll be going right back as soon as my apartment is fixed up.

Then again, why the hell would he or any of the Scorpion Kings offer to shelter me in the first place?

That question has been an ever-present curiosity in my mind since I walked out of my studio and got into the car. The Scorpion Kings are supposed to *hate* me. This whole fucking town hates me. Why would they bother to help me now?

"Come on," is all Nolan says, turning and heading up the front steps.

I follow behind him at a sedate pace, watching him as he unlocks the front door and holds it wide for me to pass through. I duck under his arm and look around. The first room reveals a small living area with a single three-seater couch, chipped box-like coffee table, and a lamp in the corner that belongs in the grandma section of the local thrift store. There's only one thing on the wall—a painting that's too faded for me to see well in the dim lighting. The newest thing in the room is the flat screen mounted on the wall.

The front door closes at my back and the lock is flipped, the sound of it echoing around the square room. Glancing back at Nolan, I swallow around a dry, swollen tongue.

"Where's your..." I don't finish. I was about to ask where his parents are before I remembered that Nolan's dad had gone missing a few years back.

'Missing' meaning he'd probably up and run away from his responsibilities. At least, that's what most of the town assumed. Though there had been a good month or so following that people had speculated that Nolan, himself, had killed the man. Considering how well he's taking my own recent murder, I'm starting to wonder if he actually did kill his father.

Would it bother me if he did? I wait, anticipating a rush of disgust or even unease, but nothing comes. Why would it? After all, if he's a killer then so am I now. *Either I'm fucked in the head or I just realized there are worse things to be than a killer.*

"My mom's on night shift," Nolan says, answering my unfinished question. I nod, and he gestures to the hallway to the right of the living room. "Bedrooms are this way."

I trail Nolan in silence, letting him lead me through the house and feeling almost detached from my own body. My feet shuffle forward as my earlier questions come back to haunt me.

The Scorpion Kings *do* hate me, don't they? They have no reason to like me. But enemies don't get rid of bodies for each other. I narrow my gaze on the back of Nolan's head.

It's a debt, I remind myself. *A debt that they'll no doubt collect at some point.*

As I follow Nolan down the hallway, I rub my hands up and down my arms. My skin, though clean, feels stretched tight over my bones. So tight that any added movement on my part pulls and tugs at the flesh, making my body feel too small. I've never felt as if I were too big for my own skin. I don't like the sensation.

Nolan leaves the hallway light off, bypassing the switch, but stops next to a tiny slit of a doorway and reaches inside. I flinch when dull yellow light illuminates the space, and though he doesn't seem to notice my reaction, he pulls the door to what looks like a bathroom mostly shut. The action leaves only the barest sliver of light to shine over the faded dark carpet underfoot.

Nolan points to the room across from the bathroom, gesturing for me to go ahead of him. "In here."

I stop on the threshold. "This is your room." It's a statement, not a question.

"Yes, it is." Nolan nudges me, and I take one halting step inside.

The bedspread is a dark plaid pattern that can be bought at any general store. It's folded back, the double mattress bed made with military precision. Aside from that, there's little else in the room. A bench press, some weights, football gear in the corner, and a rickety-looking desk and chair combo that I refuse to believe Nolan actually uses.

Looking at the desk's practically concave seat and then back at the man eyeing me with dark curiosity, I shake my head. He's far too fucking big to sit in that chair. He's built like the football player he is. It'd break under the weighty mass of him.

"Disappointed?" Nolan asks when I don't say anything else.

I don't respond, instead taking another step into the room and turning in a circle. There's no sour smell, no hint of body odor or days-old sweat. It's clean and fresh, the scent more like laundry soap and cotton than what I'd expected a man's room to smell like.

Warm heat touches my back and my gaze unfocuses. The room goes blurry for a split second as Nolan's hot breath hits my ear, nearly burning my skin when he speaks. "Did you think I was rich, Princess?" His voice is low, deep. "There are only two bedrooms, and I'm not asking my mom to give up her bed—she works too damn hard to give it up for someone like you."

"Someone like me?" I pivot to face him. "What kind of person is that?" Before he gets a chance to answer, more words shoot out of my mouth. "The kind whose parents are criminals and deadbeats? The kind who kills a man that tries to rape her?" I laugh, but the sound is anything but amused. "Hell, maybe I belong in the gutter more than any of you. Maybe it was just an accident that I was born a Donovan and this is the universe's way of righting that wrong."

Nolan's dark eyes stare into mine. He doesn't speak and doesn't respond to my assessment. Instead, the two of us stand there, our gazes locked in battle. The only problem is ... I don't know what we're fighting for.

"We're bunking together," he says, breaking the tension.

I back away from him, my breaths rushing in and out in uneven spurts. He's too close, too big, too much. The bare hint of light from the bathroom in the hall does nothing to help me. Without the overhead light on, I'm reliant on that singular beam of illumination as well as the moonlight coming in through his bedroom window.

Nolan steps closer, following my retreat. My heart jumps against my ribcage, thumping in a rapid unsteady beat. The urge to flee overwhelms me. He must see that in my eyes too because upon his next shift forward, he speaks. "Where else are you gonna go, Jules?" The question is presented in a low tone. It's not sarcastic, it's not cruel, but merely curious.

When I don't answer immediately, he reaches out and flicks the light switch. The whole room is bathed in the yellow glow, and I close my eyes against the glare. Relief slides through my veins a split second before I snap my eyes open again when his fingers brush my arm. I take another step into the room, the backs of my legs bumping into the bench press, causing me to stop and glare up at him.

"I can go to a motel." I *can*, but I don't want to. Not that I'll tell him that.

"You got the money for that, Princess?" He arches a brow. "I thought you didn't even have the cash to pony up for a phone."

I grit my teeth, annoyed and far beyond humiliated. "That's none of your fucking business."

Nolan tilts his head to the side, a strand of sable hair falling over his forehead giving him a boyish look. It's not fair. He shouldn't look boyish. He should look like the conniving and manipulative motherfucker that he is.

Why did I come here again?

I supply an answer even as I think the question—I'm still in shock. He used that to his advantage.

Or maybe you don't want to be alone after what happened, a snide inner voice whispers back.

Nolan backs away just as quickly as he advanced. He turns and hefts the duffle bag from his shoulder onto the bed and strides to the open closet in the corner. Reaching inside, he withdraws something and then heads back for the door.

"I'm going to get changed and grab a drink," he says. "Do you want anything?"

I shake my head before I realize he can't see it with how he's facing the doorway. "No, thanks." Gratitude sounds a bit awkward considering who he is, considering who *I* am, but I get the words out anyway.

Nolan doesn't taunt me for it. He just gives me a firm nod and leaves the room, shutting the door on his way out, leaving me alone. I'm not leaving. There will be no motel, not just because he's right—I don't have the money for one—but because it would be stupid to be alone right now. Even if Nolan is the last man I'd ever have expected to offer me this kindness, I'll take it.

Kindness for outcasts like me is in short supply.

As soon as the door shuts behind him, I feel something in my chest crack wide open. I stumble under the weight of it and slump onto the edge of the bed. Staring down at my hands, I blink and try to focus, but they're moving all over the place. It takes me a few more seconds to realize that it's not my vision but my hands. They're shaking, practically vibrating as I bring them closer to my face.

I killed a man tonight.

The memory is fresh in my head. Yet, even as I draw it back up—it feels hundreds of miles away, collected into a bubble that's attached to me, but only by the thinnest of strings. All it would take is one little snip and it'd float away, never to be seen again. My breath comes faster, sawing in and out of my throat as I push the heels of my palms into my eye sockets.

They, the man who'd tried to rape me had said. *They told me you'd fight harder.* What did that mean? Who the fuck is *'they?'*

The logical conclusion would be that someone had either paid the man or convinced him to harm me as revenge for my father's crimes. Although I'd asked about calling the police, the truth is that they wouldn't protect me, and I don't need them to anymore anyway. That fucker had tried to take something from me, and I'd killed to protect it, to protect myself. Lowering my arms from my face, I sigh and look up.

There's nothing really to look at in Nolan Pierce's room. No mementos, no photographs, nothing to hint at any of his interests other than living, breathing, and working out—as if he, himself, is little more than a guest in his own life. I find myself staring at the laptop sitting in the center of his desk. The screen is dark, offering a reflection of my face. My arms close around myself, rubbing up and down once again as a chill seeps into my body. I rock back and forth.

"I don't regret it," I tell myself. "I don't regret it. I did what I had to do. I don't regret it." The truth burrows into me. I don't regret it, but I *should.*

A roil of emotion swarms me, swimming through my veins. I curl inward, dragging my legs up until my feet hang off the edge of the mattress and I can wrap my arms around myself. I'm too close to the edge, sure that with little effort, I'll splinter apart and pieces of me will be lost forever.

My stomach is a ball and chain hanging in my body, weighing me down. It tightens and contracts as if someone is punching me right in my abdomen, over and over again. The pain moves up to my head, the repetitive *thud thud thud* taking root in my temples.

I killed a man tonight, and I'm not sorry.

"Jesus ... who the fuck am I?"

I don't even realize I've spoken aloud or that Nolan's bedroom door is open again until he replies to my question. "You're someone who's had a bad night, Princess," he says, causing me to lift my head to meet his gaze.

My eyes widen in shock. *Oh ... my ... God.*

Nolan Pierce is ripped. In the back of my mind, I knew he had to be. He's a football player after all. He has weights and a bench press in his room. His friends work out at Cory's Gym. Reality is far different when you just know something versus when you can see and experience it for yourself.

I can't stop the way my gaze drops over his wide chest, down to the grooves of his abdomen and then the juncture of his hips where two diagonal lines disappear beneath the waistband of the plaid, cotton pajama bottoms he's wearing. Standing in the now open doorway with a bottle of water in one hand and what looks to be his old clothes in the other, he casually tosses the shirt and jeans into the nearby plastic white hamper and shuts the door behind him.

Stop fucking looking, Jules.

Nolan strides to the bed, those abs getting closer and closer, shifting with each step as he passes me, and then he picks up the duffle off the bed and drops it to the floor. I release my legs and let my feet touch the floor again. He sets the bottle of water on top of the chipped TV tray table that acts as a nightstand and turns on the lamp stationed there. No wonder all of the girls at school want to fuck the Scorpion Kings.

Even as numb as I am, when Nolan turns to reach for the light switch on the wall, I nearly fall off the bed. Scars. A fuck load of them. They line the length of his spine, almost like ... whip marks. Some are wide and some are slender, but there's no doubt that they're old. Beneath them, the muscles of his back flex and shift as he walks. He doesn't even seem to notice that I'm staring and I quickly glance away. As much as I want to, I shouldn't ask about them. He flips off the main light, casting the rest of the room in the light glow of the lamp.

"Shoes off," he tells me, turning back around and pointing to my feet, "if you're sleeping on the bed."

I glance over to the tucked-in sheets because I really need to look somewhere other than the soda cans he's smuggling under his fucking stomach muscles. With him facing me again, it's hard to focus anywhere else. There's no way he's real. I thought the Adonis belt was a fantasy that desperately horny people made up. It's just not physiologically possible—is it?

"You're letting me take the bed?" I ask because that doesn't seem like him at all.

Nolan snorts and then folds down the sheets and blankets, straightening the top of the bed as he does. Reaching into the pocket of his pajama bottoms, he withdraws a cell phone and hooks it to a black charger on the TV tray table.

"Letting you take the bed?" He looks back at me and gestures for me to hurry up and get in.

Left with little else to do, I slowly get to my feet and then look down. I'm still wearing my converse. Stepping on the back of one shoe, I toe it off and then do the same to the other, leaving them next to the bench press before I move towards the bed and then bend down, crawling onto the surprisingly clean sheets. His room is a little cluttered, but it's not dirty. Bran had been a fucking slob, too used to having a maid clean his room and make his bed every day to concern himself with even the simplest of tasks.

Once I'm far back onto the bed and against the wall, Nolan slips onto the mattress. I slap a hand out onto the sheets and sit up. "Wait, what the hell are you doing?"

A scowl overtakes his handsome face. "It's a fucking double," he snaps. "Unless you want to sleep on the floor, you'll deal."

"I am not sleeping with *you*." No way in fucking hell.

Nolan points to the floor. "Then you're welcome to the floor, Princess, because I'm not giving up my fucking bed."

My hand curls into a fist. "You're such a dick," I hiss.

Sinking down to the mattress, he punches the pillow behind his head and stretches out. I glance down when the sheets shift. His feet damn near hang off the bed. "Make up your mind," he says. "Three ... two ... one..." Reaching over, the last light goes out, plunging the room into near-total darkness.

31
JULIET

Fuck. My whole body goes rigid. My breath comes in short staccato bursts. I didn't realize it until now, but he pulled the curtain over the window shut and now it's blocking out the moonlight. The thin yellow glow under the gap beneath the door to the hallway isn't enough to tell a man from an asshole. Wait. Both are the same, right?

I try to force myself to laugh at the silly thought, but it locks into my throat and refuses to budge. My heart gallops like a horse on steroids in my chest. A shadow dances in front of me. I scramble backward only to slam into the wall. My head bangs against it, but the pain is a distant thing that blossoms in the back of my skull. I'm too concerned with the darkness surrounding me and the monsters it hides. I can't do this. I need the light. I need to know who's here with me and I can't know if I can't see.

"Turn it back on," I croak out. "Turn the light back—turn it ... turn it back..." Oh, fuck me. I can't breathe. More shadows creep out of the corners of the room, growing larger and larger, taking shape. I'm surrounded by them. "Turn ... turn it..." My ability to speak abandons me completely. I blink rapidly, staring at the shadows that become men as if I can will them away.

It's not real. They're not there. I'm not...

My nightmare creeps into reality. An old ghost that has haunted me for years. A familiar, handsome face smiling at me. *Pretty girl ... pretty, pretty girl.* A shudder of revulsion works through my body and my throat turns to fire as acid rises from the pit in my stomach. He grins down at me with razor-sharp teeth and wide, hungry eyes, forcing me to acknowledge his existence.

A scream rockets out of my throat as a hand touches my shoulder. Without thought, I slam my fist into the very real man that's next to me. My knuckles connect with a jaw that feels like granite. Pain explodes in my knuckles, but I'm too out of it to care.

"Fuck!" Nolan's curse penetrates my head, but the hand—*his*, I recognize—doesn't go away. It only grips me harder as he begins to talk. "Jules, you're fine. You're okay. I'm not going to hurt you."

I gasp for breath, my hands shaking as I reach up and grasp at him. Skin, hot and smooth under my palms. "Turn on the light." *Is that my voice? Is that pathetic, scared trembling voice mine?* "Please. *Fuck.* I need the light."

"Shhh." Nolan reaches around and cups the back of my skull, pulling me away from the wall until my cheek is against his shoulder. "Shhh." He hushes me, rocking back and forth in slow, soothing motions.

"Turn on the light," I repeat even as I lean into him, holding on as a broken piece inside me wiggles free and stabs at my insides.

"I'm not going to do that." Despite his words, his voice is gentle—more so than I ever expected from him. "I can't."

"*Why?*" My nails dig into him. Is this how he wants to torment me? Is he truly this cruel?

With my breaths puffing against his skin, I try to slow my

heart rate by counting backward from ten and start over when I reach zero. Still, I don't feel as composed as I want to be. It's not fucking working and if I didn't want to lose it in front of one of the goddamned Scorpion Kings all over again, I'd cry. I'd actually cry.

I don't want to open my eyes and see if those shadows are closer, if they look like the man I killed or worse. I press my forehead into Nolan's chest and shoulder. "Turn the light on," I say again. His heat is a fiery thing and I can't help but soak it into my skin, needing the warmth if only to stay sane.

His hand continues to hold me to him. When he speaks, his tone is even, unyielding. "I'm not going to turn on the light because you can't stay afraid of the dark for the rest of your life, Jules. If I let you sleep with the light on now, then it might take you a hell of a long time to sleep without it again."

"I can sleep without the light on, I just need…" My throat closes up.

In the studio, there was always moonlight to see. There was the light from the oven and microwave clocks and when my head got really bad, I could always leave the bathroom door cracked with the light. In here, in his arms, there is only shadow and dust and darkness.

I'm suffocating.

"No, you're not." It takes me a moment to realize that Nolan is responding to me. Even my thoughts are slipping out. I've lost all control. "I won't let you suffocate, Jules."

I take several deep gulps of air before I manage a response. "You don't give a shit about me." The words come out on a croak. "Are you sure it's not because *you* don't want to sleep with the light on?" I challenge.

His chuckle is low and raspy, the sound of a man both amused and tired. Suddenly, I feel bad about keeping him awake. He and the others didn't have to come to my rescue. No one asked Gio to break down my door. No one asked them to get rid of the body. No one asked them to help me. It would have been easier for them to leave me be—to let Silverwood find out and turn me into a criminal too.

"Maybe it's a little of that," Nolan admits, distracting me from the direction of my thoughts, "but you have to know I'm right."

I swallow around a thick, struggling throat and sag into him. *"Fuck."* It's all I can say.

He nods against me, the feel of his hair brushing my temple when he bends a bit more making me shiver. "Yeah," he says. "'Fuck' is goddamned right."

Nolan doesn't move for a long time, just holding me there as I get my breathing under control and my heart rate slows back to what can probably pass for normal on a screening. A yawn stretches my jaw and nearly pops it.

"Better?" he inquires as I finally push away from him. My cheeks feel too hot and I'm mortified that I just let him—fuck, I have no idea what this was, but I do know I felt vulnerable around him and I don't think that's such a good idea.

"I'm fine," I say, silently praying for the words not to be a lie.

Though I can't see him, I have the distinct impression that Nolan is surveying me in the dark like the guy has night vision or something. I scrub a hand down my face, an odd bout of self-consciousness rearing its ugly head.

"So," I say, "are the guys coming over here or…"

"They're going back to their own places," Nolan says as if I didn't just have a whole mental breakdown against his chest. "I can ask them to come over, though, and stay the night if you want." He pauses as if hesitating and then, "Do you want them to come over? To make you feel safe?"

"I feel safe." The words shoot out of my lips and this time, no amount of praying will make them the truth. They're a defensive mechanism and a lie.

The sound of air and a soft *whoosh* and *thump* as I assume Nolan flops back onto the bed and his pillow tells me he isn't fooled. "Fine," he says. "Then sleeping shouldn't be a problem."

I remain sitting up, my line of sight no longer blocked by Nolan's body. The shadows are back in the room, lingering just beyond some invisible barrier that keeps them a few feet from the bed. My eyes strain to see them for what they truly are—my imagination.

My imagination is a cruel bitch, though, because they remain.

"Tell me something," I say, needing more of his distraction.

"Hmmm?" Nolan's sleepy hum is the only sound in the room other than my own breathing.

"Why did you come tonight?"

He stills in the process of pulling up the sheets. Forcing my eyes down, I focus on the build of a man—a real one—next to me on a bed that feels too narrow for both of us. I have to admit, though, it's a hell of a lot more comfortable than my futon.

"Go to sleep," Nolan says, repeating his earlier words. "No more questions."

"I want to know," I insist. Patting the bed, I reach out, not stopping until I feel the hard muscle of his body. My fingers skim down and I realize that I'm much lower than I meant to be when I touch several lines in succinct procession. Ripping my hand away from his abs, I hold the offending limb to my chest and silently curse myself.

"No, you don't, Princess." Nolan doesn't sound sleepy anymore. He sounds angry.

With my hand against my chest, between my breasts, I part my lips and say the one thing I know will make him talk. "He tried to rape me."

The temperature in the room before those words were verbalized had been a comfortable, warm. As soon as they leave my mouth, however, it drops significantly. A shiver steals over my shoulders and down my spine. I lift my legs up, pulling them from beneath the sheets, and wrap my arms around my knees as I had before.

"He was going to rape me," I clarify, "and I let him think he could so he would get close enough so I could stab him in the back." My teeth rake over my lower lip. "Then … I pushed him off the balcony and watched him fall to his death."

Nolan knows all of this already. I told the Scorpion Kings everything when they showed up at my apartment. It had seemed stupid to hide it when Gio had seen the results of my actions.

I squeeze my eyes shut and press my forehead into my palms. When, after several beats of silence, I finally lift my head, Nolan is sitting up. The outline of his upper body illuminated by the soft light of the moon coming in from the window.

"Do you want to talk about it?" he asks.

We are *talking about it,* but I know he doesn't just mean the action itself. He wants to know if I need to unleash all of the shit that's now in my head. I contemplate the question. Logically, I recognize that the events of the night only happened a few short hours ago, but somehow my mind has fast-forwarded me through it. Almost as if time has warped becoming both longer and too fucking short. I feel detached from the hours between then and now. All I can focus on is where I am here, with Nolan, or there, with *him*. It could have been a second before now or years in the past, and yet … I don't know how my emotions can ever fade.

After a beat, I turn my cheek from one side to the other. "No," I whisper. "I don't think so. I just"—I squeeze my arms around my legs a bit tighter, until my chest constricts and aches—"I just think I needed to say it aloud."

Nolan watches me, the one eye that I can see is dark, his pupil nearly swallowing the ring of cinnamon that is his iris. "How did killing him make you feel?"

Of all the questions I might have guessed he would ask, that was certainly not one. My lips part, jaw dropping. "What?"

He tilts his head to the side, examining me. "You heard me," he says. "How did it make you feel?"

I want to snort at his question and tell him that he sounds like some sort of gangster therapist, but I don't. Instead, I find myself thinking back to the moment the intruder had been on top of me, how his body had pressed me down into my shitty futon. The smell of him, rank and stinking of tobacco. For the last several months, I've felt nothing but anger, pain, abandonment, and utter loss. There's no place for me in this new world I'm unaccustomed to, no room for someone who doesn't belong.

All those short skirts ... your tiny, little cheerleading uniform. Do you dance around like that just for me, pretty girl? I want to swat the ugly words away.

I wish I still had those meds my mom had gotten me. My nightmares ... they're not real. Just fear brought to life by anxiety. It's easier to focus on the events of tonight. Those are undeniable.

When that man had broken in, when he'd held the knife to me and threatened me with a fate worse to many than even death ... it had become so clear to me that not only do I not belong, but no one would even care if I died. No one would care if I was raped. Even if they heard me scream or beg, no one would have come—but then someone had. *They* had.

Knowing that no one cared if I lived or died or if something worse than either was happening to me had been the final nail in a coffin I didn't know I was already lying in. My grave is built and I am dying. Suffocating.

Holding that knife in my hand felt like I was fighting back against fate. As if I had finally found a home. A home in which I'm not a victim. I don't have to be one. I enjoyed making him hurt. The warmth of his blood on my fingers had created a fire inside me, and it made me whole again. It's a bad idea to admit this to anyone, much less someone like him, to a Scorpion King.

"Powerful." The word is a rasp on my tongue. "It felt powerful to stab him, to kill him." To make him hurt the way he hurt me. To take back control and make it my bitch.

Nolan's eyes are steady on mine, unwavering. I'm more than a little astonished to find no judgment in them, no condemnation. Then again, knowing who he is—a gutter rat like the rest of them no doubt used to the violence that life has to offer in the streets—perhaps I shouldn't be so surprised.

"Good," is all he says. One simple word and I feel ... *accepted.*

For the first time since my life fell apart, I feel like someone is looking at me and they're not seeing what they want to. He's not seeing Allen Donovan's daughter, the child of a criminal. He's seeing the real Juliet—no blood ties, no family, no past.

I sway towards him, my eyes falling from his gaze to his mouth. I wonder if his lips are as soft as they look. Before I can close that distance between us though and make what I'm sure is a stupid mistake, Nolan is already there—erasing the inches of space.

His mouth presses into mine with a readiness that both confuses and incites me. My hands arch up around his neck and I open my mouth without thought.

Kissing Nolan is delicious.

It's nothing like making out with my ex. Nolan's kiss is more devouring than those lame pecks and cool, boring licks. The difference is like that of a kitten and a lion. Nolan is all predator, crawling over me and pressing me back into the bed as his hands grip my hips and his body surges forth. His hard cock is against my belly, rubbing back and forth, but I'm not scared. I want more—more of his mouth and lips and touch. It doesn't make any sense. I should be traumatized by what happened tonight—maybe I am, but I'm not scared of Nolan Pierce. I'm not scared of the way he makes me feel.

A gasp escapes me, and when my lips part, he delves inside, sliding his tongue along mine. Fire dances along the surface of my skin, turning me to ash. I am a creature of pure sensation under this indelible beast.

Nolan kisses me and I am afraid that it's the kind of kiss I will never be able to forget.

Pressing one hand to the center of his chest, I push him back just enough to separate our mouths. Hot puffs of breath echo between us, and for the first time in a long time, the dark doesn't feel quite as oppressive.

"What?" Nolan sounds strained, the single word he lets out is taut and hungry.

"You hate me," I breathe. "Why are you doing this if you hate me?"

A low groan rumbles up his throat and his lower body sinks down harder against me. I can feel his erection, hot and hard, where it's trapped between us. I don't feel threatened by it though.

"Does that matter?" he asks.

"Doesn't it?"

I can't see his eyes in the dark, but I can feel the penetrating heat of his gaze on me. "Maybe I'll hate you again in the morning, Princess," he says, "but not tonight."

I blink up at him, trying to see him clearly even though it's impossible. "Why?"

Wide palms cup either side of my head, holding me in place as he leans into me and his head dips. Soft lips brush back and forth across mine. "Tonight," he whispers, "I think you and I can just be Nolan and Juliet. We don't need to be a Scorpion King or a Donovan."

Does that mean that come dawn he'll hate me again? As much as we might want to pretend all of the issues between us are gone, in the morning, they'll be back. I'll always be a Donovan and he'll always be a Scorpion King.

My hands smooth further up the hard, muscled plains of his chest until I come to his shoulders. I open my mouth, letting my tongue wander out to slick across my lower lip and touching his at the same time. A low groan echoes out of him. His sight in the dark must be better than mine—or maybe it's just that I'm trying to ignore all of the shadows of my mind and he doesn't have that problem—because he growls like he saw the movement.

"Make your decision," Nolan orders. "Are we doing this or not?"

I close my eyes. This is a bad idea. A very, *very* bad idea, but after the night I've had, I want to take something back. I want a reward for what I've gone through and fuck if I'm not ready to take it from him.

"Not all the way," I tell him.

I have to keep something for myself. Something that is just mine. I don't trust easily, not anymore. The last guy I fucked was a boyfriend that cheated on me with my best friend and vanished when my family fell apart.

Does it make me a little fucked in the head to think it has something to do with me? Maybe. Do I care? Not at the moment.

Nolan groans again. "You're fucking killing me, Princess."

His hand comes up and closes around my throat, a threat and a promise. When his lips touch mine again, they're even more demanding than they were before, but I open for him anyway. Hot, wet kiss after hot, wet kiss merges between us. His body slowly rocks against me. I could laugh at how high school this all is, the two of us grinding on one another as we make out like teenagers.

We *are* teenagers, but I haven't felt like one in months. It's kind of nice to remind myself that this is what I am, this is what I'm meant to do. Sneak in and out of boys' rooms.

Kiss them. Pretend for just a fucking second that I'm normal.

"Stop thinking," Nolan growls, sounding annoyed.

"I'm—" I start to defend myself, but he cuts me off by releasing my throat and sitting up. His hands touch the hem of my shirt.

"No penetration is fine," he tells me, "but I need your tits on my chest."

That's all the warning I get before he's ripping the tanktop right off me and dropping it to the floor. Then he's back and my nipples harden into little points as if seeking him out. My breasts feel heavy and swollen as Nolan reaches down and lifts one of my legs to wrap around his waist.

With an annoyed grunt, he pauses and disappears. A second later, the fabric of my sweats is yanked straight down my legs. I snap them shut, but he forces his way between them, falling back into the same position as earlier. Nolan curls my legs over his waist and lowers himself right down.

The new position pushes the head of his cock right against my core. The only thing separating us is his sweats. A moan rumbles up my chest. He rubs again and again until I have to close my eyes and arch back. "There you are, Princess," Nolan urges. "You feel my cock against you? You like that? Yeah, you do. Fucking ride it."

I roll my hips, tentatively at first and then with more force, pushing against him over and over again. When his hand lands on one of my breasts and squeezes, I barely notice. So caught up in the sensation of his cock head teasing my clit through the folds of his pajama bottoms, I whimper as sparks dance behind my eyelids.

He pinches my nipple and I scream as the orgasm I'd been on the cusp of reaching for fades just enough for me to lose its pleasurable edge. I open my eyes to glare at him. Somehow between our grinding and kissing, the shadows have been pushed back and it's easier to see him. He's grinning down at me. One hand holds my hip in place as he thrusts in methodical movements back and forth against me, mimicking the act of penetration that I won't let him complete.

"That hurt," I complain, and yet it had also felt good too, like electricity racing through my skin.

He tweaks my nipple again, rolling it between a thumb and forefinger, causing my back to arch. "You like it," he counters, and damn him, but I do.

"Nolan…" The moan is a whine in my throat. I don't recognize the sound because it's definitely not one I ever made with Bran.

"Yeah, that's right, Princess," Nolan replies. "Call my name because I know it makes you wet for me."

Wet? No. I'm not wet. I'm fucking soaked. Drenched. Dripping down my inner thighs with each pass. I'm starting to hate my demand for no penetration, but I won't take it back.

Fingers release my nipple and delve down my stomach. My eyes flash up to meet his. I can't see their color in the dark, but I know they're burning just as hot as I am.

"Tit for tat," Nolan whispers. "I get you off and you return the favor."

I grit my teeth as his fingers slip through my folds. A hiss escapes him as if he's been burned. "Should've known you'd be like fire on my fingertips," he murmurs, as if he's talking to himself. His head tilts down and his eyes fix squarely on where his hand rests against me. One finger rubs in circles around my clit, putting just the right amount of pressure on the bundle of nerves that makes me cry out again and arch against his touch. A gush of wetness sluices out of me. He takes the finger away and I want to claw at him to force it back. Thankfully, he's not leaving me hanging and that finger, joined by two more, spears right into my cunt.

Nolan leans closer, breaths panting against my ear as he groans out his next words. "You're fucking gripping my fingers like a vise," he tells me. "Makes me wonder how tight you'll choke my cock when I get inside of you."

More of those sparklers appear, dancing around and around. My body is scalding hot, fireworks pooling low in my belly, getting ready to go off. I reach for the man hovering over me, my nails scrape his bicep.

"Make me come." I don't know where I get the courage to order him around, but I'm not going to think about it too hard. I'm too desperate for this release. There's ecstasy waiting just over the hill I'm cresting, and I want it more than I've ever wanted anything.

Nolan's dark chuckle rumbles against my cheek, low and foreboding. As if my demand is nothing but a role he's been given and he's more than happy to play the part. "As you wish, Princess."

His thumb moves up and over my clit, pressing, rubbing. His fingers withdraw and push back inside. I gasp as he nuzzles down and then latches on to one of my nipples. Lips. Teeth. Tongue. Fingers. It's all over me. Inside me. My hips follow the movements of his hand, seeking out the pleasure that he can give me. I cry out, gyrating faster and faster and still my orgasm doesn't come. Nails against his shoulders, scratching, scraping. Raw. Bloody. Wicked.

"Nolan!" I sob his name, begging for something I'm not entirely sure how to make happen.

"Remember," Nolan replies as he shuffles down further on the bed. "This is an exchange. Tit for tat, Princess. You're gonna be such a good girl after I'm done, aren't you? You're gonna suck my cock so fucking good. Gonna show me how an elite princess drinks my cum."

Sweat coats my chest, beads against my temples, slides into my hair. I'm insane for thinking this was a good idea. He's trying to kill me. Torture me in both the sweetest and worst way possible. A groan and a plea leave my lips. Both of his hands are on my hips now, dragging one of my legs further up and hooking it over a wide shoulder as Nolan settles himself lower. Shock has me looking down as I set my elbows into the mattress beneath me and sit up. Though I can't see his face as clearly as I want to, I can feel his breath against my core.

Thumb easing one of my pussy lips to the side, Nolan blows a single stream of air over my heated flesh. "I expect to be rewarded for this, Juliet," he states. "I want more than just praise. I want you to come all over my face and tell me how much you love my mouth on your cunt afterward."

God, his mouth. No one would ever know it by just looking at him, but Nolan Pierce has the kind of mouth that only the filthiest of devils possess. I didn't think I'd be into that, but I have to admit it now as my pussy gushes with liquid heat—I am.

"Come on my tongue and beg me for relief, Juliet," Nolan demands. "Let me give it to you. Let me feel you."

Delirious with lust, I'm ready to give him anything he fucking wants if he'll just finish me when Nolan finally lowers his head and sucks my clit into his mouth.

I'm lost. Broken.

Being eaten out by Nolan Pierce is an out-of-body experience. Like dying and coming back from heaven—if there is such a place. His hands move again, digging into the flesh of my inner thighs as he widens me for more of his mouth. A hiss escapes from between my lips and my hands snap down, fingers sinking into the rich silk of his hair. Holding him to my pussy, I rock back and forth, relishing in the lips and tongue action he gives me. He laps me up like a hungry animal, sucking my wetness straight from the source before sliding back up and nipping at my clit. I jerk, a whole body movement that I can't stop even if I wanted to.

There's no hiding here. No fear. Just him and me and the wet trail of liquid on the inside of my thighs as Nolan devours me. Digging into his scalp, I lock my legs around his head and arch upward as pleasure spirals inside me. My head presses back into the pillows behind me as my spine practically leaves the mattress. The rolling wave of sensation waits until that moment to attack, stabbing into me with all of the violence of a murder.

I come against Nolan's face and mouth in an instant of uncontrollable surrender. Shudders wrack my body and all the while, the man between my legs doesn't let up. He pushes me higher and higher until I realize there's not just one orgasm there, but a second, a third. Fuck me, he really *is* trying to kill me. The scream that rips free from my throat echoes around the room and back again until it's all I can hear and still, Nolan goes down on me. Licking up my wetness, sucking it back. He shoves my legs apart, freeing himself from the clasp of my thighs. With one hand under one knee and the other mimicking the same on the opposite, Nolan pushes me back, bending my body nearly in half as his mouth latches on to my core and his tongue drives into me. Over and over again, I come against his face. Fisting the sheets beneath me doesn't do shit for bringing me back to reality when he holds the keys to my body.

I lose track of how many times I come, but when it becomes too much and each sensation seems to compound against the other, I press a palm to his forehead and shove him back. "No more," I rasp. "I can't..." My breathing is shaky, hell, my whole body is a trembling mass.

How the fuck does he expect me to reciprocate when I can't even see straight?

A low, masculine chuckle vibrates through the room and I close my eyes at the sound.

Yeah, I bet he's real pleased with himself. To be honest, I would be too if I were him. No guy that's ever gone down on me has ever done so until I orgasmed once, much less multiple times.

I lie there, panting, sweating, trying to catch air in my raw lungs when the sensation of fabric driving up my calves makes me open my eyes again. Nolan doesn't say a word as he drags my sweats back up my legs and I lift my hips until they're in place. Then he grips my hands and tugs me, groaning and cursing, into a sitting position. With one last flick of a nipple that makes me want to call him every vile name in the book, Nolan hooks the neckline of my previously discarded tank over my head and then tugs it down into place, helping me weave my arms through the correct holes.

My mind is foggy and lax. I haven't felt this relaxed and sated in months, if ever before. I flop back onto the bed like a ragdoll.

"Thought you wanted tit for tat," I grumble even as my eyes slide shut again.

Nolan rolls me to the side, nudging me over until I'm between him and the wall as he sinks back onto the mattress and reaches for the sheets down by our feet. Pulling them up and over our legs, he answers, "Next time, Princess."

If that's a promise or a threat, sleep takes me into a different kind of darkness before I can consider it too long.

32
JULIET

Monday morning rolls in with a dusky pre-dawn light. Distantly, beneath warm sheets and the solid mattress versus my futon, I hear the sound of a front door opening and closing. My whole body goes rigid where I lie, but a firm hand lands on my hip. The heat of Nolan's palm delves past the fabric of my clothes as he leans in and whispers against my ear. "It's fine," he assures me. "Just my mom getting back from work. I'm going to go check on her."

He doesn't give me a chance to respond before his hand is gone and cool air hits my back when he slides out from under the covers, and on near-silent feet, leaves the bedroom. Once he's gone, I roll over and stare at the room in a newfound light.

Last night was real. The evidence is in the soreness of my clit from his attentions and the still relaxed muscles of the rest of my body.

What the hell was I thinking?

Reaching up as my eyes pass over the bench press and football gear, I press two fingers to my lips. They still tingle from last night's memory. Why did I agree to let Nolan go down on me? Why hadn't he demanded his payback? Is he going to wait for me to deliver? My mind rolls with question after question to which there are no answers. Only one man can give me those and I'll be damned before I ask him straight up. I'm not entirely sure what he's planning for today, but I promise myself that if he acts like nothing happened, I'm just going to do the same.

I lie in bed and listen to Nolan talking to a woman in the distant part of the small house. I'm not entirely sure if Eliza Pierce knows I'm staying in her house, but on the off chance Nolan is keeping me a secret, I stay in his room until I hear footsteps in the hall and the sound of a door across the hall opening and closing.

Nolan comes back a moment later. "My mom's gone to bed," he tells me.

I flip back the covers and sit up, glancing at the cell phone on his TV tray nightstand. Reaching over, I don't ask for permission to thumb the screen and light it up to reveal the time. "Do you mind if I take a shower before school?"

He eyes me in that way of his—as if he's trying to penetrate the layers of flesh and bone to see what's going on inside my head. I'm almost glad that X-Men and mutants don't exist because if anyone could do it, I swear it would be him.

Nolan steps away from the door and over to his closet. "Knock yourself out."

Crawling out of bed, I rifle through the duffle for actual clothes and head out of the room, stealing across the hallway and into the small bathroom. Though I feel dirty down to my bones—and not because of what I'd done with Nolan—I only allow myself two passes of soap and rinsing. Last night feels further away with each passing second, and I'm almost grateful for my lapse in impulse control regarding the head Scorpion King. If anything, what we'd done has helped me forget my attacker's hands on my body.

It felt like he allowed me to take back ownership of my

own body even if I technically hadn't been raped. I close my eyes and think of Nolan's mouth on my pussy. That, more than any soap or scalding hot water, seems to wash away the lingering unpleasantness.

Once I'm done, I get out and dress in a pair of jeans and a loose-fitting shirt that was once a solid tee before I cut the sleeves off. Months ago, I wouldn't have been caught dead wearing something so pedestrian as jeans and a self-made tanktop. Or rather, my mother wouldn't have let me be caught dead.

The reminder of my mom, when Nolan's is so close, makes my head throb. No doubt if I were to check my emails now, I'd find more from my dad's lawyer, asking for me to visit him. I wonder if Dad knows that Mom left town. That she left *me*.

Gathering my wet hair, I rake my fingers through it and tie it into a loose ponytail before brushing my teeth with my finger and the paste I find on the bathroom counter. I should've gotten my toothbrush out of my duffle, but I'd rather get everything over with quickly. Spitting into the sink and rinsing out the last of the minty taste, I turn my head from side to side, examining my reflection in the mirror. The bruises aren't so bad in the morning light, more sore than anything else. I don't want to bother with answering any uncomfortable questions, though, so I dig through the drawers of the bathroom sink and sigh in relief when I come up with some old makeup. *Thank you, Nolan's mom.* Hopefully, it hides the worst of the color.

Minutes later, I step out of the bathroom, holding my dirty clothes, and find Nolan waiting on his bed. His face is turned down to the phone in his hand and his brow is furrowed. I leave my PJs next to the duffle and find my converse and a pair of socks before dropping down onto the mattress next to him to pull them on.

"Problem?" I ask, hoping I sound casual when I feel anything but.

Nolan doesn't respond immediately, his fingers swiping across the electronic screen with concentration. "No," he finally says, slipping the cell into his back pocket. He must've dressed while I was gone because the wide, muscled planes of his body are hidden behind a black t-shirt, jeans, and a leather jacket that looks older than he is it's so faded. "Everything's good."

With that, he stands, and just as we're about to leave, he pauses and reaches back into my duffle. I scowl but don't say anything as he withdraws the box and removes the cell phone. He doesn't hand it over to me, but instead slips it into his own pocket.

I eye him warily. Boys are fucking weird, and Scorpion Kings—despite their reputations and the fact they got rid of the body of the man I killed over the weekend—are the same.

"Come on." Lifting the keys to Gio's Firebird and jangling them in front of me, Nolan leads me out of the house and to the driveway.

In the light of day, the street is just as cozy as it was the night before. Students hang out at the opposite end of the road waiting for the bus, and there are a few older ladies already in their gardens, bustling about with their curlers still in and their moo-moos billowing in the light morning breeze.

No one in this neighborhood has any obvious grand wealth, but neither do they seem to be scraping by. Middle class. Normal. Comfortable. It's nice. And it's not a place I belong.

Nolan hits the unlock button as he gets into the car. As I slide into the front seat, I frown at the sight of my backpack sitting on the floorboards. It hadn't been there the night before.

Almost as if he reads my mind, Nolan chuckles. "The guys dropped it off for you last night," he says. "They didn't want to wake us up."

I don't know how to reply to any of that—not the fact that they'd cared about not waking us up or about the fact that they went out of their way to drop off my backpack—so I don't say anything at all as I buckle up. Nolan reaches into the console, hooking up the phone Lex had given me to a charger before he cranks the engine.

The Firebird rumbles to life with a low growly purr that resonates through my bones. I sit back and close my eyes. Once I'd actually fallen asleep the night before, there'd been no more nightmares. At least, none of the fictional variety. Now they haunt the waking world with their presence, never once leaving me alone or letting me get too comfortable. Nolan drives in near silence, the only sound that of the vehicle and a classic rock station set to a low volume. I'm so far out of my depth and only in the light of early morning do I finally recall the problem that might assail me the second I show up to Silverwood Public with not just one of the Scorpion Kings but *the* head Scorpion King. Their leader. The powerhouse of the seedy underbelly of the youth of Silverwood.

By the time the Firebird pulls into the school parking lot, I've got a plan. A shit one, but it's a plan nonetheless. The second we're parked, I grab my bag and get out, slinging it over my shoulder. Every single person in the parking lot standing next to their shitty cars with their rusted rims and taped windows stares my way. I keep my head up, but I don't acknowledge anyone watching me.

"Well, I'll see you in class," I say quickly. "Thanks for the ride."

Nolan arches a brow at me as he steps out from his side and shuts the driver's side door. I just need to get the hell away from him before the others show up. There will, of course, still be gossip, but if I can avoid them for the rest of the day, maybe it won't be so bad.

Before I can make my way towards the school building, a black SUV swerves around in front of me, cutting off my escape as it pulls into the parking spot next to the Firebird. The roar of a motorcycle isn't far behind, and a second later, Nolan's Indian speeds down the row of cars and stops next to the SUV and Firebird. All three of them are here. And me. *Together.*

"*Fuck.*"

Nolan shoots me a look as the curse slips free. "It's not going to be that easy," he tells me, as if he knows exactly what I'd been trying to do. I glare up at him as he stops in front of me and holds something out. When I glance down at what it is, my glare turns into a scowl.

"I don't want that." I push his hand—and the phone in it—away.

"I don't care." Nolan reaches down and grabs my hand. He doesn't even seem to notice when I attempt to yank away from him but merely moves forward with his intentions. He forces my fingers to uncurl and drops the cell phone, now somewhat charged, into my palm.

"I'll dump it," I warn him. "I'll throw it away."

Nolan just stares at me, dark cinnamon eyes burrowing into me with a silent warning. "Someone is obviously out to get you. Keep it. You need it for emergencies. It's got a little bit of a charge, but it's new so it might only last the school day. You can charge it in Gio's or Lex's car after we get out."

"I don't need a fucking phone," I insist, gritting the words out through clenched teeth.

He ignores my words and continues. "If I know Lex, then it's got my number as well as his and Gio's. Meet back here after school so one of us can take you home."

"My home?" I ask, hopefully.

On the other side of the Firebird, Gio removes the biker helmet and clips it to the handlebar of the Indian before hopping off.

"We've already contacted your landlord about the

damage," Nolan tells me, "but I doubt it'll be ready to move back into yet."

I look back to the phone in my hand, fingers closing around it. "You can't control me with this." I'm not entirely sure why I say the words, but it feels necessary to tell him where I stand. To let him know that this doesn't buy me—nothing will. This phone isn't just a kind act or a gift. It's a leash. Just like everything in my past life was. The house. The friends. The school. Nothing was ever mine. If it was, then it couldn't have been lost so easily.

Arching a brow, Nolan nods to the gathering crowd of students watching us. "You really want to fight about it here?"

What I *want* to do is shove this phone so far up his ass that he can read the texts it receives by blinking.

"Keep the phone." The words are a command, not a suggestion. "Don't hurt Lex's feelings."

"What makes you think I care about his feelings?"

Lex's SUV turns off and the creak of the driver's side door echoes over to where we stand.

Nolan shrugs and drops his arms. "Maybe you don't, but you do care about money and we're not like your old friends, Princess. We aren't rolling in Mommy and Daddy's cash. Lex had to work to make his own money and he used that money to buy you a phone. So keep it or don't at your own risk."

Fuck. Him. I practically snarl as the implications of his words hit me. *Fuck all of them. Goddamn it.* I want to curse and stomp and scream like a child, but he's right. It actually does mean something that Lex bought me this phone. It means more than any of the thousand-dollar tennis bracelets or Jimmy Choos Bran or Avery ever got me for Christmas or birthdays. They hadn't worked for a damn thing they gave me, but Lex had, and damn Nolan, but yes, that does mean something to me.

A mixture of irritation and guilt burns a hot fire in my gut. I glance down at the simple black screen of the phone in my hand. It's cheap, but that doesn't mean shit to me. I no longer place value on things based on their price tags. Without giving myself a chance to think any harder about this decision, I shove the phone into my back pocket and whirl away. Hiking my bag up further on my shoulder, I start walking. Halfway to the building, I hear Gio—not Nolan—call after me.

"Meet back here after classes, Prep Girl!" he yells. "Don't even think of running or we'll come looking for you."

Clenching both hands into fists at my side, I raise one over my shoulder and offer him and his friends a silent middle finger.

"Why did Erin Kennedy tell me you arrived in Giovanni Vargas' car this morning with Nolan Pierce?" Roquel jumps on me the second I enter first period, her question shooting out of her mouth before I even get a chance to sit down.

"I don't know who that is," I say honestly. "So, I don't know why she'd tell you shit about me."

She points a chipped No. 2 pencil at me. "You don't deny it though." Roquel is a hound dog when she's locked on a target, and right now that target is me and the juicy piece of school rumor that's going around. *Is it a rumor if it's true?* Roquel's chair scrapes across the cheap tiled floor as she scoots closer to me. "Spill."

I cut a look her way out of the corner of my eye. Leave it to the gossip mill to get her to talk to me again. When I don't say anything, she groans and slumps over, turning her head so that her short crop of black hair flutters delicately all to one side.

"Come on," she whines. "Your first day out of in-school suspension and you show up with all three Scorpion Kings in tow. Are they backing you now? Is Megan out? Are you dating one of them?"

The memories of what I'd done with Nolan the night before resurface and I shove them down as I focus on responding to Roquel. "I don't know what they're doing with Megan," I tell her, "and I don't care. I needed a ride. That's all."

Roquel sits up, her brows rising to graze the underside of her bangs. "That's it?" She gapes at me. "They just gave you a ride?" She shakes her head. "I know I'm not the brightest bulb in the box, but even I can tell that what you just said is complete and utter bullshit." That No. 2 pencil makes another appearance as she jabs the pointed end in my direction.

The door to the classroom opens then, and I'm saved from further questions as the teacher enters and jumps straight into calling attendance. My previously absentee guardian angel is either finally sober or luck is on my side today, because, somehow, I manage to escape Roquel's clutches as first period comes to a close. At lunch, ignoring the gnawing hunger in my stomach, I find a quiet spot in the library and avoid the primary dining areas—and Roquel's barrage of questions about my relationship with the Scorpion Kings. Even in the library, though, I find myself bearing the brunt of people's curious stares. They're all wondering the same thing. I can't even blame them, not that I have any intention of feeding the hungry masses their drug of choice. *Information.*

Halfway through final period, I nearly leap out of my seat when my ass vibrates. No, not my ass. The phone I'd forgotten in my back pocket. Subtly withdrawing it, I hide it under the desk as I swipe across the screen and spy a text.

GIO: Meet in parking lot after school

Glancing up to ensure the teacher isn't paying any attention, I type a quick reply and hit send.

JULIET: I have to work. I'm going to catch the bus.

Gio's response is almost instantaneous.

GIO: No.

With a barely restrained snarl, I shove the phone into my

pocket again without responding. Ten minutes later, as the last of the class ticks past, it vibrates again. Double-checking the teacher's position a second time, I pull it back out for the new message, this one from Nolan.

NOLAN: Don't make me send Lex.

Using each other as threats. How original. I roll my eyes. I can't even say it doesn't work though. Of all the Scorpion Kings, Lex is one of the deadliest.

Fifteen minutes later, as the final bell ending the day rings out, I snatch up my shit and am out of the door, powering through the hallways towards the cafeteria and bus loop before the rest of the classes have fully unleashed. I'm practically sprinting to make it before they realize I won't be meeting them in the parking lot. I should've known it wouldn't be that easy.

I get one foot out of the cafeteria doors and into the dull sunlight of autumn when a muscled arm covered in tattoos comes around my waist and plucks me right off my feet. "You were warned, baby." Lex's soft but deep baritone settles right next to my ear.

I go impossibly still and don't fight as he turns me away from the surge of students coming out of the cafeteria doors, making their way over the circle of big yellow monstrosities idling against the ring of concrete to take them home. There are more eyes on the two of us, but it's pointless to try and stop the staring. Tapping Lex's arm, I release a sigh of annoyance.

"Fine," I say. "You've caught me. You can put me down now. I won't run."

He seems to hesitate for a long moment. So long, I wonder if it's not because he doesn't believe me or if he simply wants to keep carrying me. I open my mouth to repeat my words, but then my feet touch the ground and he nods back towards the building, directing where we're supposed to go without saying a thing. Grumbling under my breath, I hitch my bag higher on my shoulders and start walking away from the buses towards the student parking lot. Lex leads me back into the main hall and out a set of double glass doors. I spot Gio and Nolan, both who have adapted mirroring expressions of smug satisfaction, their arms crossed and eyes solemn.

"What was the point of that, Prep Girl?" Gio's grin makes me want to sock him right in his handsome face. "Your shit's at Nolan's anyway. It's not like you can run from us."

"Who said I was trying to run?" I ask defensively. "I need to head to work and I don't know the closest bus stop to Nolan's."

Nolan jerks his chin at the Firebird behind them parked right next to Lex's SUV. "We've got practice, anyway," he says.

"I'll take her to work and be back—" Lex begins.

"No." Nolan gestures to the Firebird again as Gio drops his arms and palms his hips. "G will take her; you're with me."

Lex doesn't so much frown as his entire face pulls back, the skin tightening over the sharp jut of his jaw and cheekbones as his lips peel away from his teeth. "Don't," Nolan barks. "You and I need to talk."

I glance between the two of them, but Lex doesn't say another word. Instead, he turns and stalks away, back across the parking lot in the direction of the gym and beyond that, the football field.

"Come on, Prep Girl." I nearly stumble under the weight of Gio's arm as he slings it over my shoulder and directs me toward the passenger door of his Firebird. He opens it and holds it out for me. "Get in."

I frown at him, my eyes moving down the bare flesh of his forearm and over the various whorls and lines of ink there. Each of them is tattooed, but Gio's appear more out of sync—there's no rhyme or reason to the lines that stroke over his skin. They almost look like veins rather than images or designs as they span across his arm and disappear into his sleeve.

"This is ridiculous." I put a hand on the top of the car and turn towards him. "We're not friends. Why are you guys even bothering to do any of this?"

Nolan speaks up again, reminding me that he's still there as he rounds the back of the Firebird and comes towards the two of us. "That's a very good question, Princess," he says.

I whip around and pin him with a glare. His long legs eat up the distance between us in an instant. I sway backward, my ass bumping into the car's door, but he doesn't let up. Hard fingers grip my waist from behind and hold me in place—Gio's—as Nolan stands in front of me. I'm trapped between the two of them, their bodies creating walls on either side of me.

My eyes widen in realization when I spot a familiar face over Nolan's shoulder. *Roquel.*

We're in public. They should *not* be doing this.

Roquel lifts her head and comes to a halt between a set of beaters that both have matching rusted undercarriages. Her jaw drops and her brow creases, but she doesn't move towards me. She just watches us as if she's waiting to see what will happen. Just like every other person still in the student lot.

Nolan's head lowers inch by minuscule inch until the hot fan of his breath drifts over the top of my ear. "Why do you think we're doing all of this?" His voice is practically a purr. Cruel arousal stabs viciously at my insides and I beat that shit back with all of the self-control I can muster.

Needing the distraction, I force my attention back to Roquel. As soon as I do, a spike of unease slams into me. There's something about her expression that bothers me, but before I can decipher what it is, Nolan's lips brush the tip of my ear. I gasp, swinging my gaze back to him.

"What are you doing?" I choke out, reaching up and clamping a hand over the side of my head.

"Isn't that the question of the century?" Gio chuckles behind me.

Neither man moves away, and I have the distinct impression that they're doing this on purpose. They're all over me in the school parking lot and there are dozens of eyes on us.

Reality is a cold-hearted bitch. "You're using me." Slowly lowering my hand back to my side, I turn my head to gaze at Gio over my shoulder. He frowns. I pivot back and meet Nolan's eyes and let emptiness fill me as my tone comes out flat and even. "Did you already tell everyone?"

Nolan's brows dip and twin lines form between them as he backs up a step. "Tell everyone what?"

The Scorpion Kings saved me.

The Scorpion Kings drove me to school.

The Scorpion Kings are practically dry-humping me in front of the entire student body.

I've been played. *Again.*

"Did you tell everyone that you fucked me? That you got into the ex-prep girl's pants?" I look back at Gio. "He did by the way—get in my pants that is," I say truthfully. "But he didn't fuck me. Was that the plan?"

The hands on my hips disappear and Gio looks like I just slapped him. I don't care. Turning, I get into the car, ripping my backpack off and throwing it onto the floorboards as I grab the door handle and slam it shut behind me. Neither man stops me; both remain outside, staring down through the tinted glass of the passenger side window. After several beats, they move away from where I'm sitting to the rear of the car.

The back of my skull meets the headrest as I stare up at the ceiling of the car. I was a fucking fool last night. Of course Nolan doesn't actually want anything else from me but what he can use. There must be a reason they came to my rescue after the attack. Hell, what if the Scorpion Kings are the ones who instigated it in the first place?

My thoughts are driven away as the driver's side door

opens and Gio gets in. Silence stretches between us as he cranks the engine and puts on his seat belt. A large part of me wants to call him and his fucking Scorpion brothers out on the shit I'm just now starting to work out, but another part of me warns me to stay quiet. If they're responsible for the attack last night, then they'll learn I'm not just an ex-prep princess; I'm the girl that will ruin them.

I stare at Gio's profile as he backs up and heads towards the parking lot's exit. "You don't know what you're talking about, Juliet."

Juliet. Not Prep Girl. I smile, and I know it's anything but sweet and amused. "Are you mad because Nolan got to me first?" I ask.

He doesn't respond, but the skin of his knuckles turns white as his hands tighten on the steering wheel. They're not the only ones who can play this game. They're not the only ones full of venom.

"Nolan didn't fuck you," Gio finally says, the words sharp and angry.

I laugh. "But he wanted to." Worse yet, *I'd* wanted him to. Like an idiot.

Gio's eyes flash to mine, dripping with venom. "Look in a fucking mirror, Prep Girl," he snaps. "Any man with a working cock would want to."

"The whole school knows I'm involved with you somehow now," I say, ignoring his claim. "You know what they're going to start saying."

"Fuck what they say." Gio slams a palm on the steering wheel. "You think we care what they say?" The Firebird jerks to a stop at a red light and he turns to face me. "People in this town talk; it's what they do." He glowers at me. "You should know that better than anyone. If you think we feel any need to hide simply because you don't want people to talk..." He lets his words drift off because his meaning is clear.

I face forward and cross my arms over my chest. "The light is green," I snap. "Drive."

Gio curses and the Firebird eases forward, but not before he gets one last statement in. "We're not your enemies, Juliet. Sure, we tested you when you first got to Public, but I'm sure you've noticed how everyone's stopped shoving you in the halls. How they've all stopped leaving trash or rotten food on your desk and in your locker. We saved your ass last night, and if that doesn't prove you can trust us, then nothing will."

But I *can't* trust them. Maybe it's not even about them. I can't trust anyone. I've been stabbed in the back too many times and I'm tired. Tired of trusting and tired of betrayal.

If history has taught me anything, it's that I'm a poor judge of character and nothing has changed except my zip code.

33
NOLAN

She's right not to trust us; even I don't know what the hell we're doing with her. I consider Juliet's words as I jog towards the gym. Lex is already there in the locker rooms when I arrive. His back is to me as he yanks his t-shirt over his head and tosses it into his open locker. I glance down the row of doors and into the adjoining shower room, but for now, it appears, we're alone. With a sigh, I let the door close behind me and move slowly towards Lex.

"Hey, man…" My head throbs as I approach.

Lex stiffens at the sound of my voice, his back muscles tightening in bunching jumps before he reaches into his locker and yanks out his practice jersey. He's angry and I get it. He's so close to having what he's always wanted—a way out of Silverwood and … her. It's not the escape that has him so insane, it's the girl.

Juliet.

"I know you're upset because I'm not letting you spend time with her, but—"

He whirls on me, pinning me with a look so dark it's closer to that of a mad animal than a human being, and I shut right the fuck up. "That is not what I'm pissed about," he snaps.

The jersey dangles from one hand, his fist gripping it as if he's strangling it in lieu of me.

I close my eyes. "It..." What do I say? That last night was an accident? It wasn't. I'd been one hundred percent sober and I liked it. I wanted it then and I want it again. I reopen my eyes. When I do, Lex is staring back at me, nostrils flaring as if he can smell her sex on me. Logically, I know that doesn't make sense, but ever since last night, I swear I feel as if I'm branded by her.

"I don't want her to drive us apart," I tell him. "I won't let her."

"I don't care," Lex bites out, "that you fucked her. I care that you won't let me fuck her too."

My hands fist at my sides. "I did *not* fuck her." Each word comes out through clenched teeth.

Lex drops his shirt and steps up to me, our chests brushing against one another as he gets in my face. "She was mine first," he snaps. "I should've been the first one to have her."

He's not listening to me. He's breathing heavy, chest rising and falling as he, too, seems to rein in the desire for blood and violence. "Who said you get to decide who does what? Who takes her to work? Who takes her home? Who fucks her?"

I narrow my eyes on his. "You did," I bite out. "You and Gio. You know how we work. You never had a fucking problem with me calling the shots until her. If you want to keep her all to yourself then why haven't you made a move before now, huh?"

Lex doesn't respond. Of course, he doesn't. "Because you're scared," I tell him. "You've been obsessed with her for thirteen fucking years and not once have you done anything more than watch and jack off to her pictures in your fucking house."

The punch is expected. I let it come, not even bothering to avoid it as it sends my head snapping to the side. "Fuck you!" Lex bursts out. "I'm not a virgin."

Slowly, I turn back to face him. I work my jaw, tasting blood on the inside of my cheek. "No," I say. "You're not a virgin. You pay hookers and strippers to come to your house and dress up as your little obsession so you don't have to step over whatever barrier you've built for yourself. You're living in a fantasy when it comes to her and now that she's dropped into your reality, you don't know how to deal."

A muscle jumps in Lex's jaw. My own aches. Fuck, but he hits hard.

"You want to piss on her too?" I ask. "Mark her as yours so every asshole in school knows it? Think she'll let you when she finds out about that room of yours?"

The snarl that escapes him is more predator than man. I hold my arms out on either side of my body. "Do you want to talk?" I demand. "Or do you just want to hit me again?"

"I want to do a hell of a lot more than fucking hit you, Pierce," Lex bites out. He only ever uses my last name when he's pissed as hell, and for what it's worth, this kind of anger from him is rare. Unfortunately, that only makes it all the more dangerous.

"Then let's go," I offer. "But just know that even if we beat each other bruised and bloody, we'll still have this talk after."

Lex takes a step back, rocking onto the balls of his feet as if he's contemplating my offer. I watch him and I wait, my own body tensing as I take in each minuscule twitch of his form. When he doesn't move after several moments, I still don't relax. I've seen Lex fight and he's a nasty, manipulative son of a bitch. He'll make you think he's done, that he's letting you go—and then he'll go for the kill. It's why Darrio likes using him for enforcer work so much. It's why he likes using all of us for enforcer work—we're all bastards when it comes to survival.

"Why Gio?" he demands, and I know what he's really asking. Why not him?

I release a slow breath and let my body finally relax. "Because we needed to talk."

"About what?"

I take a step towards him and then think better of it, but unwilling to back down, I go still, remaining right where I am.

"I didn't fuck her last night," I tell him. *Truth.* "I wouldn't do that to you." *Lie.* What a fucking liar I am. I wanted to have her last night and only by the grace of some unseen God had I managed to drag my desire back from the brink.

I could have taken her so easily. She'd been so open and ready for me, her wet slit practically weeping for a good, hard ride. As ashamed as I am to admit my folly, it wasn't Lex's obsession with the girl that stopped me, but the bruises hidden beneath her clothes. Tit for tat, my ass.

I'd wanted to do more than just devour Juliet Donovan's cunt; I wanted to flip her over and fuck her hard enough to pile drive her through a damn wall. With my hands on her skin, moving over the places that fucker had touched her before she'd killed him, I'd finally understood why Lex is and has been six feet under her thrall for so fucking long.

Juliet Donovan is pain personified and men like us love a little bit of agony.

Lex doesn't move. He just continues to stand there, staring at me as if he can see past all of my bullshit and right to the heart of the problem. I wanted to fuck Juliet Donovan last night. If it'd just been a fuck with no emotion attached, I might have done it, but for some fucking reason, Silverwood's public enemy number one has scrambled my fucking brains.

I reach up and drag a hand down my face, releasing a low curse.

Honesty. That's how our friendship works. I never keep shit from Lex and G. They know all of my dirty little secrets and I know theirs. This can't be any different. She can't be any different.

"I didn't fuck her," I repeat my words from earlier as if

they will lessen the power of the next ones, "but I did ... go down on her."

Lex barrels forward and I don't try to stop him as he grabs ahold of my shirt and slams me back into the wall of lockers. With dark eyes locked not on mine, but on my lips instead, he heaves great breaths as he lowers himself. When you're faced with monsters of all kinds in your childhood, you learn when it's best to remain still and when you should run. Right now, I know better than to move a single inch. I'd let my body atrophy and turn to stone right here before I'd break the spell that has fallen over my friend.

"You ... put your mouth on her?" he asks.

"Yes."

His eyes widen slightly, nostrils flaring as he pulls in more oxygen, as if he can smell the taste of her even after hours have passed. "You wouldn't let me take her home last night." A statement, not a question.

I answer it as if it were one anyway. "You couldn't handle it." If Juliet Donovan disappears now, no matter that ninety-nine percent of the town wants her dead and gone, people will ask questions. As far as I've heard, her father's old partner is still trying to get her to stay with him. If anything, Morpheus Calloway will look for her if *someone* decides to lock her up and keep her captive in their basement.

Not that Lex has a basement, but he does have a very nice —hidden—house that has a fuck ton of cameras, a closet full of bondage because he doesn't like the hookers touching him when he fucks them, and a shit load of mental obsessive issues.

Lex's upper lip curls back and he continues to stare at my mouth as if he's debating whether he wants to rip my face off or kiss me. I close my eyes. There's no attraction between us, but when it comes to Juliet, Lex isn't always sane. I doubt he's ever been. If it brings him closer to the object of his affection, I have no doubt that he'd do any number of things.

"I brushed my teeth this morning," I warn him. "You won't get anything of her from me."

The curse that erupts from him is knowing but no less disappointed. He releases me with a sharp shove against the lockers and my eyes open to find him stalking away from me and reaching for the football jersey on the floor. He pulls it on over his head.

"She's not yours," he grits out.

I hate to say it—I really fucking do—but someone needs to remind him of the other truth he refuses to admit. "She's not yours either."

Silence. Stone. Cold. Fucking. Silence.

"I can help you." Damn me, but I'm going to. Lex is my brother, not by blood but by circumstance and she's the only thing he's ever truly wanted.

Gun metal gray eyes swing my way. He doesn't say anything but waits for me to continue. "You're not the only one that wants her anymore." Neither am I. All three of us want her.

I don't know why it has to be her for him, or me, or Gio. She doesn't share our pasts. She doesn't know us. We hardly know her. Perhaps, it's part of human nature to desire that which will hurt us. She's venom in our veins and an addiction none of us can let go of.

"There's nothing that will change my mind," Lex says. His eyes lift to mine again. "I want her enough to do whatever it takes."

I nod. I'd known as much. Juliet Donovan might not be her father, but she's just as dangerous.

"Are you going to get in my way?" Lex asks. "Or are you going to join me?"

"So, you're saying yes?"

"I'm saying this is what I've wanted from the beginning so, yes, Nolan. *Whatever. It. Takes.*" He repeats the words with a note of finality.

"Okay, then." I guess I have my answer. I've seen the way Gio looks at her. I know he won't be hard to convince, but now we need to discuss our other important matter.

"Have you heard from her father lately?"

Lex grunts as he turns back to his locker and shucks his jeans. I take a seat on the bench. "Allen Donovan has been in touch," he answers. "I don't have anything for him yet, but I know his lawyer has been emailing Juliet regularly to get her to visit him in prison. The longer he goes without hearing from her, though, the more desperate he seems."

"He has a lot to lose," I say.

"He's already lost everything," Lex replies. He grabs his football pants and pulls them on one leg at a time. "I don't have any evidence that will help him yet."

"Let me know when you do," I say. "The whole town is following the story and his trial is coming up in a matter of weeks." Eight to be exact. Two months and then Allen Donovan's face will be splashed across the media all over again—and no doubt Juliet's will be too.

"What about that other matter?" I ask, hedging at the events from last night as I cast a look over to the door. It's not locked, but everyone else is at practice right now. No one else should be here. As it stands, I won't be going and Coach will only have Lex to beat on for being late.

"It's done," Lex says, tying the front of his pants and reaching for his cleats. "No one will tie Otis to Juliet."

"Did you find anything on him that might explain the attack?"

With a shake of his head, Lex turns away once more. "No, but I know where he was staying. He was transient for the most part. He was bunking with some of the meth heads by the old train tracks in the abandoned car lot back there."

"What else do you know about Otis?"

He looks over his shoulder as he speaks. "He wasn't necessarily a violent offender. A piece of shit and an addict, but he had no history of violence against women or rape."

Which can only mean one thing. Otis attacked Juliet because someone likely paid him to.

"We'll figure it out," I say, stretching to my feet with my arms over my head. My back muscles pop and I repress a groan. "I've got to head to work. Darrio has me running some errands this afternoon." I eye Lex as he yanks on his shoes and quickly does up the laces. Without giving myself a chance to think too hard, I say, "Why don't you pick Jules up from work and drop her off at my house later?"

His head lifts, his expression morphing into one of excitement. Like a kid on Christmas. "Just me?" he asks.

I nod. "Yeah, but don't fuck around," I say. "Text me when you pick her up."

Lex agrees readily, his whole demeanor changing in an instant. Lightness exudes from him as he hurriedly finishes getting ready for practice despite the fact that he's a solid half-hour late. Even if he knows Coach is going to murder him on the field for tardiness, now that he knows he'll see Juliet afterward, he doesn't even seem to care.

I shake my head as I leave the locker room. I almost pity the girl. She doesn't realize it yet, but Juliet Donovan has attracted a monster and he has every intention of caging her. Before too long, the people of Silverwood will forget what her father did and who her father is. They'll forget all about her, and then he'll strike.

34
JULIET

The Dionysus Lounge is full today. Each massive circular booth the hosts use to chat with their 'guests' has at least one man. Sensual instrumental music pours out of invisible speakers. I stop by one of the tables and set down a fresh bucket of ice and a three-hundred-dollar champagne. Margo, the host, frowns my way when her client isn't looking. She'd been outside when Gio had driven up and dropped me off. Even outside of Silverwood, I can't escape their infamy.

Once I'm done with my task, I turn tail and head back to the bar. Mads stands there, waiting with a tray in hand as the bartender pours drinks while the ticket machine beeps and spits out another order. Mads straightens and smiles as I approach.

"Hey, how are you?" she asks, her tone hesitant as if she's not sure of her welcome.

I sigh, turn, and prop my hip against the side of the bar. "I don't know if I have an answer to that," I tell her honestly.

The soft look of understanding she sends me makes me want to shove my head through a glass window. At least she means it though. One thing I've managed to discern from

Madison Torres is that she's every bit as kind as she acts. She's not one to gossip or spill other people's secrets. I've watched her listen to Roquel drone on and on about other people's problems. She never says a word about any of them, never agrees, but always listens. I wonder if she'll listen to me if I tell her about the Scorpion Kings.

Another waitress comes up and practically snatches the tray from Mads' hands, grabbing the three drinks that the bartender plunks down and loading them up before disappearing. Mads watches her go, her hands now empty with a creased brow. When she turns back to me, the long golden blonde hair that she has pulled into a high ponytail swishes over the nape of her exposed neck.

"I assume it has to do with the Scorpion Kings?" she hedges.

"When is it ever *not* about them?" I groan. Now that I'm no longer in the fold of Silverwood Prep—the Scorpion Kings are all I know. I haven't even been able to go to Cory's gym anymore because now I know that Gio goes there too. Then again, I'm staying with Nolan. If there's no avoiding Gio, then I guess I can start going back. I've missed it.

Mads is quiet for a moment more, her gaze turning down. She looks contemplative. I don't mind the silence. My eyes move over her in her dark wash shorts and shimmery low-cut blouse. It's not real silk, though it does a great impression of it. Real silk isn't that shiny.

"Can I..." Mads stops and lifts her head, a blush stealing across her cheeks. She ducks down again. "Never mind, it's none of my business."

But now I'm curious. "Can you what?" I prompt her.

Her jaw firms and this time, when she raises her head, her eyes connect with mine and they don't leave. "I want to offer you advice," she admits. "But ... I don't normally do it unless someone has asked, and you..." She gestures to me.

"Haven't?" I finish.

She nods.

Setting my tray on the end of the bar, I cross my arms over my chest. "Go ahead," I tell her.

She starts talking as if she's worried she'll lose her nerve before the words are out. "Be careful," she says. "With them, I mean."

I arch a brow. "With the Scorpion Kings?"

Her chin jerks down. "I'm sure you think you know them because you've lived in Silverwood your whole life, but you don't know them—the *real* them."

It takes effort not to let myself go cold at her words. "And you do?" I inquire cautiously.

Madison's lips press together for a brief moment as if she doesn't want to answer, but then she does. "Maybe not as well as they know each other, but I've gone to school with them a lot longer than you, and I…" Her words drift off and the look she gives me is almost helpless. "I know I might seem out of touch with everything at school," she continues. "People ignore me, though—they forget that I'm around and they say things they may not otherwise reveal."

Now, she has my interest. "What do you know?" I demand, leaning closer, dropping my arms.

Her brow furrows. "It's not what I know, it's just that—" She closes her arms around herself, rubbing up and down as if she has a chill. "The Scorpion Kings aren't boys. They're dangerous, and I like you. You're not what I expected."

I know what that means. "I'm not a cold, stuck-up bitch?" I ask, arching a brow.

Her snort of laughter is warm and relieving. She lowers her arms back to her sides and shakes her head. "No, you *are*," she corrects and then grins, "but I think I like that about you."

I smile back at her, surprised by how easy it is. It's easy in a way that it isn't with Roquel. With Roquel, there's a score, a debt. She got me a job and I give her information—gossip. She feeds on it. I appreciate the kindness she showed me in my first introduction to Silverwood, but at the end of the day, her friendship comes with strings. It's clear that Mads' doesn't. It almost makes me want to try again. *Almost.*

"I know what I'm getting into," I tell her. "It doesn't take a blind man to see that they're using me for something." The fact burns something foul in my gut. Anger is red hot, a seething demon prowling for release in the back of my mind.

Yeah, I definitely need to hit up Cory's gym again soon. I've let the frustration build up far too much.

Mads' next words shock me back into the conversation. "I don't know that they're using you," she comments, teeth sinking into her lower lip as her face contorts in thought. She releases it with a huff and gives me a sad look. "You have to understand. All three of them have had a rough upbringing—a lot of kids in Silverwood Public have, but they're different."

"I know that Lex's parents are dead," I state, "and that Nolan's dad took off a few years back." Even if I'm not from their side of the tracks, everyone knows everyone's business in Silverwood.

"Lex's dad killed his mom and then himself. Lex was with his aunt at the time—his parents were being investigated by social services—it's probably the only thing that saved his life," Mads says. "And Nolan's dad was abusive to his mom. A lot of people in town think Nolan killed him after his mom was sent to the emergency room. She was pregnant and she lost the baby due to a beating he gave her."

A dull throb pulses behind my right eye. My chest aches and clenches. I can't keep looking at her as she tells me this shit, so I turn and look out over the lounge, not seeing a damn thing in front of me.

A soft hand finds my arm and I know it's Mads. "I think a lot of people were surprised that you came out of your parents' mess as strong as you did," she says, her voice low. "None so much as them."

"What does me being 'strong' have to do with anything?" I

snap, looking back at her. "Do you think they're hanging around because I didn't bow to their commands the second I stepped into school?" I doubt that's it. Nothing is ever so simple.

Mads doesn't even flinch at my tone. She keeps going as if I'd never spoken in the first place. "The Scorpion Kings are survivors and so are you. I see that. *They* see that. Your strength is something they crave. They're addicted to it. Their attention—their *blessing*—is the same as drinking a scorpion's venom straight. If you're not careful, soon you'll start to bleed just like them. I don't want to see you get hurt."

I don't have it in me to tell her it's too late. Dead people can't feel pain and that's exactly what I am. Juliet Donovan died months ago on the front lawn of her childhood home as her father was taken into police custody and her mother broke down in front of the entire town. I flatlined that night and my corpse is the one calling the shots now. No one even seems to notice.

Carefully, so as not to frighten her, I extract my arm from her hand and take a step back. The bartender slaps down several drinks on the end of the counter and I move towards it numbly. I gather the drinks and put them on the tray.

Mads' expression is full of sorrow when I turn back to face her. "Think about what I said," she tells me. "And know that if you ever need a friend, I'll be here."

I don't respond. I have nothing to say. Her words hit far too close for comfort. They're a warning, alright. A tale of cautionary dangers—get too close to the Scorpion Kings and they'll kill me. They'll drain me dry of this supposed strength of mine and when I show even the slightest bit of weakness … what then?

Hours later, when my shift ends, I'm still thinking about her words as I shrug into the clothes I'd worn to school and stuff the rest into my backpack to be taken back and washed. I head out into the parking lot, but instead of Gio's Firebird, I spot Lex's black SUV with the headlights turned off at the back of the lot.

Lex. Not Gio or Nolan. My heart threads an unsteady beat in my chest. I march towards the SUV, wishing I'd brought a jacket, and round it, popping the passenger side door. Lex smiles from the driver's side. I don't say anything as I slide into the seat and close the door behind me.

It's warm in the cab and there's a familiar emo rock song playing on the radio at a low volume that almost makes me relax. It's something I'd listen to if I were on my own—a musical taste that I used to hide from Bran and Avery because every time something like it came across one of their mainstream stations, they'd scoff and roll their eyes in annoyance before changing the channel.

Rich girls aren't supposed to like Hollywood Undead. They're not supposed to scream to Disturbed or cry with Linkin Park. Rich girls are supposed to like things that aren't as deep, easy repetitive beats with lyrics shallower than a kiddie pool. They aren't supposed to relate to the songs about betrayal and heartache and neglect. Only weirdos listen to those songs. Only the kids who hate themselves walk around dressed in black all of the time and make a hobby out of slitting their wrists. At least, that's what society believes. Doesn't matter that it's bullshit. Anyone can hurt. Anyone can love good music, and now I can too.

Maybe my dad's betrayal hadn't fucked up my entire life. Because of him, I can do whatever the fuck I want now. So, I lean forward and turn the dial-up, letting "The Kill" by Thirty Seconds to Mars drown out all of the shit in my head if only for a few minutes.

Lex is quiet as he drives out of the parking lot. Street lights pass overhead, illuminating the inside of the vehicle briefly before disappearing us into the dark once more, until the next one arrives and does it all over again. Hanging a right, Lex drives us onto the on-ramp for the interstate. As he speeds up, the front of the SUV trembles slightly and then calms as it gets over whatever hurdle had sent the hood shaking. Signs pass us on the highway. Silverwood 32 miles. Eastpoint 190 miles. Eastpoint. I wonder if that would be a good place to rebuild my life when I graduate. Eastpoint University was my top college of choice last year. This year, I'll have to apply for the underprivileged program if I want to make it in.

They're survivors ... Mads' words circle in my head like a pack of starving vultures, plucking at any stray thought and reminding me of our conversation. I cast a look in Lex's direction.

Survivors are dangerous because you never know what they did to become one.

"Juliet?" Lex's voice penetrates my maudlin thoughts. "Are you okay?"

Silverwood 20 miles. My chest constricts. "I'm fine," I say. Minutes pass, and Lex doesn't respond to my obvious lie. Instead, when the next off-ramp comes up, he diverges from the road. I sit up.

"Where are we going?" I demand as the SUV veers onto the exit.

The illumination of yellow gas station lights draws closer. Lex doesn't answer me as he directs the front of the car into the lot and then pulls it up to a pump. I relax back into the seat but watch him out of the corner of my eye. Lex shuts off the vehicle and gets out, keys in hand as he goes to perform the task of fueling the car.

When he gets back inside, Lex cranks the engine, but instead of pulling around to the exit, he drives forward and parks along the side of the gas station where a shitty diner faces towards the interstate. I frown at the open sign as he shuts off the vehicle once more and gets out.

He rounds the front of the SUV and stops next to my door, popping it open. I eye him. "I'm tired, Lex," I say. "I want to go home."

Not that Nolan's house is my home. For that matter, neither is my currently unlivable apartment. His gaze pierces me, then he leans in close. My breath catches as the smell of him invades my personal space. Cheap soap and shampoo should not be that enticing.

I'm so focused on how close he is, how the heat and scent of him comes over me in waves even though he hasn't even touched me, that I don't notice that he's unsnapping my seatbelt until the thing loosens against my chest and slides back.

"What—" I reach for it, but he stops me with a hand and a shake of his head.

"Come on," he says quietly, nodding back to the diner. "I'm going to feed you."

"I'm not hungry." As soon as the words leave my lips, my stomach chooses that moment to announce its dedication to Team Lex in an aggressive rumble.

I close my eyes again and silently curse. Doing a quick tally of how much I have in my bag from tonight's tips, I look across the way at the shiny interior of the diner. With disgust at my easy capitulation, I get out of the vehicle. Lex shuts the door behind me and moves towards the entrance. Keeping my arms secured around myself, hands gripping my elbows as if they're a lifeline, I don't look up as I follow him into the building.

The smells hit me—burned coffee and something sweet and sugary. I lift my head and spy the small glass case by the register to the side. Various deserts from pies to cookies decorated with bright cheery colors are on display. My mouth waters. When was the last time I had something sweet?

A strong male hand reaches back and pries one of my arms out, fingers locking around first my wrist and then moving down until our palms are against one another. Lex doesn't look back at me as he pulls me along, leading me down a row of red-vinyl booths. He gets to the last one and gestures for me to sit down. I glance back at the direct line to the exit and then to the seat he wants me to take.

With my free hand, I point to the booth seat with its back against the wall. "Can I sit there?" I ask.

Ash gray eyes watch me and Lex releases my hand as if that's his answer. I hurry by him and feel my shoulders relax marginally with something solid at my back. When he takes his seat across from me, he shifts uncomfortably, and for a moment, I wonder if he has the same issues as I do. Before I can ask, though, a harried, rail-thin woman appears at the edge of the table with a notepad in hand and not one, not two, but three pens stuck through the bun at the back of her head.

"What'll it be?" she asks expectantly.

I scramble for the menus set towards the window, but before I can even lay a finger on the grease-stained plastic folders, Lex speaks up. "Two waters, two specials—one with no mayo—a coffee, and a slice of apple pie with ice cream on the side."

I gape at the man across from me, but the woman wastes no time in scribbling the order on her pad and disappearing back down the row of half-empty tables and booths.

"Did you just order for me?" I ask.

Lex meets my gaze and nods.

"Why?"

"I've been here before," he says. "I know what you'll like."

I shake my head. "What makes you so sure?"

"It's a turkey club sandwich with fries," Lex replies. "Without mayo. I know you don't like it."

"And the coffee and apple pie?" I ask. He can't know what my favorite dessert is. *There's no fucking wa—*

"Coffee is for me," he answers. "Apple pie and ice cream is for you."

Something about the way he stares at me tells me it isn't. I press my back against the worn seat and frown. A prickle of awareness stings the back of my neck and to calm my racing heart, I turn away from the man in front of me to examine the interior of the roadside restaurant. There aren't that many customers at this time of night. A plump woman with a rambunctious little boy bobbing his head and swinging his legs to some silent tune in his head as he scribbles on a piece of paper sits in a booth towards the entrance. There's a flannel-wearing truck driver by the counter and an older couple at a lower table on the opposite side of the entire restaurant—as far from the convenience section of the gas station attached to this place as they can get—their white hair barely puffs above the chairs and booths between us.

I clench my hands into fists and then release them only to repeat the action. I don't stop until the waitress returns, two glasses of water and a small mug of coffee in tow. Setting everything down along with creamer and sugars next to the black coffee that smells more like motor oil than the real—non-instant—stuff, she heads back around the corner as a cook rings a bell in the slit of a window above the drink machines.

Needing to do something, I reach out and snatch several napkins from the black and white container pinning the menus against the window. Slowly, methodically, I pull apart the two-ply paper and then scrunch the centers. I'm aware of Lex's eyes lingering on me as I work, but it takes considerable effort to do this without ripping the cheap tissue paper and still make it turn out the way I want it to.

"Flowers?" he finally guesses as I finish the first one and set it aside to grab a few more napkins.

"Yeah," I mumble, starting the process all over again. "I was on the Student Council Committee at Silverwood Prep for Junior year. We sponsored the prom." Both Avery and Brandon had bailed on helping.

"Public has a prom too, you know," Lex mentions.

"Yeah, I'm sure it does." I snort. "I doubt I'll go."

"Even if someone were to invite you?"

I freeze at that question and the waitress appears in that moment, tray in hand. She passes both clubs onto the Formica tabletop and points out the toothpick marking which one has no mayo before ordering us to let her know when we're ready for the apple pie. Lex deftly slides the mayo-free club in my direction and I swipe the remains of the torn tissue flower to the side. My stomach grumbles again, but I'm already putting one corner of the perfectly cut club into my mouth and biting down.

Several moments of peace pass as I consume one half of the club and then the second before picking at the fries. Lex finishes his meal before me, seeming to devour the sandwich and fries in short bites.

"Well?" His prompting question has me dropping a fry to my plate smack dab in the middle of the mound of ketchup I'd squirted onto an open section.

"Well, what?" I reach for a fresh napkin, this time to wipe my mouth clean of any crumbs.

"Would you go to prom if someone asked you?"

I roll my eyes. "No one is going to ask the pariah of Silverwood to prom," I say. "So, it's a non-issue."

"*I'm* asking you."

The napkin falls from my hand, landing right over that fry in the ketchup mountain. I raise my head and stare at him. His hair is still wet at the ends from a recent shower, the ends curving just below his ears. His face is lean and well-defined, with high cheekbones, and a few scars here and there—no doubt from fights or football injuries—but overall, he's handsome. Had he been born on the north side of Silverwood, the prep girls in my old life would've been all over him.

But he wasn't, I remind myself. He was born on the wrong side of the tracks and he's mastered the art of manipulation. Only I don't know why he'd be using it against me now.

I sit back in my seat. "No."

One dark slash of a brow arches. "No?" he repeats, a questioning tone in his voice, though he doesn't sound particularly surprised or bothered by my answer.

"No," I affirm. "I'm not playing this game with the three of you. I'm not going to be used and passed around like some prize between you, Nolan, and Gio. So, whatever bullshit you're trying to pull, you can cut it out right now. When you drop me off at Nolan's, I'll pack my shit and go back to my place. I'm not doing this."

"The complex hasn't fixed anything yet." Lex leans forward, placing both of his elbows on the edge of the table. He doesn't deny my assumption of the reasoning behind his sudden offer to take me to prom. "And what exactly am I trying to pull?"

I push my plate away. "You know exactly what you're doing."

When Lex tilts his head, it's with an odd sort of animal grace. As if he's as connected to his body as a hunting lion, no sign of the awkward stilted movements of a boy. He's all man.

"Enlighten me." His words are a challenge and I rise to the bait.

"I don't fucking need to," I say. "We both know what game the three of you are playing—it's the reason Nolan's letting everyone at school assume I'm fucking you. It's a power play. Let me ask you something; when are the threats going to make an appearance?" A snarl builds up in my throat.

Why did I let them help me? Was it just because I was vulnerable and needed someone and they were in the right place at the right time? Then again, they hadn't really given me much choice, *but then again*, I didn't really fight all that hard, did I?

"Threats?" His question is quiet.

"Yes," I hiss. "Threats. Suck my dick or I'll tell everyone your secret. Spread your legs or you'll go to prison just like your daddy. Let me and my friends treat you like our little whore or—"

"I am *not* threatening you to get you into my bed." Lex leans forward, cutting me off as his gaze darkens. His shoulders seem to swell with each breath he takes, his nostrils flaring as he glares back at me.

An image of Nolan surfaces. His big body on top of mine. His tongue in my mouth. Mine in his. I shake my head, trying to rid myself of the memory.

Fuck this. I'm not waiting here a second longer. Standing up, I dig into my pocket and withdraw a twenty. Slapping it onto the table, I glare at him. "I'm not interested in any more lies," I tell him, "and I'm done talking about this. I called your fucking game. I'll find my own way back to Silverwood."

I leave the booth and stomp towards the exit and out into the parking lot. The moon hangs fat and heavy overhead. I glare up at it before taking a look around, wondering if there's a bus stop nearby or if I'll have to hitchhike my way back to Silverwood proper.

I don't make it ten feet across the lot before Lex is storming out of the diner and making a beeline for me. With a growl, I hold up a hand and flip him off. "Get lost, Lex," I call out. "I'm not dealing with—"

He doesn't stop. Doesn't even slow as he drives into me, grabbing my arm and swinging me around to back me into the side of his SUV. "If you think I'm going to leave you out here in the middle of bumfuck just because you've got an attitude, you don't know shit."

"An attitude?" I'll show him a fucking attitude. Shoving him back, I slide out from beneath him and stomp over to one of the gas pumps. Right next to it, as if someone had dumped it out of the back of their truck when they pulled away, is none other than a thick red brick.

It calls to me like a beacon. Anger sits inside me and there's no escape from it. My nightmares. My attacker. Megan. The school. The goddamn Scorpion Kings. Fucking everything is compounding and I'm out of control. I feel torn open and exposed, like my protective cover has been ripped free and everyone can see my wires. I just want them to look away. To leave me alone. To stop blaming me when I didn't. Do. Anything. Wrong.

"Juliet." Lex's voice is a warning. One that I ignore as I bend over and pick it up.

My hands are immediately coated in dust and grime. The burning rage inside me makes it so that I don't care. Rage can do a lot of things. It can numb you to pain that would otherwise be debilitating. It can make you stronger, faster, and a hell of a lot meaner.

"How's this for fucking attitude, Lex!" I scream as I heave it up and hurl the damn thing right towards the back window of his SUV.

The second the brick leaves my hand, it's like the whole world slows down. I watch it fly the short distance and with as much anger and force as I'd put behind it, I'm not shocked when it collides with the black glass and shatters it upon impact. Glass rains down against the pavement, pinging and skidding every which way. The cracking sound echoes around the near-empty parking lot, and for several seconds the two of us just stand there. It's as if neither one of us can believe what just happened—what I just did. I don't even think. I just run.

Anywhere as long as it's away from here. Away from him.

35
LEX

It's instinct. The chase. The thrill. The desire to hunt and feast. That's why we're taught not to run from predators. Running triggers their basic instinct to hunt. Only prey run from predators.

Now, Juliet is running from me and I am chasing her.

What I'll do when I catch her ... well, we're both about to find out.

Juliet tears off across the parking lot, her blue hair flying behind her as she runs. My limbs are sore, not just from practice but from the extra punishment Coach heaped on me for not only being late, but for also being the only one of my brothers to have shown up at all. I give chase anyway, my legs devouring the space between us. I'm taller, and though she's strong and fast, I'm fucking faster. I catch her at the far edge of the parking lot right where the road leads to the on-ramp of the highway. Before her feet can cross the strip of dead grass, I reach out and capture her.

A scream echoes back to my ears—not one of fear, but one of anger and annoyance. My lips twitch in amusement. This right here is what I'd been missing in all of our years apart. She couldn't curse at me from photographs like she is now as I lift her in my arms, hefting her and throwing her over my shoulder in a quick move. No video could truly capture the warmth of her fists hitting my back as I carry her back to my SUV.

"Put me down!" she yells.

My hand lands against the deliciously rounded backside squirming over my shoulder with a loud clap. She freezes for a single second right before she's back to cursing and hitting me, harder than before. Yeah. This is nice.

"You fucking asshole!"

Glass crunches under my shoes as I round to the passenger door. I pop it open and deliver her into the seat. Her punch slams into the side of my face the second she's right side up and I react on pure impulse. My hand snaps out and grips her around the throat. I thrust her head back against the seat and glare down at her.

Blue eyes flash up at mine. Dangerous. Oh, my baby is so fucking dangerous to me. She's not going to come willingly. She's going to kick and scratch and make me bleed the whole way. The end result will be the same—she'll be mine—but if she wasn't like this, I wouldn't want her. She's a fighter and I'll love all the scars she gives me. They'll be far nicer than any my parents gave me.

"*Behave.*" It's an order.

"Bite me." She spits words like the foulest bile, but what she doesn't understand yet is that I'll do anything she asks of me—even if she regrets asking.

Tipping her head back, I lean into the cab of the SUV. I shift my hand up just enough to bare the length of her throat. Her t-shirt gapes to the side, revealing where her neck meets her shoulder. Without giving her a second to fight me, I sink my teeth into that place.

Pleasure bursts across my tongue. Her gasp echoes in my ears. She tastes like salt and vanilla. My teeth take her harder, digging down until her gasp turns into a sound of dismay and annoyance. Her little hands shove against my shoulders, but I take my time. I stroke my tongue over the bite mark, my lips quirking up when—as I pull back—I see the red half-circle imprint of my teeth on her skin.

"You fucking bastard..." The words are a breathy rasp.

When I straighten and look into her ocean-deep eyes, I work to keep my voice steady. Even so, when I speak, it's through a deep growl. "Punishment is coming, baby..." For her or me, I'm not sure yet.

My thumb strokes along the curve of her throat and up to her jawline. She's so fucking beautiful—like fire and ice captured into one infinitely human soul. I want to die like that. Again and again. In her arms. First by her flame, then by her frost.

Juliet's chest rises and falls in rapid, sharp movements. I release her and step back, closing the door with a quick snap. I watch her dive for the handle with a scowl, but I'm ready for her. I press the button on my key fob and the doors lock.

Her eyes widen on the other side of the glass when she realizes that, unlike newer vehicles, my SUV has the old school knobs at the top of the door that disappears into a hole. She stares at it for a moment and then tries to lock her fingers around it. I hold the lock button down as I circle the front of the SUV. By the time I get into the vehicle, she's fighting back more curses.

"What is wrong with you?" she demands. I crank the engine and reverse out of the parking spot. She yanks on the useless handle. "Let me out! This is kidnapping."

I don't bother to tell her to buckle up; we're not going far. The breeze rolls in from the shattered back window and my lips twitch. I should be pissed, but I'm not. If anything, I'm amused by her reaction. Besides, Nolan has been wanting a reason to fix up the SUV.

Less than five minutes later, I pull onto a small, dark road just far enough off the main one to be hidden and less used.

Directing the front of the SUV onto the shoulder, I slam it into park and remove the keys, deftly slipping them beneath the front seat as Juliet stews in hers.

I suck in a long breath. I knew it would come to this sooner or later. Now that she's here, with me, in reach, I can't help but find myself nervous.

What if she doesn't like me?

What if she doesn't like what I do to her?

What if ... the fantasy is better than the real thing?

All of my fears collide into one in my head, but as the woman next to me turns and faces me, her expression a stony mask, I push them away and focus on her.

"What now?" she demands. "Are you going to leave me in the middle of nowhere and tell me to find my way back on my own?"

Ignoring the ridiculous question, I glance over my shoulder at the backseat. Thankfully, it looks like none of the glass reached there. No doubt it's littering my trunk space though. It'll be a bitch to clean out, but worth it since letting Juliet break my shit brought us both here.

I get out of the car, hitting the unlock button as I do, and hear her outraged cry of, "Where the hell are you going?" behind me. Juliet glares at me through the windshield as I circle around to her side. She tenses as I open her door and reach for her. Her hands ball into fists and she resists, pulling back as I lock my fingers around her wrists and drag her from the car. No more punches though. She learned that lesson.

Her head tips back as I press her against the side of my SUV. Soft moonlight drifts over her features, making her already blue hair appear even more vibrant in the night. My chest is against hers. I'm close enough I can count each pulse of her heartbeat in her throat.

Now that I have her here, I'm practically vibrating with the need to get inside of her.

I didn't fuck her... Nolan's earlier words penetrate the fog of desire that's descended over my mind. No, he hadn't fucked her, but he tasted her. He knows the intimate details of her sex. What kind of flavor rolls across the tongue of the man blessed enough to kneel at her feet. It's not fair. I wanted her first.

"*What?*" Juliet's voice makes me realize I've left off looking at her face and am now slowly moving down the rest of her. She wears a plain t-shirt and jeans like a supermodel. Her body lithe and strong beneath the fabric.

"You think my brothers and I want to hurt you?" I rasp out the question.

"I know you do," she replies.

"You're right," I tell her, "and you're wrong."

She smells so fucking good. It makes me want to bend my head down into the place I marked with my teeth and inhale until I get high on nothing else but her. Juliet Donovan is my drug of choice.

Juliet's body bumps mine as she shifts against the SUV. "Just get on with it," she snaps, gesturing to the road that's unlit by any street lights. "Go on."

"I'm not planning on leaving you here," I tell her, leaning close—so fucking close. I dip my head, holding myself just far enough away that our mouths don't brush, but I can still feel the heat of her breath.

"Then what are you going to do?" She looks at me, so full of defiance and challenge. It would be such a shame to deny her.

The truth is all I have for her. "I'm going to show you exactly why you're wrong about us."

"I hate you, Alexio Medicci…" she whispers. She says my name like a prayer and a curse. It sounds so fucking good on her tongue.

"No, you don't, baby." My mouth hovers incredibly close to hers. The barest of inches separates us. "You hate that I see you. You hate that none of the people you trusted ever saw the real you. But I do. *We* do."

I brush my lips across hers. Once. Twice. By the third time, her breathing hitches and her hands creep up the sides of my arms.

"This doesn't mean shit," she warns me. *Lie.*

"It means *everything*." I grip her waist and let some of my weight rest against her until she can feel the hard ridge of my cock in my jeans.

The moment my mouth finally meets hers, I know we're both lost.

Love? Hate? It doesn't matter anymore. What we feel can't be described by the written word or a simplified emotion. What we feel transcends conscious thought and all that's left is fire and ice.

36
JULIET

Lex's fingertips against my body dig deep, prying me away from the outside of the SUV as his mouth slants over mine. His kiss begins soft, almost reverent, but I don't want that. I want violent. I want wrathful. I bite down on his lower lip hard enough to draw blood and the groan that echoes up his throat rebounds up into the night sky. We're surrounded by nothing but a long stretch of infrequently traveled road and trees. Out here, anything could happen. He could set me loose, tell me to run, and hunt me through these woods.

Just like my dreams…

My fury is waning, slowly being replaced by desire. I latch on to it, the tension coiling low in my belly forcing me to act in a way I never have before. I grip Lex's shoulders and lick away the blood from his mouth. He shoves me back into the SUV's cold, hard surface and takes my mouth in another desperate kiss.

He's big enough to block out most of the area around us, his broad shoulders a mass of darkness that cages me in. Muscles ripple under my hands, against my chest. Lex's hips roll into me, the hard length of his cock rubbing between us—a warning and a promise.

You hate that I see you. You hate that none of the people you trusted ever saw the real you. But I do. We do.

Damn him. Tears prick at the back of my eyes. I push them away, stuffing the ache that those words had caused in my chest so far down that I hope they disappear forever. Never to be seen again.

I kiss him back with renewed energy, as if letting him consume me will erase the hurt his words caused. There is a darkness inside me that has swallowed me whole. It eats away all of the pain and the fear until there is nothing left but bone-aching emptiness. I have become a void of morality.

In a move that speaks of his upper body strength, Lex reaches down and plucks me off the ground. He lifts me up and my legs part immediately, wrapping around his waist. One of his hands leaves my backside and slaps the door of the vehicle. My hands creep around his neck as I hang there against him, nothing but him to keep me afloat. Lex shifts his head, trying to find the perfect angle. His tongue twines around mine, stroking, teasing then withdrawing. I gasp for breath, dragging in lungfuls of air before he dives back down. He licks at my lower lip and then sets his teeth to the soft, vulnerable skin there. My chest burns, but I don't stop kissing him. Instead, I reach out and entice him back into my mouth, curving my tongue around his and playing at the seam of his lips.

Lex drags his head away, breaking the kiss. There's a sudden rush of wind and Lex turns and shifts the two of us to the left before he yanks the back door of the SUV wide open. My ass hits faux leather seats and I'm shoved, unceremoniously into the backseat of his car. I crawl backward, my chest heaving for more breath. Ember dark eyes are locked on me, Lex's face shrouded in shadow as he bends his head low. For just a moment, a beam of moonlight hits him at the crest of his forehead and the image it presents sends a shiver of fear down my spine. His face appears skeletal, the shadows of his brow covering the hollows of his face, but nothing can hide the square cut of his jaw or the powerful muscles beneath his t-shirt. Fear and desire war within me, both fighting for survival.

As if sensing the direction of my thoughts, he hooks a booted foot into the floorboards of the car and leverages himself inside. The door is left hanging open and the cold night air slips over my too-hot flesh from both that and the broken window at the back of the vehicle. A window that I broke—fuck, what was I thinking?

Slowly, Lex's eyes drift over my face and down to my t-shirt. My nipples pebble against my bra, so hard that they poke out and throb in time with the beat of my heart pulsing in my ears. His gaze stops on my tits and his jaw clenches. His shoulders rise and fall with the force of his own breaths.

My chest constricts. The air I was so readily sucking down seconds before evaporates. I can't fucking breathe. I blink quickly, pressing against Lex when he leans over me.

No. Everything's closing in. His body, the car, the seat at my back. I close my eyes, but that only makes the sensation worse. They shoot back open and Lex's face swims in front of mine. His hands hold my face, keeping me in place when I start to fight against him.

"No," he says. "It's okay, baby. Calm down."

Everyone can see me. Everyone is watching. They see the damage. The blood seeping from invisible wounds. My lashes flutter. They're always there, always staring, always judging. Bile starts to crawl up my throat.

Why was I attacked? Why did someone try to rape me? Why me? *Why. Me?*

"*Juliet!*" Lex barks my name like a command and I blink, focusing on him. When he notices my attention, his tone gentles. "What's my name?"

"W-what?" I stare at him, confusion pushing aside the panic.

"What is my name?" he repeats the question calmly.

"Lex."

He nods. "Good. Remember that when I make you come so hard you forget everything else. I want to hear you screaming my name when you see God so he knows who sent you."

He silences me with his mouth before I can utter a reply. Air whispers across my stomach as he grabs my shirt and tugs it upward. The fabric moves higher and higher, revealing first the rounded curve of my stomach and then the undersides of my breasts contained in a black bra. His tongue invades like a marching army, erasing my panic and my rationality.

When Lex reaches the front of my jeans, I manage to rise back from the depths of his kiss. Shoving against his shoulders, I rip my lips away from his. Gasping, I reach for his shirt too. Grabbing the hem, I rip it up and over his head.

Fast. We're going so fast. Wind whips through the SUV and I shiver, pressing closer to the heat of his skin. He has tattoos just like his friends. His are a bit different though. I trace the curling limb of a snake as it moves over his shoulder and down his bicep, disappearing onto his back.

Like Nolan, Lex is built from granite. All muscle and hard sinew with olive skin stretched over it. My fingers trail further down until I stop at the waistband of his pants. There's something written over the curve of one side. I touch it with the pad of my pointer finger, following the script to the end.

Vivere est militare.

I lift my gaze to his, noting that he's panting as if he's run a marathon. "What does it mean?"

His nostrils flare. Shadows dance over his features. The light coming in through the moonroof is dull and shifty. There must be clouds because one moment it reveals all of the lines of his expression—tight and hungry—and the next, we're cast back into darkness.

"To live is to fight." It takes me a moment to realize he's answering my question.

"To live is to fight," I repeat the words, contemplating how they feel on my tongue. Did he get them in memory of his parents? I wonder. Or for something else? For that matter, does he share any tattoos with the other Scorpion Kings? It'd been near pitch black when I'd been with Nolan. I hadn't seen much of him. Only felt.

Lex returns to my jeans and unbuttons them. Backing up until he's out of the backseat and standing on solid ground, he reaches down and rips off my sneakers before divesting me of my pants and tossing them somewhere onto the floorboards. There are so many reasons this is a bad idea. Still, I don't utter a single protest as I lean back, sprawled out on the backseat of his SUV in the middle of nowhere, and let him touch me.

Rough hands skim up my legs, lifting them, smoothing over the surface of my calves and then my thighs. I close my eyes and drop a forearm over my face, letting the other hang at my side. He reaches for my t-shirt and lifts the fabric again, higher and higher until I'm forced to open my eyes and lift my arm away from my face for him to pull it over my head. My skin burns under his gaze as my shirt goes the same way as my pants and I'm left in nothing but my bra and underwear.

"Tell me something..." I swallow at his words, but a moment later gasp as one of his fingers smooths over the place between my legs. He presses down against the crotch of my panties, and I know he feels how wet they are. "Did you like Nolan's mouth on you?"

I grit my teeth, not answering. If he's going to turn this into some sort of inquisition on who's better—him or his bestie—then maybe I should stop this right now. I shift, sitting up again only to have him yank my legs up, putting one over his shoulder. My spine slaps the seat once more.

"Did he kiss you down here?" Lex prompts. "Lick you? Did you scream when you came for him?"

The questions keep coming, but this time he doesn't pause to even give me the illusion that he wants an answer. Lex's head descends and he sucks at me through the fabric of my plain black underwear. The combination of heat and wetness sends my senses into overdrive. A shocked cry escapes me and I reach out with both hands, shoving them into his hair as I practically come off the seat. The sensation of pleasure is muted due to the barrier between my pussy and his lips, but the heat promises to drive me to insanity. Lex nuzzles between my legs, his mouth and jaw moving back and forth across the soaked crotch of my underwear. Then the soft glide of something to match my wetness strokes up, pressing the delicate fabric between my lower lips. *His tongue.*

I'm letting it happen again. I don't know how they manage it—but every time I think I'm getting away from them, they drag me back into the gutter. Where they reign, mayhem follows.

Lex grips either side of my underwear and drags them over my thighs, lifting my legs until my calves are at the ceiling of the SUV so he can get them completely off me. A rush of air slides over the soaked flesh of my cunt. It takes all of my self-control not to moan at the sensation.

My legs are draped over Lex's shoulders and down his upper back. His head settles between my thighs, his mouth hovering right over my core. The heat of his breath drifts softly over me, each exhalation making a wave of goosebumps rise along my flesh. A low masculine groan leaves his mouth and rumbles through the air, and my eyes slide shut at the first touch of his lips on my pussy without anything between us. Such a fucking bad idea ... and yet, so incredibly hot. He drags his nose up through my folds, inhaling me right before his tongue drifts out, lapping at my wetness.

"You taste like sin." Lex's voice vibrates against my pussy. "My favorite sin."

A moan finally breaks free as the revelation of his words move over my clit. I arch up into him, and a moment later, I'm rewarded by the firm stroke of his tongue—down one side of my labia and up the other. My fingers clench against his silky black hair, nails digging into his scalp as sparklers flare to life under my flesh. Higher and higher, his tongue moves and then is drawn away completely. Before I can cry out in despair, however, his lips close over the bundle of nerves at the apex of pussy and he sucks. My back bows.

"Ah!" The sparkles burst into fireworks. A girl could get used to this—having multiple men eat her out like they're starving monsters and she's the first meal they've had in decades.

With hard hands, Lex clamps my thighs against him and dives down again—rougher than before. His tongue swipes across my clit, making me shudder, and then delves deeper as he slips towards my opening. He laps at the wetness oozing out of me, the sound of his lips and tongue devouring everything in his path deviant in the otherwise quiet interior of the SUV. It's not even cold anymore. All I can feel is the heat of his body pressed to mine.

My breaths are loud, ricocheting around the car as I gasp and pant and moan. He tightens his hold, keeping me in place when my hips jerk, and the shock of white-hot pleasure makes me want to pull away. I shouldn't, but I like that too. All I can do is ride the tidal wave that is Alexio Medicci.

Sweat beads pop up along my skin, sliding from my temples and back into my hairline as my hips rotate and grind up into his lips, teeth, and tongue. Lex is a master at eating pussy and making me forget just how fucking dumb I am to let him between my legs. One of his thick fingers finds the opening of my cunt and presses in as he strokes his tongue back up over my clit. Back and forth, back and forth as he thrusts inside. A cry is dragged from my throat and tears burn my eyes, staining my eyelashes, and making the strands cling together.

"*Fuck*." I moan, tossing my head back and forth on the seat. The faux leather no longer sticks to me. The sweat rolling off my body has me sliding across the surface as I try to thrust into the finger entering me, mimicking the action of sex.

Lex moans and my lashes part as I glance down at the man between my legs. He backs away from my pussy, watching me with those dark eyes of his—burning embers threatening to consume every hint of gray in their depths. The rigid shape of his cock strains at the front of his jeans, a hard dangerous thing. I stare at it as my teeth sink into my lower lip.

"Don't look at me like that." Lex's voice is a feral growl.

"Why not?" I challenge him. I can't seem to help myself. I always have to defy them—thrust myself against the hardness of their existence and see if they're as strong as they claim to be. Maybe if they're strong enough, they can keep me from falling apart.

"Because if you keep looking at me like you want me to fuck you, then I might just do it."

I blink. "I thought that's where this was going," I say.

He grins, and the sight of it makes him look positively evil. "Is that what you want, baby? Do you want me to fuck you?"

Do I? I don't know what I want anymore, but I do know that my body is practically crawling with the need to get closer to him. To feel his strength all over me, like a lion between my thighs dependent on me to bring him pleasure—what a high that would be.

My desire is a primal thing; it's all teeth and blood hunger. The way he smooths a hand up my outer thigh, urging my legs to close tighter around him, makes me lose my breath. Lex turns his head and kisses the inside of my leg. I almost whimper when he backs away and straightens.

"No." I reach for him. Damn it, I was close. Now that I know what kind of pleasure these men can give me, it's not fair that I don't get it when I want it. If I have to put up with their pushy, asshole behavior then I should at least get something out of it.

"Shhh." Lex hushes me with a calm tone and gently lifts me up, reseating himself in the backseat. The muscles of his arms bunch as he raises me until I'm no longer on my back and sets my ass right down on his lap. I blink.

I'm not a tiny slip of a woman. I've got muscle and a stomach and an ass. I'm not easy to manhandle, and yet, he'd moved me as if I weighed practically nothing. It's hot—the feeling of being completely weightless in his arms.

I look down between us. His chest is bare, but his jeans are still on. Lex's hands move up my back and untwist the clasp of my bra. The cups sag forward and he peels the straps off, tossing the material to the side as his gaze lights on my nipples. They pucker and tighten in the cold air.

"Fuck, you're beautiful, baby," he murmurs, eyes locked on my chest. His hands clench and unclench on my sides. I've never felt so soft, so malleable as I do in his arms. He's rigid and hard, a statue full of warmth and life.

"Touch me." The words are out before I realize I've even spoken. The look in his eyes is full of so much yearning that it makes something inside me respond.

Those storm-cloud eyes of his flicker over my face before they return to my breasts. One hand moves up my side and then he's cupping me. My head tilts back as a gasp explodes from my chest. He pumps my tit in his hand and squeezes right before his fingers grip my nipple and pinch down.

A shocking bolt of pain that quickly turns into pleasure rockets right down into my cunt. My hips roll on automatic impulse, coming down against the hard length of him straining in his jeans. A groan rumbles up from his chest. The vibrating echo moving from his body and into my own. Lex grabs my other breast, and together, he repeats the action. Squeezing both before pinching my nipples and releasing. I grind against him as lightning travels through my veins. Over and over again, I sink against his cock, the sensitive flesh of my pussy moving atop the rough fabric of his pants.

Sweat beads pop up along my spine and trail downward. I close my eyes and forget everything else. I forget where we are, who he is, who *I* am, and I just *feel*.

Grinding against Lex's cock without taking it inside me is so vastly different from any other encounter I've ever had. It's as if the two of us are on the verge of doing something so wrong, so taboo, that we're questioning our own minds. Yet, once we start down the path, there is no stopping.

Our breaths mingle together as he leaves my breasts, my nipples sore and achy from his ministrations. His hands grip my hips and pull me down harder against him. He forces me to move faster, higher and then lower. My eyes open and I look between our bodies, where my cunt leaves a wet spot over the hard bulge in his pants. Panting, sweating, gasping, begging silently for a release that's just out of reach, I grip his shoulders and whimper as his fingers dig into my skin. I'm going to have marks tomorrow. The smell of sex is heavy in the air, only lessened marginally by the wind that slips in through the open back window and door.

It doesn't even occur to me that I'm out here, in the middle of nowhere, with a man I consider my enemy, naked on his lap as I grind my way to an orgasm that threatens to wreck all of the others in my past. I'm overwhelmed by him, consumed by him, and I revel in it.

"That's it, baby," Lex grits out through clenched teeth. "Take it. Use me to make yourself come. I want to see you fall apart."

His eyes are on me, no longer between us, but on my face. I should be embarrassed. I should feel ashamed. I don't. I've long since stopped caring what others think of me. Why should I when I'm the only one who has to be me? I'm the only one who has to live in my skin and be who I am. They don't get to decide what I do with my body or my life. They can walk away, but I'll always be me.

"Ride me, baby," Lex urges. "Ride me like you want me to come inside you and fill you up."

I'm shaking, so damn close to the edge that I can practically taste the pleasure on the other side. Something holds me back. Something is keeping me from reaching it, and the longer I try and fail to get there, the more frustrated I grow. My head throbs as I rise and fall harder over Lex's cock.

I've never met another guy who would ever let a girl do this. Use him without taking his cock out and using it, but that's exactly what he's doing. His hand cups my ass, moving me faster as his pants collide with my body. He groans and his other hand moves between my legs, sliding through my wetness until he finds the pearl of my clit.

A scream lodges in my throat. I'm there. So close. Almost...

He slips right past my clit and I swear if I could kill him with just my thoughts alone, he'd be a pile of ash. The low chuckle that reverberates through his chest and into mine is both amused and pained. *Good,* I think. At least I'm not the only one in agony.

"I'll take care of you, baby," Lex promises. "I swore I would. I knew you'd be like this—so pretty, like fire in my hands."

I feel like fire. Smoke and flames cascading up to the marked and imperfect ceiling of the SUV. My hips jolt as he slides a thick finger inside me. A cry of pleasure escapes my throat and I bite down on my lower lip hard enough to taste the rusty flavor of blood. His finger continues thrusting and then a second one is added. I whimper, arching against him as he stretches my opening. It's been so long since anything felt this damn good, since I wasn't thinking about bills or school or work or how much I hate the world. The tears lingering in my eyes and on my lashes break free, slipping down the sides of my face. I have to stop this. This is too much like what happened with Nolan. I can't do that with both of them—not the same way. That would be like treating them as if they were the same person and they're not. Nolan is ... Lex is...

"Lex," his name comes out hoarse. The sound only seems to drive him to move faster, harder. He holds me against his chest so that there's hardly any room between us—just enough for him to keep fucking me with his fingers.

Stars dance in front of my vision. My insides flood with renewed wetness, the gush of liquid between my legs making the slicking sound of his fingers that much more prevalent. Denim scrapes against the inside of my thighs, yet another piece of the kaleidoscope of sensations that drives me up that final cliff.

Lex leans forward and takes my lower lip between his teeth. He soothes the split I created with his tongue, licking away the blood. That's what does it. Not the fingers in my cunt. Not the grind of his cock against me. Not even the sore throbbing of my nipples in memory of how he'd pinched and twisted and played with them. His kiss, filthy and tasting of raw blood and pain, sends me into my orgasm. My thighs shake and quiver and I collapse against him, my body locking down as pleasure swarms me. So sharp and sudden that it makes my eyes roll back into my head and my insides clench around the fingers still thrusting into me.

I don't know how long it takes for the orgasm to ease, but when it does, I find myself in much the same position. Sitting on Lex's lap with my head pillowed on his shoulder as he holds the back of my head. Between my still trembling thighs, his cock is no longer hard, but there is a decidedly far wetter spot than before. Exhaustion pulls at my limbs, wrapping long tendrils around my body and forcefully dragging me closer to the dark. I can't let it win.

Lifting my head, I gaze down at the man beneath me with a frown. He stares back at me. For a long moment, neither one of us says a word.

Then I ask the one question that no one has been able to answer yet. "Why?"

Lex shifts forward, pressing his forehead to mine. I swallow roughly, feeling as if my tongue has swollen to an impossible size. "Because," he whispers back, nuzzling his head back and forth, "you've always been mine."

My throat works but no words come out. The need to deny him, to tell him that I belong to no one is right there at the tip of my tongue. They hang there, a silent rejection that never comes and now I wonder if they ever will.

37
JULIET

The Scorpion Kings are obsessed. That fact wouldn't be such a problem if it weren't for one teensy, tiny little detail. The object of their obsession is me.

It's a conundrum, considering that the rest of Silverwood hates me.

The week following my *night* with Lex, it becomes increasingly clear that they have no intentions of letting me get away. Every morning, I'm driven to school by Nolan and every afternoon, I either hang out in the library doing my homework or, if I have work, either Lex or Gio drives me over to Tangier.

It's all anyone is talking about—the fallen princess of Silverwood Prep has become the Scorpion Kings' little whore. I honestly can't tell if this was their plan all along or if the guys really don't give a fuck.

"Hey." A bag drops next to my head where I lie on the edge of the amphitheater's stage. I look up as Mads sits down next to me and swings her legs over the side. "Is this where you've been all week?" she asks casually. "I haven't seen you around."

I wave a hand through the air. "Just trying to avoid all the prying eyes," I tell her.

She snorts but doesn't respond. Instead, she lifts her bag into her lap and begins rifling through it. Plastic crinkling noises precede her hand appearing in my line of vision, a bright yellow bag dangling from her fingertips. "Here," she offers. "I figure the Kings haven't been feeding you much."

I take the bag but don't correct her assumption. If anything, I'm actually eating better staying with Nolan than I had when I'd been on my own. Nolan is basically an empty pit that food disappears into. I wonder if he has to eat so much just to keep up with his muscle mass.

Mads and I sit in silence as I crack open the bag and withdraw a sliver of salty goodness, popping the chip into my mouth and chewing. A fog has settled over the parking lot beyond the school building, the rain from the days before settling on the ground and turning everything wet. The amphitheater stage is one of the only dry places to sit out here which is why we're practically alone.

"So," Mads begins, "are you going tonight?"

I don't have to ask what she means—it's been all over school. The Silverwood Scorpions have a game tonight and they're playing none other than my ex-alma mater, Silverwood Prep. I pop another chip into my mouth and chew thoughtfully before answering.

"I think they expect me to go," I hedge. And I don't know how I'll be able to get out of it. After all, I don't have a car anymore, and I've been relying on the guys to get me to and from school since I'm no longer at my apartment.

Mads sighs and leans back on the stage, placing both of her hands flat on the concrete and swinging her legs back and forth over the edge. "If you need a seat buddy, I'll go with you," she says.

"It's probably not a good idea for me to go," I say.

"Why?" Mads looks down at me. "Because your ex will be there?"

I shrug. "It won't be just him," I admit, "but yeah, I'd rather not run into anyone from my old school. They never come to this side of town, so it hasn't been a problem since…" I let my words trail off, but Mads knows what I mean; I haven't seen anyone from my old life since I left it behind to strike out on my own because of my dad's arrest.

A beat of silence passes and Mads fixes her attention on the parking lot, her expression disappearing from my view as I look back to the bag of chips in my hand. My stomach rumbles as if demanding more. I acquiesce, popping another into my mouth.

"Well, I have to go." Mads finally breaks the silence. "I'm a photographer for the newspaper and they didn't have anyone else available for the game. So, if you need a partner, I'll be there."

Finishing off the rest of the chips, I sit up and crack my neck to the side. Peering at her from the corner of my eyes, I contemplate her offer. It's been a surprise that Roquel hasn't been dogging my heels all week since Monday when I first arrived at school with the Scorpion Kings. Despite my earlier prediction that I could handle Silverwood Public on my own, I'm starting to wonder if maybe I wasn't wrong. I'm exhausted being around the guys twenty-four-seven for the last week. Mads is promising me a break from them and a buffer. I'd be crazy not to accept the olive branch.

"Yeah," I say, crumpling the bag in my hands. "If I can't get out of going, I'll hang with you."

Her head turns my way, a bright smile lifting her lips. "Does this mean I can get your number?" she asks, quirking a brow.

With a groan of annoyance, I pull out the cell phone I'd been forced to carry since moving in with Nolan and hand it over. "Here, put your number in and text yourself," I tell her. "I'm gonna go throw this away."

Mads takes the cell as I get up and stride over to a trashcan that sits just outside of the awning. I toss the empty chip bag in before returning to her side. By the time I reach her again, she's holding up the phone for me and getting to her feet.

"I'll message you later," she says as the first bell rings for lunch to end.

I grab my bag, and together the two of us head inside, separating and heading in opposite directions the second we get inside. The main hall of the school is flooded with bodies in an instant and the crush slams into me as I try to make my way to my next period. Gritting my teeth, I ignore the jostling and semi-purposeful shoulder checks. This week has been marginally easier than previous ones, and I'm under no illusions that it has nothing to do with the Scorpion Kings.

When a hard foot slams down on mine, I've had enough. I shove the bitch that made the move to the side and step out of the crowd, pushing my back against the wall to let everyone else move past me. I'd rather be late to class than get into another altercation. No matter what Principal Long thinks, I never make it my mission to start fights, but I certainly won't let myself be the school's punching bag.

Not thirty seconds since I step out of the line of students rushing for their next class than a bulky arm slings around my shoulders and I'm sent against a chest that smells like cheap cologne. Wrinkling my nose, I push back and look up.

"Hey, Scorpion Slut." I recognize the guy as one of the football players, but not just that—he's the very guy that Roquel had fucked at the bonfire party. Hudson Grey. The insult strikes my ears a split second later.

This time, when I push him, it's with far more energy and anger. I shove against his body enough that his arm slips off me. "Don't fucking touch me," I snap. "And don't call me that."

Hudson grins, completely unperturbed by my annoyance. "What's wrong?" he asks as one of his friends—another I recognize from the bonfire, though his name escapes me—comes to stand behind him. "Don't like the truth being put out there like that?"

"What's the point in hiding it now?" his friend asks, leaning closer. "Everyone knows you're the Scorpion Kings' little plaything now, Donovan."

I clench my hands into fists at my sides. "You don't know shit."

The two exchange a look and then smirk at me. What could they know? Maybe I'd had something with Nolan and then Lex, but I'm anything but a whore. I hadn't fucked either of them.

Hudson leans closer, his expression rapt with interest. His friend, however, hangs back, looking over his shoulder as if he expects someone to pop out behind them. I frown. A second warning bell rings throughout the hall and I glance over to find that most of the students have disappeared down the side hallways towards their classes.

I shake my head and take a step back from Hudson and his buddy. "The both of you can fuck right off," I say, turning to go.

"We'd rather fuck you," Hudson calls after me. "We hear you give it real good and you don't mind fucking the guys in the gutter now."

Don't. React. Every muscle in my body tenses as those two words ring out in my head. *Don't you dare give them the satisfaction of seeing you lose your shit.*

It's there though. The urge to turn and go absolutely apeshit on the two of them. The image of their snide smirks disappearing as my foot connects with their dicks hovers in my mind—a blaring reminder of what I'd rather do. I put one foot in front of the other, though, and leave them behind.

I make it to class just in time, the final bell ringing as I step through the doorway, earning a reproving glare from the teacher. I ignore her and take my seat, spending the rest of the period fighting back the rage that swells in my chest. It's been far too long since I've been to Cory's gym.

The phone in my pocket buzzes halfway through the class and I slip it out from under the cover of my desk to check the screen. The first text is a simple 'hi' from a new number and it takes me a moment to realize that this must be from Mads' phone. After saving it into my contacts, I move onto the reason for the buzz. A new message bubble pops up on the screen.

GIO: Got practice before the game. Come to field after school.

I scowl at the message and choose not to respond. That is obviously the wrong move because as the bell for next period rings to signal class changes, I step out into the hall to find Gio waiting for me. His back is against the wall of lockers, his head tipped back with a smart-ass grin on his too-handsome face.

"Hey, Prep Girl." He lifts a hand in my direction.

"Ugh, even if I have to put up with you outside of school, can't you leave me the hell alone here?" I demand.

Students stream around us, their eyes locked on our exchange. The very fact that we're being watched like a television show premiere makes the skin on the back of my neck itchy. I turn towards my next class and Gio follows, easily falling into pace beside me.

"No can do," he says. "You didn't reply to my text."

"You didn't ask a question."

His eye roll is more felt than seen because I keep my gaze centered forward. "Come on, Prep Girl, you ain't got work tonight and you won't have a ride back to Nolan's since we'll all be at practice before the game. You might as well come. Where else are you gonna go?"

I hate being reminded of all the choices I don't have.

When I don't offer Gio a reply, he groans and swivels in front of me, stopping suddenly and forcing me to do the same or risk slamming into him. My scowl deepens.

"*Move.*" I bite the word out, narrowing my eyes.

He holds his hands up in a placating gesture. All it does is make me want to punch him. "Okay fine," he says. "How about I make you a deal?"

Before I can tell him where exactly to place his deal—so far up his ass that he chokes on it—Gio reaches into the back pocket of his jeans and withdraws a set of keys. He waves them in front of me.

"I'll give you the keys to your freedom for a few hours," he begins, dangling the silver keys over my head for a moment before dropping them and swiping them out of the air with his opposite hand before they hit the floor, "and you'll come to the game tonight."

I roll my shoulders back. "Whose keys are those?" I demand. They don't look like the keys to his Firebird and I wouldn't put it past the Scorpion Kings to lull me into a false sense of security only to set me up to be arrested for driving around in a stolen vehicle.

Gio grins. "Well, since you fucked up Lex's ride," he hedges, his lips twitching with amusement, "he had to borrow a ride from the garage."

"From his job?" I clarify.

Gio nods. "Yup. It's probably not any sort of ride you're used to"—there it is, that reminder that I'm not on the same level as they are. That I was once in a league completely separate from them and everyone else in this school and therefore, a reminder that I'm not one of them—"but it'll get you from point A to point B."

I cross my arms and force myself to look at his face and not those keys. The idea of being by myself for the first time in a week is so enticing that it's almost worth the risk of being set up. I could go to Cory's gym and get some of this anger worked out of my system. I could go to my apartment and pick up some things they hadn't thought to pack. I could just ... keep driving straight out of town. As soon as that last thought occurs to me, though, I correct myself. I won't drive out of town and certainly not in someone else's car.

"And the only stipulation for this 'freedom'"—I lift my hands and curve them into air quotes—"is that I come to your stupid game tonight?"

Gio arches a brow. "You used to be at every game for Silverwood Prep," he reminds me. My breath catches as he steps closer, not stopping until our chests are brushing. The heat of him burns into my front and I refuse to back off. I won't give him the satisfaction. "You might not be getting credit for it anymore, but you can still cheer for me if you like, Prep Girl."

I snatch the keys out of his grasp and start to walk off, not bothering to respond to his unnecessary taunt. I get halfway down the hall when his amused call sounds behind me.

"See you at the game, Juliet!" he yells, causing several more heads to turn our way. "I left you a little present in the front seat."

Without missing a beat, I lift one hand over my shoulder and offer him my middle finger as I keep walking.

38
JULIET

The vehicle is a piece of shit pickup truck that looks as if it's normally used to haul building materials. Pressing the button on the key fob attached to the ring I'd taken from Gio, the lights flash a dull yellow and I walk towards it. I don't even care how rusted out the undercarriage looks or that there is a crack that crawls up through the center of the windshield. It's a car I have access to and I'm all alone.

Unlocking the driver's side door, I hop in and slide the key into the ignition. It takes a few tries, a lot of sweat, and breath-holding, but the truck finally turns over—the engine revving to life in a violent cough. I sigh in relief before turning to the seat next to me to find the 'present' that Gio had left behind. My excitement over being left alone for a short length of time is utterly ruined by what I see.

With a grimace, I lift the frilly cheerleader uniform that's dyed in the indigo blue and white colors of the Scorpion's team colors. The outfit is similar to the one I'd worn while attending Silverwood Prep. Except that the prep academy's colors had been silver and white and the skirts had been separate. Public's cheerleading uniform is one long suit, and lo and behold ... there are no boy shorts sewn in. I roll my eyes and toss the offending piece of fabric onto the floorboards.

I back out of the parking space and head towards the road, enjoying the sense of being in control of my direction for the first time in months. The window is an old manual crank, but I don't care. I carefully roll it halfway down, letting the cold air spill into the cab as I head towards my apartment complex, bypassing the ring of yellow buses that circle the side of the high school's building.

Twenty minutes later, after dodging far too much traffic, I pull into my complex's lot and direct the front of the truck towards the office. Shutting the vehicle off, I leave the window down and my bag in the front seat and walk straight into Mrs. Ritchie's office without knocking.

Mrs. Ritchie sits at the front desk with her wrinkled hand clutching the old-fashioned mouse as she plays a singles game of solitaire. When the front door chimes, she glances up and I see the moment she recognizes that it's me. The initial reaction of politeness morphs into a look of annoyance.

"Can you tell me when the damages in my apartment will be fixed?" I ask, not bothering with pleasantries.

Mrs. Ritchie sniffs, directing her already pointy nose up at me. "It'll be fixed when we can get to it," she says haughtily. "We have a lot of work orders in right now."

Yeah, probably because this apartment complex is falling down around everyone's ears. Instead of saying as much, I offer the older lady a tight smile. "Can you at least give me a timeline?" I persist. "I'd like to move back in as soon as I can."

Mrs. Ritchie looks away from me and clicks something on her computer screen. "It'll probably be a few weeks," she says dismissively. "Perhaps you should think about that next time you decide to have a party." She pauses and looks back at me, tipping her face down until the glasses perched on her nose slide precariously close to the end. "Also, partying is a violation of your lease. We don't allow parties on the premises."

Bet they don't allow murder on the premises either.

"I didn't have a party," I remind her. "Some ... guys from school played a prank on me." The lie falls off my lips in a stilted fashion, but it's the very same story Nolan told me they'd given to the Ritchies to explain the damage to my apartment. "And I'm pretty sure you were offered extra money in exchange for fixing the apartment sooner."

The old bat of a landlady straightens again and huffs out a breath. "Yes, well, we have to get a contractor out here to ascertain how bad the damage is," she quips. "They have full schedules."

I grit my teeth as foul rage simmers just beneath the surface. "Well," I state, reaching for one of the business cards sitting on the holder at the edge of her desk. I pull the thing out and grab a pen from her pen cup. "I have a new phone number." I scribble the information down on the back before sliding it her way. "If you could please let me know when you have a timeline, I'd really appreciate it."

Mrs. Ritchie looks down at the business card I'd written on as if it's a bug that's invaded her personal space. "Yes," she says, "we'll be sure to do that."

I just look at her for a long moment, wondering if I should even bother to call her out on the lie. No matter what I do, though, she won't care. I turn around and walk back out of the office. There's only one place that will help me right now and it's not my damn apartment.

I get back into the truck and thank the universe that the engine turns over on the first try. Putting one hand on the steering wheel and the other on the back of the bench seat, I contemplate how much of a work out I'll be able to get in wearing the jeans and t-shirt I'd thrown on for school this morning. At least, I'd thought to wear sneakers.

Ten minutes later, I direct the borrowed vehicle into the

parking lot just behind Cory's gym. My chest tightens, and it isn't until I slam out of the car and stride into the building that it finally eases. For a moment, I just stand there, the scent of body odor and cleaning spray filling my senses. Then my shoulders relax and come down from around my ears.

"'Ey, girl, ain't seen ya by in a while!" a familiar voice calls out from the back of the gym.

A smile pulls at my lips and I step around a set of treadmills, heading straight for the dark-skinned man with a wide smile and his dreads pulled back into the same ponytail he always wears.

"Hey, Cory. You got time for a sparring session?"

Cory arches one bushy brow, his gaze traveling down over my clothes. He shakes his head. "Ya disappear for weeks and the first thing you ask for when you walk back in is a fight?" He chuckles, turning away and gesturing for me to follow him. "Come on, girl. Let's get ya skinny ass geared up."

I laugh and follow after him. Skinny ass or not, a good fight might make the football game tonight worth it.

Three hours later, I'm sore and sporting a few new bruises and a split lip thanks to one of Cory's fresh trainees—and the fact that I've been out of practice for far too long. Despite it all, I've never felt more calm as I hop into the cab of my borrowed truck. Unfortunately, my clothes are a little worse for wear, covered in sweat and a little bit of blood.

I look down at myself and grimace as the vehicle rumbles to life. My eyes move over to the uniform Gio had left for me. There's no way I'm putting that shit on. Instead, I resign myself to smelling like male body odor, and head to the school.

Halfway there, the phone in my pocket buzzes. I reach for the radio before remembering I'm not back in my old BMW. I don't have a car anymore and this one is certainly not hightech. There is no Bluetooth button. With a grimace, I slow to a stoplight before fishing it out of my pocket, press the green button, and make sure it's on speaker, then set it next to me on the bench seat.

"What?" There are only a few people who even have this number.

"Hey, did you decide to come to the game tonight?" To my surprise, it's none of the assholes but Mads.

"Uh, yeah, actually I'm on my way there now," I say.

Mads lets out a relieved sound. "That's great. I'm actually already here, I'll wait for you."

"Sounds good." With that, I end the call and concentrate on the rest of the drive.

Minutes later, I pull into the school's student parking lot and spot Mads' familiar head of white-blonde hair. She's waiting on the sidewalk near the path that leads around the school to the football field. Parking the truck towards the back, I hop out and head in her direction. Her eyes widen as she watches me approach.

"What the hell happened to you?" she says.

I frown and follow the direction of her eyes. "It's not that bad, is it?"

"That looks like blood on your jeans," she states. "Did you get into a fight?"

I sigh. "It's not mine," I say.

She narrows her eyes on me. "Somehow, that's not reassuring." Mads shakes her head. "You can't show up to the game like that."

The sweat cooling on the back of my neck makes the tendrils of my hair stick to my skin. I blow a lock out of my face and frown. "I don't have anything else to wear." And I'm certainly not putting on that stupid cheerleading uniform Gio left for me. I'd burn the stupid thing before giving them the satisfaction.

Mads reaches out and grabs my hand. Looping the strap of her camera over her neck, she pulls me in the direction of the building. "I've got some extra clothes in my locker," she tells me. "You can borrow them."

I eye her much shorter frame with doubt, but let her pull me along anyway. In hindsight, with how much the Scorpion Kings have been hovering, I wouldn't put it past them to lose their shit over a little blood. Not that I care how they'll react. Nope. Not at all. But it's easier on me when I don't have to defend myself.

That's why I'm letting Mads do this or so I tell myself.

39
JULIET

The bleachers on the home side of the football field are filled with a sea of indigo blue and white. Mads and I stand to the side as a raucous group of guys with their shirts off and the same colors painted on their bodies barrels past, screaming, "Fuck the Spears!" My lips twitch in amusement. Tonight, the Silverwood Scorpions are facing off against my old school, the Silverwood Spears.

Even before my family lost their prestige and money, I never cared for football or school sports. My mother had insisted I be on the cheerleading squad for two reasons—it would look good on college transcripts to be involved in school events, and more importantly to her, it would keep me from getting fat. I glance down at my current body, covered in a pair of longer boy's basketball shorts and an old jersey with the number '35' stamped on it.

Mads told me it was her ex-boyfriend's football jersey. I didn't really care then, but now I wonder why she'd bother to keep the jersey of the guy who supposedly made a sex tape of her for the whole school. I side-eye her as she waits for another group to bypass us up the bleachers before she waves for me to follow her.

"Come on, I have to head down to the field," she says.

Without a word, I glance out to the green below and trail after her. I've neither seen nor heard from the guys since this afternoon and it feels odd. I'd been excited by the prospect of being away from them, but now it's starting to worry me. It's difficult to go from being with three people twenty-four-seven to not talking to them for several hours.

Mads and I make our way down the main part of the bleachers to the field below. Wet grass gets crushed beneath our sneakers as we stop and she lifts her camera, snapping a few shots of the students filling the stands. Across from our side, the silver and white colors of Silverwood Prep shine like a beacon under the field spotlights. I close my arms around myself and try to focus on anything but looking in that direction. Irritation creeps along the back of my neck and down my spine. My skin feels stretched over bones that are too big. My stomach rolls.

Mads moves forward, striding down the length of the field towards the big banner as the speakers crackle to life with the team announcements. I watch as Mads gets to her knee and aims her camera. Music plays, nearly drowning out the roar of the crowd. It's too loud.

The paper banner with the words "Silverwood Scorpions" scrawled across it in big, block letters rips in half as the team comes sailing onto the field. The response from the bleachers at our backs is deafening. I wince.

Looking up, I scan the seats, noting the teachers who have arrived and the parents with their arms laden down with popcorn and drinks from the concessions. There are little kids too—dozens of them, all dressed in jackets and some even with their faces painted to represent the Public school. My breath comes out in little white puffs in front of my face, and I wish I'd thought to bring a jacket.

"Alright." Mads stands up. "I think I got enough for the

paper. Let's head up and take our seats. I'll take a few more from the front row."

Thank fuck. I pivot back towards the bleachers when Mads reaches out and stops me. She points behind us and I follow the line of her finger. Three bodies separate away from where the team is gathered and head in our direction. I'd know those bodies anywhere. I watch as Nolan, Lex, and Gio approach.

Nolan is the first to take off his helmet, followed by the others, but Gio is the first to speak. "Hey, where's the outfit I left you?" he asks.

Mads shoots me a look that I ignore. "I'm not a cheerleader anymore, dipshit," I say. "And I'm not your doll."

Gio continues to frown at the jersey. He reaches for me as if he means to tug at it and I easily dodge him, sliding around Mads to her other side. "I don't like it," he snaps. "Take it off."

"No!" Even if I wanted to, there's no way I'm undressing in front of more than half of the school. I can feel sharp gazes on the back of my neck anyway and it sends tingles up and down my spine. I don't care what they think of me but I'm tired of feeling like I'm trapped under a microscope every second of the day.

Gio reaches down, gripping the hem of his own. "If you wanted to wear a fucking jersey—"

Just before he can pull it off, Nolan reaches out and smacks him upside the head. "Keep your fucking clothes on, asshole."

Gio lets go of his jersey but narrows his eyes on me. "Whose fucking jersey is that anyway?" he demands.

I roll my eyes. "It's none of your bus—"

"Do you have a cut on your lip?" Nolan's question cuts me off and I scowl.

"Oh my God, can you back off for like two seconds?" I snap, stepping away from all three of them when they step forward in unison, like they're about to attack me.

"Where did you go this afternoon?" Gio's voice holds a dangerous note. "Did someone fuck with you?"

I roll my eyes. "I was at Cory's gym," I admit. "I got it while sparring, but like I was trying to say, it's none of your fucking business. Lay off."

All at once, the three of them ease up, their stances relaxing. Lex shuffles forward, his helmet in one hand as he reaches up with his other to touch the cut. I freeze, the warmth of his fingers smoothing across my cheek and lips.

"You should put some hydrogen peroxide on this," he murmurs. "It'll help it heal."

I can feel Mads' wide-eyed gaze on all four of us and the heat rushing to the surface of my skin. I tug my face away from his hands and take a healthy step back. "I'll be fine," I say, gesturing to the field. "You need to go get ready for the game."

Gio gives me one of his signature grins—all seduction and swagger. "You gonna cheer for us, Prep Girl?"

"Who says I won't cheer for the winner?" I shoot back.

His smile widens. "That's what I said."

Oh, his confidence is *so* in need of some leveling. "We'll see," I hedge, shaking my head.

Mads scoots closer to me, returning the strap of her camera around her neck. Nolan offers her a smile and a head nod. "Stick to this side," he tells us. "I don't want to have to head off any trouble while you're here."

My upper lip peels back away from my teeth as I scoff. "Bite me."

Nolan's cinnamon-colored eyes laser in on me. "Is that a challenge or an offer?"

I flip him the bird and turn to walk away, Mads hurrying to catch up as I reach the stairs that lead us back up to the bleachers.

"Wow, they really look after you," Mads murmurs as we

exit the field and make our way over to the front row where a few seats have been left open.

I snort. "No, they like to control me," I state plainly. "And I like to give them a run for their money." She hums in the back of her throat, but it's not a sound of agreement. I wait until we're both seated, my ass freezing to the icy cold metal bench of the bleachers, before I respond.

"What?" I ask her.

Mads lifts her shoulders in a delicate shrug as she pulls the lapels of her sweater closer around her. I rub my bare arms absently, waiting.

"They don't really act like guys who hate your guts." She turns and eyes me. "Was that one of their trucks you were driving? I thought you didn't have a car anymore."

"It's Lex's loaner from the garage Nolan works at. His SUV is ... erm ... being worked on."

The focus of Mads' gaze on the side of my face sears into me. She hums again, and I'm really starting to hate the sound. On the field, the players line up and the screaming crowd at our back finally calms enough that I don't have to work to hear my own thoughts.

As much as I try to focus on the field in front of me, it's hard not to lift my gaze and scan the bleachers across the way. There are several faces I recognize, old classmates and teachers. When halftime hits, I nearly swallow my tongue as Avery jogs out across the green in her tiny Silverwood Prep cheerleader uniform. My gaze shoots to the benches and sure enough, Brandon is right there, watching her like a drooling dog. My insides churn.

Yanking my gaze back, I find myself turning and scanning the bleachers around us. There are more parents here than I expected. It reminds me where mine are—or rather, where they aren't. *Here.*

Halftime ends and my stomach rumbles with hunger. Mads leaves and comes back a short time later with a bucket of popcorn that she shares as we huddle together for warmth. Salt and butter coat the back of my tongue as we watch the last few moments of the game, each team fighting back and forth on the field for the final point that will cause them to either win or lose.

Gio's '20' jersey plows through the line of players wearing white jerseys and Nolan backs up, throwing the football high and wide. Everyone on our side stands up and so do we. Mads and I hold on to each other, our breaths caught. The Silverwood Public running back catches it in midair and then leaps for the end zone just as the buzzer sounds and the crowd erupts into cheers.

The Silverwood Scorpions are the winners.

"Holy shit!" Mads jumps up and down against me. "That was awesome!"

"Yeah…" I huff out a laugh, a little surprised by how easy it'd been for me to actually enjoy the game despite being on the opposite side I used to cheer for.

"Come on." She tugs on my arm. "I have to get some pics of them celebrating for the paper."

I follow her a little numbly, my skin having long since chilled in the night air. My head feels full of cotton as we pass through the gate and she heads off to snap a few photos of the team jumping on top of one another. My chest echoes with a hollowness as I wrap my arms around myself and stand back on the sidelines—always on the outside.

My gaze lifts and moves over to the Silverwood Prep team as they trudge back to their coach. I used to belong there, I think to myself. Win or lose, I was one of them. Now, I don't belong anywhere.

I really shouldn't be here.

Without thinking about it, I turn to go and halt when a familiar voice calls out. "Juliet!"

My heart picks up speed as I slowly turn to face the man who hustles across the field in a crisp black and white suit that doesn't really match our surroundings. Morpheus Calloway hasn't changed much in the months since I've seen him. His hair is pushed back, slicked along the sides out of his face, but there's a shadow of beard growth that he normally shaves dusting his jaw. There are hollows beneath his eyes, and the suit—an expensive Armani—appears slightly looser than it should considering I know for a fact that he has all of his suits tailored.

"Mr. Calloway," I hear my voice even though I don't recognize the decision to speak.

Morpheus slows to a stop in front of me, his face slightly flushed—likely due to the cold. He frowns at my clothes. "Where's your jacket, Juliet?" he asks, his voice full of disapproval.

My shoulders come up in a shrug. "Don't have one with me," I state.

With a curse, he starts to shrug out of his suit coat. "Here, take—"

I hold up a hand. "No, I don't want your jacket," I tell him with a shake of my head. "Thank you, but I'm fine."

Of all the people from my old life I hadn't expected to run into here, he's at the top of the list. "What are you doing here?" I ask.

"I'm one of Silverwood Prep's premiere sponsors," Morpheus says, sounding gruff as he holds his suit coat in his hand. It's clear he still wants to give it to me, and I take a step back to ward him off.

"Oh, right…" Guilt has me looking around for an escape. Where is Mads? Where are the guys? My heartbeat threads an uneven pulse in my chest. I swallow reflexively. "Um, well, it was nice seeing you." I back away.

"No, wait!" Morpheus jerks forward and I go still as his free hand closes around my arm. "Don't go yet."

My hands clench and unclench as I resist the urge to yank myself from his grip. Why would he want to talk to me? What could he need? Is it about the business? Has my dad done something else?

I close my eyes and force myself to suck in a calming breath. I count to five before reopening them and focusing on the man in front of me. Morpheus Calloway is a good man. He'd been my dad's best friend and the one who had saved everyone's jobs when the embezzlement case had first come out. To Silverwood, he's a hero. To me, he's yet another reminder of how much I don't fucking belong.

"Your phone's been shut off," Morpheus says. "I've been trying to reach you. I emailed. Do you need money? Please, Juliet, I've been so worried about you. You know you don't need to do this. You can move back to your school. I'm happy to pay for your tuition. You can live with me. I hate that you're here."

I want Morpheus Calloway's money as much as I want his charity—which is to say not at all. "That's really nice of you," I tell him, carefully extracting my arm from his hand, twisting towards his thumb to break the hold. "But I don't want to take any more from you than what my family's already taken." I rub the back of my wrist where he'd touched and glance over to the Scorpion team. When will the guys be done? How much longer am I going to have to be here?

"You didn't take anything from me, Juliet," Morpheus insists. "Please, I consider you part of my family. I've watched you grow up."

"You're not my real uncle," I remind him quietly. God, I don't want to hurt this man, but how terrible of a person would it make me if I relied on him after everything that's happened? He's lost so much because of my dad, and I just ... I can't do the same thing. I can't take from him because he's a good person. I can't be like my parents.

Morpheus sighs, his shoulders slumping in defeat. "I know," he says, "but that doesn't mean I don't care about you."

"I appreciate it." I feel numb and unable to move, like my legs are full of lead.

"Have you heard from your mother?" he asks.

I shake my head. "Not since she left me the note."

The note he'd given me. The note that had explained that she was sorry, but that she needed to be away and that Morpheus Calloway would take care of me, that he would take care of everything. As if I would allow that. As if I would be just as selfish as her.

"I'm sorry to hear that," Morpheus says. "I've talked to your father a bit. He misses you."

That has me lifting my head and meeting his eyes. "You've talked to him?"

Morpheus nods. "Yes, he'd really like to see you." He shifts closer and I still can't seem to move. My legs remain firmly planted on the ground. "I know you sold the BMW, Juliet. I wish you would've let me help you. I know you can't drive yourself, but if you need a ride—I'd be happy to take you to visit your dad."

In prison. Because he's a criminal. I bite down on my lower lip hard enough to taste blood. I can never get away from this. From the emails from my dad's lawyers to Morpheus, the one man who should be the angriest at my father, everyone seems to think that giving my dad another shot is important. Why though? Why should I? He didn't just betray the town. He didn't just steal from starving, struggling families. He fucking ruined his own.

"Thanks, but I'll handle it myself," I say, my voice biting with frost as I grit the words out.

"You should talk to him, honey." Morpheus' hand hovers over my shoulder as if he wants to pull me against him, as if he wants to offer me comfort.

I urge my legs to step back, to move away, but they don't. I don't want comfort. I want justice. I want the man who wrecked my life to pay for his crimes. What would talking to him do now?

"Hey, are you okay, Juliet?" Nolan's voice penetrates the tension between Morpheus Calloway and me. A warm body sidles up next to me and Morpheus immediately takes a step away. I can breathe again.

"I'm fine," I lie. "I was just saying hi to an old family friend." My feet start to move, Nolan's interruption giving them new life. I pivot away. "Thanks for the offer, Mr. Calloway," I call back over my shoulder as I reach for Nolan's hand and tug him with me. "I'm okay now though. You don't need to take care of me anymore."

Nolan doesn't say a word, and he doesn't force me to stop walking and turn back. To my utter relief, he merely swings an arm over my shoulders—the scent of grass and wet dew heavy on his sweaty body—and ushers me over to where Mads is waiting with Gio and Lex. Gio's eyes move from Morpheus to me, questions in their depths. I look away.

No, I don't need Morpheus Calloway to take care of me. If there's one thing I've proven in the last several months, it's that I'm more than capable of taking care of myself.

40
GIO

Juliet is eerily quiet as we drive back to Nolan's house so he can shower in private—Nolan in Lex's truck and Juliet in my Firebird. When we pull up to the single-story millhouse, Nolan gets out of the Firebird and heads up the front steps. I glance over to the passenger seat.

"Hey, you want to go get changed?" I offer. "We're going to a party to celebrate the win. You're gonna get cold if you stay like that." I gesture to the basketball shorts and jersey she's wearing.

Juliet gives me a look that says everything and nothing at all. As if she knows what's going through my mind because, yeah, it's not just the cold I'm worried about. Fact is, I don't like that she's wearing another guy's jersey—even if he's already graduated.

In a blink, I can see her in my mind wearing my jersey and nothing else. Her long, toned legs parting as the blue and white fabric rides up. I shift against the seat and shut that shit down as soon as I realize what I'm doing. I really don't want to get a hard-on here.

"Can I stay behind?" she asks, nodding to the house that's illuminated by my headlights.

"No."

She sighs and then nods. "Then, yeah, fine, I'll get changed."

I nod and shut off the engine, killing the lights as we both step out of the vehicle. Letting Juliet cross in front of me first and head for the front door, I wave over to Lex to let him know we'll be back. He nods and lifts his phone, typing away on it—no doubt still managing to work even after a grueling game.

Together, Juliet and I head into Nolan's house. The sound of squeaking pipes sending water through the walls echoes back as Nolan showers down the hall. "Grab a jacket too," I tell her as she scurries towards the hall, but she's already disappeared, ignoring me.

Shaking my head, I turn away from the hall towards the kitchen. Eliza, Nolan's mom, usually keeps a couple of bottles of tequila under the sink when she's had a rough day. I find them and the shot glasses. Pouring three shots, I take the first, wincing as the burn cuts down my throat like a knife.

"Jesus!" I mutter, but that's cheap tequila for you. I pick up the second one before thinking better of it and setting it back down. Maybe I'll pawn it off on Nolan or Lex. With Juliet hanging around, the likelihood of me actually getting laid tonight is low. I only really need to drink if I'm gonna fuck some chick to relieve the stress.

"Starting early?" Juliet's voice comes from the kitchen's open door. I grin and turn to face her as she steps into the darkened room.

My eyes trail down her body. The basketball shorts and jersey have been replaced by jeans and an oversized hoodie that all but swallows her up. Her blue hair has been tossed up into a messy bun and ... did she wash her face? Her makeup is gone, and it's only now that I realize the sound of water pumping through the pipes is gone. Nolan must be out of the shower.

I arch a brow. "I told you we were going to a party," I remind her.

She frowns as she rounds the counter and stops next to me, her eyes on the two remaining shot glasses. "Yeah, I heard you the first time," she replies. "Are you going to drink both of those?"

I ignore her question. "If you know that, then why aren't you more dressed up?" I ask. "You took your makeup off." There's a vicious twist in my gut as I imagine her all dressed up, kitted out, and ready to seduce. "Have you given up on finding a rich sugar daddy to take you back to your rightful place?"

The look she sends me would burn me to a crisp if it had the ability. "I'm not looking to be rescued," she snaps.

"No?" Shut up, G. Despite the internal command, I can't seem to help myself. "Seems to me you could use a bit of rescuing. Why not get prettied up so you can find some knight that'll take you under his wings and protect you from the big bad scorpions."

"Maybe I'll kiss a frog and he'll turn into a prince," she says in the same snide tone.

Why don't you kiss me and find out, Prep Girl? I manage to keep the offer from falling off my tongue but just barely. The sight of her dressed in some other motherfucker's number still has me riled and I need to calm down.

Juliet shakes her head and reaches for one of the last remaining shots. "Take your shot," she tells me, lifting the glass.

"I didn't say you could have it." The words leave my lips as she puts the rim to her impossibly full lips and tips her head back in a quick jerk. The clear liquid disappears into her mouth and her throat works as she swallows it all down.

Fuck. Me.

When her head lowers back down, she grimaces and sets

the now empty shot glass on the counter. "This needed salt," she murmurs, "and a lime."

My breath saws in and out of my chest as her pink tongue comes out and licks over her lower lip. A groan works its way up my throat and I squash the urge. Gulping it down hurts worse than the shitty tequila. What do those lips feel like? I wonder. How would they feel wrapped around my cock?

All thoughts of trying to keep my dick under control have fled and the rock-hard erection I'm sporting now tents my jeans. With gritted teeth, I fight for control, twisting away from her and gripping the edge of the counter until I swear I can hear the wood creak under my hold.

Deep breath in and exhale. I repeat the action, counting backward from ten and restarting when it doesn't feel like enough time.

"*Gio.*" The sharp snap of my name finally draws me out of my reverie and I turn to face Juliet once more, hoping she doesn't notice what's happening down below. Before she can, though, the sight of Nolan standing in the kitchen doorway makes my cock deflate in an instant.

"I can't make it to the party," Nolan says.

Juliet frowns. "What do you mean you can't make it? That's why we came back here."

Nolan doesn't bother to glance at her. His eyes are rooted squarely on me which means I should know why his plans have suddenly changed. I do. Only one person still alive can put that look on his face. Darrio. My father.

Without hesitating this time, I reach back, grab the last shot, and down it in one go. "I got it," I tell him. "I'll take care of her. Do what you gotta."

"I'm taking Lex with me," Nolan says.

That's unusual. I glance over my shoulder. "Do you need me?" As much as I'd love a good after party, not fucking around with Juliet there dampens the fun of it, and with both of the guys off on some job for my dad, I'll be too busy thinking about what the old man is planning to do much partying.

"Wait a second, hold up!" Juliet gapes between us. "What the hell is going on? Where are you going?"

"Don't worry about it," Nolan tells her before redirecting his attention to me. "I don't think I'll need you, but keep your phone on you, and G?"

I tense. "Yeah?"

He nods to the glasses at my back. "If you're driving anywhere else tonight, let that be your last shot. I don't know when I'll be back."

I hear what he doesn't say—if I get pulled over with alcohol in my system, he doesn't know when he or Lex will be back to get me out. I nod my understanding and with that, he's gone—heading out the door as Juliet stares after him.

"Where is he going?" she finally asks, turning back to me.

I pick up the empty glasses and dump them in the sink. "Work," is all I say as I rinse them and lay them upside down on the drying rack.

"The garage isn't open this time of night."

Slowly, I turn around and raise both brows at her. She's not a stupid girl and I damn well know that when she was hanging out on the north side of Silverwood with all of her rich, preppy friends, she'd seen the evidence of our side hustle. Our main jobs as my dad would put it.

Her lips press together and dip into a frown. "You're still dealing?"

"Never stopped." Can't stop ... even if we want to. Not yet.

I slip past her in time to see Lex's truck back out of the driveway. I watch them go. Is there really any point in going to the party now if they're not going to be there?

Damn my father. Why tonight of all nights? He hadn't

even bothered to show up for the game and then he pulls both Nolan and Lex into a job but not me. I should be grateful he waited, at least, until after the game was over. My hands clench into fists at my sides as I stare through the front window into the empty street. I'm not going home tonight.

"If we're not going to the party now, I'm gonna go take a shower and change for bed," Juliet says at my back.

She doesn't wait for me to respond but disappears down the hallway towards the lone bathroom. The sound of the door shutting a moment later echoes through the house. I wait a beat more until the pipes start to clang with fresh water sliding through them yet again. Then I lean down and lock the front door before heading back into the kitchen.

Grabbing two of the still-wet shot glasses and one of the tequila bottles from under the sink, I follow the same path and end up in Nolan's room. Much like my own, his room is almost utilitarian in its sparseness. The only difference is the fresh scent of shampoo and soap lingering in the air—as well as the open duffle bag full of Juliet's clothes.

I wonder if Eliza knows she's been housing Silverwood Public's enemy number one. She hardly ever sees Nolan because of her constant night shift duties. It's convenient even if it's a bit depressing.

I take a seat on Nolan's bed and kick off my shoes. The tequila bottle meets the TV tray nightstand and the shot glasses settle right next to it. I close my eyes and lean my head back against the wall, the soreness of my limbs from the effort of the game slipping deeper into my bones.

For once, it's not Lex or Nolan with her. But me. Alone. With Juliet Donovan.

Fifteen minutes later, the door to the bedroom creaks open. "What are you still doing here?" Juliet asks.

I open my eyes to find her dressed in a pair of sweats and a tanktop with her hands toweling off the extra moisture from her hair as it cascades around her shoulders.

"Can't leave you alone, now, can I?" I shoot back.

She snorts but comes in and marches over to her duffle. Dropping what I assume were the clothes she'd been wearing earlier on top, Juliet turns to me and lets the towel just hang from her shoulders. "Are you staying the night then?" Her tone is resigned when I expected a fight.

Frowning, I reach for the tequila. "You impressed me with how well you took that first shot," I say instead of answering her question. "I thought I'd find out how well you can take another."

She hums in the back of her throat, one brow arching up over those glittering blue eyes of hers. I'm like a starving man dragging himself, inch by inch, towards an oasis. She's the water I so desperately need. Without it, I might die.

"Come on," I wheedle, shaking the bottle at her. "How about a game of truth or dare?"

Her eyes sharpen on me and she edges closer. I can tell what she's thinking as if it were written on her face. She wants answers—answers none of us have bothered to give her yet, and if she plays with me, she might just get them. I can't contain my smile.

Oh, poor little Prep Girl. I've got you now, don't I? Even an ex-queen can't help but fall for the illusion of control.

"You're not afraid to lose?" she taunts, reaching for the bottle.

I watch her as she twists off the cap and then sets it on the TV tray. "Not at all."

She's so close I can see the outline of her nipples through the thin fabric of her tanktop. They're pebbled against the surface, just begging for someone to lick them, suck them. Nolan and Lex both had their time with her. Now, it's my turn.

Juliet pours two shots before setting the tequila down and picking one up. The next thing I know, she's shoving my legs to the side and crawling past me until she's resting with her back against the only other wall that touches the mattress. A low chuckle rumbles up my throat.

"Alright, Gio," she says, a challenge in her tone. "Truth? Or Dare?"

41
JULIET

There are two types of tequila. The kind that I grew up drinking—smooth, easy, and fuck all expensive. Then there's *this* kind.

"Truth."

I roll my eyes. "Pussy," I say before launching into my first question. The only reason I even agreed to this game. "Where are Nolan and Lex going?"

Gio's whiskey-brown eyes linger on my face right before he lifts the shot glass and downs a mouthful of tequila. I gape at him. "That was an easy question!"

He shakes his head and grabs the bottle to refill it. "Your turn," he says. "Truth or Dare?"

I narrow my eyes on him. "Truth."

The smirk he sends my way lets me know he's thinking the same thing I said when he chose the same answer. "What did Morpheus Calloway talk to you about at the game?"

I blink, surprised by his question. Tilting my head to the side, I contemplate my shot. Do I take it or answer? Saliva collects on the back of my tongue, the after taste of the shot I've already had reminding me how fucked I'm going to be in the morning if I have much more of this shit. With a sigh, I lower the shot and balance it on my thigh before answering him. "He was checking on me," I say. "Wanted to make sure I'm doing alright."

Gio snorts. "Try again, Prep Girl," he replies. "That's not a real answer."

I glare at him. "You didn't ask for specifics," I snap back. "Your turn. Truth or Dare?"

"Truth."

"Ugh." My fingertip finds the rim of my shot glass and I stare at the clear firewater. "Why won't you talk about where Nolan and Lex are going?" I ask, then before he can respond, my eyes shoot up to his face. "Be specific."

His square-cut jaw tenses for a brief second. I expect him to raise the glass to his lips and deny me once again. When he relaxes a moment later, I lean forward. "Because," he says, "knowing could get you into trouble you're not ready for. Besides, it's none of your business."

"Oh, but my life is yours?" I arch a brow. "That's a bit hypocritical, don't you think?"

Full, masculine lips curve upward. "Just a bit," he admits. "Now, you. Truth or dare?"

"Dare."

His eyes widen and I grin.

"What? Did you think I'd keep playing it safe?"

Gio shakes his head, but his smile doesn't leave his face. "If anything, I'd say choosing 'dare' is safer than truths," he argues. "But if you want to puss out, then..."

I scowl and flip him my happy middle finger, earning a deep, vibrating chuckle. The sound of his laughter fills the quiet room, reminding me that the two of us are alone here and I've already proved to myself how stupid I can get when it comes to these men.

"Take your shot, Prep Girl," Gio says gesturing to the shot glass perched on my thigh.

My brows draw down. "What? Don't think I'll do the

dare?" I will. No matter what it is—just to prove that I'm not a chicken shit.

Gio stares back at me, our eyes colliding. Both of us refuse to look away now that we're locked in place. "I don't think you're ready for the dare I have for you."

"Try me."

Liquid gold and bronze swirl in the depths of his gaze. His pupils dilate and I don't think I need to look down to know that he's hard as a rock. *What will it be?* I silently challenge him. *Are you going to dare me, Playboy?*

Slowly, Gio sets his shot glass on the TV tray and leans across the mattress. His fingers come out and pluck the shot glass from my leg. "You want me to dare you?" he asks.

I tip my head back as he comes over me, hovering closer and closer. My heart rate kicks up a notch. "Do you need *me* to dare *you*?"

That chuckle of his makes a second appearance and he reaches up, cupping my chin in his massive paw of a hand. I forget, sometimes, how much bigger he is than me. Maybe it's because when he's surrounded by Lex and Nolan, he appears smaller—shorter. The fact is, though, that Giovanni Vargas is built like the linebacker he is. Athletic. Ripped with muscle and corded with strength.

Gently nudging my head back, he stares down at me and it takes me a second to realize that he's not gazing into my eyes but at my lips. "Open your mouth, Prep Girl," he whispers. Instinct has me automatically pressing my lips together and one corner of his mouth twitches upward. His eyes flash to mine. "Unless you'd rather I forget about the dare."

"Not a chance." The moment the words pass my lips and he responds with a wide grin, I realize how easily I fell for his trap. It's too late now though.

Gio urges my head back even more and then lifts my shot to his lips. He sucks the contents back and my brow furrows in confusion just before he tightens his hold on my jaw and dips his head. I part my lips in time for his own to do the same. Tequila flows from his mouth into mine, sliding like fire down my tongue and to the back of my mouth in one long, continuous stream. I swallow automatically and when it's all gone, we stay there like that for a moment more. Our lips barely brushing but no kiss passing between us.

Gio sits back, his hand easing as I'm freed from his grasp. "Truth," he says before I can ask the question.

I eye him, and I have to wonder who the real chicken shit is here. Him or me?

Over an hour later, the two of us are laid out flat on Nolan's bed, the bottle of tequila between us. What had once been a full glass container is now precariously low and the room is spinning. I lift my hand to the ceiling, staring at my fingers as I try to count them.

An indelicate snort escapes my lips, and I drop my arm back to the bed when I get to eight. That's funny. I didn't think I had eight fingers on one hand. How'd I go my entire eighteen years without realizing that?

"What?" Gio asks. Even though I know he's had just as much alcohol as I have, he doesn't sound nearly as drunk as I feel.

A giggle bursts out and the next thing I know, Gio is sitting up and staring down at me. I clamp a hand over my mouth but more laughter spews forth.

"The hell is wrong with you?" he demands.

I can't help it. My eyes start to water and I have to pinch my nose shut to stop myself. Only that doesn't work as well as my intoxicated mind seems to think it will and a snort rockets out. Suddenly, I'm covered from head to toe by a massive, bulky body. Fingers find my wrist and peel my hand away. Gio glares down at me as tears leak from the corners of my eyes, sliding towards my hairline.

He sways in front of me, and a second—more transparent —version of Gio hovers a bit to the side. "There are two of you," I say, or at least that's what I try to say. It comes out as something more like 'thar ssss twoovve you'. How many shots had I taken?

"Jesus Christ." Gio shakes his head. "You're fucking trashed, aren't you?"

I roll my shoulders in a shrug. "Might be." I'm totally trashed because I'm not even bothered by the fact that Gio Vargas is crouched on top of me, both of his thighs encasing mine.

After a moment, my laughter and amusement finally die down, but Gio doesn't move away. Instead, he looks down at me, eyes glimmering in the shadowed room as he takes me in. One of his hands comes out and my breath catches when he cups my cheek.

"What did Morpheus want from you tonight, Juliet?" he asks.

Not 'Prep Girl' this time but my name. It's impossible to sober completely just because of one question, but some of my earlier drunken reverie slips away. I stare up at him. Should I tell him?

"We're not playing Truth or Dare anymore," I say.

That thumb of his strokes slowly up and down the side of my face, the rough calloused texture of his palm like a brand on my flesh. I want more of that touch, that heat. Ice has crept its way into my chest and formed a cave there. I've been alone for months, cold and unwanted. Afraid to even consider reaching out to someone that I should've trusted without thought. Morpheus Calloway is my dad's best friend. He's been there for every birthday, every Christmas, every major milestone in my life.

So, why can't I rely on him?

"He wants me to move in with him," I find myself saying when Gio doesn't move.

He frowns. "You don't want that?"

What I want is ... so far outside of what I can have.

I turn my cheek and his hand slides off my face. "Answer me," he presses. "Why don't you want to live in a nice big mansion, safe on the better side of town?"

The way he says the word 'better' comes out of his mouth like a sneer. I push against his chest. He doesn't take the hint. He doesn't move. Instead, Gio grabs me by the wrists and holds my hands against him until I'm forced to return his stare.

"Why does it matter so fucking much to you?"

The varying shades of brown in his eyes swirl as he looks down at me. Then he says three words that seem to change everything. "Because you matter."

My throat closes up tight. My eyes burn. I matter? Bullshit. I want to scream at him but my muscles remain lax, unwilling to fight back against the garbage spewing from him. Fine then. If my body won't fight, then my mouth will.

"If I mattered so much then my dad wouldn't be a fucking criminal," I snap. "If I mattered so much then my mom wouldn't have skipped town. If I mattered so much then this whole goddamn town wouldn't—"

"Shhhh." Gio hushes me with a quiet noise and I fall silent. I swallow against a too-tight throat, willing the tears at the back of my eyes to remain right where they are. No damn way do I want to cry in front of one of the Scorpion Kings. I've already allowed myself to be too vulnerable in front of them.

"What else did he want, Juliet?" Gio's question is a quiet beseeching sound in the deadly silence that surrounds us.

I don't owe him any answers. I don't owe him shit, but … "Why do you want to know?" My voice comes out as a croak. I'm viscerally aware of Gio's body pressing down into my own. My back is against the mattress and he's draped over me so that there's nowhere I can feel where he's not touching me.

The room is still spinning slightly, the world slowing down to give me a chance to keep up. Gio holds my hands, pinning them over my head, stretching my body beneath him so that my breasts are shoved upward into his chest. My nipples pebble against the thin fabric of my sleep tank. I should be screaming and trying to knee him in the balls, but for some reason, my body relaxes beneath his. As if it knows that we're not under any threat by this man.

"I already told you," he whispers, lowering his head until they're nothing but a hair's breadth away from mine. "Because you matter. Because I want to know."

I should not feel as good as I do, and yet, there's at least one thing that makes it better—the fact that I'm not the only one affected by our position. Gio's cock stretches against my belly, tenting the fabric of his pants. My breath releases from my chest and I slowly peel my eyes away from his to look down the strong length of his body.

Holy. Fuck. They can't all be ripped with muscle and packing some serious dick game ... can they?

When I glance back up at Gio's face, his pupils are blown wide as fuck as he stares down at me. He doesn't even try to shift his hips away or hide the fact that he's hard.

"Do you really think your boys are going to be happy with this?" I mean for the words to come out as a taunt, and though they start that way, by the end of the question, I sound as breathless as I feel.

One single dark brow arches. "We didn't grow up like you, Prep Girl," Gio replies. "We've always had to share our toys."

I freeze under him. *"What?"* Those words can't mean what I think they do.

Why not? a snide voice in my head asks. *It's what you expected anyway?* That they would use you, play you, and fuck around with you just to prove that they could. No one really wants the fallen princess of Silverwood. No one cares.

His whiskey eyes narrow. "I'm not going to like what's going through that pretty little brain of yours, am I?"

I buck my hips and his eyes widen a fraction just before he settles himself more firmly on top of me, letting the weight of his hips pin me underneath him. His cock nestles against my belly button and sinks against my stomach as if it's planning to make a home there soon. I've gotten it on at least somewhat with two of the Scorpion Kings and now, here I lay, ready to make the same mistake with the third and final one.

What the fuck am I doing?

Gio leans down and I tense as the brush of his jaw, covered in a stubbly beard growth scratches along my cheek just before hot breath touches my ear. "Confess, Prep Girl," he commands against the side of my face. "We don't keep secrets from each other."

"I'm not one of you," I remind him, and I never will be…

"You could be." Each breath blows hot air over my earlobe making me shiver.

"No," I whisper back, almost afraid to break this quiet space between us. "I can't."

He arches back up, his eyes meeting mine in the darkness. "You could have stayed at Silverwood Prep." The words are a statement, not a question, so I don't bother to respond. I just lie there, feigning a relaxed pose beneath him to keep this man from realizing just how bothered I am by his nearness. "Tell me why you didn't."

"I couldn't afford it," I say.

"Morpheus Calloway would have taken you in," he says. "He would've paid your tuition."

"Morpheus Calloway isn't my father," I snap back. "He's not even my uncle—not really." *Thank fuck for that.*

"Blood doesn't mean shit." My formerly pseudo-relaxed pose tightens for a brief second before I realize he's not taunting me. Gio's face is dead serious. "Blood doesn't earn you love or respect or even loyalty," he says. "It's just another way for people to control you. If Morpheus Calloway wanted to take care of you after you lost everything, why didn't you let him?"

I stare back at Gio with an extra caution that I hadn't

before. His words are ones that I happen to agree with. "Because…" The word comes out soft, almost nonexistent in the tone I use that's just below a whisper. "I can't trust that his help doesn't come with strings…" Or that it won't just disappear tomorrow.

No one helps another person out of the goodness of their hearts. People's hearts aren't so kind. Hearts are vicious, greedy creatures and mine died a long time ago.

"Juliet." My name on his lips sounds so odd now. I'm more used to him calling me 'Prep Girl' even though the nickname is an annoyance.

I squirm under his hold and his gaze. "What?"

"You can't go through your life without trusting another person." His tone is soft and warm.

I twist my head and stare across Nolan's room. In the computer screen sitting on his too-small desk in the corner, I spy the reflection of us—Gio hovering over me like some hungry beast, and me, splayed out beneath him like a sacrificial lamb. That's what I am to this town. The sacrificial lamb to their rage. They can't get to my father, they can't get to my mother, but they can get to me, and they will. They'll take it all out on me if I let them.

One of Gio's hands passes both of my wrists into a single grip and he reaches down to take my chin between his fingers. He turns me back to face him, forcing my head up until our gazes are locked. "Tell me, Juliet," he urges. "You can trust me."

Tears burn at the back of my eyes. No, I can't. I really fucking can't.

"They want me to see my dad." Despite my thoughts, the words escape, and I can't pull them back once they're out.

"Who does?"

"Everyone," I tell him. "Morpheus. Principal Long. Dad. His lawyer."

Gio seems to take that information in. His gaze doesn't shift away. "What do you think?"

"Why would I want to see the man that ruined my life?" That's what no one seems to understand, I'm just as much a victim of his crimes as they are.

Gio sighs. "I hate my dad," he admits.

My lips part. I hadn't been expecting him to say that ... not at all.

"He's a piece of shit," Gio continues. "He used to beat my mom when I was too young to do anything about it. He doesn't hit her anymore though."

"You stopped him?" I guess.

Gio jerks his chin down in a nod. "I got my ass beat, but I started to fight him every time he'd smack her around. He doesn't do it anymore, but she still refuses to leave him. He still talks shit, calls her fat and ugly, and complains that she can't cook and she doesn't treat him as a woman should." Each word from his mouth seems to make his jaw clench tighter and tighter. "She loves him even when he doesn't deserve her devotion."

Slowly, judging his willingness, I tug at the bonds of his hands. He releases me, but his body stays on top of mine. My hands sink down, my arms coming over his shoulders. His muscles bunch and contract beneath his t-shirt as my hands run over his back. I want to tug it up and off him, to feel his skin. Maybe if I were a bit more sober, I wouldn't do it, but here, now, in this place, when I want something—I make it happen.

Gripping the hem of his shirt, I pull and Gio doesn't fight me. He lets me take it off and toss it over the side of the bed. One of his hands presses into the mattress next to my head, holding himself up, while the other plays idly at the hem of my tanktop. There are dips and hollows that hide his chest in the shadows, but with how close he is, there's no camouflaging the absolute state of him. He's bulky and shredded with muscles.

When I touch him, he breathes harder—as if it's taking severe concentration for him to let me. Like Nolan, Gio is the kind of man who enjoys being in control. Maybe he needs control to accommodate for everything else.

"I don't want to be like that," I whisper. "I can't be a woman that lets other people shit on her because she's too trusting."

Gio's one hand curls into a fist by my head and his other hand halts at my waist. "You're not."

"And I won't be." I shake my head. "It's why I can't let Morpheus take care of me." It's stupid of me to admit this much to him, but I've had too much tequila and I can't seem to stop the words from coming out.

"Your dad..." Gio sucks in a breath when one of my hands falls down the ridges of his abdomen and hovers precariously close to the waistband of his jeans. His cock is still straining beneath the fabric, promising me a wild ride that I haven't gotten yet from any of them. I'm surprised by how much I want it.

"What about my dad?" I ask the question because I don't care much about his answer. I just want to keep him talking as I drag the pads of my fingers along the seam of his jeans.

"Whatever you decide..." His breath catches and I love the sound. "I don't want you to regret it."

I hook one fingertip into the loophole, popping the button free. "I don't want to talk about my dad anymore," I admit. "Even if I wanted to go see him"—I flick my nail over the lip of his zipper. His hips jerk and his breath explodes against my face—"I don't have a car."

I drag the zipper down and ... my mouth goes dry. Gio goes commando. There's no underwear to hide the thick base of his cock as it comes into view, surrounded by a patch of dark hair. He's as thick as I expected and my eyes widen at the flash of metal. He has a pubic piercing, a little bar with dual balls on either side.

"I'll take you!" The offer bursts from Gio's lips and I don't know who is more shocked by them—him or me.

"What?" My hands still and he breathes heavily through his nose as his eyes meet mine.

"Let me take you," he practically pleads, "to see your dad."

His cock is in sight, right there, and practically ripping at his jeans to be free and he's offering to take me to see my dad … in prison.

I shake my head. "You are…" Strange. Insane. Absolutely confounding.

I reach into his pants and free his cock. That one piercing isn't alone. Gio's cock strains between us, a second flash of metal stealing nearly all of my attention—and no small amount of my sanity. Right through the head of his cock, a metal piercing slips into his slit and out through the underside of the thick, veiny shaft.

Gio's hand shoots down, wrapping around my wrist to stop me when I go to fist him. "Say yes," he orders.

My eyes snap back to his. "*Seriously?*"

"*Yes.*" He hisses when I test a squeeze around his length. My fingers don't even touch around the other side. What will it feel like to have him slamming this monstrosity inside my cunt?

"I've got my hand on your dick and you want to drive me three hours away to visit my dad in prison?" I demand.

Dark eyes of molten whiskey and earthy soil bore into me. "Say yes and I'll let you continue."

I roll my eyes and my fingers slacken around his length, but he doesn't let me go. Instead, he takes my hand and wraps it carefully back around his cock, forcing me to hold him against my palm. He's hot and hard and practically pulsing with the need to come. My thighs press together as a rush of responding wetness oozes out of my pussy, saturating my panties.

"Say yes," he repeats, bending his head low. Right before his lips press to mine, he stops. "Say yes and I'll let you keep going."

"I wouldn't get anything out of giving you a hand job."

"You'd get to see me wild for you," he whispers back. "You would control the pace, the strokes. You would get to see how I come, Prep Girl, and more than that, you'd get to see how I come *for you*."

Gio, a man who so obviously needs to feel in control, is offering *me* a chance to take the reins? My brain short circuits as he drags his mouth across mine in a chaste, teasing kiss.

"Say yes…" He breathes over my lips, and I can't help myself. I do.

"Yes, Gio."

"Thank fuck." He releases my hand and I palm his cock, stroking him.

The head of his cock is an angry red and purple, weeping at the slit. The metal there glimmers. When I drag my hand up the length of him and get there, I swipe a thumb over the piercing. The pad comes away wet and I meet his gaze as I release him and raise my hand to my mouth. His lips part as I suck my thumb between my own and lick the taste of salt away.

His chuckle is low and vibrating. *Wicked.* "I knew you'd be a vixen, Prep Girl," he says right before he nods down to his bobbing erection pressed between us. "Take me in your hand again."

I would roll my eyes at the commanding tone in his voice if that wasn't exactly what I already planned on doing. I reach for him, palming the wide shaft and squeezing around him. Gio groans, the sound filling my ears as he plants both of his hands against the mattress. He pumps into my grip, his cock dragging over my belly, the piercing at the tip catching at my tanktop. It shifts upward until my stomach is bare. My lungs fill with air as I tighten my hold and he groans, the sound ricocheting into my ears.

His face tightens and he bares his teeth, the row of straight pearly whites almost appearing like fangs in the fantasy of the dark. This is so wrong and deviant and yet, I can't stop. Not now.

Gio's cock pulses in my hand, begging for release, and my body responds. My breasts swell and my pussy flutters with a tingling sensation. I rock into him as well, letting him feel my restlessness as it matches his own.

"Shit." Gio's hissed curse reaches my ears a split second before he moves. His hands grip my shirt at the collar, right above my tits, and with hardly any effort, he rips it straight down the front. Air washes over my nipples as they're bared to him. His fists punch the mattress on either side of me once more.

"Harder," he growls. "Stroke me harder. Make me come for you, Prep Girl."

Focusing on the velvety skin of his cock against my palms, I grasp him tight and pump him hard. I squeeze him, my fingers rippling over his shaft as his hips continue to thrust against me. His eyes stay on my face, glittering dangerously. I swallow, my mouth dry as I keep looking from his face to his cock.

My nipples are hard little diamonds. I suspect I know where this is going. Therefore, when Gio rips himself away from my hands and takes his own cock in one too-tight fist, I'm not surprised. My belly quivers as I suck in breath after breath. I want it, I realize. The feel of his cum splashing over my skin.

He directs the head of his cock to my tits. "Hold them," he commands.

I do, reaching up and grasping my breasts, pushing them together. I pinch my own nipples, needing the stimulation. A moan escapes me and he bares his teeth in response. Gio's hand flies over his dick. He doesn't even seem concerned by the metal piercing him. Each time he strokes up to the head, his knuckles practically whiten with how hard he squeezes. So obsessed with watching the way his hand moves, I hardly notice when his other hand moves up and clasps around my throat. When it does, though, that's when he has my attention. I stare up at him as his fingers tighten around the sides of my neck but never push inward. I can breathe, but the sudden loss of blood flow makes the whole world go hazy.

I moan, undulating beneath him as he jacks off over my tits. He's barely leashed control and hot olive flesh. He pumps his cock far more roughly than I did and within seconds, his groan of relief is filling the air. A scalding hot wash of cum shoots out and lands on my skin. He covers me, directing the streams of his orgasm all over my tits and paying special attention to my nipples. He bathes them in his release, seeming to get a sick sort of satisfaction in seeing me covered in him as his fingers contract around my throat.

My teeth sink into my lower lip as the world dances in and out of focus. My hands drag upward, moving through the liquid on my breasts. I trace my fingers through the cum there and circle my nipples. Gio curses, the sound equally as turned on despite the fact that he's already had his release.

I feel floaty and empty-headed. The alcohol is finally doing its job. I don't even care that there are too many shadows around us. I'm warm and tingly and for the first time in a long time, I feel safe—even if that, too, is an illusion.

42
JULIET

A bolt of sunlight smacks me square in the face and a groan rumbles up my throat. I slap at the bed, searching until I find a pillow and then I yank it over my head, blocking out the light. My head *pounds*, but a low masculine chuckle has me lifting it again anyways. For a moment, I have no clue where I am. The room isn't mine. The bedsheets aren't mine. Hell, the mattress isn't mine. Then I remember.

I'm at Nolan's house, in his bed. Slowly, I turn in the direction of male amusement where I find none other than Nolan himself, sitting in that tiny scrap of a piece of furniture desk chair. He's watching me with his elbow propped on the chair arm and one leg drawn up and crossed over the knee of the other. There are shadows under his eyes that make me wonder if he even slept the night before.

I glance down at myself, frowning when I don't recognize the gray t-shirt I'm wearing because it's definitely not what I put on for bed. The events of the night before come back in small increments, reminding me just what happened to that black tanktop. Another groan comes from me as I collapse back on the mattress and reach for the pillow once more.

"Too much tequila?" Nolan inquires, his tone light.

Lifting a hand from the bed, I flip him the bird and burrow back into the sheets and covers. I could sleep for a week and it still wouldn't be enough.

"Come on." The bed dips under a heavy weight and the pillow over my head is plucked away. "We've got plans today and you can't stay here."

I arch up onto the mattress, ready to spit bile his way when a water bottle is suddenly shoved in my face along with his open palm where two little blue pills rest. Scowling, I snatch the pills and water, downing them in record time. Glaring at Nolan as he waits patiently for me to finish chugging a good half of the bottle, I finally catch my breath and release it only for him to snag it from my hand and get off the bed.

"Breakfast is already ready, Princess," he calls over his shoulder as he shakes the bottle in my direction. "Best get up and get ready for the day. We have a shit load to do."

With a snarl, I dive for the pillow now sitting at the end of the bed and throw it at the back of his head. He laughs, easily dodging it as he slips out of the bedroom and closing the door.

Fifteen minutes later, I'm dressed, my face is washed, and I'm feeling marginally more human as I enter Nolan's kitchen to find that we're not alone. I carefully avoid looking in Gio's direction as I head to the counter where a stack of pancakes wait on a plate as Lex scoops the last one on top. The back of my neck prickles with awareness as I grab one of the paper plates and fork over a couple of the pancakes before turning towards the others.

Nolan kicks out one of the four chairs surrounding the table as I approach and I take that as my cue to sit. All of the fixings for a good pancake breakfast are already set out, so I snag the butter and syrup and drench my breakfast in the sugary combo before spooning up some peanut butter right on top.

"Lex, your SUV is ready for pick up," Nolan calls out as I stab a fork into the first bite and lift it to my lips.

Raising my head as I chew, I watch the goings on surrounding me as Lex pulls up the final chair with a plateful of his own breakfast. Gio has thankfully turned his attention to his food as he digs in and fiddles with his phone absently.

We've always shared our toys...

His words from the night before choose that exact moment to enter my head, reminding me of my idiocy. Peanut butter sticks to the roof of my mouth and I swallow roughly, trying to get it to go down. All around me, the guys act completely casual, as though they don't know what I did with Gio in Nolan's bed. Surely they do. Gio admitted as much—they don't keep secrets from each other. Minutes pass in an odd sort of discomfort where I'm the only one who seems aware of their every word, every move. I finish my breakfast quickly, grateful for the pills Nolan had given me earlier because my hangover headache is finally abating.

I pick my plate up and snag Lex's and Nolan's on the way to the trashcan. I ignore Gio's completely since his is still half-full of food. When I turn back around, I realize all three sets of eyes are on me. I lean back against the countertop, propping myself up as I cross my arms.

"Okay," I finally concede. "What are we doing today?"

Lex smiles and arches a brow. "You're not going to fight us?"

I glare his way. "Is there a point?"

He seems to think about it for a moment before shrugging. "Not really. You'll just wear yourself out and we'll make you do what we want anyway."

Yeah, I expected as much. "Then, no," I say. "I'm not going to fight. I'm too tired and hungover to do much." And this is the first Saturday in well over a month that I've not had to work. I don't really remember what other people do on their days off.

"We have work to do," Nolan says. "Gio, you need to go check up on your mom. I'll run Lex to the garage so he can pick up the SUV."

"I thought you were working last night." As I say the words, I watch the three of them. Just as I expected, they tense and go quiet. *Yeah,* I think sardonically. *Errands, my ass.*

Clearing his throat, Nolan recaptures everyone's attention. "My mom picked up an extra shift at the hospital this morning, so I wanna run over something for her to eat." He refocuses on me. "Then we need to go see how the Ritchies are doing with your place."

My arms tighten around my chest. "I went yesterday," I admit. "Mrs. Ritchie made it seem like it'd be a while more."

Nolan nods. "I want to go in and talk to her myself. Mr. Ritchie is a cheap bastard. If you're not kicking up a massive fuss, he'll take forever to get shit fixed. Then we really do have shit to do today."

I contemplate the three of them as Gio stabs the last of his breakfast and swallows almost an entire pancake whole. I'm surprised he manages it without choking, but once it's gone and he drains his glass of orange juice, he's up and out of the chair. He bypasses me to drop the paper plate into the trash and his glass into the sink. Just when I think I've gotten away from the awkward morning-after encounter, he stops right in front of me. My arms drop to my sides as he cages me in against the counter. Right there, in front of his boys, Gio Vargas leans down and puts his lips right in front of mine. I go still.

"Next time," he says, voice low and deep and vibrating up through his chest, "I wanna see you come all over my cock."

My lips part and he swoops in, damning me with a hot as fuck kiss. His tongue slips in and duels with mine, tangling together in an intimidating rush of heat. Then, he's gone, slipping back out and stepping away.

"Remember what we said—find out when visiting is at the prison and one of us will drive you to see your dad."

"Wha—"

But he's already gone, disappearing through the living room and out the front door before I can even reconnect my brain with my body.

A beat of silence passes and then Nolan lets loose a low whistle. "Well, he certainly doesn't beat around the bush."

"You knew that." Lex passes Nolan a look I can't decipher.

Face threatening to go hot with a blush, I spin away from both of them. "Do you have things to do or not?" I snap as I head back down the hall to grab my shoes.

Behind me, I hear the two of them laugh and the weird little belly flip that happens in my stomach doesn't make me feel any more grounded than that kiss Gio planted on me.

After breakfast, I'm squished into the white pickup between Lex and Nolan to drive over to the garage that Nolan works at. We drop off the truck and trade places into Lex's freshly fixed up SUV. I frown as I hop into the back seat and glance back.

"Is it just me or does this thing seem higher off the ground?" I ask.

Nolan chuckles as he gets into the passenger seat up front and Lex starts the engine. "I've been wanting to deck out Lex's ride for months," Nolan admits. "Your little tantrum gave me the excuse I needed."

Rolling my eyes, I click on my seatbelt. "It wasn't a tantrum," I mutter, sitting back.

Neither of them reply and we roll out of town. Lines of trees go by, flying past the windows as Lex takes the winding back roads that lead to the edge of Silverwood's town limits. Just before he reaches the outskirts, he hangs a right and we veer off onto a gravel road.

"Where are we going?" I demand, sitting up straighter as I glance back towards the main road.

"I need to stop by my place to pick something up," Lex says. A few minutes later, we pull up to a rusty gate and Nolan slips out, running up to unchain the lock and hold it open.

The SUV ambles forward and Lex stops again a few yards in for Nolan to run and hop back into the vehicle. They leave the gate open as we drive further down the path where we pass an old-looking farmhouse with a wraparound front porch and a bed of half-dead flowers out front. The place looks a bit on the rough side, but it's clear whoever lives there does their best. The paint is new even if the front steps appear saggy.

We don't stop, though, until we're a good half mile further behind the farmhouse. My eyes widen at the small structure there. It's a plain, undecorated square of a building that looks like it has three old wooden doors almost big enough for a small car to fit through. On top, there are small windows set over each door. A metal rooster shaped weather vane sits atop twin arrows with the letters 'N, S, E,' and 'W' underneath.

"What is that?" I ask, leaning closer to the window.

"My great-something granddad used to fix carriages back in the 1800s," Lex says. "He built an extra-large carriage house back here for when some of the folks in the city would bring them to be refurbished or whatnot."

"The 1800s?" I frown. "Don't tell me you still use the carriage house." Even as I say the words, the evidence of the well-used building is staring me in the face.

The carriage house appears almost as well kept as the farmhouse we passed. There are no cracks in the windows, no grime coating the outside of the structure, and a light above the door along the side of the building makes it clear it now has electricity running through it.

Lex parks the car and glances back at me. "I live here," he says before popping his door open. "Stay here. I'll be right back."

I watch him walk up to the carriage house and pull out a set of keys from his pocket. He lives here … in a carriage house. What? I look to Nolan only to find him staring back at me. In the time since we passed the gate, he's found a pair of aviators and pulled them on. The shiny reflective surface of the glasses makes it impossible to see his eyes and know what he's thinking.

Something warns me against getting any deeper with these men, against asking questions that they might not be willing to answer. Once the questions circle in my head, though, they won't be stopped.

"Why does Lex live out here instead of with his aunt?"

Nolan glances from the quaint looking carriage house that looks so very different from what I ever expected of Lex and back to me. "Lex's aunt didn't expect to take in a kid when she did," he admits. "She got him through his younger years after his parents…" He drifts off, but he doesn't need to remind me. Before my own father's criminal dealings, it had been one of the worst scandals to break in Silverwood. A supposedly kind, loving couple had come under a social services investigation for abuse of their young son. Rather than risk being shamed, Sancho Medicci had killed his wife and then himself. "He prefers it out here," Nolan finishes after a beat and faces the windshield as the door opens and Lex climbs back in.

"All done. Let's go."

Lex quickly backs away from the carriage house. When we get back to the gate, Nolan hops out and locks it back up, and then we're on our way once more.

The more time I spend with these men, the more I start to wonder who they actually are. Are they criminals? Are they manwhores just looking for a good time? Football players hoping to make the most of their high school career? Lost kids with few people to look after them and guide them in the right direction? Or are they something else entirely?

I'm almost afraid of the answers I might find.

Once I'm back at school, I'm forced to face the reality of Principal Long's stipulations. *Counseling.*

Julia Beck is one of those women whose face is ageless. There's no hint when you look at her face. She could either be one of the teenagers walking the halls of Silverwood Public or she could be a woman nearing her forties. Sitting in front of me with black-rimmed glasses perched on the end of her upturned nose, she clasps her hands on top of her desk and stares back at me. She's analyzing me as much as I'm analyzing her.

"It's my understanding, Miss Donovan, that you don't necessarily want to be here," she says.

"*Yup.*" I pop the word out as I lean back in the relatively comfortable seat across from her and turn my head to look out of the window in her door.

Since coming back to school, the guys haven't left me alone. I know it's because they worry about the man who attacked me and whether or not there will be a second attempt from whoever put him up to the task. As the days go by, though, I am starting to forget there was ever a time where I wasn't surrounded by them twenty-four-seven. I fall asleep in Nolan's bed, wake up in Nolan's bed, ride to school with one of the three of them, and sit next to them at lunch and in classes. I'm quickly growing accustomed to my new normal even if it disturbs me how easy it's becoming.

"You've had a lot happen in the last several months," Miss Beck says. "It's understandable that you'd have a lot of emotions about it."

My eyes cut back to her. "Can I ask you a question?" I deadpan.

She blinks, seeming surprised by my ready engagement, but brightens almost immediately. "Yes, please do." She leans closer.

"What did you lose when my dad fucked over the rest of the town?"

Her expression falters. "I'm not sure that I—"

I hold up a hand, stopping her. "Please," I say. "No bullshit. If I have to be here, then I'd rather get the hate out in the open than have to play this back and forth, 'Oh no, you poor thing,' 'Well, other people have issues too and it's because of your father's garbage.'"

The counselor's face goes rigid in an instant, guarded and closed off. "I don't care for the rude and inappropriate language," she states. "However, I do appreciate your candor, Miss Donovan. So, in light of your transparency, I'm happy to offer you some of my own."

I wait for it. The blow that's sure to come. How this is her job and she's just doing it, but she doesn't care to help someone like me. Oh, she won't say it like that. She'll make it a point to use those big educated words to tell me that my issues aren't as important as other people's and how just because I'm displaced doesn't mean I can act as I want. No more beating bitches' faces in. No more acting out in class and causing an issue. No matter what anyone else in this school does to me, I should just sit here and take it and be grateful they don't think of a reason to throw me in jail along with my dad.

Not that they'd have to look far for a reason...

Nolan had said they hid my attacker's body, but how well was it truly hidden? What if they're just holding on to it to use it against me later? Where would they even hold a body for long periods? The carriage house?

"Six weeks after the initial story of the Donovan-Calloway embezzlement scandal broke and stocks of the company plummeted, my fiancé killed himself." Miss Beck's announcement stuns me.

I close my eyes. *Fuck.* When I reopen my eyes, I'm shocked to find no emotion on Miss Beck's face. There's no consternation, no animosity, no rage. I frown in confusion and one corner of the woman's mouth tips up.

"My fiancé was a lot of things," she continues. "An intelligent investor was not one of them. He sank everything he had into Donovan-Calloway." Like many others, no doubt, I keep my mouth shut. "Another woman in my position might hate your father," she says. "But you … you're not Allen Donovan, are you, Juliet?"

"What do you know about who I am?" I bark the question at her.

Before Miss Beck can answer, though, there's a sharp knock on the door and it swings open. The two of us look up to find none other than Gio standing there. He glances over Miss Beck before his eyes find mine.

"Come on," he says, jerking his chin behind him. "Your hour's up. Time to go."

"Mr. Vargas," Miss Beck begins.

He merely shakes his head. "Sorry, Miss JB," he says with a grin. "We've got to steal her away. Don't worry, she'll be back for her next sesh."

Like fuck I will, but I don't say as much as I stand up and snag my backpack off the floor. I don't know how or why the counselor lets Gio tug me from her office, but as he does, her voice filters back to me. "I think you should do it, by the way," she calls out.

Curiosity stops me and I press my lips together briefly before glancing over my shoulder.

"Do what?"

She smiles, and it's an easy, kind thing. She really has that saintly air about her. Her fiancé committed suicide and she doesn't seem to hate me for it. It's odd, to say the least. "Go to see him," she answers.

There's no question about who the 'him' is. I swivel to face Gio as the door closes behind me. "You told her?" My hands curl into fists.

"Me and Miss JB go way back." Gio heads for the hallway and I follow him out of the counselor's waiting room into the corridor. "Yeah, I told her I convinced you to go see your dad."

"What the fuck, Gio?!"

He reaches into his pocket, seeming unconcerned by my hissing wrath. "I've got a date set up," he says. "Had Lex call the lawyer—they're expecting you this weekend."

"*This* weekend?" As we arrive at the doors that lead out into the student parking lot, I come to a stop. He shoves the door open and then curses as rain begins to sprinkle over us.

"Shit, we're gonna have to run to the car," he shoves his phone back into his pocket and darts off across the lot. I follow but at a much more sedate pace. I don't even feel the fat drops of rain that fall on my face and shoulders.

I'm going to see my dad. *This weekend.* Less than two days away. *Am I fucking ready to face him after he blew up my life?*

Gio gets to the Firebird first and hops into the driver's seat. I'm slower to slide into the passenger's side. He cranks the engine.

"Gio—I'm—" Freaking the fuck out.

"It'll be okay," G says. "But I knew you'd put it off if you could."

I face him. "That's my choice to make. You can't just decide this for me."

He doesn't even flinch at the harshness in my tone. "It's done," is all he says.

It's done. Those words hit with an awful finality to them. "No." He arches a brow. I cross my arms over my chest. "No it's not just 'done'."

Gio's expression remains calm as he stares back at me for several moments, not saying a word.

I growl in frustration. "It's been months since I've seen my dad. The last time I talked to him was over the phone." It'd been a quick 'it'll all be okay, honey' lie that I hadn't believed then and certainly don't believe now.

"You won't be alone this time." My heart stutters to a halt in my chest. Was that why it had felt so terrible the last time I'd talked to my dad? Because it'd been right after I'd moved into my apartment. Mom was gone and I was ... alone.

Heat rockets into the car, driving away the cold from outside, and a wide palm finds my thigh, gripping and squeezing in an all-too familiar gesture. "I'll be right there, Prep Girl," he murmurs. "No matter what happens, you don't need to face him all by yourself."

A familiar burn starts up behind my eyes and I turn in my seat to face the windshield. I'm only distantly aware of Gio putting one hand on the steering wheel as he leaves the other on my leg as he reverses and peels out of the lot. The school building disappears in the rearview mirror.

This weekend ... more rain falls outside the car, sliding down the windows. Gio turns on the windshield wipers. The combination of the heat pouring out of the vents, the sensation of his hand on my thigh, and the fog filling my head consumes me and I fade, growing further and further away as the road disappears beneath our wheels.

Above all, I feel the wash of relief that maybe ... he's right. Maybe if I'm not alone, facing him will be easier.

43
GIO

I stare at my wrapped knuckles, covering the light smattering of almost invisible scars I've gotten over the years. The sounds of the others in Cory's gym behind me fade as I contemplate the last week.

The memory of Juliet sprawled out beneath me, her shirt torn and her tits on display is branded into my head. They'd been perfect, the right amount of softness, full enough to almost overflow my hands, and the way she'd gripped them and held them up for me as I'd jacked my cock … fuck. I have to stop thinking about it or I'll pop a fucking tent right here.

Turning away from my reflection in the floor-to-ceiling mirror, I finish tucking the tape in place and bound into the ring where my opponent waits. Cory stands nearby, his eyes scanning an old, cracked iPad with a pair of reading glasses I've never seen him wear perched on the end of his nose. He looks older with them and the sight bothers me for some reason.

"Alright, asshole," I say, redirecting my gaze to my opponent—a lanky guy with a mottled bruise on the side of his face from an earlier sparring match. "Are you ready to do this?"

"Far more ready than you, pretty boy," he sneers.

I arch a brow. Yeah, I know I'm pretty, but this guy must not know me from my reputation—or at all. Just because my packaging is a lot nicer than most guys' doesn't mean I can't lay his ass out.

"Keep it civil, G," Cory calls over to us, not even bothering to look up from the iPad. The fact that he said anything though, tells me that just because he looks distracted doesn't mean he's not well aware of everything going on in the gym.

"Got it, old man." I refocus on the guy in front of me, narrowing my eyes on his smug expression. The sooner I wipe it off him, the better I'll feel.

We begin to circle each other, my feet sliding across the ring's mat-floor with comfortable ease. The echoing sounds of grunts and repetitive thuds from the other men in the gym echo all around us, as well as the low sound of rap music that Cory keeps on most of the time. It's just loud enough for anyone who forgot to bring their own music, but not so loud that I can't hear myself fucking think—or hear the intake of breath that preludes my opponent's first move.

Dodging to the left as he barrels towards me, I watch the moment the guy realizes his initial plan of attack hasn't worked. He whirls back towards me. We go back to circling. The next time he attacks, I capture his arm and bend it backward.

Using his own momentum, I swing the man around and turn his thumb up, shoving it into his back until he screams like the little bitch I knew he was. With an eye roll, I squeeze tighter for a second until Cory's head comes up. Then I release the fucker and push him away.

"Is this really the best you could come up with?" I ask, directing my question to Cory and not my fight partner.

Cory shakes his head. "Didn't say he was the best," he says. "Boy's in training."

"Well, he's too cocky," I reply.

"Fucking asshole." The 'boy' as Cory had called him mutters as he rubs some feeling back into his arm.

I ignore him and slip out from the ropes of the ring to find my footing on the floor next to Cory. A light coating of sweat covers my upper body and trickles down the side of my face. Not necessarily because of the fight, but because it feels hot as fuck in the gym with so many people here today. My gaze moves across the room to the morning sky outside. I've got to hurry up and go home soon for a shower if I'm gonna pick Prep Girl up in time. A three-hour drive with just the two of us … alone. It's impossible not to think of the last time we'd been alone.

Cory lowers the iPad to his side and eyes me. "'ow's our girl?"

I sniff and wipe away a droplet of sweat from my upper lip with the back of my tape-covered knuckles. "She's fine."

More than fine, she's a fucking work of art. Those nipples of hers had been a rosy hue, so tight and puckered as she'd undulated against me, practically begging me to spill my seed all over her.

Stop. Thinking. About. It. The mental reprimand is a blaring warning in my head. Not that it does me much good. I check the clock on the wall reminding myself we need to leave soon if we're gonna get there by the start of visiting hours. I'd promised Lex, too, that I'd slip a note from him to one of the guards to give to Allen Donovan sometime later. The security of the prison is pretty good, but a prison guard's salary can always use a bit of padding and he's been hard at work tracking connections for the Donovan trial. It's coming up soon and I'm sure seeing her father will remind Juliet of that fact.

"She came in for a bit," Cory says, dragging me back to the present and my plans for later.

"Yeah?" I start to unravel the tape on my fingers and Cory's brow arches.

"She missed the place," Cory says, though he doesn't comment on my actions.

"I'm sure she has." And Nolan doesn't live close enough to the gym for her to walk. "She's been working a lot."

Cory hums in the back of his throat as I ball up the first bit of tape and toss it into a nearby trashcan before working on my next fist.

"Hear she ain't been to her apartment in a while," Cory hedges. When I don't respond, he huffs out a breath. "Is she staying with you?"

A snort escapes me before I can stop it, but I shake my head. "What do you think, man?" I rip off the last of the tape and it goes the same way as the rest. "She wouldn't be safe at my place." My own mama ain't safe at my place, but I don't say as much.

"Darrio don't like her kind," Cory agrees with a solemn nod.

An understatement if I ever heard one. It's not that my father hates Juliet specifically, but everything she once was—and everything he isn't. A more jealous, envious man there never has been. Darrio Vargas wants what everyone else has—money, power, fame, and respect. Not that Juliet has any of that now, but for a long while she did. For most of her life, she'd been a queen. Just because she's fallen into the gutter with the rest of the peons doesn't mean she's one of us.

But you could be ... the reminder of my own words to her that night circle in my mind. I hadn't realized how much I wanted them to be true until they'd come out of my mouth. Juliet Donovan could be a Scorpion if she really wanted—she's strong enough, brave enough, and doesn't give a fuck what anyone else thinks.

She's the kind of girl that'll burn your house down and then fuck you in the ashes, and if that doesn't make her the hottest woman I've ever known...

"You taken care o' her?" Cory asks.

I take a step back from the old man and move to the cubbies as I call an answer over my shoulder. "Don't worry about her, Cory. She's tougher than she looks."

"That ain't an answer, boy!" Cory shouts.

I grab my bag from the cubby I'd chosen earlier and swivel to eye him across the room. It's on the tip of my tongue to tell him that Juliet Donovan is Scorpion property now, but I don't. I hold it in. Juliet isn't mine. She's not any of ours—no matter how much we might want her to be.

"See ya later, old man," I say instead, giving his frowning expression a wave as I turn and head to the exit.

The sound of footsteps behind me stops me from fully leaving the building though. Surprised, I turn back just in time for Cory to drop the iPad he'd been holding onto the front counter before heading in my direction. My brows lower and I pause, waiting there with my hand on the door handle.

"You let her know she's welcome here whenever she needs a good bout of stress relief," Cory says, his tone brooking no argument. It's not a question but a command.

I arch a brow. "That how it is?"

"Yeah." He places his feet shoulder-width apart and stares at me. "It is." It's easy to forget that Cory wasn't always just a small-town gym owner. He's a calm presence that has a way of smoothing over even the roughest of guys. All kinds enter his gym from fighters to gangbangers to regular bar brawlers. They work out here to let loose some of their masculine anger, but it's not the machines or the always well-maintained fight ring that brings them around again and again. It's this man right here.

Cory is a big man, but not the biggest I've ever known. Everyone around Silverwood knows Cory's got some good connections up north in a place called Eastpoint. Unlike a lot of kids from southern Silverwood, he'd gotten out for a time—entered a talented program at a university there. Why he'd ever come back, no one knows, but one thing is for sure, Cory never let anyone get away with shit that wasn't right.

He's a great personal trainer, but he's an even better ally. His strength isn't in size, but in the way he cares about people, and to him, Juliet is one of those people now. When no one else gave a shit about her, he did. He taught her. He took her in. He gave her a place to release her anger.

Did Juliet know that when she came into his gym that first time or was luck just on her side?

I reach into my duffle and pull out the keys to my Firebird. "She's gonna be just fine, Cory," I assure the man. "We're looking out for her."

His brown eyes move from my face to the keys dangling in my grip. Cory flicks one of the longer dreads hanging down his shoulder back before leveling me with a wary look.

"You ain't messin' with her, is you?" he demands. "You and those boys o' yers?" A cold sort of look enters the older man's eyes, and for a second, I feel as if I'm staring into the face of a man who could go against my own father.

I put a hand up to ward off Cory's anger. "She's under our protection," I tell him honestly. "If anyone can use it, she can."

Cory's eyes narrow. "You three ain't known for offering up your protection for nothin'," he says.

I repress a groan. Convincing Cory that we don't mean Prep Girl any harm feels more daunting than the idea of seeing Allen Donovan, her actual father. "She's ... fuck, Cory," I grit out. "I don't know what to tell you. She's different—at least, for us she is. We're not fucking with her. Even if we were, do you really think she'd stand for it?"

Cory gazes at me for a bit longer before the tension in his body eases again and he rocks back on his heels with a decisive nod. "You right," he admits. "She'd knock yer asses out."

Yeah, she would. I shake my head and push open the door. "Now, I really gotta go or I'll be late—and if you're right, she'll knock my ass out for that too."

The husky laugh from the other man follows me out the door into the cold morning. A smile graces my lips and my hands clench around my keys. I start to reach for my phone in my pocket to let Juliet know I'll be there soon when I realize I left it in my car. With a sigh, I head around the gym building and cross through the alleyway to the back lot.

I'm so focused on getting to my car that I don't hear the sound of footsteps at my back until it's too late. Frowning, I turn slightly just as something hard and rounded slams into the side of my head. Staggering as the jolt of agony shoots through my skull, I slam into the opposite wall of the empty building next door, hands scraping against the stone exterior. My duffle drops to the ground. My keys slip free from my fingers and my knees hit concrete. Air whooshes out over my head, but I misjudged my opponent, and a knee slams directly into my face on my way down. My vision tilts and blood spurts from my nose.

"Fuck!" The garbled curse ricochets up the walls as a body slams on top of me.

Ignoring the pain in my head and face, I kick out, my sneaker connecting with someone's leg. There's the deep baritone of a male voice and then a fist comes swinging towards my face a second time. I roll away, rocks and gravel digging into the thin barrier of my t-shirt and shorts.

The sweat still on my skin makes the dirt and grime stick to me as I struggle back to my feet, swaying. Liquid drips down over my upper lip and the vile taste of rust and blood fills my mouth. When my vision clears enough for me to see my attackers, I grit my teeth. There are three of them—covered in black from head to toe, black balaclavas over their faces to hide their identities. The first dives for me, fist outstretched, but I spin out of his reach and shove him, face first, into the wall. There's no time to enjoy the sound of bone on brick crunching and his responding scream before the second and third rush me at once.

I take a right hook to the face as I kick out at the other's legs. Blood. Sweat. Pain. It fills me from the inside out. I fight—punching, kicking, panting, cursing. I struggle against them until my vision blurs again, going black at the edges. Something wet oozes down the back of my head and I realize that the first hit must have been done with an actual weapon of some sort.

I'm bleeding both in the front and back. Something slices through my t-shirt, right over my abdomen, and I gasp as pain cuts through my flesh—freezing in shock. The man with the knife leans in close, pressing his lips almost against my ear as he speaks.

His voice is even and clear. "We were asked to deliver this message," he says. "Leave the Donovan girl or else."

The knife is ripped free and I go down hard on my knees, the bits and pieces of rock and gravel on the alleyway floor cutting through the skin of my kneecaps. A cloud of dust rises around the front of my shorts as I cup two palms over my stomach.

Glancing down, I swallow hard as I see the red slipping out from between my fingers.

"Hey! What the 'ell you doin' out here!"

My lashes flutter as I hear the sound of Cory's angry tone reach my ears. Never in my life have I ever been so fucking happy to hear that old man than I am now. Pain sears through my stomach and more blood seeps into my shirt, staining the gray fabric a crimson brown.

Rushing footsteps fly past me as the world tilts and the ground comes rushing up to greet me. Just before my face connects, the last thought in my head is ... *Prep Girl's gonna be so pissed.*

44
JULIET

The time that Gio was supposed to pick me up comes and goes. I send a text to him fifteen minutes later when I still haven't heard from him. At the half-hour mark, I try to call him. No answer. I send more texts. I call a few more times. Still, there's no response.

I could just … not go. No one is waiting for me but my dad and it's not like he deserves my presence. Yet, now that I've decided to see him, I'm set on it. I have questions and no one else can answer them.

When it's over an hour later and Gio still hasn't bothered to answer my multiple missed calls or text messages, I grit my teeth and walk out the door. I should've known better than to rely on him, than to rely on fucking anyone. I don't bother to lock the front up because, even though I've been staying with Nolan for weeks now, I still don't have a key. I text Nolan, who's supposed to be working at the garage, but there's no answer from him either.

The phone that Lex had given me is at least good for something. I'd forgotten how hard life was without a phone, but now that I have one again it's easy enough to find the public transport system website and pinpoint the nearest bus stop. Thankfully, it doesn't take long for the next bus to arrive and I find a spot by a window at the back.

I stew there the entire length of the ride to Hansgard Correctional Facility with *Bad Omens* and *Three Days Grace* screaming in my ears thanks to the headphones I'd pilfered from Nolan's desk. Every passing minute is another sharp slice to my chest. Somehow, I can't stop myself from checking my phone repeatedly for the several-hour bus ride.

No calls. No texts. Just ... nothing. As if they forgot I exist. As if ... Gio's promises never happened. My teeth grind down hard enough that my jaw begins to ache and it takes actual concentrated effort to loosen up. I lean against the bus window and stare at the passing scenery without ever really seeing any of it. I have to wonder if this isn't how kids in the system feel.

You're lucky, Miss Donovan. At eighteen, you have a lot more options open to you. Mr. Calloway is offering to provide for you at the very least until you finish your senior year. Other kids would kill for an opportunity such as this. You won't even have to leave your current school.

I close my eyes, remembering the words of the social services lady who had come to see me after my mom had left that note. *Lucky.* She'd said the word with no small amount of derision, her obvious distaste for me and my family name evident in everything she did. From her words to the curl of her upper lip, she'd made it clear that she didn't care to be there. No doubt another Silverwood resident had been fucked over by the whole ordeal.

When the bus slows, my eyes open and I spy the large gray building that makes up the Hansgard Correctional Facility. Before we come to a full stop, I get up and pop the headphones out of my ears before stuffing them into my pocket and heading down the steps.

It's time to see my dad.

Less than two hours after I entered the doors of Hansgard Correctional Facility, I slam out of them again with burning eyes.

Liars. That's what they are—that's what they all are. The Scorpion Kings and my father. They're the same.

I storm towards the parking lot with my throat tight and my whole body shaking. Stopping halfway down one of the rows of beat-up trucks, cheap Mazdas, and a few minivans, I press my fists into my eye sockets and tip my head back.

"I didn't do this, sweetie. I'm innocent." My father's words sink into my head, spinning around and around.

Why did I even bother coming? Why does he think proclaiming his innocence as he has since he was taken in months ago is going to change anything?

Maybe it's best they didn't show. Taking a deep breath, I drop my arms away from my face. A drop of wetness lands on my forehead and my eyes open. Dark clouds hover overhead, the perfect shitty kind of weather to a perfectly shitty day.

"I just need a little money, Jules. Morpheus isn't answering my calls and your mother hasn't—"

More bits and pieces of the conversation I'd just had with my dad invade as another droplet hits my cheek this time. Dropping my head, I stare at the sneakers I'm wearing, fixating on the scuff marks over the toe as those two drops of rain turn into a light mist.

"I don't have any money, Dad. The government seized all of our assets—you know that. Mom's gone. She left."

"What do you mean she left?" I can still see his shocked face. At least one parent seems rather surprised that the other would abandon their only child. That has to count for something? Wasn't Morpheus supposed to tell him?

"She's gone, Dad. She left town. I haven't seen her in months."

And I don't think she's coming back.

I hadn't had the heart to tell him my suspicions, not when the news of Mom's desertion had made him sit back on the rickety plastic stool of the meeting room we'd been allowed to see each other in.

"You must be staying with Morpheus, then…"

I hadn't corrected that assumption either. Despite how angry I've been—how angry I still am—seeing my dad sitting in handcuffs and a garishly bright orange jumpsuit had hit me much harder than I thought it would. He's aged in the months he'd been incarcerated. The gray at his temples has begun its takeover, moving from his temples to the sides of his head and even a few streaks at the top. His eyes had been heavy with dark circles, and more wrinkles than I'd ever seen on him had lined his lips.

Just for a moment, when I walked into that big room with all of those tables—bolted down for safety purposes, of course—I'd looked at him and wanted to turn back into a scared little girl. I'd wanted to run up to him and throw my arms around him and start sobbing. I wanted to beg him to make it all better.

He hadn't even opened his arms. How could he have when he hadn't even been able to stand up from the table? The security guards had handcuffed him to a loop in the metal surface.

Just when it was all starting to get better—just when I thought I might be okay…

My new cell phone rings in my back pocket. Taking it out, I trudge towards the glass overhang for the bus station a block away from the facility. More rain falls, soaking into my hair as I lift it to my face and see the caller.

A spark of resentment crawls up my throat. *Nolan.* Of course, he calls me now. I'm more surprised it's not Gio, since he was the one that was supposed to be here. The one that lied. My chest constricts as I swipe the green button and put the phone to my ear.

"Where are you?" he demands.

"Where the fuck do you think I am, asshole," I snap back. "At the correctional facility."

"What?" Nolan's shocked voice slaps me. "Why would you be there? Gio didn't—" He stops and takes a breath. My lower lip trembles and I bite down hard to stop it. He knows. He knows Gio didn't pick me up. Had they just pressured me to do this only to take it back not thinking I'd come all this way by myself? Why? To humiliate me? Remind me that no one gives a fuck about me? Why make promises if they had no intention of keeping them? Why even bother to be kind to me when it was only half-assed? I was so much better when I'd been relying on myself. It was easier when it was just me. No stupid Scorpion Kings buying me shit or making me feel like I'm not alone.

Being alone isn't the hard part—it's thinking you're not and then finding out no one gives a shit about you. It's easier to be in a room by yourself than to stand in a crowd of people without a single one of them reaching out to help when you're in danger.

"Listen, you need to come back," he says.

"You're not surprised that Gio forgot," I state instead. "Or did he forget?" My damn chest tightens up again, a coil winding around and around until it hurts. "Did he ever intend to actually bring me?"

There's a brief moment of silence on the other side of the line and I laugh out loud, a broken, achy sound. "The answer's no, isn't it?"

"No, it's not," Nolan says. Then just as quickly, he barks a curse. "Fuck." That's it. That's all he says.

I nod as if he's right in front of me and hop onto the sidewalk. A streak of water slides down the side of my face.

"Yeah, fuck is right," I tell him. "Fuck you."

"Juliet, I didn't—there was a situation."

"Let me guess," I say. "You had to go collect more money from poor business owners and take it to your boss?"

I stomp on each crack in the pavement, breathing heavily as I throw the words out like bullets.

"What we do for work is none of your business." Nolan's voice is low, a warning. "Where are you now? Are you done there?"

"It's none of *your* business," I say, throwing his words back in his face.

He growls. "I'm not fucking around, Juliet. Where the fuck—goddamn it. You know what…"

The bus stop is in my line of sight and I spy a couple of people already standing there, waiting, taking up most of the space underneath the minuscule overhang. I'm going to look like a drowned rat by the time I get back to Silverwood.

Nolan says something, the sound of his voice slightly muffled as I assume he turns away from the phone and talks to someone else. When he comes back, it's with the same frustrated tone. "Did you turn off your fucking location?"

I grin at the question. Yes, I had. I'd been so angry with them that as I'd ridden into Hansgard via the bus, I'd found the location-sharing app on my cell and promptly deleted it.

"I don't think you should worry about my location anymore," I say. "In fact, don't fucking concern yourself with me at all anymore. When I get back to Silverwood, I'm going home—back to my apartment and you can fuck off for all I care."

"The door still isn't fixed," Nolan says. "It's not livable."

"I don't care as long as it's away from *you*," I seethe even as I start to tremble from the chill burrowing into my bones from the rain. "From all of you."

Stopping beneath a tree that offers some reprieve from the rain a few yards away from the bus stop, I wrap my arms around myself and clench my teeth to avoid chattering. "I'll ship Lex's phone back to him. I don't need shit from you."

I never did. I'd just forgotten that.

"*Juliet.*" My fingers clench around the phone in my hand at how he says my name—it's both a caress and a threat. "You don't need to stay with me, but you can't go back to your apartment."

"Yeah? Who am I going to stay with then? Gio?" I snort in disbelief. "Didn't you warn me how much Darrio Vargas hates me? What would the slum lord of Silverwood do if he found out that Juliet Donovan was living in his house, huh? Do you think he'd beat me? Rape me? Sell me to the highest bidder?"

Would any of that be any different than how I'm being treated by the town of Silverwood now?

"Maybe it's a good thing my dad's locked up," I mutter. "He didn't even know my mom had skipped down."

"*Jules.*" This time his tone is softer. I can't let it get to me. "I'm sorry you had to go there alone. I know we promised—"

A droplet of water slides down the center of my cheek and I quickly wipe it away, not sure if it's a tear or rain. "Yeah, well, promises get broken, don't they?" I snap, my chest squeezing impossibly tight. "Or do you consider them broken promises even when you never intended to keep them?"

"I—we did, Juliet, I swear to you. We've had shit going on. We meant to keep our promise. You shouldn't have gone off on your own; we could have rescheduled."

"Right, because my entire life is supposed to revolve around you now, is that it? Am I supposed to be your *Scorpion Girl*?" I hiss the last two words like the vilest of curses. "There for your beck and call at all times?"

When am I going to learn this lesson? I ask myself. Nobody really wants me, they just want to use me.

"Of course not—you're coming back from Hansgard, right? Where are you—"

"No?" I cut him off. "You've treated me like a Scorpion Girl. First you and then Lex. Gio's the only one who hasn't tried to fuck me—which is a miracle considering he's the manwhore of your little group. I assumed he would be the first."

Nolan growls again, a sound of pure animal rage. "I did not try to fuck you, Juliet." His voice dips deeper with each word. "Believe me, if I'd really been trying—there would be no guessing. I would have fucked you good and hard."

"Yeah, but now you'll never get the chance, will you?" Water splashes onto the sidewalk and I look up to see the public bus careen around the corner down the street.

I move out from under the cover of the tree and head towards the bus stop. "Just..." Nolan sighs. "Just come back and let's talk about this. You don't have to stay with me if you truly don't want to. We can figure it out."

"No," I tell him, nearing the stop. "Like I said, there's no need. I'll figure it out myself. I always do."

"You are coming back, Juliet," Nolan growls. "If I have to track you down myself, you are coming back here. You can't escape us."

"Yeah?" I feel dead inside. "Watch me."

"Jul—" I end the call before he can get another word out and when it immediately starts ringing, I turn it off.

Letting an older woman with a cane and a short bulky looking man get on the bus before me, by the time I enter the mildly warm interior and swipe my card, I'm drenched to the bone. My sneakers make squishing noises as I stride down the aisle and find an empty seat towards the back. Thankfully, there aren't that many passengers at this time of day so even as the bus starts up again and heads off to a new stop, most people decide to stick close to the front.

I recline back against the hard bus seat and turn towards the window. The phone in my pocket is a heavy weight, a reminder of the stupid trust I'd given them. Pointless. Utterly pointless. I bite down on my lower lip as it begins to tremble and then squeeze my eyes shut as those start to burn. I shift around in my seat, turning my head to rest against the cool glass of the window.

Everyone chooses themselves or they always choose someone else.

The Scorpion Kings choose each other, and I thought … maybe … but I'd been wrong. As always, I'd been wrong. I'd misjudged Avery and Brandon and now the Scorpion Kings. A deep, wicked voice in my head points out that between my old friends and the Scorpion Kings, there's only one common denominator—me.

My eyes reopen. Maybe I'm the problem. Maybe I'm just … not worth choosing.

Actual tears fill my eyes turning the whole world into a blurry mess and I lower my head biting down harder until I taste blood. I force my eyes to stay open in the hopes that not blinking will stop the tears from falling, but I fail at that too. More and more come, leaking from my face and falling all over my lap.

To never trust again. Because trusting someone only ever ends in pain—and I'm always on the wrong side of misery.

45
NOLAN

"*Fuck!*" I dial Juliet's phone and when it goes straight to voicemail—*again*—I haul back and throw the damn thing. The phone crashes into the wall—leaving a good-sized dent before it clatters to the floor. Lex stands in the center of the living room, his brows drawn low.

"She can stay with me," he says. "When she comes back, we'll go get her, and she'll stay at my place."

Lex's place is a far cry from what someone like Juliet Donovan is used to. I scrub a hand down my face. "And what about your room of secrets, huh?" I point out. "You wanted her involved with us. You wanted her in the middle. Well, congratulations, you got your fucking wish. She can't find out about that or she'll run."

"She's already running," he tells me.

I groan. He's right. We fucked up. Darrio fucked us up. I thought waiting until right before we left town would be the best time to get rid of him, but over the last few weeks, he's been up our asses more and more—up Gio's ass to spend more time with the gang. Then today…

"We don't have time for this," I say, shaking my head.

"No, she's not staying with you. She'll come back here even if that means I have to tie her to my goddamned bed every night."

Lex frowns. "I won't need to go in the room often if I have her with me every night. I can lock it too. She won't find out."

How did we let her disrupt our lives like this? How did *I* let her?

I stride across the room and pick up my phone. When I hit the button on the side and nothing happens, I curse, tossing it onto the coffee table. I shove a hand up through my hair, gripping a mass of it and yanking hard.

"I'll get you a new one," Lex says, nodding to the phone. "Don't worry about it. What we need to do now is find her."

"She's on her way back from the prison," I say. "She's probably on the bus."

"Then we wait for her to show up here." If someone had told me at the beginning of this that one day Lex—the fucking stalker—would be the voice of reason, I'd have punched them. Now, though, it's the truth.

"She's not going to show up here." She'd been too angry, too hurt. "But at least we know where she'll be. She'll go back to her apartment. She has nowhere else to go."

Lex nods. "Alright then, you go to her apartment and I'll go get Gio."

Gio. My head throbs with an impending migraine. The last several hours have been all kinds of fucked up and the worst has yet to come. "His mom's with him at the hospital," I say. "But we should go see him before he gets out. He'll be fine for now—whoever got the jump on him didn't get away with just a few minor scratches. They've got to be hurting. I'll scope out the hospital to see if they show up until it's time to go get Juliet."

Lex rocks back on his heels. "Do you think that's wise?"

I shoot a look his way. "Would you rather I leave him on his own?"

"No, that's not what I mean."

I grit my teeth, frustration making the ache in my head pound all the harder. "Then, enlighten me." Each word comes out clipped and even.

"She's pissed at you."

"She's pissed at all of us," I shoot back.

"Juliet is hurt. She thinks we forgot her. She doesn't know about Gio."

"And we're not going to tell her." I lower my voice and glare at him.

"Why not?"

"Because she's not involved. The less Darrio Vargas knows about Juliet Donovan, the better. That man would gut her if he could."

It's not hard for Lex to pick up on what I don't say. "Do you think he had a hand in Otis breaking into her apartment?" The careful danger in his tone would make a lesser man step back.

"I think if there's anyone in town with unsavory intentions towards the daughter of Allen Donovan, it would be Darrio Vargas. He's always had a thing against the Donovan family." He'd always had a deeply rooted hatred for anyone he saw as better than himself. It explained why he hated his own son so much.

Lex's hands ball into fists and he glances at the door. "I'll kill him." The words aren't spoken like a man angry or a man just spouting bullshit. They're spoken with a tangible hint of daring, a man who's killed once and has no compunction about doing so again. If I let him, Lex could fall very deeply into an abyss that would steal him away from Gio and me. He would cease to be himself behind his screens and cameras, finding his targets easy to track, and then learning every one of their weaknesses before he took advantage and they found themselves six feet under.

I take two steps toward him and put a hand on his shoulder, redirecting his attention to me. "We will," I assure him. "It's always been the plan—we'd never leave Gio's mom here with that bastard when we leave. He won't hurt her or Juliet. For now, we need to go check on Gio. We need to make sure whoever went after him won't try to take him out when he's weakened. He needs us."

Lex's brow furrows. "I need my laptop," he says. "But..." He shakes his head as if trying to ward off the need for violence that rides him, a feeling I know all too well. "I don't know that you should make it obvious that you're watching Gio. If whoever hit him thinks he's protected, it might make it harder to find out who was involved."

It's a good point and one I hadn't considered, but the fact is that we need more information than what Gio's mom had given us. The woman had been in hysterics, sobbing and worried over her son. I had to wonder if Darrio hadn't had a hand in his own son's attack. It was suspicious that he'd called in both Lex and me and not long after, Gio had been attacked. Gio was a good fighter; if he was in the hospital then there was a chance he'd had more than one assailant. Unfortunately, the cops would likely be unhelpful. Everyone in Silverwood knows who Gio's father is. They'll expect Darrio Vargas to avenge his son or to handle everything in his little gang of criminals.

I squeeze Lex's shoulder and then drop my hold. "All I need now is an extra phone," I tell him. "I'm going to head over to the hospital to look after Gio and his mom. I'll wait until the bus is supposed to show up and go grab Juliet from her apartment."

"What do I do?" Lex cracks his neck to the side, his body rife with tension. His hands are no longer balled into fists though, so that's an improvement at least.

"Go home," I tell him. "I'll send you what I find out from the doctors and Gio. I want you to start by tracking the cameras in the area he was in before the attack, see if whoever attacked him was stupid enough to slip up."

Every hint. Every clue. It didn't matter how small, we'd find it and we'd use it. No one hurt one of our own and lived.

46
JULIET

Fire is cleansing. Fire is cruel. Fire is licking up the side of what was once the only place I could call my own. Not my parents'. Not a charity case handout. Mine. My apartment complex sits like a beacon to all as flames tear over the side of the building, consuming everything in its path. Numbness eats away at my limbs as I watch the procession of firefighters and the flashing lights.

Several people—other residents—stand on the sidewalk, watching as the red and gold glow throws lights and shadows across the parking lot pavement. I scan the crowd, somehow knowing they should be here.

I'm not stupid.

Just hours ago, I'd yelled at Nolan. I'd told him and the other Scorpion Kings that I would never trust them. That they were all liars. Well, they might be liars about some things, but never about what *they* wanted. Nolan had said I'd have to come to them and he'd made sure I had no other choice. I bite my lip as my emotions threaten to take over. Closing my eyes, I let the soft cool wind of autumn soothe my too-hot skin. I'm not close enough to the fire to feel the heat. No, there's a different fire here—it burns inside me with all of the violence of an impending volcanic eruption.

You can't escape us.

Nolan's words rumble in the back of my mind, in that delicious deep baritone of his. The voice of a man who knows how dangerous he can be, who's confident in himself and his power.

Because unlike me, Nolan Pierce has power in Silverwood. It might be dirty, filthy power, but it's power nonetheless, and he made sure he came through on at least one promise today. Too bad it wasn't the right one.

I open my eyes as I hear a man shout out something garbled. I can't hear the words, but a moment later two of the firefighters rush towards the front of the building, dragging a long hose behind them. There's more shouting and then water jets out, dousing the front, crashing right through the windows. A part of me wants to ask them what the point is. It's a smaller series of units and a quick pass around the parking lot sees that all of the residents and neighbors I'd grown used to seeing come and go from the building are outside. At this time of night, almost everyone is home from work, and no one is screaming for the firemen to save their friend or husband or children.

The building is old and the fire is tearing it apart like an animal ripping through the carcass of its prey. The back of my head throbs and the pain stretches up towards my temples.

All of the money I'd gained from selling my BMW was in that apartment. Most of my clothes. The pictures I'd kept. My futon. It's all gone now. Everything is gone, and I can't even seem to cry about it. No matter how hard I think about crying, nothing happens. My eyes remain dry and my chest remains an empty cavern. I'm burning up inside, a strange sort of heat stealing over each of my limbs—eating away at my sense of self—but there's none in my eyes. No pain. No burning. No heat. I've cried myself out and there are no more tears. They took those too. My tears are theirs now.

There is still one thing left that they don't have. One thing they haven't taken and it's the only weapon I have left.

I take a step back and then another and another. The scent of wet wood and burning embers rises into the night sky. My eyes linger on the metal railing and staircase. That will likely be the only thing standing tomorrow morning when the last of the fire has been put out, but even that won't be the same. It's already started to warp under the heat of the flames. When dawn rises, that building will be a charred pile of wood, broken glass, and melted metal.

No one watching the scene of the burning building even notices me as I stride across the street. The bus that dropped me off is long gone. I'd been the only one that had disembarked and I'd been so stunned as I stared at the flaming mass of wood outside of the window that I'd almost missed my stop. I wonder now if I shouldn't have just kept going—shouldn't have just let the bus keep driving me right out of town.

What would they do then? If I just up and disappeared. Went somewhere far away, changed my look again, maybe even my name?

I stop in front of the dollar mart and glance down at the blue streaks of my hair. I lift one lock to the light that's pouring out from the storefront. I can't remember why I chose blue. Maybe I was depressed. Maybe it was because I wanted to look as different from my old self as possible.

Some people believe that hair holds memories. Mine has held nothing but pain and loss.

This hair, though, isn't the same. I refuse to believe that this is pain—the ache in my chest. Betrayal. It's so easy to let shit happen to you, but it's hard to fight back and still, I'd tried. I'd tried and I'd tried. Fighting is exhausting. It's dirty work.

But ... that's what had caught their attention, wasn't it?

They were all surprised that someone like me—a fallen Silverwood princess—could fight back.

Well, I'm still fighting.

I lower the lock of blue hair back to my shoulder and start walking again, past the dollar mart and then past the next block. My heart hammers in my chest and I shiver, wrapping my arms around my chest the further I get from the fire. A new sort of chill bleeds through my still somewhat damp clothes.

The Scorpion Kings want to play games?

They want to cut me off from any other avenue?

They want to fuck me and fuck me over?

Fine.

We'll see who wins.

One foot in front of the other, I walk until my legs ache, until my muscles are drained and sore. I walk until I near the edge of the town where the houses grow further and further apart and sidewalks disappear entirely. I walk until the bottom of my shoes touch only grass and faded road pavement.

There's only one thing left to do, one place left to go.

The Scorpion Kings are going to regret everything they've done. They might think they've trapped me with them, but they're wrong. I'm not trapped with the Scorpion Kings ... *they* are trapped with *me*.

Before this is all over, I'm going to make them fucking *bleed*.

Thank you so much for reading The Venom We Bleed. Please make sure to review it here and grab book 2 here!

ABOUT THE AUTHOR

Lucy Smoke, also known as Lucinda Dark for her fantasy works, has a master's degree in English and is a self-proclaimed creative chihuahua. She enjoys feeding her wanderlust, cover addiction, as well as her face.

When she's not on a never-ending quest to find the perfect milkshake, she lives and works in the southern United States with her beloved fur-baby, Hiro, and her family and friends.

Want to be kept up to date? Think about joining the author's group or signing up for their newsletter below.

Facebook Group - Reader Mafia
Newsletter - lucysmoke.com/subscribe
TikTok - @Lucy_Smoke

ALSO BY LUCY SMOKE

Contemporary Series:

Gods of Hazelwood: Icarus Duet (completed)

Burn With Me

Fall With Me

Sick Boys Series (completed)

Forbidden Deviant Games (prequel)

Pretty Little Savage

Stone Cold Queen

Natural Born Killers

Wicked Dark Heathens

Bloody Cruel Psycho

Bloody Cruel Monster

Vengeful Rotten Casualties

Sinister Arrangment Duet (completed)

Wicked Angel

Cruel Master

Iris Boys Series (completed)

Now or Never

Power & Choice

Leap of Faith

Cross my Heart

Forever & Always

Iris Boys Series Boxset

The *Break* Series (completed)
Break Volume 1
Break Volume 2
Break Series Collection

Contemporary Standalones:
Poisoned Paradise
Expressionate
Wild Hearts

Fantasy Series:

Mortal Gods Series (completed)
A Sword of Shadow & Deceit
A Reign of Storm & Madness
The Blood of Gods & Monsters
A Haven of Brimstone & Darkness

Awakened Fates Series (completed)
Crown of Blood and Glass
Dawn of Fate and Valor
Wings of Sunfire and Darkness

Twisted Fae Series (completed)
Court of Crimson
Court of Frost
Court of Midnight

Barbie: The Vampire Hunter Series (completed)
Rest in Pieces
Dead Girl Walking
Ashes to Ashes

Sky Cities Series (Dystopian)

Heart of Tartarus

Shadow of Deception

Sword of Damage

Dogs of War (Coming Soon)

Made in the USA
Coppell, TX
02 March 2026

73061363R00268